MW00579472

SUMMER
AFTER
SUMMER

SUMMER AFTER SUMMER

A Novel

LAUREN BAILEY

alcove
press

This is a work of fiction. All of the names, characters, organizations, places and events portrayed in this novel are either products of the author's imagination or are used fictitiously. Any resemblance to real or actual events, locales, or persons, living or dead, is entirely coincidental.

Copyright © 2024 by Lauren Bailey

All rights reserved.

Published in the United States by Alcove Press, an imprint of The Quick Brown Fox & Company LLC.

Alcove Press and its logo are trademarks of The Quick Brown Fox & Company LLC.

Library of Congress Catalog-in-Publication data available upon request.

ISBN (Hardcover): 978-1-63910-655-4
ISBN (ebook): 978-1-63910-656-1

Cover design by Sandra Chiu

Printed in the United States.

www.alcovepress.com

Alcove Press
34 West 27th St., 10th Floor
New York, NY 10001

First Edition: May 2024

10 9 8 7 6 5 4 3 2 1

For David

CHAPTER ONE

June 2023

On the day I leave Wes, I get into my car in a state of shock and drive out of New York without looking back.

It took longer than it should have to move out of our apartment, but it feels like less time than it takes to get to the Hamptons on a Friday in late June.

Though it's been years since I've made this journey, I should've remembered how the snarl of the Long Island Parkway makes my heart race and my palms sweat against the steering wheel. How the unpredictable stops of the other cars mean that I'm constantly slamming on the brakes and skidding to a stop just before I hit their bumper, my eyes racing to the rearview mirror to see if I'm about to get rear-ended.

I should've left earlier, but it didn't work out that way. Instead, I'm caught with all the other hopefuls, stop-starting our way to the first weekend of summer, trying not to cry.

My car is packed to the rafters with my things. I didn't have time to sort/keep/toss; once I'd made the decision to go, I just needed to bounce. So, I threw as many of my belongings as I could into a set of suitcases I'm pretty sure are mine, and a few large black garbage bags, and stuffed them into my car. I don't even know if I have everything I need for the summer, but I'll figure that out when I get there.

Home.

I'm on my way to Southampton to help my father clear out the house my family's owned for generations. I grew up in that house, but as much as I love it, I haven't lived there for more than a summer since I went away to college.

The sale has been a long time coming, my father's money draining away like a leaky boat. He's never been good with money, though it's his "job" to manage the family's generational resources. Until the markets collapsed in 2008, he'd run the enterprise well enough to keep the roof intact and the grounds tended. Since then, there've been more and more financial hiccups, like the aftershocks of an earthquake. One year, the taxes weren't paid. Another, the power got turned off for a week. You get the idea.

When asked what he was doing about it, my father would always stare off into the middle distance, as if he was trying to recall something from long ago, and not the five "Final Notices" from the power company sitting on his desk, unopened. Then he'd change the topic, telling some story about a friend he'd run into in town and how *old* he looked, how very *run down*.

But expounding on the neighbors' physical deterioration didn't solve the problem of too much property and too little cash flow. We'd been trying to convince him to sell for years, until the bank took the decision out of his hands. The sale was negotiated swiftly and without any involvement from me at my request, the bare details sent in an email. The closing is at the end of August. My father and all of the family's possessions need to be out of the house by then.

My older sister, Charlotte—who still lives at home, but never made any effort that I'm aware of to stop the financial slide—called two weeks ago, in a panic, to tell me that he hadn't even started packing.

"What am I supposed to do about it?" I asked, holding up a finger to Justine, the student I was working with after school in the music room.

"Come," Charlotte pleaded. "Help."

"Take over, you mean. Get it done."

"Well . . ."

This is always the role I play in the family, even though I'm the middle child. I'm supposed to be the irresponsible one, but somehow, after our mother died when I was fourteen, it was suddenly my job to make sure the school fees got paid and we all had uniforms that fit when the semester started.

"I'll help," she said, but I doubted it.

"What about Sophie?"

"She's got the kids. She already complains constantly about how they're too much for her."

I couldn't help but nod in agreement while Justine pounded the piano keys in annoyance. She was eight and still thought the world revolved around her. My sister, Sophie, is the baby of the family, and she's clung to that role fiercely, even though she was the first to marry and the only one of us to have kids. The truth is, I'm not close to either of my sisters, but that's as much my fault as theirs.

"I can't just drop my life, Charlotte. My husband. It's going to take months to clean out that house."

She ignored my reference to Wes. "Doesn't the school year end in a couple of days?"

"So?"

"Well . . ."

I stared at the colorful wall, painted in a mural of dancing instruments. "Can you please say what you mean instead of speaking in ellipses?"

Charlotte sighed. "You know you're the only one Father listens to. And you don't want everything to end up in a dumpster, do you? Not all of Mom's things."

Now *I* wanted to pound the piano keys. Charlotte can be manipulative when she wants to be, which is more often than she should. "You'd do that?"

"Why should it be my responsibility? Just because I live here? He's your father too."

"I know."

"I'm not going to be the only one to take care of him."

"I didn't ask you to."

"You kind of did, though, Olivia, when you moved away and never came back."

I wanted to contradict her, but she was right. As much as I loved it, Southampton was a crucible of bad memories, and I'd insulated myself from them as much as I could, returning rarely—and lately, not at all.

I agreed to think about it and hung up. Then I spent the next twenty minutes calming Justine down, who'd felt *ignored* and was going to tell her mummy that I wasn't giving her the right amount of attention. I knew better than to try to reason her out of her tantrum. Her mother paid extra for her lessons, and the income I made teaching kids like her to play mediocre piano after school was an important supplement to my inadequate teacher's salary.

Despite the guilt Charlotte laid at my door, I'd decided I wasn't going to go. But then it turned out that I *could* just drop my life *and* my husband; that I had to because I couldn't breathe in New York anymore, and so here I was.

Another car stops suddenly in front of me, and I apply the brakes as my heart skips a beat, praying they don't give out. My car is ten years old and hasn't had a tune-up in years. I never remember to do stuff like that, but Wes is always telling me he worries whenever I drive it. Not enough to take it in himself, though, and over time, the tone of the concern has shifted from fretting about my safety to saying things like, *"If you end up killing someone with that thing, don't blame me."*

When your husband switches from caring for your well-being to worrying about the safety of others, well, let's just say it's a warning sign—and in my case, one of the many reasons my things are stuffed into this death trap.

My car stops right before the black bumper in front of me, and I breathe a sigh of relief, my heart racing like I've been sprinting through the rain. There's a sticker on it that reads: "If you can read this, you're too close." I let it get a car's length ahead of me and check the upcoming sign. It's my exit. I just have to navigate across three lanes of traffic, and I can be free of this particular hell.

I get off the highway and drive through town, passing familiar restaurants and new logos in old places. I cut away before the main street, not wanting to get caught in the stop-and-go traffic as the tourists pop in and out of the cute candy-colored stores. I turn onto First Neck and aim for the beach, turning right when it morphs into Meadow. I pass the Crowder's massive turreted home with its thatched roof, then a new build I don't recognize that looks like it belongs in Malibu, not Cryder Beach.

And then I'm at Taylor House, its weathered shingled sides rising from the long pale grasses that grow out of the sandy dunes that surround it, its lighthouse windows glinting in the sun.

The house is a pile, built at the beginning of the last century, when the family was still accumulating money rather than watching it dwindle. We'd never been able to settle on how many rooms it had—twenty-six or twenty-seven, depending on who you asked and whether the secret room behind the library shelves counted. (Obviously, yes.) Either way, it was more rooms than anyone needed, and more rooms than this family could afford.

As I bring my car to a stop, I stare up at it, feeling nostalgic. Memories click through my brain with a swiftness that leaves me breathless, and I'm relieved that soon I won't have this place to remind me anymore. Another family will build a life here, for good or bad, and it won't mean anything to me.

I wonder for the first time who bought it and whether they're planning to tear it down and build some post-modernist collection of boxes like so many others have done. I promise myself that I won't be around to find out, that this is the last summer I'll spend here. Once the past is tucked away, and Charlotte and my father are settled somewhere reasonable, I'll lock up my memories and throw away the key.

Charlotte comes out of the front door, summoned by the sound of my tires on the gravel drive. She's wearing an off-white linen jumpsuit, tied at the waist with a tight cinch. A pair of oversized black sunglasses hide her dark eyes.

When I get out of the car, I can't help but notice the weeds poking through the stones, and the overgrown flower border; how much slumpier the place looks in general from the last time I was here.

Charlotte, though, is the same—thin and waspish, her long, dark brown hair still glossy and blunt at her shoulders, her clothes hanging off her because she doesn't eat, she never has. At thirty-seven, she could still pass for twenty-five. She has one of those faces, both thin and plump enough that it doesn't seem to age, especially since she's always been careful about the sun.

"Olivia!" She tips her sunglasses down to peer at me. Her skin is almost the same color as her outfit. "*What* are you wearing?"

I check myself, unable to recall what I threw on before I tossed the last bag into the car. I see a pair of black leggings that are a size too small and a T-shirt for a Bon Jovi concert I forgot I even attended. I haven't had a haircut in months, and the lack of sun and general malaise I've been feeling for too long has turned my hair mousy. Add in the fact that I spent too much time in the sun with too little sunscreen for years, and I doubt anyone would guess I'm one minute younger than the thirty-five I am.

"My white jumpsuit is at the cleaners."

Charlotte isn't sure how to take this, so she air-kisses me instead, one kiss near, but not quite on, each cheek, an affectation she picked up during a summer in Montreal to learn French. Her vocabulary never made it past ordering off the menu in a pretentious way in French restaurants, but Charlotte isn't the sort of person who accepts personal limitations.

"Well, you look dreadful. Thank *gawd* the garden party is tomorrow."

"Garden party?"

"Didn't I tell you? We're kicking off the summer with a hurrah in the garden. Don't worry, I've arranged everything."

"Smoked salmon sandwiches and gin?"

"Precisely. You'll be there?"

It's the last thing I want to do, but that's what this whole summer's going to be like. I might as well accept it now. "Yes."

"I assume you have something else to wear?"

I point my thumb at the car. "Somewhere in there, I'm sure."

"I've put you in your old room—hope you don't mind. It'll be hot as blazes most nights. The air is on the fritz, and we aren't going to be fixing it before we leave."

"William must be complaining about that."

"We've put window units in his room and mine. They do all right. He spends most of the day at the club, so it's not too bad, really." Charlotte smiles, proud that she's managed our father's whims to a degree that kept his complaining to a minimum. William doesn't suffer, well, anything, and has always been vociferous in his complaints at the least hint of discomfort.

"Is there a window unit for me?"

Charlotte raises a bony shoulder. "I didn't know you'd be coming when I bought them."

"Fair enough."

Most days, the breeze from the ocean keeps the house tolerable for sleeping, but on a still night it can be murder on the third floor. When we were kids, we used to sleep in the summer house, but I'm not sure it's hospitable now.

"You want to get your things?" Charlotte says. "It's hot out here."

I walk to the back of my car, not waiting for Charlotte to help, based on experience, but she surprises me by coming up to my shoulder and peering into the cargo area. "Is that all of it?"

"Everything but the furniture."

"He'll take that, I suppose?"

"I don't care where it goes."

I reach in and grab one of the suitcases and a large satchel that has my toiletries and overnight things. I decide to move the rest of it later. It's coming up on five, and if there's one thing I know without having to ask, it's that cocktails will appear shortly, on the veranda. I need a gin and tonic (or ten) to wash the taste of today out of my mouth.

"Is Aunt Tracy here?" Every summer since my mother died, her best friend has been making us delicious meals. Cooking is her passion.

"She arrived a couple of weeks ago."

"How's she taking the sale?"

Charlotte shrugs, then tilts her head back and looks at the house. You need to do that to get it all in one view. "It's funny to think of not living here. Sometimes I'm quite *sad* about it."

She sounds sincere, but it's often hard to know with Charlotte. It's hard *to* know Charlotte. She's always been a self-contained unit, even before our mother died. Afterward, she grew a shell around her that was hard to penetrate. Eventually, I stopped trying.

"Where will you go?"

"Not sure yet. But *that man* paid enough to settle all the debts and keep Father until the end of his days and then some. We'll each get our share, so I'll buy something, I think."

All of this is new information to me, and my head's playing catch-up. I latch onto the least confusing part of what she just said. "Who ended up buying it? No one told me."

Charlotte turns toward me, her eyes as dark as beads. "You haven't heard?"

"No. Who is it?"

"I can hardly believe it myself, and where he got the money, I don't know, but it was Fred."

CHAPTER TWO

June 2003

"I'm *so bored*," Ashley says, swatting at a fly on her long, thin, already tanned legs.

We're sitting at the pool at the Southampton Lawn and Tennis Club, facing the ocean. Justin Timberlake's "Rock Your Body" is playing on a loop on Ashley's iPod, which is sitting between us on a small table, with two sweating Diet Cokes.

"You've only been here for two days," I say.

Ashley checks her pale pink nails. *"Bored."*

"I'm not the program director."

"But you are."

"Why don't you take a tennis lesson?"

"One tennis freak in my entourage is enough."

"I'm not a freak."

"Uh-huh. That's why you have a list of tournaments you want to win and the ages you want to win them at?"

"It's bad to have goals?"

"It's weird to basically already have a job when you're not even sixteen."

"But this is when I lay the foundation, I . . ." I glare at her. "You're trying to push my buttons."

"It's so easy to do it!"

"Fine, fine. No tennis for Ash. Got it." I think about it for a minute. "You could swim?"

Ashley puts her hand in front of her mouth and pats it in an exaggerated way. Her chunky highlighted hair flows to her narrow shoulders in beachy waves.

"I'm out of ideas," I say, and scrunch down on my pool chair. My own hair is sun-bleached and pulled back in a high ponytail, still wet and smelling faintly of salt from my workout.

Unlike Ashley, I'm perfectly happy to sit around and do nothing in the hours I have to myself, which aren't many. Every day is the same—three hours of tennis in the morning, starting at the crack of dawn, then an hour in the gym. Late afternoon is for piano lessons, which I want to give up. But it was my mom's favorite thing, and since she died last year, it's the only way I feel connected to her.

In between, I hang with Ashley at the club. It has ten fenced-off lawn tennis courts, a saltwater pool, and an old clubhouse with a gabled roof, weather-beaten cedar shingles, and a long wrap-around porch. It's stuffy and exclusive, all the things my father loves and I kind of hate. But it's where my tennis coach is in the summer, and my scholarship is attached to him.

"What about your birthday?" Ashley says.

"What about it?"

"Sweet sixteen and never been kissed."

"I have too."

"Spin the bottle doesn't count."

I turn over onto my stomach so she doesn't see me blush. My sixteenth birthday is a week away, and I haven't had a real kiss. I'm obviously pathetic. "Who has time for boys?"

"Uh, *everyone*."

"The boys here are all dumb."

"But are they cute? That's all that matters for kissing."

I rest my chin on my hands. I can hear my Aunt Tracy telling me to put sunscreen on my back, but I ignore her voice in my head. I love her, but when she tries too hard to mother me, it's more than I can take. "Hmmm. Well, let's put it on the list then."

"Top ten goals for summer?"

"That's the one."

"Perfect." Ashley reaches into her pastel beach bag and pulls out her bright pink day planner. She flips to a page that she's marked with a Post-it: *Ash and Olivia's Top Ten Summer Goals.* The words are surrounded by stars and fireworks, and she's left slots one to three open. Number ten is *Perfect tan.* She puts *Olivia gets kissed* at number two.

"What are you saving number one for? Sex or car?"

Ashley's been going back and forth on which one she wants more since yesterday. Even though it doesn't make sense for a sixteen-year-old in Manhattan to have a car, she wants a BMW 3 series for the "status." I'd poked a finger in my mouth and pretended to hurl when she said that, and she left the space blank.

"I've decided on sex." Ashley stretches her arms above her head. She's wearing a tiny bikini with black and white polka dots that I'd never feel comfortable in. My shoulders are too broad from tennis, and I have more muscles than normal everywhere else. I'm happy in my tankini that doesn't make me feel like everyone's looking at me.

"Bold choice since there's no boy in sight."

She sticks her tongue out at me. "Ooh, I know what we should do!"

"What?"

"Go to the beach."

"You want to go to the beach? With the *sand*? And the *tourists*?" Ashley's inherited her parents' snooty attitude toward the vacationers who are just like them, minus the millions of dollars they had to buy a house in one of the new developments a mile from here.

"I was thinking more of the umbrella boys."

"Oh." I sit up. The public beach near the club is staffed with teenage boys for the summer. They rent out chairs and umbrellas and run the concession stand. "That's mostly guys from the local high school."

"So?"

"I know all of them already. Since kindergarten."

"Maybe they've grown up since you switched to Hampton Prep."

"I guess."

Ashley checks her flip phone quickly. "It's almost lunch time. If we go now, we can get food from the Shack."

The thought of one of their lobster rolls does sound good. "But what about the calories?"

"It's first week. No diets." She stands and starts stuffing one of the club towels into her beach bag.

"You're not supposed to take that off the property," I say, then regret it. Ashley knows the rules, and I don't need to be reminding her like I'm her mother. She still has one of those.

Ashley brings her Vuarnets down over her eyes. They're pink and cat-eyed, and she brought me a pair too. "I thought you weren't the program coordinator."

"Yeah, yeah."

"Come on, let's go."

I collect my things, shove my feet into my flip-flops, and follow Ashley out of the club grounds, walking single file behind her down the narrow path through the dunes. The club owns its own strip of beach, the Atlantic stretching out in front of it, the cold waves rolling in and crashing into the white-sand shore. As usual, the club's beach is abandoned, but the public beach is full. There's music blaring from the speaker on the lifeguard's station, and the blue and white umbrellas they rent out are twisting in the wind.

"You sure you want to do this?" I say to Ashley, watching the sand fly up from the back of her flip-flops. They're Lanzarote she told me, as if I'm supposed to know what that means.

She glances back. "You have a better idea?"

"I think we've already established that I do not."

She grins, her straight teeth newly free of the braces that she'd hated. "Well, come on then. Your future awaits!" She points her arm to the sky, mocking herself and our mission. But she doesn't stop and neither do I. Instead, we clamber over the berm that separates the two beaches, and plop down onto the public side as the wind whips my ponytail against my neck.

"Who looks like a good prospect?" Ashley asks as she shades her eyes from the sun. The sunnies are cute, but they don't block out much light.

I scan the crowd. Six guys our age are standing by the umbrella station, wearing khaki shorts and white polos. I recognize five of them from middle school. Guys named Dave and Dan and Mike, who thought it was funny to pull on my braids and tear down my art projects from the teacher's honor wall. I have no interest in speaking to them.

But there's another boy—tall, athletic, with dark hair that curls across his forehead—I've never seen before.

"Ooh la la, who is *that*?" Ashley gives a low whistle.

"Shh!"

"He can't hear us. Come on—let's say hi." Ash tugs on my arm.

"Ouch."

"That wasn't hard."

"I wrenched my shoulder when I was playing this morning."

"You should give that up."

"The ticket to my future? No way." Ashley doesn't understand my passion for tennis, or why I work so hard at it. But she still has a trust fund, so I don't blame her.

"Maybe you're about to meet your future right now."

"On Cooper's Beach? I doubt it."

"Come on, quick. Before Becky gets to him."

She points to where Becky Johnson, a girl Ashley refers to as—no joke—her *nemesis*, is talking to the new guy and flipping her butter-yellow hair over her shoulder. She's wearing a small bikini top and cut-off jean shorts.

Ash hustles me over the hard white sand, past multiple families with bickering children and babies in sagging diapers.

"Excuse me," Ash says with a voice that's strikingly like her mother's. "We'd like to rent an umbrella."

New Guy stands a little taller at the tone and picks up a clipboard while Becky shoots daggers at us. "Name?"

"It's for my friend here." Ashley nudges me forward.

Our eyes connect, mine and New Guy's, and it's not like in the books. There's no jolt of attraction or thunderbolt or anything, but there is a warm feeling in my chest because this boy is very cute. His eyes are a deep blue—*like the ocean after a storm*, I can't help but think, even though I feel silly, and he has a small trickle of freckles across his straight nose. He's tall enough that I feel small next to him, which doesn't happen often when you're five eight and the boys haven't finished growing yet. His name tag says "Fred."

"Name?"

"Olivia Taylor."

He writes it down with a black gel pen. "You want a lounger too?" He says the word in a way I haven't heard before, the *un* sound elongated.

"Where are you from?"

"Boston. Here for the summer. You?"

"From here."

"You're the first person I've met from here." He smiles at me, and maybe there *is* a jolt of something. Whether it's Ashley's elbow in my back or the annoyed stare I'm getting from Becky, I'm not sure. It could be Fred, though, which is . . . I don't know what this is.

"We do exist."

"Ha. Yes. I know. My aunt and uncle live here."

"Where?"

He mentions a house and a street name, and I know exactly which one he's talking about. An older couple without any children bought it during the winter, and for a week it was the talk of the town. The talk of my father anyway, who's always extremely interested in the pedigree of anyone new who moves to Southampton.

"So, did you want the lounger?" Fred says, showing his accent again.

"Do we, Ash?"

"It's ten dollars more."

I blush at the mention of money. I hadn't even thought about the fact that we'd have to pay, which is stupid. At the club, everything is paid for by chits that get collated once a month and mailed out to our parents. Or that's how it works for Ash. I teach clinics three times a week to the younger kids, to work off what I spend on Diet Coke and burgers.

I can't say any of this to Fred, so I pat myself down like I've seen my father do too many times when he's "forgotten" his wallet at his favorite restaurant. When William does this, the maître d' makes cooing noises and says he'll add it to his tab, but that's not going to work here.

"I've got it," Ashley says, taking out a Black Amex that belongs to her father. "You take cards?"

"Cash only."

"Hmm." Ashley taps the card against her chin. "We're good for it, obviously."

"I'm sorry, but I've got to get cash up front. Don't want to get fired during my first week."

"Of course not," I say, tugging on Ash's arm to keep her from embarrassing me any further. "We'll do it another time."

"I'm here every day," Fred says to me with that same slow smile.

The tips of my ears are burning, and it's not from the sun. "Good to know."

He raises his eyebrows twice quickly, then turns back to Becky, who's got her arms crossed in a way my mom always used to tell me made me look like a spoiled brat.

"Come on," I say to Ash. "Hopefully they take your card at the Shack."

We walk toward the parking lot where the Shack sets up its food truck in the summer. I glance back at Fred, hoping to get a last look at him so I can memorize what he looks like. Becky's still talking at him, but he's watching us, watching *me*, and when our eyes lock, his grin goes wide, and I'm definitely feeling something, though it's hard to describe what it is.

I think it means I want him to kiss me, but that's silly because we only just met.

"I told you going to the beach was a good idea," Ashley says as Fred gives me a friendly wave.

My hand raises to repeat his gesture. "I'll never doubt you again."

CHAPTER THREE

June 2023

"Fred Webb?" I say to Charlotte as I struggle to bring my bags through the ornate front door. As predicted, Charlotte's interest in my things was purely sociological.

"Do we know another Fred?"

"I don't know," I say petulantly. "Do we?"

"We do not."

I pull the suitcase over the threshold and drop my bags onto the black and white marble floor. Cold in winter, slippery in summer, it's classically beautiful and totally impractical. But my mother loved it, and like too much in this family, if she dictated it, then it stayed.

"Why didn't you tell me?"

Charlotte gives me an elegant shrug of the shoulder, but I know why. If I knew that Fred had anything to do with the sale, I wouldn't have come home, no matter how much I wanted to get out of New York.

Damn it.

I breathe in and out slowly as the house's smell envelops me. Lemon-scented cleaner and the deep tang of the ocean that you can hear if you stand still. It was the lullaby of my childhood, and even now, whenever I sleep near the ocean, I feel at peace.

But not today.

"Have you seen him?" I ask. "Fred?"

"It was all done through the lawyers."

I can hear my heart hammering in my ears. Fred. Fred. *Fred.*

If I were smart, I'd wheel my bag right back out of here and drive somewhere else.

But I've never been smart where Fred is concerned.

"What could he want with Taylor House?" I try to keep the anguish out of my voice while I gesture to the crumbling plaster and the walls that haven't been repainted in twenty years.

"Honestly? He'll probably tear it down and build one of those ultra-modern places like everyone else does."

But why this *house,* I want to shout. *He could do that to anyone.*

But I already know the answer.

It's *this* house because it's mine.

* * *

"Oh, Olivia, you're here," my father says as we walk into the front parlor. When he's not at the club, he has a set pattern through the house during the day, following the best light like a sundial. "Good, good."

He opens his arms, gesturing for me to come closer. He's wearing what I always think of as his summer wardrobe—madras golf shorts and a matching polo. At sixty-five, he has the body of a bon vivant: a veined nose and a paunch that sticks out too far, but he's still charming and handsome with his shock of white hair, bright blue eyes, and an easy smile that falls into a laugh when he's amused, which is often. Despite his tendency to complain, he's always been a good-time Charley, cheers of *"William!"* following him wherever he goes.

I kiss him on his left cheek. He smells like cinnamon gum and Old Spice, and I start to choke up as he pulls me into a brief hug. It's been too long since I've seen him. I've been so wrapped up in my own drama, I didn't make the time for him that I should have.

But I'm here now, and despite the fact that I'm still reeling from hearing that Fred Webb bought this house, I'm glad.

"Let me get a look at you." He holds me by the arms and inspects me.

I cringe, thinking about what he's seeing. My skin is pale because I've been inside all semester, and my face is somehow both gaunt and swollen from too little eating and too much drinking. I can tell by his expression that he thinks I look frightful, and he's not wrong.

His mouth is twitching as he fights the urge to say it. "Good to have you here. The salt air will do you good, I'm sure."

"Thanks, William." I started calling him that after my mother got sick when I was twelve, and it stuck.

Back then, everyone thought I was precocious. Now, it's a habit that everyone accepts. The truth is, I did it to create distance between us. Because if parents were going to be people who died unexpectedly, it was safer to keep them at bay.

I wait for him to ask me about Wes, but he doesn't. Instead, he says, "Shall we have a drink?"

Drinks on the veranda occur every day at five, rain or shine, sleet, or poverty. The liquor bill is the only one that always gets paid on time. And William avoids messy topics, such as leaving one's husband, like the plague.

Not that I've told any of them many details. I just texted the basics to Charlotte and Sophie in our rarely used group chat and told them when I'd be arriving.

It's the WASP way, after all. My family are gold-medal recipients in stuffing things down and withholding emotions.

"Sounds good," I say about the drink.

He crooks his arm through mine, and we walk through the patio doors. The veranda's a wide expanse of porch and patio, partly covered, that stops at the bright green lawn. A local boy mows it twice a week for a minimal fee, so it's well maintained in a way that most of the grounds aren't.

I stop and take in the view. The sky is that clear blue of early summer before the heat haze sets in. There are high, puffy clouds gliding lazily above it, and just over the grass-covered dunes is the ocean, its roaring waves dulled by the distance. I breathe in and out deeply again, like I did in the hallway, taking in the salt air, feeling some of the anxiety and sorrow seep out of me.

It will do me good to be here, the past and Fred notwithstanding.

"What do you think about this sad business?" my father asks, his hands on his hips, facing the view.

"Selling?"

"What else?"

"We've been trying to get you to do it for years."

"Yes, yes, but the way the bank just stepped in and . . . I was getting around to it. They didn't have to act so hastily."

Aunt Tracy comes outside carrying gin and tonics on a tray, along with small bowls of cheese straws. I eye them hungrily, feeling weak and needy. There won't be any dinner, or any more cheese straws, until eight, and what with the hasty packing of everything I own, I didn't get lunch.

I bury my instinct to grab one of the bowls and shove its contents in my mouth. Instead, I take the tray from Aunt Tracy, put it down, and pull her into a hug. "It's so good to see you."

"It's been too long since you were home," she says when we break apart. Aunt Tracy's coloring is dark, with white streaks in her short, thick chestnut hair, and laugh lines on her honey-colored face. She's wearing light gray slacks and a white poplin shirt with a coral necklace.

"I know. Don't scold me."

"Your father's been missing you."

"He'll be sick of me by summer's end."

She smiles. "I'm making your favorite for dinner."

"Seafood paella? You're the best." I pick up a gin and tonic and a bowl of cheese straws, and drift toward where Charlotte and my father are talking over their own drinks. His is half gone already.

"So, what's the plan?" I say. "Where should we start with the clean-out?"

Charlotte shoots me a look. "We were talking about the garden party tomorrow."

"Ah."

"You'll be attending, dear," William says.

"I guess so."

"Good, good. All the usual suspects—the Phelps and the Thorpes—and your sister's family."

"And I invited Ashley," Charlotte says.

I ignore Charlotte's addition. "Sophie made it down okay?"

Sophie's husband's family has a place a mile from here, where they spend the summer, letting their boisterous boys run around while her husband, Colin, commutes back and forth to Manhattan. I like Colin, but I find my nephews exhausting, even though I work with children. Maybe it's because of that. It's one thing for kids who aren't related to me to give me a hard time. Another entirely when it's my blood.

"She's been down for a week, complaining daily," Charlotte says.

"What's it this time?"

"Her back, apparently."

Charlotte and I exchange a glance, tamping down our laughter. One thing we've always connected over is how Sophie is old before her time.

"That's a shame."

"To already have problems with your back," William says, "and so young too. I blame the children."

"Naturally."

"They run around like banshees. You should see them when they come here. Climbing all over me and the furniture. Your mother wouldn't have liked it."

"Mom would have loved it," I correct. "She was always scampering around with us."

"Was she?" He sips at his drink with that faraway look he usually reserves for financial matters. I long ago decided that his vagueness was a deliberate choice. A way of pre-creating an excuse when he lets the details of life get away from him. He can be as sharp as a tack when he wants to be.

"She was," I say gently, then turn to the view again. I sip at my drink, that bitter mix of alcohol, tonic, and lime I always associate with home.

"Be that as it may . . . the garden party. She always loved the garden parties."

"She did."

"And everyone will be so glad to see you. Only, perhaps you could dress up for it?"

"Don't worry, I won't wear my sweatpants."

"That's all right, then. Barry, the lawyer, is coming too, and his daughter. Have you met her? She and your sister have been spending a lot of time together."

There's a trace of a blush on Charlotte's cheeks. "Ann's a lawyer too, Father. She works with him. They're partners. And there were a lot of details to work out."

I'm intrigued. It's so rare to see Charlotte discomfited. "I'm looking forward to meeting her."

"And the new owner, of course," William says, rocking on his heels. "A rich man from London. Though I hear he's American. He bought the place sight unseen; can you believe it?"

A lump forms in my throat. "Fred. You invited him?"

He rattles the ice around in his glass. "Who's Fred?"

"Mr. Webb. The man who bought the house."

"Ah yes, that's right. Some bigwig in shipping, they tell me. Or is it a cruise line?"

"Shipping," I say through clenched teeth.

"Made a fortune, I understand. And bought this place, like I said, sight unseen." William shakes his head at the marvel of it.

"He has seen it."

"The virtual tour, you mean. They came and filmed that one day, and it took hours. I had to shoo them out eventually, but then they insisted on taking drone shots, flying that little buzzing thing up there over the house. What for, I can't imagine."

I finish my drink in one long gulp. I can't tell whether he's deliberately misunderstanding me or not. It's possible he's forgotten all about Fred. His daughters' personal lives aren't the sort of thing he keeps track of so long as the G&Ts flow nicely at five PM, and dinner is on the table promptly at eight.

"He's really coming to the party?" I say to Charlotte, pulling her aside as William walks out into the lawn to stretch his legs.

"Father insisted on inviting him."

"You could've warned me. You could've warned me about all of it."

"You're not *still* carrying a torch for him are you?" Charlotte's tone is incredulous, but her eyes are filled with curiosity. "After all these years?"

"It's not '*all these years*,'" I say, then bite back the rest of my answer. It's been five.

CHAPTER FOUR

June 2003

I do go back to the beach the next day. After an afternoon of hanging with Ash, but thinking about Fred, it feels like I don't have a choice. Like my legs would've taken me there even if I was trying to go somewhere else. It's a crush, I think, but I'm okay with that. I haven't had a proper crush in years, not since I moved to an all-girls school in ninth grade that let me have the afternoons off to play tennis.

This time, I leave Ash behind with an excuse about having to run an errand that I'm not sure she believes, and I bring enough money to rent a deck chair and an umbrella—a twenty I stole from my father's wallet because I don't get my first paycheck until next week.

I'm nervous as I chain my old ten-speed to a wooden fence post, then scramble over the dunes. I don't know how to do this—talk to a boy—and now I'm regretting not bringing Ash along to do the talking for me. She can be a lot sometimes, but that's probably what's needed.

But Ash isn't here, so I pull the belt on my beach coverup tighter and gather up my courage. Under the coverup is a tankini two-piece in a light blue color that makes my tan pop and emphasizes my strength in a good way.

I pull my hair back into a ponytail, then walk to the umbrella station. Fred's standing with the other guys, the ones who used to torture me in middle school. They're horsing around the way guys do, slapping asses and punching shoulders.

I stand there, frozen, a lump in my throat. I should go, I think. He hasn't seen me yet.

Then Fred looks up and gives me that slow smile I remember from yesterday, and my nerves travel from my stomach to my fingertips. I try hard not to stare at him, but I want to memorize his face so when I'm thinking about him before I go to sleep, I get the details right. Last night, I wasn't sure I remembered the freckles properly, or the exact color of his eyes. But now I see them, plain as day—six freckles in a straight line across his nose, and his eyes really are the same color as the ocean.

He takes a couple of quick steps toward me. "Hey, Local. You came back."

"I did." I jut out my hip in a way I've seen Ash do, and something pops. Ouch. "I even brought some money this time."

"I can't be bought."

My throat is dry. "I . . ."

"I'm just teasing. You want a chair or an umbrella or . . .?"

"Can I get both for twenty?"

He smiles again, right at me, and even though my knees are weak and there's a small possibility I'm going to pass out, I'm proud of myself for coming here. I can do this. I can talk to a boy.

"Doesn't it hurt to stand like that?" Fred asks with an eyebrow arched.

"Oh, um . . ." I pull my hip back into place. My cheeks are burning. "Yeah, it kind of does."

"Looks funny too."

"Gee, thanks."

"I didn't mean . . ."

"No, it's fine. I'll take that lounger?"

Now *he* has the beginning of a blush creeping up his neck. We stare at each other for a moment, then Fred grabs a lounger and an umbrella, tucking one under each arm. "Where do you want to sit?"

"Where do you recommend?"

"Well, those people over there"—he motions his chin toward a family where the mother is reading a novel and two cute kids are playing in the sand with plastic shovels. The dad is on his back, fast asleep, his belly alarmingly red. "They usually have a big screaming match right around lunchtime."

"Not near them, then." I scan the beach. There's a couple sitting on two chairs, chatting. "What about over there?"

"How do you feel about older men checking you out in your bathing suit?"

"Ugh, no."

"Didn't think so. Come on, I've got the perfect spot." Fred walks between the chairs until he gets to an open area that's far enough away from the other umbrellas that I won't have to listen to someone else's conversation.

"I can't believe this space is still free."

Fred puts the gear down and opens the lounger. "I saved it for you."

"You did?"

He tucks his chin down, concentrating on driving the umbrella into the sand. "I thought you might be back." He opens the umbrella, and it casts the perfect circle of shade. Then he looks up at me, shy. "I hoped you would, Olivia."

"Oh, I . . ."

"Don't worry, I don't bite."

I laugh and the tension breaks. "Are girls usually worried you're going to bite them?"

"Not that I've heard."

"That's good then."

He holds out his hand. "Towel?"

I take my backpack off and pull out the towel I brought from home. It's dark blue with red lobsters on it. "You don't have to lay it out. I can do it."

"All part of the service." He takes it and smooths it out over the lounger, tucking the corners down into small clips that I wouldn't have known were there. "Voila."

"That looks great."

"Trick of the trade."

"But now I know your trick, so I don't need you anymore." I can't believe it. I'm *flirting*.

He looks up at me, his perfectly arched eyebrows raised. "I have others."

My heart thumps. He's flirting too. "Such as?"

"You'll have to come back to find out." He steps toward me and takes the twenty out of my hand. He does it in a way that tangles our fingers for a moment, and a warmth spreads from that skin on skin to my chest. Then his fingers are gone, and it feels like I might've imagined it. Only the blush on his neck has crept to his cheeks.

He clicks the end of his pen. "Olivia Taylor, right?"

"That's right. And you're Fred . . ."

"Webb. Rental is good till four."

"I'll have it back to you before then. Thanks again for saving this spot."

"No worries." He puts his hand on my shoulder and lets it rest there. "If you need anything, just holler."

That heat starts to build again, making my throat tight. I don't know how to handle it, so I duck away, pulling my book out and laying it down on the towel. It's *The Amber Spyglass*, the third novel in the His Dark Materials series.

"It would be so cool to have a daemon," he says.

I check his face to see if he's teasing. He isn't. "You've read them?"

"Of course."

"They're my favorite books."

"Mine too." He reaches down and picks up the novel, thumbing through the pages. "What would your daemon be?" He's referring to the animal spirit that each character has.

"I've always loved foxes."

"You're joking."

"No. Why?"

"Only because that's *my* daemon." He hands the book back and our fingers brush again. All of this casual contact is making me feel dizzy. "Team Will or Team Roger?"

"For Lyra? Will, of course."

"So we don't agree on everything."

We grin at each other. "I can't believe there aren't going to be any more books," I say.

"Agreed."

One of the Dougs or Daves whistles from across the beach. Fred turns and puts his hands up in a *what?* gesture. The guy motions for him to come back.

"I've got to get back, or Dave will have a fit."

"Is that Dave Dale?"

"You know him?"

I nod. "Keep him away from peanuts."

"Is he allergic?"

"Nah, he just gets super hyper when he eats them. Or at least he did when we were kids."

He taps my breastbone lightly. His touch feels like it will leave a mark. "Right, local knowledge."

I clear my throat. "That's me."

"Come say goodbye before you leave?"

"I have to bring back the chair, don't I?"

He raises his shoulders. "Most people just abandon them."

"Most people suck, then."

"Nah, it's the job. Enjoy the read."

I smile. "Reread."

"Ha! Later, Local."

I think he might touch me again—I want him to—but instead, he gives me a small wave, then turns on his heel and skims back over the sand to where Dave is waiting.

Dave gives him the requisite punch in the arm while looking at me. I'm sure he's placed me by now and is telling Fred all about my most embarrassing fifth-grade moments.

And in that moment I wish I *was* Lyra, that the spirit part of me was something detached that I could send after those who might do me harm or protect me like a charm.

CHAPTER FIVE

June 2023

Waking up in my bedroom on the third floor feels both familiar and awful.

I had too many gin and tonics last night, followed by too much wine at dinner after Charlotte pulled me aside and finally asked what happened with Wes. I didn't give her the gory details, but she figured out the basics. I was here, wasn't I, when I'd said I couldn't be. She knew something was broken in my marriage.

How broken was too much to think about. So instead, I escaped to my stuffy room, threw both windows open to let in the night breeze, and turned on an old fan that rattled as it turned on its axis. Then I stripped down to my underwear and a tank top and tried to fall asleep, which, after a long night of sweating and a carousel of regrets, I finally did.

This morning, my heart hurts and I miss the large king bed I picked out with care, enjoying the expensive Egyptian cotton sheets Wes had insisted we splurge on in our perfectly temperature-controlled apartment. Even though this room is exactly as I left it, it's not mine anymore. I am essentially homeless. And that's hitting home like some terrible metaphor.

And then there's Fred.

I'm going to see him tonight. Just the thought of it sets my body quivering in anticipation and dread. Fred. Fred. *Fred*. His name echoes through my thoughts like it always has. And it feels like it always will.

I turn on my side and squeeze my eyes shut against the intrusion. I don't have to see Fred. I can skip out on the garden party. If I do, he might frown in that way he has when he's disappointed, but I won't be there to see it. My father will tut-tut about how I never think of anyone but myself, and Charlotte will get sick of having to answer for my whereabouts because she hates when the attention isn't entirely on her.

I can live with all of that except for the fact that it would make me a coward. I still have a competitive edge in me somewhere. The fire I used to use to stare down my opponents on the tennis court and make them think they were going to lose before I even hit the first shot— that's still buried in me.

So, I'm going. I'm going.

I just have to get out of bed first.

* * *

"Where do you want to start?" Aunt Tracy asks as we stand at the end of the second-floor hallway later that morning.

There are four paneled doors in front of us, like a choose-your-own-adventure of memories. My parents' room, where William still sleeps; Sophie's room, unused and as frozen in time as mine; Charlotte's bedroom; and my mother's day room.

The day room was her private sanctum, where she could retreat to read all night if she was having one of her bouts of insomnia, or to nap in the afternoon when she wasn't feeling well. It was the first place we looked for her when we were kids and the last place I saw her before she died. I haven't been inside in twenty years.

"I'm not ready for Mom's room."

Tracy hugs me from the side. "I don't blame you. I don't know if I could face it either."

"Charlotte can clean out her own room. And Sophie."

"Agreed." She looks around as if they might materialize. "Where are they?"

"Charlotte said something last night about being tied up with organizing the garden party."

"*The soiree*," Charlotte had called it, confirming numbers over breakfast while William nodded in approval.

"And Sophie?"

"You know Sophie."

"I do." She sighs. "So that leaves—"

"Their room. Mom's side of it anyway." I swallow hard. It won't be the same as going through the day room, but it's where all her clothes and jewelry still are. My father never bothered to take the time to clear away her things. "Maybe I can face that with your help."

"I always knew you were the brave one."

"We'll see."

We step to the door at the end of the hall, and I grip the wrought-iron door handle and twist. It catches, not wanting to give, like it senses my reluctance. I put my shoulder to it and push. The door opens with a pop, and I almost tumble into the room.

"The clumsy one too," I say as I right myself and take in my surroundings. The walls are butter yellow, with matching curtains with small flowers running over them. There's a heavy oak bed that's made up with a light cream coverlet, and two dressers, William's— that's still full of his knickknacks and daily use items, and my mother's—covered in silver-framed family photographs. There's a portrait of her as a young woman on the wall, and the far wall stares at the ocean.

I walk to the Juliet window. There's a small balcony off it. "I forgot how good the view is from here."

"The best view in the house."

I open the door and walk out. The balcony is high enough that the dunes aren't an obstruction to the view. The tide is out, and the beach is dotted with colorful umbrellas and children freed from the shackle of school. The salty tang of the ocean fills my senses, mixing with the faint hint of my mother's gardenia-scented perfume, which lingers like a ghost.

I shove my rising sadness and turn. "Where should we start?"

Tracy's kind eyes cloud with sadness. "Her closets? She's got some vintage pieces that we can sell if you're not interested in them."

"I don't think they'll fit me. Maybe Charlotte." My mother was petite like Charlotte and Sophie.

"You're smaller than you used to be," Tracy says. "You might be surprised."

"Am I?" I look down at myself, trying to see a difference. It's true that the linen slacks I'm wearing are loose. "I haven't been trying to lose weight."

"I hate you." Tracy's always been plump, but it suits her.

"Probably Wes's fault."

Things had been rocky for us all year, which I'd confessed to Tracy when we had lunch in the city in March. I thought we could work things out, then.

"Him too."

"Do you want to talk about it?"

"No." I grimace, then walk to my mother's closet. There's enough sadness in this task that I don't need to bring Wes into it.

When I checked my phone this morning, I realize that he texted me last night, asking if I'd arrived okay. I'd answered with a terse *yes*. We hadn't discussed whether we were keeping the channels of communication open. Neither of us has ended a marriage before, if that's what we were doing.

"I wouldn't recommend the wine and Sprite diet, but I guess it's effective for weight loss." I open the double closet doors. A moth flies out, even though the smell of mothballs is overpowering. "I have a bad feeling about this."

"No one's touched that closet in twenty years."

"Things fall apart."

"They do."

Tracy stands at one end, and I take the other. I've got the casual clothes, pedal pushers and light linen shirts, her summer wardrobe. Her winter and more formal clothes are at Tracy's end.

"Do you think it's weird that William never cleaned out any of this?" I ask.

"Maybe he liked having her things around."

"But what about . . ."

My father's never said, but I assume he's been with someone in the time since my mother died. Did he ever bring the women here? Or was Charlotte's presence a deterrent? I haven't asked, which Charlotte would say is more evidence of the fact that I've left her to *"deal with everything."* And maybe I have.

"If you're asking if he's had women, as far as I know, no. He did love your mother, you know. Very much."

"That doesn't mean he has to be alone forever."

Tracy smiles, the laugh lines around her eyes spreading out like spiderwebs. "You probably don't remember this, but the divorcées did circle after the funeral, bringing casseroles and offering to help look after you girls. Your father shooed them all away, and eventually they gave up."

"Maybe they were scared of you."

Tracy had lived with us for a full year after Mom died. Sometimes I'd fantasize that she and my dad would get married, but when I mentioned it to her once, she laughed and kissed me and said that there were many kinds of love. I knew that meant I wasn't getting her as a stepmom.

"That's possible. What about this?" Tracy says, holding up a white shift dress. It has blue and green flowers embroidered around the collar.

"That was one of Mom's favorites."

"You should try it on." She holds it out to me, and I hesitate. I have so many memories of my mother in this dress. She wore it often when she and William had garden parties like the one scheduled for tonight. "Don't worry," Tracy says. "It's not haunted."

"This whole house is haunted."

"I've never felt that."

"I always have."

I take the dress from her and walk to the old-fashioned changing screen my mom had installed in the corner of the room. I used to hide back there with Sophie and watch her get ready for a night out. She had this beautiful strawberry-blond hair that she'd brush and brush until it fell like a shimmery curtain down her back.

I step out of my clothes and into the dress. It's narrow in the hips, but broader in the shoulders. On my mother, it fell beneath her knees, but for me, it stops above them, a more modern length.

"Will you help me zip up?" I leave the screened area and turn my back to Tracy. She tugs on the zipper and raises it slowly up my back. It feels like a miracle when it goes all the way.

"How does it feel?"

"I can breathe."

"Turn around." I do and Tracy's eyes well up. "Oh, honey. Look at you." She takes my shoulders and turns me toward the full-length mirror on the wall. The dress fits perfectly, like it was made for me. "You look so much like her."

I lean forward, trying to see what she sees. I'm pale, and the strawberry strands I had when I was young have mostly leached out of my hair, but our blue eyes are the same, and the weight loss has given angles to my face I've never seen before. "I miss her."

"I know, honey—me too." Tracy hugs me from the side again, and we look at each other in the mirror. Tracy smiles, and I smile back. It's easier than crying. "You should wear this tonight. Fred won't be able to take his eyes off you."

My smile slips, and I dip away from her. I walk back behind the screen and reach for the zipper. It's hard to undo on my own, but I manage it after a few false starts.

"I'm sorry. Did you not know he was coming?"

"No, I did. I just . . ." I poke my head around the screen. "Why do you care what he thinks about me? You never liked him."

"That's not true."

"Come on, Aunt Tracy."

Her hands flutter. She's wearing several chunky rings, and they click against one another at the movement. "Okay, yes, I did have my reservations. You kids were so young. I . . . I stand by what I said then, but . . ."

"Now that he's rich and he bought this house, and my marriage is probably over, you think I should give him another chance?"

"I wouldn't put it that bluntly."

I pull my head back behind the screen and step out of the dress. It's lovely and I'm going to keep it, but tonight has enough memories in it. I don't need to be wearing one. "Why do you assume that there's another chance left to give?"

"You don't think so?"

I stare at the wall. There's a large crack running up it, like a crooked mouth. "We didn't leave things . . . I doubt he'll even want to talk to me."

"Why buy this house, then?"

I put my own clothes back on and step out, the dress folded over my arm. "I don't know."

"We don't have to talk about it."

"Good. Though, on a related topic, Charlotte mentioned something yesterday about us all getting a share of the sale. Do you know what she's talking about?"

"Fred paid twenty-five for this place and the property around it. That's more than enough to pay off what your father owes and set him up with an annuity that will pay for a house and his living expenses until he passes on. The rest will be divided equally between the three of you."

My mouth is dry. "Twenty-five million?"

"That's right."

"I never thought it was worth that much."

"The market's been crazy these last few years. And old places like this, right on the beach with so much land—they almost never change hands. Your father agreed to settle five on each of you."

I feel like the wind has been kicked out of me. "Are you sure?"

"Yes, of course. After Charlotte mentioned it as a possibility, I saw to the details myself. You know how your father is, and frankly, I didn't trust Charlotte not to make some sweetheart deal for herself and leave you and Sophie out of it."

"But . . . why?"

"Half of this place belonged to your mother by rights, once they got married, and your father most certainly does not need that much money. I made it clear it was what your mother would've wanted, and he agreed."

I sit on the edge of the day bed, feeling weak. "I don't know what to say."

"You can thank your father. He's the one who agreed to it."

"Only because you told him to."

"No," Tracy says. "Your mother did."

CHAPTER SIX

July 2003

When I go back to the beach the next day, Fred pushes Dave aside and insists on being the one to take my lounger and umbrella to another perfect spot. I avoid the smirk Dave aims my way and give a big smile to Fred instead.

"How's this do you?" Fred says twenty feet from the water.

"Perfect."

He sets the equipment up for me, and I hand him my towel to spread over it to give our fingers a chance to touch again. I thought about his hands a lot last night. How his skin felt against mine. How I wanted something more than those brief touches that was hard to describe.

"All set," he says, patting the lounger.

I sit down where he indicates, and he sits next to me. Now the side of our knees are brushing, the light hair on his leg slightly ticklish.

"You know how to do that?" He says, pointing to a set of kids bodysurfing in the waves.

"Of course."

"You want to teach me?"

"Really?"

"I've always wanted to know how."

"Let's do it then."

He stands and starts to peel off his polo.

"Oh," I say, dragging my eyes away from his chest, which is a bit pale but defined. "Now?"

"I have a break."

"Great."

I turn away and pull my coverup over my head, with my heart quickening. I didn't think about being in a bathing suit in front of him when I got ready to come to the beach. My cheeks are already burning at the thought of it.

"Ready?" Fred asks.

I turn around. He's taken off his khakis too, revealing a blue and white striped bathing suit that sits low on his hips. They're narrow and his stomach is flat and . . . *Stop looking at it, Olivia. Eyes up!*

I meet his amused glance and turn a darker shade of red. Then I turn on my heel and sprint toward the water, yelling over my shoulder. "Last one in pays for snacks!"

We spend ten minutes in the waves as I show him how to wait for the perfect arc, when to lift your feet up and swim. He's strong in the water, his strokes sure, and he picks it up almost immediately. We catch the perfect wave and surf it in together, laughing with delight as it dumps us on the sand. He helps me stand up, holding onto my wrists longer than necessary. Our eyes lock, and a shiver of something goes through me, making my arms turn to gooseflesh.

"Again?" I say, and it takes him a moment to answer.

"I have to get back, but . . . tomorrow?"

"Yes."

* * *

The next day we head right to the water and swim out past the wave break. It's a placid day, and we tread next to each other in the gentle surf, enjoying the sun and the calm.

"Who introduced you to the His Dark Materials series?" he asks as a wave pushes him closer to me. We're facing each other, and our swirling legs keep touching. Even though the water's calm, I'm out of breath. "Most people I know have never heard of those books."

35

"My mom. She . . ." A lump forms in my throat. "She got sick a couple of years ago, and she spent a lot of time reading because it made her feel better."

Fred's eyes darken, and he reaches out to touch my arm. "Is she okay?"

"No, she died."

"Oh, Olivia, I'm sorry. I know how hard that is."

"You do?"

A gentle wave comes in, pushing us up, then down. When it passes, we're almost in an embrace. I can feel his breath on my face, our eyes level. I count his freckles to keep myself from kissing him.

"Yeah. My dad . . . he died two years ago this September."

"I'm sorry, Fred." I put my hand on his arm this time, and it tightens beneath my grip, supporting me in the water. "Was he sick?"

"He was a firefighter. One day, his luck ran out."

I'm close enough to see the tears pooling in Fred's eyes, matching my own. I want to take that last move into his arms, to comfort him, to comfort me, but instead, we stay like we are, floating, looking at each other in a way I've never done before, our breaths matching as they go out and in. Like we want to get closer, but we're scared of what might happen.

"Olivia, I—"

Someone blows a whistle and we start apart.

"Fred!" Dave yells from the beach. "Break's over."

"Guess I better go," Fred says, but he doesn't move.

"I think I hate Dave."

He laughs. "Right now, I kind of do too. Tomorrow?"

"Yes."

He squeezes my arm, then runs his hand down the length of it until he reaches my fingers. My whole body responds, clenching in reaction, and I finally tear my eyes away from his. He runs his hand back up, then swims away.

I watch his sure strokes and then continue to watch as he walks out of the water to where he recovers his clothes from the sand and ties a towel around his waist. My heart is beating too fast, and my limbs feel weak, but it feels safer here in the water than exposed on the land, and so I stay.

* * *

We have a week of days like this. Sun-kissed afternoons where we find excuses to touch each other in the water until Dave blows his whistle on us.

We talk too about anything and everything. What his life is like in Boston. What mine is like here. Why I love tennis so much. Music and TV shows and stupid things that don't mean anything serious but are a way to distract ourselves from whatever is happening between us.

We haven't kissed, even though it's all I think about. But it's coming; I can feel it. Why else would he rest his hands on my waist under the water, his thumbs making slow circles on the small patch of skin between my bathing suit top and bottom? Why else would he look at me so intensely it's hard for me to concentrate?

We just need to find a minute where we're not on display.

I haven't told anyone about Fred. He's a secret, *my* secret, and my mind is full of him no matter what I'm doing. Coach Matt tells me I'm distracted, that I need to get my head back in the game as I spray forehands past the baseline. My piano teacher tut-tuts as I screw up basic passages I'd mastered at seven. I smile about him over dinner, happy, for once, that my self-involved family is too busy with their own lives to notice.

I even keep him as a secret from Ash. I want to share, to gush about Fred and discuss every little detail and touch and what it all means, but I also want to keep him—*us*—to myself for a while until I figure out what's going on. So I tell her I'm doing extra training for tennis and can't hang out, and she pouts her disappointment but doesn't question me.

And now it's July 3rd, the day before my birthday, and I'm trying to think of how I can see Fred outside his work hours, when Ash catches me at the gate that separates the club from the beach.

"OMG, I knew it." Ash's arms are crossed, one foot jutted out in front. She's got her hair in a French braid, and she's wearing pink terry shorts and a matching sweatshirt.

"Knew what?"

"You've been ditching me. For a *guy*."

I can't keep the blush from creeping up my cheeks. "I . . ."

"You *are*."

"I didn't mean to."

Lauren Bailey

"Yeah, you did."

I yoke my arms around her neck. "Are you mad?"

"No, I'm impressed."

We start to laugh. "Didn't think I had it in me, huh?"

"Not in a million years."

"You want to come with me?"

Ashley cocks her head to the side. She's wearing a shade of bright red lipstick that she calls her Lolita look. *"Gross,"* I said, when she told me that. *"Did you even read the book?"*

"I don't have to," she says, responding to my invite.

"I want you to."

"You're a terrible liar."

"It's true. But come. You can . . . meet him."

Her eyes light up. "Fred? You talked to him?"

I nod because *talking* seems like too small a word to describe it.

He gets me and I get him, and the way we get each other seems impossible and inevitable. At night, when I think over our conversations, I tell myself that it feels this way because it's the first time, the first boy. But I know that's not true. There hasn't ever been another person like this in my life, and my heart feels so full I'm worried about what might burst out of me.

Love, I think. *This is love.*

"Have you kissed him yet?" Ashley opens the gate and links her arm through mine.

"No."

"So, you're what? Hanging out? Friends?"

"We haven't talked about it."

"Oh, girlfriend, no."

"What?"

She wags a finger at me. "You have to talk about it."

We turn right on the beach, the wind whipping our hair around. "Why?"

"You don't want to be put in the friend zone."

"I thought that's what girls did to guys?"

Ashley purses her lips. "Nah, it can work both ways."

"I don't think that's what's happening."

"Which is exactly my point. Has he asked you out?"

There had been some talk, yesterday, of us maybe grabbing a bite after his shift ended, but I had piano, and if my father heard that I'd skipped my lesson, it would lead to all kinds of questions. "Not in so many words."

"It's a good thing I found you out."

"Ash . . ."

"Don't worry. I'm just going to help things along. I'm the reason you met, right? You're happy I did that?"

"Yes, but—"

"Leave it to me. Besides, your birthday's tomorrow. Don't forget the mission."

"I remember."

"Good."

We get to Cooper's Beach, and I let Ash take the lead. She barrels past the umbrellas and beachgoers and walks right up to Fred with a confidence I wish I had outside the tennis court.

"I hear you've been hanging out with my girl."

He gives me a wild-eyed look before burying it in a grin. "Nice to see you again, Ashley. Hi, Olivia."

"Hey, Fred." I stand back, wanting some physical space between us so he knows this isn't my idea.

"So, I'm wondering," Ashley says, oblivious to my body language or the fact that half of Fred's fellow beach dudes are listening in, "are you going to ask her out, or what?"

I'm sorry, I mouth behind Ashley.

"Isn't that between me and her?"

"Well, it would be, I guess, but we're on a timetable."

Oh no. No, no, no.

"Excuse me?"

"It's her birthday tomorrow."

"Ash . . ."

"I'm aware."

"Our July Fourth baby," Ash says. "All the fireworks go off to celebrate her."

"As they should," Fred says, and I do love him for saying that.

"I agree. So, what are you going to do about it?"

"Excuse me?"

39

"We just agreed that Olivia deserves fireworks on her birthday, did we not?"

His eyes dance. "We did."

"So?"

"I'm not quite sure how that works here. Are you allowed to do fireworks on the beach?"

I have to intervene. I can't watch them negotiate our first date anymore.

"There's a dinner," I blurt. "At the club. This lobster night thing. And after, they'll be fireworks. I can bring a guest." My heart is pounding, and is this what almost fainting feels like?

Fred gives me that slow smile. "Are you asking me out?"

"Of course she is," Ashley says.

"Olivia?"

"Yes. I'd lo—like you to come. If you can. I mean, there'll be a lot of grown-ups and my father and my aunt, so if you don't want to, I understand."

"I can handle fathers and aunts."

"You say that. But you haven't met them."

"Are you taking it back?"

"No!"

"Good. What time?"

"It's at six. We can meet here and walk over? Or—sorry—did you want to pick me up?"

"That is usually how dates work."

I sink in the sand. He knows how dates work. Because he's dated before. Unlike me. "Okay, then pick me up. At Taylor House. Do you know where it is?"

"I'll figure it out. Dress code?"

"Oh, um, I think the guys wear jackets?" I look to Ashley for help.

She's grinning from ear to ear, pleased with herself and enjoying my discomfort. "Jacket, no tie is fine. Chinos, pressed shirt, those shoes or something better." Ashley points to his boat shoes. "Can you handle it?"

"I think so."

"Good. And you've had lobster before, right? You know about the bib?"

"Ash!"

"I've had lobster before. I know about the bib."

"No offense or anything, it's just a lot of people are surprised to see a bunch of rich people wearing plastic bibs with lobsters on them."

Fred laughs. "No offense taken. I'll see you tonight, Olivia? Five forty-five?"

"Yes."

"Did you want a lounger today?"

"Yes, please."

"I even have cash," Ashley says. "Aren't you proud of me?"

We pay and Fred walks us to my spot. I want him to linger, but I'm also nervous about talking to him in front of Ashley. So instead, I help him lay my towel out, and let my fingers tangle with his and hope he knows by my smiles and silence how happy I am, and nervous too.

"I'll see you later," Fred says when everything's set up. His eyes rest on me, and the world slows down, and again my mind fills with that word, *kiss*, but now's not the time or the place. Instead, he turns and walks away, and I watch him until he reaches the other guys. He winces at an especially hard shot in the shoulder from Dave.

"Do you love me again now?" Ash says as she arranges herself on her towel.

"I never stopped."

"Is there room in your heart for both of us?"

"Ha ha." I sit down and bring my feet up on the lounger. "Dinner at the club. Yikes."

"It'll be great. And by the night's end, the mission will be complete."

"He's not going to kiss me in front of my father and everyone."

"No, but on the beach after, during the fireworks. You'll see. It'll be perfect."

I try to imagine it, what his lips will feel like, how magical it sounds. But I'm worried about what comes before. How my father is going to react. What bringing Fred to this dinner will mean to him. "You think William will be okay with it?"

"Why should he care?"

"Fred doesn't have any money."

"This isn't Shakespeare, Olivia. He's not going to, like, ask for your hand in marriage."

"You know what a snob William is. You should've heard the way he was talking about Fred's aunt and uncle when they moved here."

Ashley flips over. In her cat's eye sunglasses and lipstick and itty-bitty bikini, she really does look like that movie poster of Lolita. "Didn't your mom come from nothing?"

"Yes, but he doesn't apply the same rules to himself, and her family came over on the *Mayflower*, so that makes up for everything."

"Oh God, I forgot about that."

"How could you? He only brings it up *all the time*."

"Well, just tell him Fred came over on the *Fortune*. That ought to shut him up."

"What's that?"

"It's the ship after the *Mayflower*. I think it landed in Cape Cod. And he's from Boston, right? It's perfect."

"I shouldn't have to lie about him."

"You're right, but since when did logic apply to parents?"

"Ha! I just hope I don't regret it."

"Regret kissing a hot guy on a beach on your birthday? You need to chillax."

"I'll try."

"Good. Now tell me everything."

CHAPTER SEVEN

June 2023

I don't end up going to the garden party, but it's not because I chicken out.

Instead, Sophie provides the perfect excuse when she shows up at the house shortly after Aunt Tracy and I finish cleaning my mother's things out of her bedroom.

I've always thought of Sophie as the biological link between Charlotte and me. She's between us in height, weight, hair, and eye color, with dark blond hair and green eyes, and a frame that will never get as thin as she wants despite perpetual dieting. Now, at thirty-three, she's the one who looks the most like our mother, despite my momentary transformation earlier when I put on her dress.

"What's all this?" she says when she comes into the house as I'm muscling the last of the garbage bags of my mother's things down the stairs.

"Mom's stuff."

"Oh, I wanted some of that."

I feel a beat of resentment. "You could've helped sort it."

"You didn't tell me you were doing it." Sophie starts to untie the top of one of the bags, her salon-perfect hair falling in a wave that blocks her face from view. She's wearing golf-length linen shorts and a tennis club sweater tied over her shoulders.

She's right, I didn't. "Charlotte told me you weren't helping. *'Too sad,'* apparently."

Sophie looks up at me. Her eyes are tired, and her cheeks are hollowed out in a way I associate with one of her fad diets. "I never said that."

"I should've asked."

"It is sad, though."

"I *know.*"

"And with the kids . . . you know how it is."

"Sure," I say, quashing a sigh. We are who we are. We're not going to change that over the course of a summer. "I made a bag for you. And maybe you could take these others to Goodwill?"

"Which one is mine?"

I point to the smallest bag. "All her Chanel stuff is in there. I think it will fit you."

She smooths down her peach-colored polo shirt. "I'm down five pounds."

"That's great."

"You look like shit."

"Gee, thanks."

"Sorry, that just popped out." She touches my shoulder. "I'm worried about you. We all are."

This brings me close to tears. *This* is the reason we stuff our emotions down. Because letting them up hurts. "Thank you, Soph."

"And I'm sorry about Wes."

Maybe I'll get to a time and place where his name doesn't feel like a knife, but I'm not there yet. "Yeah, me too."

"What happened? You said you were having problems at Christmas, but—"

"Turns out it was Wes who was having a problem. Of the female kind."

Her eyes grow wide. "Oh! How did you find out?"

I stare at the floor trying to erase the memory of the texts I found on his phone. "I don't think I can talk about it."

"No, of course. I understand." She squeezes my arm. "I'm here, though. If you need me."

Tears spring to my eyes. "Thank you. Ah . . ." I wipe them away quickly. "God, it's hot. Any idea where I can get an air conditioner?"

"The Home Depot might have some still, though I heard there was a run on them a couple of weeks ago when we had that heat wave."

"Great."

"Can you help me put this stuff in the car? My back is killing me."

I bury a smile. "Sure."

Her black SUV is parked in the driveway, and I make several trips, hauling the bags from the hallway.

"I can't believe I'm missing tonight," she says as she pushes the button to close the trunk.

"Why?"

Sophie sighs. "You didn't hear? Colin Junior has an earache, and it always turns into an infection, and my sitter canceled, so I'm stuck at home with him. God forbid Colin should miss the party and 'babysit' his son."

"He's not still calling it that, is he?"

"Don't get me started."

"But it's a party at your family's house."

Sophie crosses her arms over her stomach. "He says there are businesspeople who're going to be there that he needs to talk to. I don't know. Ever since he found out about the money, he's been acting weird."

"I thought he had his own money?"

"You know his parents decide what to give us each year."

"I didn't know that."

Sophie clutches her car keys. "Yeah, well, they're kind of judgy, to be honest. I've been telling him for years that he should ask them to settle an amount on us so we can stop having to wonder every year what it's going to be. He's never wanted to do it. But now, we'll have our own money."

"It's your money."

She shakes her head. "No, it's ours. That's how marriage works."

Wes and I had never combined our finances. I'd always thought it was a sign of our independence, but maybe it was just another sign of our failure.

"At least you have some choices now," I say lightly.

"What's that supposed to mean?"

"Just . . . you don't have to be so involved with his family if you don't want to."

"We live in their house every summer."

"Get your own house."

"Colin says we should put it in trust for the kids."

"Sure, some of it. But Soph, come on. Use it to buy some independence. A little happiness."

"I thought money didn't buy happiness?"

"That's what people without money say to make themselves feel better."

"When did you become such a cynic?"

That stops me. I don't believe half the things I said, and talking so much about money makes me feel icky. But that's a prejudice born out of privilege. My family's had money troubles for as long as I can remember, but we were also sitting on an asset that was worth millions. I've never experienced real hardship, and I don't want to pretend that I have. "I'm sorry."

She puts a hand on my shoulder. Her princess-cut engagement ring twinkles in the sun. "You sure you don't want to talk about it?"

"I am."

"Okay, well . . . Have fun tonight."

"Thanks." I wait for her to mention Fred, but she doesn't. Maybe she hasn't heard about that yet. Or maybe she's forgotten all about him and me. Just because he's taken up so much space in my life, doesn't mean he's anything other than a blip in hers.

"Come by tomorrow and see the kids?"

"I will."

"Teddy could use a tennis lesson."

"Sure."

Sophie hugs me quickly. "I'm sorry you had to do Mom's stuff without me."

"There's still her day room."

"Let me know when you're doing that one." She climbs into her car and turns it on. I step to the glass and rap on the window. She lowers it. "Don't worry—I'll clean out my room. Though I doubt I want anything in there."

"Sooner rather than later, please."

"I thought we had all summer."

I look down the length of the driveway. It's lined with large maple trees that turn a brilliant red in the fall. "I don't know how long I'm staying."

"I thought Charlotte said—"

"It's still up in the air."

"Okay. Anyway, I should get going."

"Why don't I watch the kids tonight? So you can go to the party with Colin."

Her eyes widen. "What? Are you sure?"

"I don't know any of these people anymore. It's your life, not mine."

"Thank you!"

"No problem. I'll be there in an hour?"

Sophie smiles as she puts her car in gear. "The kids will be so happy to see you."

*   *   *

The kids are not happy to see me. At best, they're neutral, giving me a cursory "Hi, Aunt Olivia!" before running off to their screens. It's my own fault. I only see them a couple of times a year, at family holidays, and the occasional time Sophie remembers to invite me for Sunday dinner. They live on the Upper West Side, and I live (*lived?*) in Tribeca, and that's enough distance for it to be like we live in two different cities.

Sophie's happy, though, and so is Colin, who I do love. I always have.

When his parents joined the SL&TC twenty-five years ago, they were the first Black members. Colin's dad was a vice-president at Morgan Stanley, and his mom was a doctor, and I shit you not, but I heard more than one member refer to them as the *Huxtables* when they were out of earshot. I can't imagine what it was like for the Martins, enduring clench-jawed conversations where people talked about the "inner cities" and then nodded to them like they must understand exactly what they meant because what else would they be doing in the Hamptons if they weren't there to escape crime?

Back then, we rolled our eyes and grabbed Colin, because Colin was cool, Colin was fun, Colin was good at everything. He and I bonded over tennis, and he'd bite his tongue whenever one of the older members asked him what basketball team he was on.

He and Sophie bonded over . . . I'm not sure what, but he was into her from the beginning. After a couple of summers, it was decided. Sophie and Colin, that was their future, and if my father had any objections, I never heard them. Colin was always welcome at dinner, Colin got to squire Sophie to the end-of-year party, and then later, the prom. They went to the same college, and no one was surprised when they announced their engagement right after graduation.

I used to resent it, because my own choices were met with a lot more resistance, but I've tried to let that go.

Anyway, Colin was going places, but then Colin made a mistake. Instead of forging his own path after he finished his MBA, he got a job at Morgan Stanley, and suddenly nepotism was a problem. He got overlooked, he got passed over, and Mr. Martin couldn't do anything about it because then that *would* be nepotism, and Colin didn't want his help. But now, eight years later, Colin's at least two levels below where he should be, and they're still depending on his parents for luxuries like private school and summers in the Hamptons.

Rich-people problems. It's hard for me to take them seriously, except I know it bothers Sophie. And Colin is disappointed in himself. But every time I encourage him to do something about it, like go to a new company, he smiles politely and changes the subject. But tonight, he's smiling at me with genuine warmth when I arrive, his wide grin lighting up his face, his brown eyes dancing as he straightens his red-and-blue-striped tie.

"Olivia-girl, you're a lifesaver."

"Happy to help."

"You know I never would've heard the end of it from Sophie if I'd gone without her."

"She does have a point."

"One she's made to me over and over."

This is their banter. He complains to me about her, she complains to me about him. Who knows what they do when I'm not around?

"Where are your parents? And Lucy?" Lucy is his younger sister.

"My parents aren't coming down till later in the summer. And Lucy's here, but she's having a drink with a friend and meeting us at the party."

"Who's the business contact you need to talk to?"

He slips on his dark navy jacket. It fits him beautifully, his body still taut like an athlete's. "No one."

"Is it Fred?"

His eyes are guilty. "I'm sorry, Olivia."

"What are you sorry about? We all owe a lot to Fred, from what I've been hearing."

"Is that why you wanted to babysit the kids?"

"I've told you and told you," Sophie says, coming into the room in a pink column dress with white piping. "It's not babysitting when it's your family."

"I think that only applies to husbands," I say. "Is that one of Mom's?"

She twirls for me. "You like?"

"It looks great. Maybe a bit much for a garden party, but . . ."

"That's what I told her," Colin says. "But does she listen?"

Sophie gives him a kiss. I look away, tears in my eyes.

I had this. I *had* this, and now it's gone. "You guys are going to be late."

"She's right, Colin. Olivia, the kids' food is in the fridge, and I left instructions for bedtime."

"I throw them chips and let them stay up as late as they want, right?"

"She's kidding, Soph."

Sophie puts on a bright, brave smile. "I know that. Love you. Boys! Be good for Aunt Olivia!"

"Okay!"

"And Junior's medication is here." She points to the cupboard next to the fridge. "If he's rubbing on his ear a lot, text me."

"Go—have fun."

They rush out in a trail of perfume and cologne, and I wander into the kitchen, happy that I'll be able to eat dinner at a more reasonable hour. Dinner at eight sounds luxurious when you have cocktails and nibbles at five, but when you're a teacher and you have to be in bed at nine because otherwise you're exhausted the next day, it's much less appealing.

Wes had trouble understanding that, and eventually he stopped asking me to join him for his after-work things. Another sign I should've paid attention to. Back then, I was just grateful for the extra sleep.

I pull some things together for dinner and make organic mac and cheese for the kids, with peas in it for their vegetables, and they deign to spend ten minutes with me while they wolf it down before they disappear back into the den. Sophie texts me once to ask after them, and I assure her that everything's okay. Then I sink into the massive couch in the great room, with the intention of catching up on something on TV, but instead I fall asleep, all the bad nights and too much emotion catching up with me.

When I wake up, Colin Junior and Teddy are jumping on the couch. Jumping on me.

"Mommy and Daddy are home!" Colin Junior says.

"And we're not in bed!" Teddy adds, wagging his finger at me like his grandmother.

I sit up, feeling panicked. I'm the worst aunt in the world. Anything could've happened to the kids while I was sleeping. But instead, they're fine, good enough to mock me for dereliction of duty.

"Okay, let's scatter. Come on!"

They giggle and I grab each of them by one hand, rushing them out of the living room and down a long hall to their wing of the house. They share a bedroom, done up in nautical blue and white, and they whip off their clothes and jump into their pajamas, leaving me to pick up after them. I shove their clothes into the hamper as they clamber into bed. I can hear the front door opening, the laughter of more than just Sophie and William. Guests. Great.

"We didn't brush our teeth," Teddy says. At six, he's the responsible one, if a pack of wolves can have a responsible one.

"You're right. Bathroom, quick."

They jump up and make fast work of their teeth, then I shoo them back into bed and tuck each of them in quickly.

"You're going to be in trou . . . ble," Colin Junior says.

"Not if we don't tell."

"Secrets are bad. Mommy said."

"Not this kind of secret. Don't worry."

Colin Junior nods, but Teddy doesn't look so sure. "I'll think about it," he says, then pulls his duvet up to his chin.

"Okay, Teddy." I kiss each of them on the forehead. "I love you."

"Love you!" they say back, and my throat is tight. I do love these little monsters, and I should spend more time with them.

I close the door to their bedroom and stop. There are at least three voices in the living room. Sophie and Colin and, I assume, Lucy.

"Olivia?" Sophie says, her voice trailing down the hall. "Where are you?"

"I'm here," I say stepping out of the shadow near the boys' door. "Just checking on them."

Sophie's cheeks are pink from drinking. "How were they?"

"If I say *angels*, you'll know I'm lying."

"Were they very terrible?"

I hug her impulsively, maybe to distract her. "They were fine. Almost like they weren't even here."

"Oh, good."

"How was the party?"

"It was fun. Everyone was there. And everyone wanted to know where *you* were."

"Did they?"

"Ash did for sure."

I'd forgotten she was going. "Ah."

"You two ever make up after your fight?"

"Nope."

"That's too bad. You were always so close. I was jealous, honestly."

"I remember you always wanted to play with us."

"And you never let me."

"Sorry about that."

"Bygones, right?" Sophie tugs at my arm. "Come into the living room for a drink, and we'll tell you all about it."

"Just for a minute. I need to get home." She turns and I follow her, realizing that I didn't ask her who's here.

But I should've known, because life doesn't let you escape your fate by playing a trick on it like skipping a garden party.

Nope.

Because when I walk into the living room, Fred is standing by the window next to Lucy.

My eyes move slowly toward his as my heart slams in my chest. When our eyes meet, he starts in surprise, like I'm not who he was expecting, then buries it quickly.

"Olivia," Sophie says. "You remember Fred Webb?"

He arches an eyebrow at me, part greeting and part challenge, and it's all I can do to keep my voice calm as I say, "I do."

CHAPTER EIGHT

July 2003

When I tell my father I'm bringing a date to the lobster dinner, he pauses and shakes the ice in his glass. Then he starts asking questions. He wants to know who the boy is, and when I tell him it's the Webb's nephew, he gets quiet, then shakes his head like he's saying no, only he doesn't say the word. I remind him that it's my birthday, and he shakes his head again because maybe he didn't remember, but it's not the Fourth yet, so I can't get mad at him.

Aunt Tracy arrives with a drink, and I follow her back to the kitchen and cry on her shoulder. She tells me that she'll make sure there's an extra ticket and not to worry about it—she'll deal with my father.

I wipe my tears away and go to bed, and in the morning I'm sixteen.

It doesn't feel any different. At breakfast, Aunt Tracy's made my favorite waffles, and Charlotte and Sophie each give me a card that I'm sure she bought for them. Charlotte says she'll take me to the DMV to get my learner's permit and give me a lesson or two, and Sophie says she's glad I'm bringing a date to dinner because Colin is going too, and it's so cute, we can double.

Then I'm late to practice, and my coach, Matt, is mad at me and makes me hit an extra basket of cross-court winners until I hit every cone he's placed on the court three times. I don't tell him it's my birthday; I just blink back my tears and hope he doesn't notice because *"there's no crying in tennis."* And then, after training, he surprises me with Ash and a special birthday lunch in the club dining room. Ash gives me this beautiful tennis bracelet, with small diamonds set in silver, and tells me she'll help me do my hair tonight, and then I cry for real, apologizing to them for being such a baby.

No one mentions my mother.

She had plans for each of us on our sixteenth birthday. It was something she liked to talk about often, how we'd get a special day with her. We'd crawl into her bed, crowding around her while she asked each of us what we wanted to do. It changed every year, except for me. I wanted to go to New York City and watch the US Open in the best seats possible, and it didn't matter that the Open was at the end of the summer—it was my birthday dream. She used to laugh and kiss the top of my head and say she'd get to work on changing the date, but just in case would I mind deferring the celebration?

Then she died on a cold and rainy January day, and birthdays became afterthoughts. If it weren't for Aunt Tracy, they wouldn't get celebrated at all.

After lunch with Ash and Matt, I skip the beach because I don't want to jinx it. I just hope Fred shows up when he said he would.

When I get home, there's a box on my bed with a note from my father that says: *Your mother wanted you to have this.*

I sit down slowly, my hands shaking as I open it. Inside is another envelope, this time with my mother's handwriting on it. She must've written it over a year ago, when she knew she was dying.

I use my thumb to peel it open and pull out the card inside. It's embossed with a lily, the flower my mom always said meant July. I hold it to my nose. It smells faintly of her perfume, a light flowery scent that always made me feel safe and loved.

Oh, Mom. I miss you so much. It still hurts every day.

She doesn't answer me—she never does—so I open the note. Two pieces of cardboard fall out, but my eyes are drawn to her words.

I couldn't get them to change the date. I hope it's everything you ever wanted anyway. I love you. Mom

I pick up the paper that fell out. It's a pair of tickets for the US Open, center court for the whole second week. And this must be because of William. I don't know how he managed it or what he sold to afford it, but when I go to find him to thank him, tears of joy still on my cheeks, I notice that the small sketch of ballet dancers he had on his desk, which was my mother's favorite thing, is missing.

So I fly into his arms, and I tell him, *"Thank you, thank you!"* and he pats me on the hand, and his eyes are misty, and he's *"so proud of the young woman I've become,"* he says. *"I know your mother thinks so too."*

I crawl into his lap the way I haven't done since I was very small, and we sit there like that until our tears dry up.

* * *

Now it's five thirty. Ash is here, finishing my hair, which is long and shiny, streaked with blond and strawberry highlights from the sun. I'm wearing a knee-length white tunic dress covered in light pink flowers and a pair of cream wedges because the party is on the sand, and I never learned to walk in heels anyway.

"He's going to *die*," Ash says, putting my tennis bracelet on my right wrist.

"I might die."

"Don't be silly. It's just a date."

"Plus a kiss," I say. "What if he doesn't want to kiss me?"

"Please." Ash grabs my cheeks between her hands. "You're so cute *I* want to kiss you."

I rest my forehead against hers. "I wish you were coming tonight."

"No, you don't. Besides, I'll meet you on the beach after."

There's a rap on my door. It's Aunt Tracy. "A young man is here for you."

My eyes fly to Ash's—*he's early.*

"See how excited he is?" she says. "He couldn't wait."

I hug her, then rush to the stairs. I stop at the top of them, not wanting to fall. I walk down slowly, turning on the landing and there he is, looking up at me, that wide smile getting wider by the minute. He's wearing a powder-blue linen shirt with a white linen blazer and dark blue chinos, and he looks so amazing I can't help but blurt it out. "You look great."

I reach the bottom step, and he takes my hand. "That's what *I'm* supposed to say."

"Don't feel like you have to."

"Olivia, come on. You're beautiful."

"Thank you."

"I got you this." He picks up a clear box from the table by the door. There's a pink rose corsage inside. "Too much?"

"No, it's perfect."

He takes it out and reaches toward my breast to pin it on. I suck in my breath.

"Wait," Aunt Tracy says. "Stop." She's holding a camera. "I must get a picture."

"Oh god," I say to Fred. "I'm so sorry."

"Don't worry, my mom is the same way."

"This is Aunt Tracy," I say. "Next best thing to a parent."

"Olivia, don't make me cry."

"Take the shot."

Fred pins the corsage on while Aunt Tracy clicks away. Then Colin arrives for Sophie, and we go through the same thing all over again, all of us lining up together.

"Again, so sorry about this."

"No worries." He leans his head toward me. He smells like soap and the beach, and I want to bury my face in his neck. He lowers his voice. "Just promise me one thing."

"What?"

"You'll write my name on the back when she gets it developed, so when you look at it a million years from now, you'll remember who I am."

"I'm always going to remember this," I say, and he reaches for my hand, curling our fingers together and pressing tight.

But I don't remember much after that. How we got out of the house or the walk to the club. I just remember the feel of his hand holding mine, soft on the inside, calloused on the edges. It feels strong and sure, and why haven't we been doing this the whole time, exactly?

We walk around to the back porch, the one facing the beach. There are about a hundred people here already, mostly adults, but some kids in colorful dresses and short pants are running around, weaving in between them. There's music playing—some big band number I'm sure my dad would approve of—and the air is full of the other guests' chatter. He and Aunt Tracy are sitting at a different table with some of their friends.

We consult the seating chart, my hand in Fred's, his index finger making a slow circle against my palm that feels so good it's distracting. We're sitting with a family I didn't know very well, but I'm happy about that. Happy to stay in our little cocoon, even if that includes Colin and Sophie.

We weave through the crowd, still hand in hand. Twelve tables are set out on the beach, with lights strung above them on poles. When it gets dark, they'll light up the night. But for now, the sun is still out, the sky starting to pink.

We take our seats, and Colin goes to get us drinks from the bar. I kick off my shoes, letting my feet sink into the soft sand. The place setting is for lobster—a cracker, a small fork, wet wipes, and napkins; and as promised, there's a white plastic bib folded on top of my plate.

Fred finally lets go of my hand, then picks his bib up and ties it around his neck. "What do you think?" It's made of cheap plastic and has a bright red lobster on the front.

"It suits you." I pick mine up, but he takes it from me.

"Let me."

I turn my back to him, and he knots the plastic ties around my neck, letting his fingers trail along the bones in my neck. I shiver, though it's not cold, and he leans forward, his breath tickling my skin. "Happy birthday, by the way."

"Thank you." My voice is high and squeaky, and I'm happy to see Colin coming back with four champagne glasses on a tray.

"How did you get those?" Sophie asks, giggling.

"I think they thought I was part of the waitstaff."

"Oh god," I say, "I'm so sorry."

"I'm not." He passes out the glasses.

I've had champagne before—my father's not that particular about the drinking age. But even he'll be upset if Sophie turns up drunk later tonight.

"One glass," I say to her. "I mean it."

"Okay, Mom."

"Not funny."

"Sorry." She raises her glass, and we all clink as they toast me happy birthday. Fred makes a face when he tastes his.

"Not good?"

He puts it down. "Not my thing."

"And all this?" I motion to the Buffys and Biffs, decked out in pastel, scarfing down champagne while their lobster bibs flutter at their necks.

"I'm very happy to be here."

"Me too. I mean, I'm happy you're here."

"Good." He pushes his glass toward me. "Some extra for the birthday girl."

"I bet they'd give you a beer."

"It's fine." He takes my hand under the table, those slow circles again. I curl my toes in the sand. "So, how does this work?"

"I don't know. This is my first date."

Fred laughs. "I meant the dinner. Is it buffet or . . .?" He runs his finger along my inner arm. His touch feels electric. "But I'm honored."

"I'm screwing this up."

"Not at all."

"They bring the lobsters out. There will be corn too."

"Great."

"God, look at her," Sophie says, pointing across the sand to Charlotte. She's sitting at a table with a man I don't know, her hand on his shoulder, leaning toward him intimately.

"Who is that?" I ask.

"Wes Taylor."

"What?" Colin says, laughing. "Your sister's dating your cousin?"

"Maybe?" Sophie says uncertainly.

"Gross," I say. "And no. It's a common last name."

"Maybe he's a third cousin once removed?"

"I haven't checked the family tree, but I don't think so." I turn to Sophie. "What do you know?"

"I listened to her on the phone the other day. I think she met him in New York over spring break."

"I'm not sure I could date someone who has the same last name as me," Fred says. "Too weird."

"Agreed." I tip my glass to him, and he raises the water glass in front of him. I take a sip of the bubbles. They tickle my mouth and make me feel bold. "If I were your cousin, would you still be into me?"

"You think I'm into you?"

"Um . . ."

He grins. "I'm into you."

"Phew."

"The answer on the cousin front is . . . can I plead the fifth or something?"

"You can. But what are you doing Labor Day weekend?"

"Why?"

I tell him about the tickets.

"That sounds amazing."

"It will be. Roddick is kind of killing it this year, but I'm hoping Andre gets one more title. I'm worried Serena and Venus will be out because of injuries, so maybe it's Clijsters's year—I don't know."

Fred is amused. "You're cute."

"I did warn you I was a tennis geek."

"It's fine. Those just are a lot of names I don't know."

"Which *do* you know?"

"Sampras?"

"Ooh," Sophie says. "She hates Sampras."

"Why?"

"Because of Agassi. Come on."

Fred's forehead creases. "I don't follow."

I pat him on the arm. "You have two months to become knowl-edgeable in the ways of tennis."

"So you're inviting me to the game?"

"Well, yeah."

"I accept."

"Good."

A chorus of *oohs* dominos across the sand. The waiters have come out with trays full of lobster and corn. In a few minutes we get served giant lobsters that are two pounds each.

"Whoa," Fred says, playing with a claw. "These are enormous."

"Do you need help or . . .?"

"No." He starts to expertly pull the small legs off, then dissects the body like a surgeon. He catches me watching him. "We summered in Cape Cod every year till my father died."

"I love Cape Cod."

"You were thinking I didn't know how to lobster."

"I'm an idiot."

He grins. "You going to eat that, or what?"

I return the smile, then dig in. The meat is sweet, like summer and the ocean combined. The corn is sweet too, out of season but somehow still good. I feel so lucky and happy as we crack claws, drag them through butter, and toss the discards into the large bowls in the middle of the table. When we're done, the waiters clear the plates and bring us more wet wipes to clean up the mess.

"That was delicious," Fred says, wiping his fingers and then his face.

"It was. But wait till dessert."

"Dessert is the bomb," Sophie says. "Right, Colin?" Her cheeks are pink, and her eyes are unfocused.

"I said one glass of champagne."

"Hey, you're not . . ."

I hold up a hand. "Don't say it."

"Okay, sorry."

"No more. I mean it."

"Yeah, yeah."

Fred taps me on my shoulder. "What's the dessert?"

"Strawberry shortcake."

"That sounds great." He smiles shyly. "I got you something."

"You did?"

"It's your birthday, isn't it?"

"I know, but—"

"No buts," Fred says, putting a box on the table. "Open it."

It's small and blue. Inside is a thin silver bracelet made up of links and a tiny tennis racquet.

"It's a charm bracelet," Fred says, taking it out and attaching it to my left wrist. "When something important happens in your life, you get a charm to remember it by."

I run my thumb over the small perfect racquet. "It's beautiful."

"It's not diamonds," Fred says, touching the bracelet Ash gave me. "That's just something money can buy. This is thoughtful. Thank you, Fred."

"Aren't you going to kiss him?" Sophie says, twittering next to me.

Fred's eyes are dancing, and I lean forward and kiss him on the cheek, feeling the heat of his skin through my lips. "I was always going to remember this night, but now I really will."

"My pleasure."

The cake comes next, and everyone sings me happy birthday, and then the music starts, and we dance to the Abba songs they play for the grownups. Then the DJ transitions to a slower number. Avril Lavigne's "I'm With You."

"Will you dance with me?" Fred asks, holding out his arms.

I walk into them for an answer, avoiding the knowing glance I'm receiving from Sophie. Most of the adults leave the dance floor, with only a few younger couples near us swaying to the music. The sun has set, the stars beginning to poke out. Fred's arms are tight around me, looped low on my back. Mine are around his neck.

"Having fun?" he asks against my ear, his lips grazing it.

The side of my face starts to tingle. "Yes."

"I know birthdays can be hard after . . ."

I tighten my grip, holding on. "I got a nice card from my mom. She wrote it before . . ."

"That's really sweet of her. I wish my dad had done that."

"Me too."

He pulls his head back, and I look up at him, our eyes connecting, a powerful pull between us. Our faces move closer together and I think it's going to happen, a *kiss*, but then Avril hits a high note, and it cuts through the moment. Fred pulls me to his chest, and I turn my cheek against it, breathing him in until the song is over.

Then we're pulled to the beach, where some of the local teenagers have set up a massive bonfire. Ash is there, and she admires Fred's gift, then tells me that she'll leave us alone so we can *"you know."* I turn back to Fred and try not to think too much about the kiss I want, the expectation of it hovering between us like the fireworks that are waiting to be set off.

Lauren Bailey

Someone presses a beer into my hand, but I put it down because the fizz of the champagne is still running through me, and I want to remember everything about this night. The salt air and the sea breeze and the way Fred's hand feels in mine, strong and sure, and the tinkle of his bracelet against my wrist, the empty links a promise of many more charms to come.

Someone attaches an iPod to a speaker. "Hey, Ya!" comes on and we *"shake, shake, shake it,"* laughing with each other, shaking our hands at the fire. Then it transitions into Nora Jones's "Don't Know Why," and Fred pulls me into his arms like he did at the club party. This time I can concentrate on how well we fit well together, my chin resting on his shoulder, our thighs brushing as we turn slowly in the sand.

Fred pulls me tighter, his arms crossed over my back, his hands resting in the depression at the bottom of my spine. I tip my head back. My body feels hot in his arms, my heart full of a happy ache. He touches my cheek, running his finger down to my chin, and I start to tremble as he looks at me like he did an hour ago, full of heat and promise.

The world slows down, and he brushes his lips against mine, then presses us together more firmly as my hands reach up and tangle into his hair.

And as the first fireworks explode above us, my mind is full of the fact that this kiss—*this kiss*—is everything I wanted it to be and more.

CHAPTER NINE

June 2023

Fred is acting weird, like he doesn't recognize me or wishes he didn't.

It's not anything he says, but his expression says it all. A slight downturn of his mouth, a wariness in his eyes. I know his looks better than my own, and even though it's been years since I've seen him, it hasn't been too long for me to misinterpret them.

He's surprised by what I look like now, a shadow of myself, and he's unhappy to see me in general, though he must've known, when he went to a party at my father's, when he agreed to come to my sister's, when he negotiated to buy *our* house, that it was inevitable.

He must've sought it out, and though I feel like I have a pretty good idea of the answer, I want to ask him why.

But now's not the time, not with him looking at me like I'm an unpleasant stranger.

"I'm going to go," I say to Sophie.

"You sure? Stay for a drink."

I eye Fred across the room, where he's sitting with Lucy, smiling at her the way he used to smile at me. Attentive, engaged, that heat of interest. His hair is short in a way that suits him, almost no curl to it, and his face is tan. My heart squeezes just looking at him, but that might be muscle memory.

"I don't think so. I'm tired. The boys wore me out. We'll catch up another time, okay?"

"How are you getting home?"

"It's only a mile or so. I'll walk."

"What? No, Colin will take you. Colin, Olivia needs a ride home." Colin stands up. He's wobbling a bit on his feet. "My pleasure."

"I'll take her," Fred says smoothly, his voice deep and steady. "I have an early call."

Lucy looks disappointed, but not jealous. Thirty, she's open and sunny, like Colin, and runs an estate sale and decorating business in East Hampton. She wears her dark hair naturally and on the shorter side, and she's wearing a burnt-orange linen wrap dress that shows off her curvy figure.

"There's no need," I say to Fred, my gaze steady, though my heart is anything but. "It's a lovely night to walk."

"Don't be ridiculous. I'm going that way. It's no trouble at all."

Fighting him is only going to cause a scene, so I gather up my things. Sophie kisses me goodnight, and Colin gives me an apologetic smile.

Fred and I walk out of the house together. The night is warm but pleasant. The moon is half full, a few clouds floating across it, the stars out, pinpoints in the night. I breathe in the bougainvillea and lilac that line the parking circle, hoping their scent will calm me.

No such luck.

Fred opens the passenger door to his black Range Rover. I climb in and put on my seat belt, folding my hands in my lap. It's a short drive. I can do this. We don't even have to talk. I need my breath for breathing anyway, which feels like a chore.

"I'm staying at the club," Fred says without me asking as he pulls out of the driveway. It feels strange to be in this confined space with him. Intimate.

I open my window and inhale the night air. The road is dark and not well lit. "I didn't know."

"It's convenient."

"Until you move into the house."

"About that—"

I pull my head back in. "Did it have to be *my* house? Really?"

He clenches his jaw. "It met all of my criteria."

"Oh my God, are you listening to yourself? *'It met all of my criteria.'* What the hell, Fred?"

"I thought you'd be happy. Grateful, even."

"Why? Because of the money? You know I don't care about that."

He grips the steering wheel so tightly his knuckles go white. "Your father was on the brink of bankruptcy."

"So, you what? Bought the house as a favor? Out of charity?"

He doesn't say anything, just stares at the dark road.

"That's what I thought." We lapse into silence, my breath coming heavy for the minute it takes to arrive at the driveway to Taylor House. "Drop me here."

"All right." He stops the car. I open the door, but he reaches for my arm before I can get out. His touch scalds my skin. "Olivia, the point is, I'm going to be around. We need to find a way to be civil to each other."

"I don't see any reason why we have to spend any time together at all."

"It's a small town . . ."

"Which I'll be leaving as soon as I help my father clear out the house and settle in somewhere else."

He releases me, a look of confusion passing over his face. "I thought you loved it here."

"I did."

"What changed?"

"Life, Fred. You've been living yours and I've been living mine, and you don't know me anymore, okay? And I don't know you."

"And you want to keep it that way."

"I think it's best."

"All right, then." His voice sounds sad, but I know that's wishful thinking.

Fred doesn't want to be in my life—he's made that perfectly clear. He just doesn't like scenes.

"Thanks for the lift."

"When I see you on court, I'll keep my distance."

"On court?"

"At the club. Don't you play there every morning?"

A lump forms in my throat because I don't. I haven't played in years. But I don't want to tell him that. I don't want to give him an inch into the person I am now because I can't stand it—not again.

So instead, I open the door and leap down onto the gravel path. I close it firmly behind me, and since I know he's going to wait until he sees me inside, I run into the night and slip into the house before the first tear falls.

* * *

"Hey, Coach," I say the next morning as I poke my head through the door of his office.

"Well, well, well. Olivia Taylor, as I live and breathe." Coach Matt walks toward me with his arms extended.

Matteo Fernandez was a long-time journeyman on the Association of Tennis Professionals tour in the seventies who never quite lived up to his potential. Sidelined by injuries and self-doubt, he retired early and took on the coaching position at the club, shepherding the next generation of players through his no-nonsense regime. During the summer months, we played outside on the grass courts, and in the fall we moved to the indoor facility, alternating between hard courts and clay. The program had produced three junior champions, two lower-level tour players, and me, *"the best of all of them,"* he used to say.

He pulls me into a bear hug, his thin frame pressing against mine, then releases me. His face is lined from years in the sun, and there's almost no hair under his ball cap, but otherwise, he looks the same: six feet, on the thin side, with strong forearms and legs.

"You looking to hit?" he asks, motioning to my tennis whites.

I pulled them out of a drawer early this morning, wondering if they'd still fit. They did, and so I wandered over here in a haze, asking myself what I was doing.

"You looking to get beat?"

"Confidence! Love it. You have a racquet?"

"I don't."

"I can rustle one up for you."

"Thanks, Coach."

66

He checks his watch. "Perfect timing. The others will be arriving shortly."

"The others?"

"The team. I assume you want to go through the whole routine?"

The whole routine is three hours of warmups, hitting drills, serving, then playing a match. "Sure, let's do it. Only, go easy on me, okay? It's been a while."

"How's the rib?"

I twist slowly from side to side. "It's good."

"So, then, no."

"No what?"

"I will not be going easy on you, mija."

I should've known. Matt's philosophy is to play through everything. Injuries, bad weather, the heat. That's how you build the toughness you need to make it on tour. If you know you've done something, then you can do it again and again.

"Let me get you that racquet." He goes into the locker at the side of his office and pulls one out. "This should work."

He hands it to me, and my hand closes around the grip. I slice through the air, once, twice. My arm feels good. Loose.

"Let's head to the courts."

I follow him through the clubhouse. There are seven kids already on court, playing mini tennis, warming each other up.

"Huddle up!" Matt yells. The kids hustle over, three girls and four boys between the ages of eight and fourteen. "This is Olivia Taylor. Some of you might recognize her from the pictures on the wall holding the annual cup. Or the pictures in my office from her tour wins. She's going to be playing with us. Now, Olivia probably wants you to go easy on her because it's been a while, but what do we say to that?"

"No mercy!" the kids yell back, and though some of them are laughing, it's still a bit frightening.

But it also lights a fire in me. The competitive fire Matt saw in me at age six, when my mom brought me to him and said she'd found me hitting tennis balls against the garage door for two hours and maybe he could help me do something a bit more productive with my time.

"All right," Matt yells. "Back to work. Cindy, you'll play with Olivia."

A spindly thirteen-year-old girl with her hair in long, blond pigtails and her socks pulled up to her knees nods with assurance. I'm her mission now. She will not be denied.

But I've seen that expression before. It used to be mine, and this old dog still has a few tricks left in her yet.

I follow Cindy to court one, which faces the back of the clubhouse, where the guest rooms are. I take the far side, so I'm looking right at them as we warm up at the net, then move back to hit from the baseline. Cindy strikes the ball hard and fast with lots of spin, but I can match her. I swing freely, years of training taking over as I get low and flex my knees and twist my body to generate power.

Whack, whack, whack, whack! Our rally is loud, each of us running down balls we might have normally let go in a warmup. She drop-shots me, and I struggle to get to the net on time to put it over, but I do. I'm out of position now, so I sprint across the net to intercept the forehand winner she's trying to put down the line. I get my racquet on it, angling it away from me, and it drops low across the net and spins out of the court. Cindy is fast, and she gets her racquet on it, but not fast enough. She dumps the ball into the net.

"Nice shot," Cindy mutters.

"That was a great rally," I say, out of breath. "Don't worry. No way I can keep up that kind of quality. I'm so out of shape."

Cindy smiles to herself, thinking that I'm stupid to tell her my weakness as if it wasn't already obvious by the way the white polo shirt I'm wearing hugs my no longer flat belly.

We'll see.

I walk back to the baseline, taking my time so I have my breath back before the next ball arrives. I turn, getting into the ready position. My focus is pulled by the twitch of a curtain in one of the guest bedroom windows. It's Fred, watching with a self-satisfied smile on his face.

Whether it's because he thinks he still knows me or he's guessed that he's the reason I'm out here, I can't tell.

CHAPTER TEN

July 2003

After the perfection of my sixteenth birthday, I go to bed fantasizing about the amazing summer Fred and I are going to have and all the things we'll do between now and Labor Day, when we'll go to the US Open. I'm filled with happiness, and if life can be better than this, I don't see how. We have nine weeks together, and my mind is filled with kisses and plans and love.

Yes, I'm sure I'm in love.

Nine weeks, I think as I fall asleep with a smile on my face, reliving our kiss over and over again. *Nine weeks.*

I get one.

It's a week of kissing and holding hands and sneaking moments. A week of making plans for our future, what we'll do when we run out of time this summer and he goes back to Boston.

We can't stop talking about it, where we'll be in six months, one year, *five.*

Somehow, that becomes our catchphrase.

"In five years, we'll..."

"You'll be about to start your junior year in college," Fred says as we lie on the lawn out of view of the house behind a big oak tree. The summer house is in front of us, and sometimes I think I'll be bold and invite him inside, but most of the time I think it's safer to stay out here on the grass, where the possibility of getting caught keeps us from going too far.

"And you'll be a freshman."

"Will you enjoy that? Dating a lower classman?"

I turn to face him. His eyes look dark blue in this light, wind tossed. "Do you *have* to go into the Army?"

"The Navy." He runs a finger over my lips. They're dry and swollen from too much kissing. "I do. Even before my dad died, that was the plan. I'll enlist and then I can do the G.I. Bill, and that'll pay for college."

"But it's dangerous. We're at war."

"That's why I want to go."

"Because of the danger?"

He moves his finger to my nose, running it along the bridge, and that pulse starts up in my body again. Then he kisses me, a medium kiss that almost dissolves into a serious one where I want to wrap my arms around him and press him close against me so I can feel all of him and he can feel all of me.

He pulls back. "I believe in service. I want to help my country out. Especially now."

"But you might not end up in Afghanistan. It might be Iraq."

"That's okay."

"But wasn't the reason we went there a lie? No weapons of mass destruction, or whatever?"

He frowns. We agree on so many things, but this is not one of them. "That's not the only reason to go. Saddam's a bad guy. And we can help set up democracy there. Think about it. I can be part of helping to get them on the right track."

"Like America is?"

"Like America can be."

I kiss him, thinking he sounds like my dad on the rare times he talks politics. Or like my dad's friends who voted for Bush and Reagan and Bush again. My mother was a lifelong Democrat, and as far as I remember, it was the only thing they fought about. But it didn't keep them from loving each other, so I don't let it bother me, I'm just worried Fred will go and not come back.

Because even though I haven't known him that long, it already feels like he'll be in my life forever. Like he already has been. I cannot imagine my life without him, or when I do, it makes me so sad I can't handle it. That's how I know it's love. Not just because my body aches for him, but because I have to keep the thought of losing him at bay.

"Promise me you'll be safe."

"I'll be okay."

"Not everyone is."

"I know, Olivia. But—and I know this sounds silly—I just know I'll be all right. You don't have to worry about me."

I tilt my head back. "I will, though."

His lips hover above mine, his breath a soft breeze. "Will you miss me?"

"What do *you* think?"

He rubs his nose against mine, then kisses me again, teasing at my lips with his tongue. It's after cocktails but before dinner, those lazy hours when he isn't expected back at his aunt and uncle's, and no one's looking for me. I like kissing him at this time of day, but I like kissing him most of all in the dark, when he feels bold enough to explore more than my mouth and I feel bold enough to let him.

"I think you'll forget about me," I say.

"No, Olivia. No."

"Some girl will catch your attention, and I'll get some Dear Olivia letter, and that will be that."

"Never." He kisses me again, his tongue lazy against my teeth. I arch up to meet his body, needing to feel that connection, and he wraps his arms around me. "You're the one who's going to forget me. You'll go to college, and you'll be the star of the tennis team, and everyone will want you." He reaches down and caresses my bare legs. I stifle a moan. "They'll want these legs, and this face, and this mouth. And maybe you'll fight them off for a while, but you'll be lonely, and eventually you'll give in."

"Won't we have shore leave?"

"We will."

"That'll be enough."

"And then in five years . . ."

I plant kisses along his jawline. "You'll come to college, and we'll find a house and we'll live in sin."

"Would it be such a sin?"

I close my eyes and feel the slow circle of his fingers just below the hem of my shorts. I'm not ready for sex—so I've told him and so I tell myself—but my body is. Oh god, it is so ready.

I put my hand on his to gain some control. "I'm speaking for William."

"He likes me, doesn't he?"

"He does."

Fred came to cocktails the day after my birthday and spent an hour talking to William on the veranda, turning down drinks and sipping on a Coke. When Aunt Tracy called us into dinner, he was invited to stay, and my father even gave him the tour of the house, trotting out his old stories about how the Taylors had acquired the acreage and how much money it had taken to build the house. "You'll not find a parcel like this anywhere on the shore. Not one with this much land and this much beach."

Fred had shown as much interest as any seventeen-year-old could in real estate, and I'd left them alone, amazed William seemed to be taking an interest in him. Charlotte whined to me that it wasn't fair because he barely talked to Wes when she'd brought him to the house the day after.

"I'm glad," Fred says. "Wouldn't want it to get all Shakespearean up in here."

"Ha. That's what Ash said."

"She thought it was going to be a Romeo and Juliet situation?"

"Not exactly . . . That's more Charlotte's situation."

"What's your dad's problem with that guy anyway?"

"I think it's because he doesn't like having a better-looking man named Taylor around."

Fred laughs. "Oh, so you think Wes is good-looking?"

"Not as good-looking as you."

"Good. Hmm. Maybe it's because he's not actually a Taylor? No *Mayflower*, no fancy house."

"That's probably it. God, I'm so sick of my father acting like he did something important with his life because he was born with money."

"It's what he knows."

"It's gross."

Fred checks his watch.

"Do you have to go?"

"I've got a few more minutes. I can stay until the first firefly, at least."

I squeeze his hand and we turn on our backs, our bodies lined up next to each other. The sun is still up, but it's slipping down the horizon, casting long shadows across the lawn. I can hear the waves against the shore, the slow beat of them cresting, then sucking out again, like the slow beat that builds in me whenever Fred touches me.

In the dark, he tells me that he's never felt this way before. He hasn't gone into the details, but I know there's been at least one girl before me. I don't want to know how far they went or if they went all the way. Thinking of him with someone else breaks me.

"What shall we do tomorrow?" I ask.

"What's tomorrow?"

"Don't tell me you've forgotten our one-week anniversary."

Fred catches at the bracelet on my wrist. I never take it off, not even during tennis. "Didn't you want to go to that party on the beach?"

"Not really."

"Isn't Ash expecting you?"

"Yes, and she complained again today that I've abandoned her for you." My Ash time has been reduced from five hours a day to two—we do the pool till lunchtime, but then after I go to the beach and hang with Fred. I know it's wrong to abandon your friends for a boy, but I can't help it. I want to be with him every second of every day. I even thought, briefly, about cutting back on tennis practice, but quickly tossed that idea away. I can love Fred and tennis in equal measure—they're both going to be part of my future, and Fred understands that.

"Let's go, then," Fred says. "It'll be fun."

"But you hate all those guys from work."

"Not hate, exactly."

"Okay, we'll go. But not for too long."

I turn my face toward him and he's right there, his lips inches away. "Not for too long."

* * *

"Hurry up, Fred will be here in a minute." It's after dinner, and Ash and I are in my room, getting ready.

"I thought he was meeting us there." Ash is trying to get her slippery hair to stay in a high ponytail to match the "fifties look" she's decided on for the evening—a halter dress in a bold print that twirls when she spins.

"What's the big deal? Here, there?"

"Because the minute he gets here you're just going to start ignoring me." Ash holds up her hand. Her nails are the same bright pink as her dress. "And don't bother denying it. You know it's true."

"I'm sorry."

She pouts. "I miss you. This was supposed to be our summer together. Now I barely see you, and when I do, all you talk about is *him.*"

"I'm not that bad, am I?"

"You are."

"Better than talking about tennis all the time, right?"

"I mean . . ."

"I'm sorry."

"You already said that. What about all our plans? What about the list?"

"What list?"

She spins in her chair. "My point exactly! The only thing you've ticked off has to do with kissing *him.*"

"We never finished the list."

"That's even worse."

"Okay, okay. What do you want to do?"

"We were supposed to learn how to surf."

I don't remember this being on the list, but now's not the time to bring that up. "Let's do it."

"Really?"

"Yeah, sure. Where should we go?" I stand behind Ash and check myself in the mirror. My hair is loose to my shoulders, which are bare in the dusty pink, strapless cotton dress I'm wearing. I've got a bulky sweatshirt out for the beach too, but for once I'm happy with the way I look.

"I think there's a place we can learn in Montauk."

"Okay, sounds good."

"Tomorrow?" Ashley presses.

I'm about to agree when I remember. "I can't tomorrow."

"Why?"

"Because I'm supposed to go to Fred's house for dinner."

"Reschedule."

"I can't, Ash. I'm meeting his aunt and uncle for the first time. It's a big deal." I put my arms around her neck. "Come on, I can go any other day. Just not tomorrow."

"You promise?"

"I do."

"Just us, right? No Fred."

"No Fred." He has to work anyway, and I assume we'll be back by dinner time.

"And then you'll sleep over?"

I meet Ash's eyes in the mirror. She's testing me. "Sure."

"Great. I'll set it up tomorrow morning."

"Olivia!" Aunt Tracy calls. "Fred's here."

"Remember," Ash says. "You promised."

I smile at her and go greet Fred. He's wearing broken-in chinos and a faded blue sweatshirt that I love, and he smells clean and fresh from his shower. I want to drag him to the backyard and hide inside the summer house forever. Instead, we walk hand in hand to the beach, Fred on one side and Ash on the other.

When we get there, there are about twenty kids gathered around a bonfire. One of them is playing DJ with his iPod and a large speaker like they did on my birthday. Inevitably, the shore police will break up the party later, but for now, it's early enough that they'll let us have some fun.

Fred gets us each a beer, and then I spend the next hour trying to pay him less attention and Ashley more. It's hard, because instead of wandering off as she usually does, she's glued to us. I'm not sure how Fred feels about it, I've never asked him if he likes Ash or not, but I can tell that Ash is still not satisfied. She's being loud and pushy, the way she gets when she's frustrated, and she keeps encouraging both of us to drink. I don't want to, and Fred almost never does, so we walk around, each with a beer caught in our fist, feeling them go warm while Ashley downs one after another.

"Maybe slow down a little?" I say to Ash two hours later. She's started slurring her words.

"I'm having fun! You two should have some fun too!"

"I *am* having fun; I'm just worried about you."

Ash waves her arms around. "I know you're just waiting for when you can go off to your kissing place."

"Ash." My eyes flash to Fred's.

"What? Fred doesn't mind that you tell me about the kissing, do you, Fred? That's what girls do. Talk about kissing their boyfriends."

"Maybe I should get you a Coke," Fred says.

Ashley walks up to him, the beer sloshing out of her Solo cup and onto the sand. She puts her hand on his chest. "Do you know that you're the first boy Olivia ever kissed?"

"You don't have to answer that, Fred."

"Why not? Why shouldn't he answer that? That was the whole point of the list, right? Right there in the number-one position. Kiss a boy on your sixteenth birthday."

Fred goes pale. "Is that true, Olivia?"

The pain on his face stabs at me. "Not the way it sounds, no."

"It wasn't a . . . challenge?"

"It was. But that's not why—"

"It was *my* plan," Ash says proudly, biting the edge of her cup. "I got Olivia to leave the club and go to the beach to find a guy, and I saw you first and I introduced you, remember? I did that. I get the credit."

Fred takes Ash's hands gently and lowers them off his chest, then steps away. He turns to me. "Is what she's saying true, Olivia? This was all some game? It didn't matter who it happened with?"

I'm fighting tears. What is happening? "Of course not. Fred, how could you think that?"

"What am I supposed to think?"

"That I met you and I liked you and everything that's happened since then is because we both wanted it. Please believe me."

"I . . . I don't know what to think."

"Fred, come on. Ashley's drunk. You can't . . . This is not a big deal."

His eyes are so dark they're scary. "It is, Olivia."

"Please don't be mad."

"I'm not . . ." He shakes his head. "I need to go."

"What?"

"I can't be here right now. Take Ash home."

"Will I see you tomorrow?"

He doesn't answer me. He just turns and walks up the beach, dropping his beer into a garbage can, leaving me there with Ash, who's swaying by my side.

"Was it something I said?" Ash giggles, and I rush past her. I want to go after Fred, but my stomach is rolling, and instead of catching up to him, I bend over when I hit the dunes and hurl.

CHAPTER ELEVEN

July 2023

For the next week, life in the Hamptons falls into a routine.

I rise early and train with the team, working through the aches and pains that are accumulating in my body. Cindy and I have developed a rivalry. *Little Killer,* I call her in my mind, because if she could kill me with her eyes each time I get a shot past her, she would. But already my steps are faster, my mind more focused. Some of the muscle tone has returned to my arms, and my skin isn't so pale, my face less drawn. Sometimes she wins and sometimes I do, and Matt looks on approvingly, so we both must be doing something right.

Training ends at ten. After a shower and a stretch, I clean out another room of the house, then fill up my car with things to take to Goodwill, the dump, my sister's. I'm working the perimeters of the house—guest rooms, the formal parlor. Rooms that don't contain hard memories or secrets, working up the courage to get to the difficult parts.

Sometimes, Charlotte helps me, spending an hour or two sorting through generations of knickknacks and the glass figurines in the dining room cupboards. Sometimes, my father stands in the doorway, peering at me over the edge of his reading glasses without comment.

One disastrous day, Sophie brings the boys. They have a glorious hour going through our leftover toys that I'd pulled out of the attic, and then they thunder away, leaving a worse mess in their wake. William retires to his room with a massive headache, and for once I can't blame him.

But mostly I'm on my own. Alone with the memories—and the mementos I find despite myself. A picture drawn in kindergarten that my mother pressed between the leaves of a book. Her copy of *The Amber Spyglass*, filled with her highlights and notes like she was studying it to write an essay on its Christian symbolism. Old letters, old photos, a life that was never sorted through when she died because we were too young, and my father never bothered.

I try to get William to engage with what furniture he wants to bring to his new house, wherever that will be. I print up listings, but he just takes them without looking. I don't know how we're ever going to get him to commit to a new place, but Charlotte tells me she's handling it, and so I decide to leave it alone. If he's still here when Fred's moving trucks arrive, that will be his problem, not mine.

At night, I sweat in my room and turn over the mistakes in my life. My tennis career, Fred, Wes. I haven't heard from him since that first text, though I check each day. I'm surprised at the silence but grateful for it too. I don't know what I want to say to Wes yet, and anytime I think about it, the rage boils up to the surface. I hate its bitter taste.

I push him away and switch to trying to decide what I'm going to do in the fall, if I love teaching enough to continue when I have the financial independence to stop. I don't arrive at any answers, and finally I sleep.

After a particularly hot night on the crest of July, I go on a fruitless search to the Home Depot for an air conditioner, where I run into Colin's sister, Lucy. We chat casually, and I wait for her to bring up Fred. When she doesn't, I find myself saying that I might need her services for an estate sale. She's more than happy to run it once we get the personal items out of the way, and this seems like the perfect solution to at least one of my problems.

I return to the house and work till four, then take a shower to clean off the dust that covers me like a film. Afterward, I change into a veranda-appropriate outfit and join the daily shifting crowd for cocktails.

Today my father's lawyer, Barry, is here, along with his daughter, Ann, the woman whose mention made Charlotte blush. I stand on the edge of the crowd and watch my sister as she flits from one person to the next, making sure their drinks are fresh. She's taken extra care with her appearance, wearing a peach dress that makes her skin look rosy. Her hair is glossy and just blown out, her makeup flawless.

She has a date, I think, or she's on one. The object of this grooming is thirty, Asian, petite, and very pretty. She's wearing a black linen pantsuit cinched at the waist by a large leather belt with an intricate design on it, and high, high heels that bring her up to Charlotte's height. She's elegant, the swift movements of a dancer evident in the way she holds her cocktail glass.

"This is Ann Clay," Charlotte says proudly as she makes the introduction. I smile at Ann and wonder if this is how my sister is finally coming out to me. Not in some private confessional, but here, on the veranda, without any pretense or air about it after years of saying nothing. *Good for you,* I want to say, but instead, I hold out my hand to Ann.

"Nice to meet you." Her handshake is firm, and I like her already. "I hear we have you to thank for all this." I gesture to the property.

"I was only doing my job."

"Don't be silly, Ann," Charlotte says. "Did you know she got Fred to up his initial offer by nearly fifty percent? And she negotiated the closing to the end of the summer. He wanted immediate possession."

I kick myself for the thousandth time that I didn't press Fred for more details when he drove me home a week ago. I see him most mornings at the club, watching the tennis from his window or eating his breakfast on the porch. We don't speak, rarely make eye contact, and he's often on his laptop or his phone. But there he is, without fail.

It has to mean something because he could avoid me easily if he wanted to. I haven't worked up the courage yet to ask him what.

"Well, thank you for talking him out of that. Cleaning out this place is a major task."

"Charlotte has been telling me."

"Has she?"

Charlotte shows zero traces of guilt. "Olivia's been such a help. Giving up her whole summer to come here to do this. I'd be lost without her."

"I'm not sure I'm staying the whole summer."

"Because of your husband?" Ann says. "Or should I say ex?"

"Charlotte tell you about that?"

"Yes—sorry. Is it a secret?"

"No . . . I . . . it's fine." I take a sip of my drink, letting a beat go by to collect myself. "I have to find somewhere to live when I go back to the city. I can't leave that till the last minute."

"Me too," Charlotte says. "It's such a chore."

"Are you staying out here?" I almost want to laugh. It's taken this conversation with Ann to attack the big subjects in our lives. But Charlotte and I have never been as close as we appear when there's a stranger with us.

"I'm not sure." Charlotte gives Ann a shy look. "But I need to make up my mind soon."

"Do you live out here full-time, Ann?"

She sips at her lemon drop martini. "I split my time between here and the city. Dad's here all year-round, but we have a small office in Manhattan, which I manage."

"I don't think I could work with Father," Charlotte says.

"Well, he's never had a job, so that makes it easy."

Charlotte's mouth turns down. She's never had a job either, though she likes to pretend otherwise. There have been charity boards and fundraisers and a gig volunteering at an art gallery, but that was years ago.

"You're a teacher?" Ann asks.

"That's right."

"Do you love it?"

"Some days. It's nice being around motivated kids, and they are, for the most part."

"Charlotte said you were a tennis player?"

"I was."

"Why not coach?"

"I was burnt out when I stopped playing. Coaching is a seven-days-a-week gig. It didn't appeal."

"I'm surprised you needed a job," Ann says. "Don't tour players make lots of money?"

This isn't the first time I've been asked this question. "If your last name is Williams. But I was never in their league. I tooled around in the low two hundreds for most of my career, which was enough to cover my expenses, but didn't leave much of a nest egg."

"That's surprising."

"Is every lawyer rich?"

"Nope."

"It's the same in tennis." I take a sip of my drink, hoping to change the subject. "Did Fred say what he wanted to do with the place?"

"He swore it wasn't to cut it up for development if that's what you're worried about. But you know he's being swarmed with offers right now."

"You didn't tell me that," Charlotte says.

"I thought you said you didn't care if they took this place down to the ground?"

Charlotte's eyes go wide. "Shh, not so loud. Father might hear you."

I laugh. "Don't worry, Ann. I've heard her say that very thing to him directly."

She'd said it when we'd sat William down five years ago to convince him to sell. The debts were mounting, and the bank was making threatening noises. Most of the capital was gone, sunk into paying taxes and upkeep. Aunt Tracy pushed gently, trying to get him to see reason. He didn't like it, and in the end he'd tried to make it about preserving the house for our memories of our mother. That's when Charlotte announced that she didn't care if the house burned to the ground. She didn't want to be *ruined*.

He'd agreed to a compromise—letting most of the staff go, selling off a smaller piece of land next door—and it had been enough to keep the wolves at bay for a few years. We all knew it was postponing the inevitable, but we'd taken our victory and gone on with our lives.

"How did he take that?" Ann asks.

"He didn't like it one bit," Charlotte says. "But it did get him to see reason, for a while."

"I'll never understand this very male attachment to land. It must be buried deep in their DNA. *'I own this. Mine.'*" Ann grunts deeply, and we laugh.

"Well, now Fred can lord over all of it," I say. "I hope he gets what he was looking for."

"I don't think that's what he wants to do," Ann says.

"No offense, but you don't know him." I take a ragged breath. "Nice meeting you."

"You too."

I take a few steps away from them and stop to regulate my breathing, but it's no use. Even though I haven't had to talk to Fred except for the short ride from Sophie's, his presence hangs over everything. Each room I clean out is a room he'll occupy; each memory I unlock is one he'll replace.

I can't take it anymore. I need to speed up this process and get the hell out of here.

I walk back to the house, wiping my tears away. I want to be alone, but there's someone standing in the French doors that I can't ignore.

Ash.

CHAPTER TWELVE

July 2003

Fred doesn't talk to me the day after the beach party.

Instead, when I go to the beach, Dave tells me that Fred's dealing with a family emergency. He doesn't know anything else, and so I worry, wondering if it's true or if he just doesn't want to see me; if *I'm* the emergency.

It feels like I am. My heart is pounding. I miss easy shots during practice. And when I go to see Ash, she's no help because she's still green and moaning in her bed, even though it's the afternoon. She says she doesn't remember anything that happened last night, and I don't have the heart to tell her what she did. I get her a glass of water, then ride my bike back to my house and pace the floor of my room.

When I can't stand it anymore, I find his aunt and uncle's phone number, and I call the house. The phone rings and rings, and no one answers. Maybe they have caller ID, and Fred is standing over the phone, looking at my last name as it pops up, waving off his aunt, telling her not to answer. Or maybe there's really something wrong—with him, with them, with some other member of his family—and he's gone.

I feel sick, and I want to crawl into bed like Ashley, but instead, I change my clothes, brush my hair, get on my bike, and ride to Fred's place.

I don't expect dinner, but I've been invited, and no one has canceled. And I need to see Fred because it feels like I am going to die if I don't.

It's a two-mile ride to his house on flat roads. I ride slowly so I don't arrive sweaty and because I couldn't make myself eat anything today, and I feel dizzy. The salt air massages my face as the sky turns rosy above me, and though I've tried to slow this down, I'm here.

The house is a two-story Cape Codder, with cedar shingles and a white wrap-around porch. There's no car in the driveway, and it has a stillness about it that makes me feel like no one's home and no one will be for a while.

I straddle my bike, trying to decide what to do. I can knock on the door, but I don't want to hear the empty echo of an abandoned house. I can't make myself leave either, so I stand there, watching the porch, my heart beating in my ears until the door opens and there's Fred.

"What are you doing?" He doesn't smile the way he usually does when he sees me. Instead, he runs his hand through his hair and frowns. Not good.

"Trying to decide whether to knock on the door."

"Why didn't you?"

"I wasn't sure you wanted to see me." I take a quick breath. "I went by the beach and you weren't there, and then I called and you didn't answer."

"I wasn't here."

"Dave said there was an emergency?"

"My uncle's in the hospital."

"Oh, Fred, I'm so sorry." And I am sorry—*I am*—but I'm also relieved. He didn't skip work because of me. "What happened?"

"A heart attack."

Oh no. Oh God. I'm a terrible person. "Is he going to be okay?"

"I don't know. I'm going back to the hospital now."

"Okay, I'll leave."

I put my feet on the pedals, but I'm too dizzy to control the bike. It starts to tip over, and I just manage to stop myself from falling. But the bike slides sideways, and the chain catches my leg. I can feel my skin ripping before I see the blood.

"Dammit." I step away from the bike and sway as I take in the blood pouring down my leg.

Fred is next to me, his hand on my elbow. "Come in the house. I'll get you cleaned up."

"But you have to go to the hospital."

"Olivia, I'm not leaving you like this." He pulls his T-shirt over his head and wraps my leg in it, tucking in the edge to tighten it. Then he puts my arm around his neck and guides me into the house. He leads me to the back of the ground floor, where there's a bedroom with a bathroom attached. His room, by the smell of it—fresh soap and the beach.

"Sit here." He leads me to the edge of the bathtub, and I sit down. He leaves me for a minute and returns with a first aid kit. Blood is seeping through his T-shirt, and my leg stings. Matt is going to be furious.

"Are you afraid of blood? Because you look like you're going to pass out."

"No, I . . . I haven't eaten anything today."

"You'll be okay." His voice is gentle. "I'm going to take the T-shirt off now."

"All right."

He does it swiftly, getting a pad of gauze and some Bactine ready to clean it up. "This is going to sting."

I look away as he uses the Bactine to clean the wound. I wince but don't say anything as he works quickly and gently. When he's done, I check it. There's only one cut, not deep, but long and a series of abrasions where the skin is puckered.

"No stiches, I don't think," Fred says.

"That's good. You don't need more people in the hospital."

He frowns.

"I'm sorry, I shouldn't be making jokes."

"It's the shock."

"Sure."

He puts a clean pad of gauze on the cut, then starts taping it to me. In a minute he's finished and cleaning up. "See if you can put weight on that."

I stand slowly and my leg starts to buckle, but I catch myself before my knee hits the tile.

"You all right?"

"I'll survive." I look up at him. "Thank you. And I'm sorry—I know you need to go."

"You didn't do it on purpose."

"I know, but . . ."

"It's fine. Accidents happen."

I limp into his bedroom. His bed is made with a simple blue coverlet. There are books on the nightstand, including his copy of *The Amber Spyglass*, and a guitar in the corner. Everything is neat, clean, organized.

"I didn't know you played the guitar," I say.

"Yeah."

"Are you good?"

He shrugs.

"I guess we don't know each other that well." I don't make eye contact when I say this, because if I do, I'm going to cry. I thought we *did* know each other—I was sure we did—but now I feel like I'm with a stranger.

"Olivia. Look at me." He's got that frown on his face again, that stressed-out, unhappy look that shouldn't ever be on any seventeen-year-old's face.

"What is it?"

"There's something I should've told you."

"Okay."

"Don't look at me like that."

"Like what?"

"Like I'm about to tell you I'm dying."

"Well, aren't you?"

"No."

But he is. He's about to tell me that *we're* dying, and that's just the same.

"What should you have told me?"

"Here," he says, sitting down on the bed and patting it. "Sit."

I sit next to him, and he takes my hand. It's the same hand I've been holding all week, inside soft, outside roughened, but the warmth has gone out of it.

"Last year," Fred says, "at school, I started dating this girl. Phoebe. I'd had a crush on her for a while, since middle school."

Phoebe. Her name is Phoebe. I hate her. "Okay."

"She never used to pay any attention to me. I . . . I was different in middle school. I was a nerdy kid who liked fantasy books, and I grew late, and I was overweight."

It's hard to imagine it, but I understand what he's telling me. He was *that* kid. The one who got picked on. The one the girls ignored until, suddenly, they didn't anymore.

"And then there was the whole dead-dad thing. Which coincided with me growing and thinning out and learning to not talk about books so much."

"Except with me."

He smiles briefly. "Except with you."

"So, Phoebe."

"It was great at first. First-girlfriend stuff. You know."

I swallow through the lump in my throat. First-girlfriend stuff. Like with us, he's telling me. Only it wasn't with me; it was with someone else.

"Right."

"I thought everything was going great, and then I found out about the game."

"What game?"

"This stupid thing the girls were doing with bracelets."

The bracelets. It had happened at my school too. Suddenly, a bunch of girls were wearing colored gummies on their wrists, and each one meant a different thing they'd done with a boy. The more bracelets, the more clout. It was gross, and when the parents found out, they were banned, and at least two girls got sent away to these super-strict boarding schools in Utah.

I'd never had any, but Ash had a couple when she arrived in the Hamptons last summer. "Were you a bracelet?"

"I was." He shakes his head. "Apparently, I was extra points because I was 'sad boy.'"

"That's terrible."

"Yeah, well, I found out that Phoebe was only in it for the bracelet. And she wasn't too careful about who she told. Or who she was getting the other bracelets with."

"She cheated on you?"

"She had a lot of bracelets." He pauses. "She broke my heart."

"I wouldn't do that."

"But you could."

This is breaking *my* heart. "Fred, I didn't kiss you for bracelets or points. That was just Ash being drunk. She's the one who put getting kissed on a list. Not me."

"But she did make you come to the beach that day. And she did force you to talk to me."

"Yes. But—"

"Look, Olivia, I know it's different—I do. But it feels the same. Do you understand?"

I think it through. "You feel like you can't trust me."

"It feels like I can't trust *this*." He takes both my hands in his and squeezes them. "And maybe that's me. Maybe that's something I need to fix. I know I have issues trusting things because of my dad. I went to all that dead-dad therapy. But I feel like once the trust is gone, it's hard to change that."

"How do you know unless you try?"

"You're right, I don't. But I'm leaving so there isn't any way to find out."

I pull my hands away. "What?"

"I talked to my mom today. My uncle is going to be in the hospital for a while, and they don't need me around. I'm leaving tomorrow."

I feel sick. "What does that mean? I'm never going to see you again?"

"I don't know. It just all seems pretty complicated."

"You don't even want to try?"

"I can't make any decisions right now."

"But you *are* making one. You're pushing me away for something I didn't even do."

He hangs his head. "I'm sorry."

I don't say anything. I can't. Yesterday, I had to hold myself back from saying *I love you* every time he looked at me. And now, he can't even meet my eyes.

"Olivia?"

"I want to go home."

"Let me drive you. You can't ride your bike like that."

I stand, woozy, and lean against him. I want to push myself away, but I'm using every bit of energy I have not to cry, not to break down and bawl like I did when I was a little kid.

Nothing has ever hurt this much; it feels like nothing ever will.

Then I catch myself. Something did. Losing my mother was worse than this, and I survived that. I can survive this. There's another side to this pain; I just have to wait for it.

"You all right?" Fred asks.

"No."

He isn't expecting this answer, but I don't have to lie about how I'm feeling. If this is it, I can tell the truth about that at least.

"Olivia."

I push myself away from him, steadier on my feet. I meet his eyes and they're sad, but not as sad as me. "I heard you, Fred, and I understand what you're saying, but I'm not okay with this. I don't have any doubts. I know we can work this out, and I want to do all those things we talked about. All the six months and next year and in five years . . . I meant all of that."

"I meant it too."

I feel a burst of anger. "No, you didn't. Because if you did, then you wouldn't be doing this right now. We'd be talking about how to figure it out. Not how to say goodbye."

"Olivia, I—"

He reaches for me, but I duck away and rush out of the room.

My leg is killing me, and I can feel the gash opening again, but I don't care. I need to get out of here and I'm not going to sit in a car with him, not even for one minute.

"Olivia. Olivia—please stop."

I get outside and pick up my bike. I step over it, getting it in position between my legs. It's only a couple of miles. I can make it home. I must.

"Olivia." Fred puts his hands on the handlebar and steadies it. "Olivia."

"What?"

"I don't want it to end like this."

"Me either, but it is."

"I want everything I said I did."

"Just not now."

"Maybe we can . . . in a couple of months . . ."

"No," I say. "I can't do that. I can't be the girl waiting to see if you want to be with me. My heart can't take it."

His hand tightens on my handlebar. "I understand."

"So, goodbye, I guess." I put my feet on the pedals. "I hope your uncle is okay."

"Thank you."

I wait for him to release me, but he doesn't. "You need to let go."

"I don't want to."

And now the tears are making my vision blurry. "You already did, though."

His face creases with hurt. "Maybe, in five years . . ."

"That doesn't work now."

"Why not?"

"Because that was us together the whole time. Now it's just going to be five years *later* with no *together* in between. It'll be five years *lost*."

He taps the top of the handlebars. "Okay, then. Five years later. I'll be here."

"You can't promise that."

"I can."

Our eyes meet one last time, that brief flash of heat where I think he might kiss me, and then his hand drops, and I'm free to go.

I can't stand to be in this conversation for one more minute, so I push hard against the pedals and crouch low over the handlebars and pump my legs as fast as they can take me.

The tears fall one second after he can't see me anymore, and soon I'm going so fast, the wind is in my ears.

I think he might be calling after me, he might be saying my name, but it's probably wishful thinking like the belief that we could ever have made it to five years from now, when the truth is—we couldn't even last the summer.

CHAPTER THIRTEEN

July 2023

Ash doesn't look any different from the last time I saw her. Thin, tanned, with her hair in immaculate beachy waves, wearing a light pink dress that must've been tailored to her. She had two children in two years, but I always knew her figure would bounce right back.

"Hi," I say.

"I was expecting *fuck you*."

"The thought had occurred."

"I don't blame you. I'm so, so sorry, Olivia. For all of it."

I blink back the tears that were already forming.

"Can we talk somewhere private?" Ash moves her hands around as she speaks, and I can see her large engagement ring flashing on her finger just above the diamond eternity band. My own rings are shoved into a jewelry box in one of the bags I haven't unpacked yet, my finger bare without them. "And maybe with alcohol?"

"That's probably a good idea."

She smiles, her teeth whitened, her skin that tight, perfect look you only get with treatments. I wish she'd left her face alone, but she wasn't the first or last woman who felt the need to adjust her approach to age. "Does William still keep a bottle in his study?"

"Let's hope."

We walk together to his study, an uncomfortable silence between us, so different from how we never used to run out of conversation.

His study is lined with bookshelves, and there's a bar cart under the window. There's a bottle of twenty-year-old Scotch on it, and two heavy tumblers. I pick them up. "These might be from the last time we did this."

"Does Scotch go bad?"

"Don't think so."

"Excellent."

We exit, and I go to the stairs, some instinct or memory driving me to my room as Ash follows. We used to do this, years ago, when the adults were asleep. Steal liquor and spirit it away to the third floor, giggling quietly so we didn't get caught. We don't need to hide now, but it still seems like the best place to have this conversation.

We enter my room. Even though I opened all the windows and left the fan running, the heat is stifling.

"How can you stand it?" Ash asks, her face already glistening with sweat.

"It cools off at night a bit."

She looks around. "It's exactly the same."

Nothing's changed in here since I moved out for college. Pale blue walls, boy band pictures, a vanity mirror, a princess bed. I remember when these things were so important to me, but now they're just evidence of the person I used to be.

I put the bottle down on the dresser with the glasses and pour us each a stiff drink. I hand one to Ash, and she sits in the old blue rocker in the corner, the one my mother bought for the nursery, that I'd dragged up here after she died, to soothe myself in.

I sit on the edge of the bed and raise my glass to her. I take a sip, the dark liquid rough in my mouth, but she downs the whole thing, not even taking the time to shudder afterward.

"You didn't come to the cocktail party the other night," Ash says, giving me that direct stare I remember from childhood.

"I was looking after Sophie's kids."

"You wanted to avoid Fred."

"An added bonus. Though it didn't work." I take another sip. Do I like Scotch, or is it just a trigger for memories? "He came back to their house with Sophie, Colin, and Lucy. Then drove me home."

"How did *that* go?"

"About how you'd expect."

Ash stands and crosses to my dresser. She reaches for the bottle and pours herself another glass. "Olivia and Fred. Torturing each other summer after summer."

"Ha."

"Is it funny?"

"No, it's sad."

She cocks her head to the side. "Why the hell is he buying the house?"

"I don't know. I tried to ask, but . . ."

"You chickened out?"

I smile. "Maybe you could do it?"

"You *want* me to talk to him now?"

That stings, as it's meant to. Ash is so wound up in me and Fred, the catalyst for our meeting, and a role in more than one of our break-ups. It's the reason we aren't talking, though I guess we are now.

"A conversation for good," I say lightly, but she grimaces.

"I think I'm going to stay out of this one."

"That's probably best. But you must be curious."

"I'm curious all right. Curious AF as the kids say."

"Are we not still kids?"

"I wish. I feel like it sometimes. Then a child walks into my room in the middle of the night and calls me mommy, and the illusion shatters."

I've never met Ashley's kids, only done some light stalking on Facebook. "How are they?"

"They haven't let me have a full night's sleep in years."

"That sounds exhausting."

"It is. You'll see."

I finish my glass. "I doubt it. I guess you heard about me and Wes?"

"What happened there?"

"He swore to me he wasn't cheating, but it turns out he's a liar?"

"Ouch."

"Yeah, well . . . the last couple of years . . . the pandemic. His business failed, and it turns out spending months together in a one-bedroom apartment exposed some flaws."

"You should've come out here, like the rest of Manhattan."

"Neither of us wanted that."

Ashley finishes her drink and picks up the bottle. "Probably a bad idea to have another."

"Probably."

"Did you want to avoid me too, Olivia? The other night."

"Probably."

"I really am so very sorry."

"You said."

"Is there anything I can do to make you believe it?"

I cup my glass in my hands. "The fact that you're here, trying, helps."

"I'm glad." She checks the gold watch on her wrist.

"Do you have to get home?"

"Do you want me to leave?"

"You can stay if you like."

She takes out her phone and taps out a text, her long nails clacking against the screen. She frowns as she waits for a reply, then her features clear. "Dave's on it."

"How is Dave?"

She sits in the rocking chair, cradling the bottle the way my mother used to cradle me. "He's good. You know, he's a great dad. It's hard to remember what a dummy he was when we were kids."

"Not a dummy, exactly," I say. "Maybe a bit of a bully."

"He feels so bad about that. We both do." She puts the bottle down at her feet. "God, we were awful, you know? Both of us."

"People change."

"Not around here."

"This house is going to change pretty soon."

"That must be weird for you?"

"It's weird going through everything, especially my mom's things."

"I assume Charlotte and Sophie aren't helping at all."

"Nope."

"Why do you let them walk all over you like that?"

I shrug. "It's the role I play. And I didn't want all of Mom's things tossed away like so much trash."

"And you wanted to see Fred?"

"I didn't know he'd be here."

She makes a face. "Really?"

"No one told me he'd bought the house."

"So many secrets."

"I'm kind of sick of them."

"Yeah." She fans herself. "Fuck it's hot in here."

"I can't find an air conditioner anywhere."

"I can take care of that for you."

"How?"

She pulls out her phone again and taps, taps, taps. "I have people."

"Air-conditioning people."

"People for everything." She puts her phone down. "Someone will come tomorrow. In the meantime, we need to get out of here."

"Where do you want to go?"

"Let's go to Bonne Amie. My driver will take us. And before you even start that eye roll you want to make, yeah, yeah, I know."

"I wasn't going to eye-roll."

"Uh-huh," she says.

"Okay, maybe a little."

"I'd be upset if you weren't. Because then that would mean I don't know you at all."

* * *

Bonne Amie is a French restaurant, on the main street, that you usually need a reservation for. But Ash has always operated by her own set of rules, so when the car drops us in front of the white and blue facade surrounded by cute black bistro tables full of people, we sail past them to the maître d', Claude.

"Bonsoir," I say.

"Good evening, madame," he replies in thick, accented English. His black hair is mussed, and he's got a very French-looking mustache, too large and droopy. He's wearing a crisp white shirt and black dress pants. He directs us to a table in the corner and pulls out Ash's chair and then mine.

"White wine?" I say to Ash.

"Please."

"Que nous conseilleriez-vous de boire? Nous aimons le blanc." For years on the tour, I had a French hitting partner who insisted I learn French, but I don't get to use it much.

"Oui, oui. White wine is good," Claude says without adding a suggestion.

"Avez-vous une recommandation?"

Claude is clearly struggling to understand me, and I wonder if it's my accent, though I never had any trouble being understood in Paris.

"We have some excellent white wines for you this evening," he says.

Ash gives the eye-roll she was chastising me for earlier and takes control. "Do you have any Domaine Leroy or Domaine Lecomte?"

Claude's eyes light up, and I gather Ash is speaking his language now. "Oui, oui, I will bring you a bottle."

He beetles off and I watch him go. "You think he speaks any French at all?"

"Doubtful."

"How stressful."

She pours water into her glass. "How so?"

"What does he do when actual French people come in here?"

"Welcome to my French restaurant, folks," she says in a broad American accent.

I throw back my head and laugh, and God it feels good. I can't remember the last time I did that, which is the saddest thing I've thought of in a long time.

"You okay?" Ash asks.

"Trying to be."

She picks up her menu. "So, am I forgiven?"

Her face is half hidden, but I can guess at her expression. "Are you really sorry?"

The menu drops. There are tears in her eyes. "I've never been sorrier for anything in my life." She extends her hand and I take it. Her fingers are cold.

"You didn't reach out," I say.

"And you didn't either."

"Was it my job to do that?"

"No. It was mine. But I was so ashamed. And then when things seemed to work out with Wes . . . I thought it was better to leave it."

That's what I'd thought too, all those times I almost called her. Better to leave well enough alone. "I get it."

"You know, I kept thinking I'd run into you in the city. Or out here. I thought—we'll run into each other, and then it will all be okay. Neither of us has to climb down off our high horse that way."

"But we didn't."

"I was always looking for you, though. For a while there were a couple of strawberry blondes in my neighborhood who thought I was stalking them."

I smile. "And I never came here."

"I know."

"So you *have* been stalking me?"

"I've been hoping that things would work out. That's why I came the other night. To finally face the music."

I let her hand go. "And instead, all there was, was Fred."

Her cheeks are tinged pink. "I didn't talk to him."

"It's okay if you do."

"No, Olivia, it's not. I said it earlier and I mean it. I know from the outside—the car, the table here, whatever ridiculous bottle of wine I just ordered—I know it looks like I'm that same shallow girl who interfered in your life for I-don't-even-fucking-know-what reason. But I'm not. Having kids changed me. Dave too. And I want you to know that I get it if you can't forgive me. But I really wish you would."

There are tears in both our eyes now. The chatter around us, the tinkling of glasses and silverware, other people's laughter and lives fade away. It's just us, Ash and Olivia, the team we used to be every summer, the team I thought we'd be for life.

I open my mouth to say the words, but Claude is there at my elbow, holding a bottle and presenting it on his arm.

"Madames, I have this wonderful bottle for you, oui oui. You will love it so much."

Ash laughs quietly, and we come back to ourselves.

Claude uncorks the bottle and pours a bit for Ash to taste. She sips it and nods, and when he fills our glasses and then leaves us again, the moment has passed.

CHAPTER FOURTEEN

June 2008

Crack!

At the Miami Challenger in 2008, it's a sickening sound that I feel all the way through my body as I reach for a passing shot down the line.

I fall to the ground, clutching my side. The pain is like nothing I've ever felt before, and I know immediately what it means. No summer trying to accumulate points with the hope of turning pro early. No tournament win, my first of the year, that I'm one game away from. No career at all, maybe, depending on how bad the injury is.

No telling either whether I'll live through the day because it hurts so much to breathe that it feels like I'm having a heart attack and drowning at the same time.

On the video that exists of this moment, it looks like I've gone to sleep, my eyes closed, my hands wrapped around my midsection. But I'm not sleeping. Instead, I'm thinking of death, and my life is flashing before my eyes in snippets, a Ferris wheel of regrets.

* * *

I spend a night in the hospital in Miami, hooked up to an IV of painkillers. One of my ribs is badly fractured, and I'm given more scans than I knew were possible to determine if anything else is broken. When they decide nothing is, I'm taped up, given a prescription, and told to take it easy for six weeks, to give myself time to heal.

I feel crushed by the news. Six weeks off isn't on the schedule. I haven't had one week off since I was ten, when I decided that I was going to try to be a professional tennis player. Time off isn't how I'm going to reach the next level. But I also know that rushing healing isn't going to work either. My roommate in my sophomore year had tried that, and she wasn't playing tennis anymore.

So I call Aunt Tracy and let her know I'll be coming home for the summer instead of shifting from city to city as planned, and she helps make the arrangements to get me there. A week later, I'm on the train to the Hamptons.

As I watch Long Island scroll by through the grimy train window, I try to take this setback in stride. Finishing college isn't a bad thing. I like my coach and my classes. I'm glad I picked education as my major, with a minor in music. When the time comes to retire from tennis, I'll enjoy teaching. I have a good set of friends, and while I haven't had a long-term steady relationship, there's a guy I'm casual with, and my life is all rolling along basically according to plan. And now I can enjoy the summer and go back in the fall and finish school properly before I turn pro, and my life becomes solely about tennis.

I'm trying to focus on the positive, but it's hard.

Instead, I text Ash: *Coming to the Hamptons, bitch!*

She answers immediately. *For reals?*

Yes! On the train.

Why?

You didn't see the video?

I do have my own life, you know.

Ash is at Columbia. Her current declared major is prelaw. She's been through premed, politics, psych, and a few others that I haven't absorbed.

I thought you were my #1 fan.

ROTFL.

You know I suck at text language.

The slightly creepy guy sitting next to me is trying to look at my phone, so I tip it away from him.

Okay I watched the video. Damn, girl.

              I'm okay.

It says you cracked a rib?

              Yeah. Six weeks of rest required.

FAN-TASTIC!

              Not so much for my tennis career.

But so much for your party career.

              Ha.

When do you arrive?

              1.5 hours.

You want a lift?

              I think Aunt Tracy is coming to get me.

I'll cancel her.

              Okay!

This is going to be awesome.

I tuck my phone away with a smile.

"You get good news?" the guy says. He's missing one of his incisors, and his breath smells rancid.

"My daddy told me not to talk to strangers."

He doesn't know what to do with this, which is the whole point of the line I came up with when men decided I was old enough to chat up every time I was alone.

I pull my headphones up from my neck and over my ears and turn up the volume on Sara Bareilles. Smelly-breath weirdo gets the message and opens a book, and I rest my head against the window and try to sleep.

Home. Summer. Lazing by the pool and parties on the beach. Laughing with Ash, reading trashy books, having nothing scheduled. It *does* sound good, like something I need. Maybe this injury is a blessing in disguise. Yes. *Summer.* A real, proper one. My mind drifts to the last summer I'd spent that way, but I pull it back. No use thinking about that. About *him.* I never let myself think about Fred if I can help it, and if sometimes, when I'm sleeping, my dreams take me back there, that's not my fault.

I close my eyes and drift off and dream the ending I wanted for myself, that last game in the tournament. I let the passing shot go, then regroup and win the next three points, and now I'm the champion and

I'm hoisting a trophy over my head, and then I'm on to the next tournament, and I'm turning pro early. And there's someone there to greet me after my victory, to hold me close and rub my sore feet, who looks a lot like Fred, and that's when I tell myself it's a dream and I should wake up.

I open my eyes. We're at the Southampton station. The guy next to me is smiling at me like he was watching me sleep. Gross. I turn away and make sure I have everything, stuffing my headphone and phone into a large, soft bag. I've got one suitcase with me; the rest is following in a few days. The smelly-breathed man takes my bag out of the bin above us, and I thank him, wishing I was well enough to do it myself.

The train stops and I walk to the exit, avoiding eye contact with this creeper so he doesn't ask for my number. I struggle to get my roller bag down the stairs and after it thunks to the platform, I look around for Ash, knowing she's always late. I decide to give her five minutes before I text her as the other passengers shuffle off the platform.

And then I'm alone, except for a man walking toward me, a tentative smile on his face.

Fred.

CHAPTER FIFTEEN

July 2023

The morning after my dinner with Ash at the French restaurant is rough. We finished two bottles of wine last night, our teasing of the faux French Claude growing by the glass. I was determined to get him to confess his sins, but he stuck to his guns and said, "Oui, oui," even when I asked him pointedly whether he spoke French or had even been to France.

I was glad for the car, and after it dropped me off and I climbed up the stairs to my hot, hot room, I stripped down to my underwear and prayed this was the last night I was going to sleep without air-conditioning.

My phone buzzing at six wakes me. At first, I think it's the alarm I'd set so I don't miss practice, but it's a text.

From Wes.

I'm sorry, it says. Just those two words floating on my screen. It could be about a lot of things, but I know it's probably about the one big thing. The worst thing. *Her.* Whoever she is.

"Someone you don't know," he promised, and then I'd held up my hand and said, *"Enough,"* because I didn't need any more of a visual than I'd already found.

I start to type an answer, then stop, because what do I want to say? I'm sure he *is* sorry. Maybe sorry he got caught, and maybe sorry that I'm gone too. But sorry is not enough, so I put the phone down and give myself a minute to decide whether I'm going to go to practice.

What I want to do is go back to sleep, but it's already hot in here, and I know from experience that once I'm up, I'm up. So instead of pulling the sheet over my head, I go to the bathroom and take a long, cool shower, then change into my tennis clothes and head to the club.

It's a bright morning and the sun hurts my eyes. I've forgotten my sunglasses at the house, so I pull my tennis cap low and pray that Matt doesn't notice the extra slowness in my step and the way I'm wincing when anyone talks too loudly.

I might be fooling him, but I'm not fooling Cindy, who crushes me in our first set. But I don't roll over that easily and I fight my way back, bringing us level at one set apiece. We're running out of time, so we play a tie-breaker, and first I'm up a mini-break and then she is, and then I rip a serve and I move up to the net, and she swings her arm back and cracks a passing shot down the line.

The world slows down, and now I'm inside a memory. Cindy's expression is the same as that of the woman who took me down fifteen years ago, and my arm is moving to try to get the shot, but my brain is screaming, *No!*

I get halfway there before I stop myself, but I can already feel the pain blooming at the site of the old tear.

The shot lands in, and Cindy puts her arms up in victory. I put my hand on my thighs, hunch over, and breathe in and out slowly. I can feel Matt's eyes on me, like he's X-raying my torso, trying to decide if history is repeating itself.

"Olivia?"

"I'm okay," I say, but it's low, mostly to myself.

Matt's hand is on my back. "Can you stand up?"

I nod, then tip myself up slowly. I rub my side. I've hurt myself, but it's not a break. I've just strained the muscles, an injury I've had more than once since the terrible break in Florida.

"Sorry," Cindy says, not looking sorry at all.

"Don't be. That was a great shot."

She smiles. "See you tomorrow?"

"Take the day off tomorrow," Matt says before I can answer. "Besides, isn't it your birthday?"

"You never used to give me my birthday off."

"I've mellowed in my old age."

I rub my side again, pressing into the muscles, trying to determine what I've done. Nothing too permanent, I don't think, but a day off is probably a good idea. Every part of my body hurts since I started playing every day.

"I'll take you up on that, then."

He smiles at me, the worry in his eyes easing. "You'll be okay."

"I will."

He releases me, and I go to the sidelines and recover my tennis bag. I wince as I bend to pick it up and stop. I'm about to ask Matt to take it for me, but then someone's picking it up.

"Let me help you," Fred says.

I rise slowly. It hurts to move, but it hurts to be around Fred too. "I got it."

Fred doesn't let his grip go; he just slings the bag over his shoulder and extends his hand like he's letting me go through a doorway first. I can feel Matt's eyes on me again, and some of the students' too, so I start to walk away, letting Fred follow me.

"You feeling okay?" Fred says. "Did you aggravate the old injury?"

"I'm fine."

"It felt like I was watching history repeat itself."

I shake away the echo of my own thoughts. I stop at the court fence and open the door. "You were watching?"

"I've always liked watching you play. You know that."

My brain leaps to that first summer when we didn't get enough time to figure out what we could be before he left. He was supposed to come to watch me play then, but we didn't make it far enough. But there were other summers. Ones I wish I could forget.

"It's not like the old days," I say as I push the gate open.

"I don't agree. You look great out there."

I grit my teeth. I thought his cold stares and clipped voice the other night were bad, but this is worse. Nice Fred. Former Fred. I'm not sure I can take it.

"Thanks." I turn to the path that will take me the short way home. "I walked here," I say. "You don't have to come with me."

"I could use a stretch. I've been in meetings since five."

I look at him now. His dark hair is mussed, and his face has its pre-shave stubble. "London time?"

"London time."

"You're still based there?"

"I'm half there, half here. But I plan to make this my base. I'm putting a team in place who will run things in London so I can be less involved."

"And get more sleep."

He smiles but it doesn't reach his eyes. "More sleep would be great."

The path to my house is narrow, not built for us to walk next to each other, and I'm grateful for that. It's easier to talk to Fred when I don't have to look directly at him.

"I hear you on the sleeping," I say. "There's no air in my room."

"I remember."

I blush. "Yes, well . . . Ash is getting her guy to take care of that today, she says, so that's good." I sound like a moron, speaking in half sentences.

"You made up?"

"You knew we weren't speaking?"

"She told me."

"Oh?" It comes out like a squeak.

"I mean years ago. I haven't spoken to her recently if that's what you're asking."

I feel a tinge of relief that Ash wasn't lying to me last night. "You've never liked her."

"That's not true."

"Fred, come on."

He lets out a sigh behind me. "Okay, maybe. But I had my reasons."

"I remember," I say with some satisfaction. Two can play at this game.

We're at the end of the beach path, and I step onto the sidewalk. It's only a block from my house now and I pick up the pace. Anxiety is pricking at my fingers, and my hangover feels like it's back for round two. I need a shower, meds, a nap. I need to get away from Fred.

"Are you thinking of playing professionally again?" Fred asks.

"What? No. I'm too old."

"You're not old."

"Thirty-six tomorrow," I say, then kick myself.

"Are you doing anything to celebrate?"

I sneak a peek at him. His face is open, candid, like he's talking to someone he just met at a cocktail party. But there's a spark of interest too. He can't quite keep that in check.

"I haven't given it much thought. I didn't know I was coming out here till right before I did."

"When you heard I'd bought the house?"

"What? No."

We're at my driveway, facing each other. The top of his shirt is open, and he has a triangle of tan between his collarbones. There's a line of sunburn too, across the bridge of his nose, following the path of his freckles.

I wish with every fiber of my being that I didn't find him so attractive. That I could forget the feel of his hands on me.

"I didn't know you'd done that until I got here."

"Charlotte didn't tell you?"

"She did not."

"You two in a fight?"

"No. Why do you ask?"

"You sound angry."

"Well, I am."

"At me?"

I cross my arms, then regret it. I'm going to need to tape my side at the very least. "Of course at you."

"What did I do?"

"Come on, Fred. You bought my family's house and didn't even tell me about it."

"Would you have taken my call?"

That stops me. I don't know what I would've done if Fred had called.

"I didn't think so," Fred says.

"You didn't give me the chance to find out—"

"Not this time, but—"

"—and you haven't told me why you bought it or what you intend to do with it."

"You really want to know?"

We stare at each other for a beat, and I can't read him. Does he want to tell me? Or is he shielding me from something that might hurt me? I can't take the risk.

"I guess not." I reach for my bag, and he gives it to me. "Thanks for bringing it here."

"Sure. I hope your side's okay."

"Thanks." I turn to leave.

"Wait, Olivia."

"What?"

"Lucy told me that you were thinking of having an estate sale?"

"Lucy told you?"

He has the good sense to look sheepish. "At dinner last night."

I want to sink into the ground. He's dating Lucy.

"Anyway, I was wondering if you had any plans for the proceeds?"

"I hadn't thought about it."

"You know there's a charity for my uncle. I thought you might want to set up something similar in your mother's name? There are some nice pieces in the house that might bring in a tidy sum."

I'm stuck between being angry at the thought that he was appraising the furniture when he was visiting the house, and the happiness of being able to honor my mother the way she should be. "Oh, I . . . I'd have to talk to Charlotte and Sophie. And my father, of course."

"Of course. Let me know what you decide, and I'll set everything up."

"You don't—"

"It would be my pleasure. I have lawyers on staff who can do it, no problem. Decide who you want the recipients to be, and we'll take it from there."

"Okay, I will."

Lauren Bailey

He stares at me, and for a moment the world slows down like it did on the tennis court, like I'm living in the past and I know what my body wants to do, but just like on the court with Cindy, my brain is screaming, *No!*

And then the moment passes, and I step onto the driveway, fighting as hard as I can not to break into a run.

CHAPTER SIXTEEN

June 2008

"What are you doing here?" I ask Fred on the train platform, my hands shaking.

His face falls. The last time I saw him, he was still a boy, but he's a man now. His shoulders are squared, his hair is short and a bit darker, and there's a definition to his features that was missing before. I can't believe this is happening. I was just dreaming about him on the train, and now here he is, in front of me, wearing chino shorts and a polo shirt—not so different from his old uniform at the beach.

"Ashley didn't tell you?"

Oh no. Oh, Ash. "She said *she* was picking me up."

"I should've known."

"It's not your fault. But . . . why are you in Southampton?"

"My uncle died last week."

"I'm so sorry, Fred."

"Thank you." He reaches down and picks up my bag. It's light in his hands, like it's nothing.

"When's the funeral?"

"Tomorrow."

I don't know what to say. My heart is beating too fast, and my palms feel sweaty. Part of me is glad to see him and part of me is furious. "You never called."

"We said we wouldn't."

"Did we?"

The days after our breakup are hazy. I kept expecting him to call or email, to tell me it had been a misunderstanding and I wasn't going to have to pay for the mistakes of some other girl. But he never did. Eventually, I stopped looking for his name in my inbox. And I didn't reach out because I shouldn't be the one to apologize. So how could I call him? What would I say? Just wait in silence for him to say the right thing? And what if he didn't? What if he was expecting me to be the one to put us back together?

It was too many questions, too many unknowns, so I let it fade to history. Us.

"It was a long time ago," Fred says.

"Five years."

"And now it's five years later."

What is he saying? That *this* is what we agreed to? That he'd reappear in my life after five years of radio silence, and we'd pick up where we left off?

"I . . . I can get a cab."

"No, I'll drive you."

I want to refuse, but Fred looks as sad as I feel. I'm going to kill Ash. "Okay, thank you."

I follow him out of the station to the parking lot. It's half full of cars, and the sun is gleaming off their windshields. Trees ring the lot, and sand is swirling across the cracked tarmac.

"I'm over here." He points to an old black pickup with rust spots on the side. He puts my bag in the back, then opens the door on the passenger side for me. I climb up into the seat, wincing as I go.

"You're injured," Fred says as I settle myself gingerly into the seat.

"Cracked rib."

"I didn't know."

He closes the door gently after me, then circles the truck and gets into the driver's seat. My brain is flooding with the questions I've been holding at bay. *Where has he been all this time? How long is he going to be here? Is he single?*

Did he miss me?

"Why did you agree to pick me up?" The only safe topic is transportation.

He turns on the engine. "I wanted to see you."

Or maybe not. "How did Ash know you were here?"

"I ran into her in town the other day."

"She didn't tell me."

He backs up and leaves the lot. His hands are sure on the wheel, and it's already one new thing about him. We've never driven together before, but I feel safe. Secure.

That's a false feeling that I need to quash immediately.

"Seems like she's keeping a lot from you these days," he says.

You're dead, I text to Ash, hiding my screen from Fred. *I killed you.* "I'm sorry she asked you."

"I'm not."

I glance at him, but he's staring straight ahead. The station isn't far from Taylor House, but it feels like a million miles. "How have you been? I mean, in general."

"Good."

I turn away; it's too hard to look at him. The same old houses flash past, tourists with sunburned arms and trucker hats. The brine of the ocean hugs the air. "Did you go into the Army?"

"The Navy."

"Right." I didn't forget, but I can't make my brain work right. "And?"

"I did my four years. I'm on the G.I. Bill now."

"What college?"

"Boston State. Studying business."

"All according to plan, then."

He glances at me now, his face a shadow across mine. "Mostly."

I sink into my seat. It hurts my rib, and I hold it gently, knowing it's another hour before I can take a pill.

"Does it hurt?"

"A lot."

"What happened?"

"I went for a shot I should've let pass me by."

"Sounds like a metaphor."

"Probably." I hug myself. "Anyway, I'm out for the summer, so I thought I'd recuperate here. What about you?"

"Here for the summer. My mom's in town for the funeral, and then I'll stay and help my aunt till school starts in the fall."

I roll down the window, needing air. We're on my street now, the dunes rolling by, the crashing waves our background music. "So we're both here for the summer."

"Seems like."

What now? I want to say, but I don't. I don't know what I want, and until I do, I don't want to make it about Fred's wishes. Assuming he wants anything from me at all. But he said it's five years later . . .

Is this my decision to make? Could we be reuniting right now if I said the word?

He turns down my driveway and stops the truck in front of the house. I don't even know if there will be anyone but Aunt Tracy to greet me, but it doesn't matter. Soon, I'll take another pill and then a long nap, and tomorrow I'll see how I feel about all of this.

"Thanks for picking me up."

"Can we . . . can we get lunch later this week?"

"I'd like that."

He smiles for the first time since the station, but it's short-lived. He climbs out of the truck, and I do the same. He lifts my bag from the back and puts it down in front of the door. "Do you need me to bring this in?"

"I can do it. Or Aunt Tracy can help me."

"Okay."

"I'm sorry again about your uncle."

He lifts his chin. "He was sick for a long time. Ever since . . ."

"The heart attack."

"Yes."

That day lingers between us, and I wonder what Fred thinks of me now. I'm five years older too. I have less baby fat in my face, and the body of a professional athlete. I'm strong, sure, outwardly confident. But inside I feel the same as I did the first time we talked on the beach. Unsure, nervous, excited.

"Where's the funeral?"

He names a Presbyterian church and I nod, my chest tightening, sadness a veil. We're lingering, not saying goodbye, but I need to leave. I need to go inside and cry and so I say, "I'll see you in a couple of days," then turn and walk to the door. I put my hand on the doorknob.

"Did you see it?" he says. "When it came out?

I smile through my tears but I don't turn around. "*The Golden Compass*?"

"Yes," he says to my back. "I wanted to call you, but . . ."

"You didn't," I say, then open the door and walk inside.

* * *

"Why are we going to this?" Ash asks the next day. We're both dressed in black, and I've borrowed Charlotte's car to drive to the funeral.

"Because Fred's uncle died."

"Amendment: Why am *I* going to this?"

"Because I need backup. And you owe me big-time after that stunt you pulled yesterday."

"You never would've called him."

I turn into the church parking lot. "That was my decision to make."

Ash shrugs. She's pulled her hair back into a bun, and with the sharp-cut jacket she's wearing, she looks like a young executive. "You should be thanking me."

"Uh-huh."

The parking lot is full. Though they hadn't been in town that long, Fred's aunt and uncle were popular. I'd see them on my visits home every year, walking together on the beach or peering into shop windows. His aunt was cheerful and friendly, and she quickly gained them entry into various charitable and other institutions, including the SL&TC.

I'd never spoken to them, though, too worried about what that might lead to. Did they even know I existed? I didn't want to find out.

I park the car at the back of the lot. "How about this? Stay out of my love life from now on."

"What love life?"

"Ha ha."

We join the somber-dressed line of people walking into the church. My plan is to sit at the back and leave before Fred knows I'm there, but that gets thrown out the window when he's standing just inside the entrance, handing out programs. He's wearing a black suit, and now, finally, he looks like the boy I remember, adorable and a little lost.

"Olivia." The way he says my name, I don't know if I'm a blessing or a curse.

"Hi, Fred. I'm sorry for your loss."

He nods to me, then hands me a program. There's a woman standing behind him who looks just like him. His mom.

"Mom," he says, tugging on her sleeve, "this is Olivia."

She turns toward me, her brown eyes warm. She's heard my name before. She knows our story. "Nice to meet you, Olivia."

"I'm sorry for your loss," I repeat, feeling inadequate.

"Thank you." She moves on to the next person in line.

"There are some seats at the back," Fred says.

I fold the program between my hands. "Okay, thanks."

Ash and I walk past him and take two seats in the last pew. The church is simple, with little adornment. The low murmur of church-talking fills the air.

"What's going on with you two?" Ash whispers to me once we've taken a seat.

"Nothing. I told you. We're maybe having lunch in a couple of days, that's it."

"Do you want more?"

I sit back on the hard seat. My rib still hurts, and I'm grateful for the cushion the pill I took right before we left gives me. "What I want is to get through this funeral without bawling my eyes out."

Ash is stricken. "I didn't even think of that. This is where . . ."

"Yes." Where my mother was buried, the last funeral I went to.

Ash came to the funeral, clutching her parents' hands. She was the only friend who did, everyone else opting out of the sad event. I didn't want to be at that funeral either, but I wasn't given a choice.

Ash reaches for my hand. "I'm sorry."

"It's okay."

"What do you need from me?"

"If I want to go, don't argue."

"Of course." She sits back and opens the program. "We'll be out of here in an hour."

"Good."

"And I'll lay off the Fred stuff."

"Thank you."

The organ starts and we go through the familiar rituals. The family walks in and takes their seats, and the minister tells us to rise and sit in a predictable pattern. I try not to think too much about what they're saying, pushing back the memories of these same words and readings from my mother's funeral. Charlotte so cold, almost frozen. Sophie in tears for days, her face pressed into my shoulder. William, solemn, sober, resolute.

When I can't help myself, I watch Fred, his head bowed, his hands holding his rolled-up program. His jaw is tight, and I know him enough to know that he doesn't want to break, and he's doing everything he can not to.

And then the minister invites him up, and he rises to speak.

I grasp Ash's hand. I want to run, but I'm rooted to the spot.

Fred coughs, covering his mouth, then pulls the microphone toward him. He's taller than the podium is set up for, so he stoops.

"Most of you know that I lost my dad when I was young. When that happened, I felt at sea. So my uncle, he did the funniest thing. He took me to sea. He came to Boston, and he chartered a boat, and he *took* me out into the bay. It was a cold day, stormy, and we really shouldn't have been out there. But he wasn't afraid. He'd seen worse he said, and so had my dad.

"I remember him standing there in his yellow slicker with the waves kind of tossing up on him, and his arms were out wide, and he said, 'Sometimes you have to embrace the sea.' And I knew what he meant. He meant that when bad things happen, you have to lean into them. You have to embrace the bad times because that's when you learn—when you *know*—what you're truly made of. He did that for me that day, and he stood by me every day after that. Whenever I needed him, he was there."

Fred pauses and wipes a tear off his cheek. "These last five years, while he's been sick, I got to give some of that back to him. And you did that too—this community. He loved living here, walking on the beach, seeing the seasons come and ago. *'Live near the ocean,'* he always used to say to me, *'and then you'll know you're alive.'*"

I lean against Ash, and she puts her arm around my shoulders.

"So, I wanted to thank you on his behalf and my aunt's for being welcoming and helping to make his last years happy ones. We're all at sea, but we're going to embrace that. I hope you'll join us."

He steps off the podium as my tears fall. His loss pierces my soul the way our ending did.

"Let's get out of here," I say as the organ starts up and the priest lifts his hands in front of him, inviting us to stand and sing.

Ash doesn't fight me, and we slip out of the pew. I take a last look at Fred over my shoulder, and something in him senses me watching. He turns and meets my eyes.

"I'm sorry," I mouth.

He nods once, then turns away, and then Ash's hand is in mine, and we make our soundless escape.

CHAPTER SEVENTEEN

July 2023

Inside, after I flee from Fred, I find Lucy talking to Charlotte and Sophie in the drawing room.

"Did I miss a meeting?" I say in the entranceway. Sophie and Charlotte are sitting on the old pink brocade couch, and Lucy is perched on a flower-covered wing chair. They're leaning in conspiratorially, like they're discussing a surprise party. They snap back at the sound of my voice.

"No, no," Lucy says graciously. She stands and invites me in. She's wearing black linen pants that stop at her ankles, and a loose-fitting white blazer. She's always had an effortless style. "I was just telling your sisters about that thing we discussed—the estate sale."

Sophie gives me a guilty look. "It would make everything so much easier."

"For who?"

"For all of us."

I know she's right, but I feel angry anyway. Charlotte and Sophie put me in charge of something I didn't want to do, and now they seemed to be revoking that license.

"And we could do a charity too," Charlotte says. "Sounds like the perfect solution."

"I agree," Ann says.

I didn't see her, tucked in the corner behind the door. She gives me a wide smile, like we're old friends, even though we've only just met.

"It sounds like it's all decided. I'll leave you to sort out the details."

"Don't be that way, Olivia," Sophie says. She stands and walks toward me, yoking her arm around my waist. "We still need you to run everything, obviously. We'd be lost without you."

Even though she's obviously buttering me up, I feel myself softening. "Can you put together a proposal?" I say to Lucy. "The cost, the timing, etcetera?"

"Of course." She stands and Ann does the same. "Why don't we leave you three to discuss it and I'll get you that proposal tomorrow?"

"Thanks."

Charlotte rises. "I'll just walk Ann out. And Lucy too, of course."

The three of them leave, and I sit next to Sophie on the couch.

"Is she going to tell us, or . . .?" Sophie says.

"Why would today be any different?"

"I don't get it. It's not like we'd care. Scratch that—I'd be happy for her."

"Me too," I say.

"Me too what?" Charlotte says, returning to the room. She reaches up and smooths her hair back, letting its dark curtain fall into place. She's dressed for tennis, though I can't remember the last time she played.

"Getting this done," I say. "I need a shower and a long bath."

"Shouldn't you pick one?"

"Nope."

Sophie laughs. "We should do this, yes? An estate sale and give the money to charity?"

"Ann can arrange everything for us," Charlotte says, taking a seat. "Pro bono."

"I should hope so after the fee she's going to get on the house transaction," I say.

Charlotte frowns. "She did great work for us."

"Do I want to know what her fee is?" Sophie asks.

"I doubt it." I lean back on the couch. It's never been comfortable, and age hasn't helped it. "Fred offered to have his lawyers set up the trust."

"Did he?" Charlotte says.

"Don't look at me like that. He and Lucy were talking about it."

Sophie leans forward eagerly. "I think they're cute together."

Charlotte watches me as I take in this information. "Why have Fred do it and not Ann?"

I try to keep my voice nonchalant. "Because he set up something similar for his uncle when he died. And he offered. But I don't care. You guys decide."

"I think we should keep it in the family," Sophie says.

Charlotte gives a satisfied smile. "I'll tell Ann."

"I meant Fred."

My throat goes dry. "Fred's in the family now?"

"If things work out with him and Lucy . . ."

"Work out how?" I say. I don't want to know, but I don't have the strength to avoid asking.

"He said he bought this place because he wants to settle down. Why not with Lucy? She's great."

"Wait, what?"

"You told me that, right, Charlotte? Or maybe Lucy did? Anyway, they've been dating—a few dinners, and I think they played golf once."

I thought they'd had one dinner after meeting at the garden party. Clearly not. "That's hardly wedding bells."

"Didn't you announce your engagement after, like, a month?"

"That's not a recommendation for a quick romance, surely."

Charlotte makes a noise in her throat that's like a growl. "This is stupid. We'll use Ann."

"No," I insist. "I want to keep this separate. We'll use Fred's team."

"Fine. Whatever. I have a match to get to." She flounces out of the room, and we watch her leave.

"She's playing tennis now?" Sophie asks.

"Apparently, she's full of secrets. Like this house."

"What do you mean?"

"I've just been thinking about Mom a lot . . . Do you think she was happy?"

"With what?"

"Her life. William."

Sophie's mouth turns down. "I remember her being happy. Don't you?"

"Yeah, I do. But we were kids . . ."

"Maybe ask Aunt Tracy? She'd know if anyone did."

"Good idea."

"You don't have to dig up the past, you know. You can just recycle it."

"You'd be okay with that?"

"Mom died a long time ago."

"You're right. She did." I stand. "I'm going to take my shower. And then maybe a nap."

"Aunt Tracy said there were workmen up in your room? Something about installing air-conditioning."

Ash had come through. Thank God. "That's the best news I've heard in a long time."

* * *

When I get upstairs, the workmen are just leaving, and I can already feel the cold air spreading like a welcome storm. I strip out of my clothes and take a long bath, stretching in the heat, then rinse off in the shower. By the time I get back to my room, it's almost cold. I decide to succumb to the exhaustion I feel and take a nap, snuggling into my blankets, leaving the air on high.

When I wake up hours later, I'm starving, and it's the middle of the afternoon. I feel disoriented, and when I check my phone, I've slept until almost three.

I change into some clothes that will do for the five PM drinks and resolve to unpack the rest of my things. Everything in my bags is a jumble, and I need to put some order to it.

But first I need something to eat.

I find Aunt Tracy in the kitchen, kneading a loaf of bread on the counter.

She smiles at me like the proud parent she is. "You must be hungry."

"I'll get something. Keep making your bread."

I open one of the fridges, rooting around until I find some sandwich things. I pull them out and line them up on the counter: whole grain bread, shaved turkey, cheese, mustard, mayo, lettuce. My comfort sandwich from childhood.

"Do you want one?"

She comes over to stand next to me. She's wearing a linen shift dress and Roman-inspired sandals, her hair flowing loosely. "That *is* tempting."

"Consider it done."

She kisses me on the cheek. "Did you have a good sleep?"

"Did you hear about the air-conditioning?" She nods. "It was heaven." I pull out four slices of bread and start assembling the sandwiches. My mouth is already watering. "I'm glad you're here."

"Me too."

"I mean, for the usual reasons, but also because I had a question."

"Anything, my love."

"Was Mom happy? I mean before she got sick."

"Why do you ask?" Tracy walks back to her bread and starts to kneed it again.

"I guess it's going through her things . . . She and William were so young when they got married . . ."

"Is this about Fred?"

"What? No. Not directly anyway."

"It must be discomfiting to have him back here. And for him to be buying the house."

I slather mayo on all four pieces of bread, then follow it up with grain mustard. "Yes, but that's not why I'm asking."

"Everyone's unhappy sometimes." Tracy pulls a bowl toward her, oiling it quickly and loading the dough into it.

I add the insides to the sandwiches and put the top on. I cut them in two on the diagonal. I put Tracy's on a plate and don't even bother with one for me. I bite into it, almost groaning in pleasure. It's been way too many hours since I ate anything.

"It's not good to dig around in the past," Tracy says. "You never know what you might turn up."

"You know something."

"I don't. I'm speaking generally." She sprinkles cornmeal over the top of the dough and makes two slashes in it. Then she covers it with a tea towel. "What happens between two people is between them." Tracy crosses the kitchen and puts her arms around me. She smells like yeast. "That sandwich looks great—thank you."

"It's pretty basic."

"So, I'm basic. Kill me. Wait. Basic is bad, right?"

"Basic is bad. But also good."

Tracy shakes her head. "I know one thing."

"What's that?"

"If your mom were here, she'd be so proud of you." She gives me one of those looks again, like it's parent–teacher night, and I've won the top prize.

And maybe I have. Despite everything and the mess my life is in currently, I've had more good than bad, overall. Not right now, but most of the time. And, like Anne of Green Gables used to say, tomorrow is another day with no mistakes in it yet.

Or something like that.

CHAPTER EIGHTEEN

June 2008

After we fled Fred's uncle's funeral, I sulked around Ash's for a while, but I couldn't settle. I felt guilty for leaving, and sad. Sad about my mother, sad about Fred. This wasn't how I'd imagined the summer would go, and it was only two days in. Added to which, Fred and I had never agreed on a day to meet for lunch, and I wasn't sure how to reach him, or even if I wanted to.

Fred had broken my heart. It had taken me a year to get over it, and every boy I'd met since then I compared to him. They never measured up, and after I while I couldn't tell if that was because I'd built Fred up in my mind or if he really was the boy I was supposed to be with. It was a lot to live with. I'd finally reconciled myself to us not being together. I didn't want to go and stir all that up again. I should leave the past where it belonged—buried in the hard ground like Fred's uncle was about to be.

When Ash tells me I'm moping too much, I leave. My side's aching, and it's time for my next pill. I take it when I get home, then make myself some food in the kitchen and creep upstairs, avoiding the family because I don't feel like engaging with that dynamic.

My room is hot, and after I eat, I feel sleepy, so I strip down to a tank top and my underwear and crawl into bed, settling under the sheet before the drugs pull me under.

I dream about Fred. About how we used to lie in the grass and kiss, our hands twined together, our legs entwined too. I remember the smell of the night, the ocean, the fresh-cut lawn that was a blanket beneath us. I remember the taste of Fred's mouth and the feel of his hands and the want that built up between us until I felt like breaking my promise to myself that I wasn't ready for the next step.

In this dream, I take that step. Fred's hands undo the buttons on my shorts. His lips trail along my collarbone to my breast. His fingers run up my thighs slowly, making my back arch. I bite down on my lip as he slips a finger inside me, thrusting it deep. The pressure builds as he moves methodically, moving his thumb in a slow circle over my—

Clink!

The sound starts to pull me from sleep, but I don't want this dream to end. I don't want this feeling to end. I want, want, want—

Shit.

I sit up, my heart beating, my rib aching. My room is dark, with only the flashlight of the moon cutting across the ceiling as it angles in through the open window. There's a noise outside, something metal clinking against itself, and then something else. A branch snapping, a soft curse.

I get out of bed and go to the window. Someone's climbing up the drainpipe in dark clothing.

It's Fred.

"What the fuck?"

"Throw me a sheet so I don't fall off this wall."

I reach back to my bed, pulling the sheet I was just tangled in from it, and dangle it out the window.

"Did you tie it to something?"

"You didn't tell me to do that."

"Shh. Someone will hear you."

Part of me doesn't care, but also, everyone else sleeps on the other side of the house and between the distance and the ocean, they wouldn't hear anything unless we yell really loud.

"Hold on." I take the other end of the sheet and tie it to the bed-post, then lean out the window again. "Okay."

Fred wraps the sheet around his wrist and uses it to climb the last ten feet. I step back as he appears in the window. He's dressed in dark jeans and a navy hoody, and with his dark hair, he looks like he's ready for a caper.

"Can I come in?"

"Bit late to ask that now, isn't it?"

I take a step back, then realize what I'm wearing. Basically nothing. I reach for a pair of shorts on the floor and slip them on while Fred finishes climbing in through the window. I sit on my bed, covering my legs with the quilt and crossing my arms across my chest.

Fred dusts himself off. There's a twig caught in his hair. "Sorry about that."

"What are you doing here?"

"I wanted to talk to you."

"And the phone doesn't work at your house?"

"It was too late to call."

"Okay."

Fred looks sheepish. "You want me to go?"

"I want to know what's going on."

"I wanted to talk to you."

"You said."

Fred holds his hands out. "This is hard for me, okay?"

"And it's not hard for me?"

"You act so cool about everything."

I almost laugh. "What are you talking about?"

He moves toward the bed and sits on the edge. "At the train station."

"I was in shock."

"And today at the funeral."

I look away. "That's where my mother's funeral was."

"I didn't know."

"It's okay."

"Hey, no . . ." Fred touches my chin with his finger. "Look at me."

I let him turn my head. What does he see as he stares at me so intensely? My hair's a mess, and my face is slack from the deep drugged sleep I was in. My body is still half in the dream, about to climax with Fred bringing me there, and now here he is, that same finger on my face, close enough to smell his sweat.

"Do you want me to go?"

"No."

"Are you happy to see me?"

"Fred."

"Just tell me. Tell me you didn't forget me."

The idea that I could forget him is so ridiculous I don't know what to say. I can't speak, and each second that goes by, I watch an ocean of feelings cross his face, from hope to disappointment to resignation. And that's what breaks me. I can't stand the thought of him being resigned to anything about me.

So, I do the only thing I can to express what I'm feeling.

I kiss him.

Not the sweet kiss of five years ago, but hard and hungry, my hands in his hair, pulling his body to me, the kisses of my dream. He meets me kiss for kiss, his hands on my hips, pulling me up and into his lap. I wrap my legs around him and press my chest to his, feeling a flood of memories, and half believing this is still an illusion, that any moment now I'll wake up for real and all of this will be gone.

Fred will be gone.

But in the meantime, Fred's murmuring in my ear, narrating how I feel under his hands. His voice is deep and husky, his breath hot on my skin when his mouth leaves mine to kiss my neck. He leans back and raises my arms above my head, then removes my top. He takes my breast in his mouth and I arch back, my hands threaded through his hair, holding him in place. His tongue makes slow circles around my nipple as he sucks on it, then nibbles gently, and I don't know how much more of this I can take.

I lean away, and we tumble backward onto the bed. My rib shouts in protest. "Ouch."

"Are you okay?" Fred asks above me, his voice gentle, his face creased in concern.

"Just my rib."

"I'll be gentler."

"Please don't."

Fred groans and then his mouth is on mine again, his hands everywhere. He undoes my shorts and dips his fingers into my underwear. I arch up to meet his palm, letting it cup me and feel how wet I am. His finger slides inside me easily, and I cry out. He moves it in and out slowly, and my God, my God, none of those fumbling boys at college ever came close to this.

I reach for the fly of his pants, and he pulls his shirt over his head, then takes his pants off quickly, leaving only his boxers. He lies down next to me. We're both breathing heavily, our mouths wet, our tongues intertwined. His fingers are still inside me, his thumb on my clit.

He pulls back, out of breath. "I didn't come here for this."

I pull him to me again, and I can feel him hard between my legs. I grind my hips into his, and he moans in my ear.

"I meant, I don't have anything."

"Oh." I pull back. "I'm on the pill, but hold on . . ." I disentangle from him and search around the floor for my purse. Somewhere in there is a two-pack of condoms. I blush at the thought of why I have them, my stupid hook-up guy at college, then banish him. After this, no matter what, that guy is never touching me again.

I fish around in the purse until I find it. I hold it up like a prize. "We're covered."

Fred smiles and beckons me with his hand. "You're beautiful."

"That's what all the guys say." He frowns. "I didn't mean . . ."

"It's okay, come here."

I climb back into bed. "Here?"

"Right here," he says, pulling me closer to him and kissing my neck. In an instant, we're right back in the moment together, only skin between us. Fred puts the condom on and positions himself over me. He looks down at me, his face in shadow, his voice full of desire. "Did you wait for me?"

"No," I say and pull him inside.

And there's nothing stopping us now as our breath turns ragged and our bodies thrust together, and I lose myself a moment before he does, burying himself deep.

* * *

Two hours later, we're still touching. His hand on my hip, mine on his flat stomach. His fingers massaging gently along my rib, then followed by kisses and promises to make it all better.

In between we catch each other up on where we've been these last five years, what we've done and seen and felt. And all that complicity we had when we first met, where we felt like our two hearts were completely open to each other, like we were the only people in the world who'd ever felt this way: that's still there—*it's still there*—and I don't know whether to stop his talking with kisses so we can start all over more slowly or talk to him until the day breaks.

"What time is it?" I ask.

He picks his watch off the nightstand. "Four AM."

"Sun will be up soon."

He smiles against my mouth. "I always wanted to do this."

"Sex?"

"Well, yes, but I meant talking all night. Being with you for the sunrise."

"But you didn't come here for this."

"I swear."

"Uh-huh."

His finger grazes my nipple and my body clenches. "Okay, okay, maybe a small part of me was hoping for a kiss."

"Fred."

"Olivia."

"What's happening?"

"We're having the reunion we deserve?"

"Okay, sure. But also . . ."

"What about everything that happened last time?"

"Well, yeah."

He turns over on his back, pulling the sheet across us. It's the coolest part of the night, before the sun comes up, after the heat of the day has burned off and been swept away by the ocean breeze.

"I was an idiot," he says.

"I agree."

"Thanks."

"We both were." I lace my fingers through his. He raises my hand to his mouth and kisses it.

"I should've reached out."

"Yes."

"I almost did a million times."

I watch the shadows cross the ceiling. Something about this night still seems impossible, but if it's a dream I don't want to wake up. "What stopped you?"

"My pride, mostly."

"Why?"

"I didn't want to be rejected again."

"I never rejected you in the first place."

"I know that now. But then . . . it was a weird time. With everything with my uncle and then that stupid thing with Ashley."

"She feels really bad about that."

"She told me."

I turn on my side and snuggle into him. "When you ran into her?"

"I think that's why she asked me to pick you up. She wanted to make it up to me."

"That's not why."

"Why then?"

I squeeze his hand. "Because she saw how devastated I was after you left. How it wasn't ever the same with anyone else . . ."

He turns to me. "Not for me either. I told you then that I'd never felt this way before, and I meant it. This. You and me . . . it's special."

My heart feels like it's melting, and we kiss, sealing something, I'm not sure what. We pull apart.

"When I saw you leave at the funeral, I wanted to leave too. And then I was lying in bed, trying to sleep, and all I could think about was how I couldn't stand to be away from you for one more minute."

I pull my hand away, feeling a chill. "This is about your uncle."

"No, Olivia. No. I was coming here this summer before that happened."

"You were?"

"Ask my aunt if you don't believe me."

"I'm not going to do that."

He pulls me into his arms. "I was coming here this summer."

"Why?"

"You need me to say it?"

"Yeah, I do."

"Because I told you I'd be here in five years, and I wanted to keep that promise. Even if you wouldn't see me. Even if I had to spend the whole summer convincing you to give us another chance."

He was coming here this summer. For me. I *am* dreaming.

"Really?"

"Really."

"And at the train station?"

"You were so . . . far away from me . . . I chickened out."

I let go of the breath I was holding. I can't remember the last time I felt this happy, and if there was another time, I don't want to remember it. Because it's probably related to Fred too, and that makes me sad. All the time we missed, all the things we didn't get to do.

"Olivia?"

"I wasn't even supposed to be here this summer."

He smiles. "Aren't I lucky, then?"

"No," I say. "I'm the lucky one."

CHAPTER NINETEEN

July 2023

"You need to get over here," I say to Ash two hours after my chat with Tracy in the kitchen. I'm standing at the window of one of the guest rooms on the second floor, which I've been cleaning out and cataloging with the app that Lucy sent me the link to. It's always been my favorite, with pretty flowered wallpaper and windows looking out over the lawn.

The cataloging is a simple if laborious process. I have to take a photograph of every piece that will be part of the auction, then put as much as I know about its age and provenance. It's taken me the last hour to do this one simple room. At this rate, I'll have to be here all summer to get the other twenty-five done.

"Please don't talk so loud," Ash says, her voice a rasp.

"Sorry."

"What's going on?"

"It's almost time for cocktails."

"Ugh, I do not need another drink, like, ever."

"You need to come here anyway."

"Why?"

I pull the lace curtain aside. My father is standing out on the veranda, with his drink in hand, talking to a couple.

"Fred's here."

"Ah."

"And Lucy."

"Oh."

I let the curtain drop. "You knew about this?"

"I'd heard they were dating."

"Bad enough that Fred is buying my house and is around all the time, but now I have to watch him with another woman? One I actually like?"

"So don't go."

"That's not an option."

"Why not?"

I peek out the window again. Fred's wearing a dark blazer and no tie, the collar on his white dress shirt open. He's got his hand on the small of Lucy's back, like he's holding her in place. "I already skipped cocktails once because he was here, and I'm not going to give him the satisfaction."

"Guess you'll just have to face it, then."

"Please come."

"I can't. I've got the kids. Dave is out tonight with his buddies."

I sigh. "I guess that's fair."

She chuckles. "I did tell you. Last night notwithstanding, my life looks a lot different these days. Tea parties, sandcastles, things like that."

"But you hate the sand."

"It does get everywhere."

"I want to meet your kids."

"I'd like that."

I turn away from the window again and walk out of the room, my phone pressed to my ear. "Tonight?"

"No. No way. You already used that excuse. And I need a night or twenty without drinking."

"We don't have to drink."

"Sure," Ash says, laughing. "We don't."

I'm in the hallway. The door to Charlotte's room is closed, but I can hear her in there. I take a step closer. Maybe she can be my wingman.

"Do I look awful?" I ask Ash.

"What do you mean?"

"When you saw me, did you think, God she's aged badly."

"No."

"You promise?"

"Yes, why?"

I hear Charlotte's voice through the door, and then another one, deeper. I take a step back. "The expression on Fred's face the first time he saw me. Like he wouldn't have recognized me if he saw me out of context."

"He didn't say that."

"His eyes did."

"Well, fuck him, then."

I smile. "Thanks, Ash."

There's a wail behind her. "I've got to go."

"I'll come over soon."

"Oh, wait! Tomorrow. It's your birthday."

"I know."

"What are you doing?"

I hear another noise from Charlotte's room. It's Ann in there, enjoying herself by the sound of it. Good for you, Charlotte. Go for it.

"Unclear."

"Why?"

"In case you forgot, my birthday hasn't always worked out so well for me when Fred's around." I back farther away from Charlotte's door and head toward the stairs. If I'm going to see Fred, it's not going to be in these dust-stained clothes.

"One time . . ."

"Yeah."

"Your next birthday was okay, though, wasn't it?"

"Sure . . . a broken rib, a summer that ended with a broken heart."

"Okay, okay." Ash clucks her tongue. "Third time's the charm?"

"More like fifth time." I release a laugh. "Are you going?"

"Yep."

"Any room at your table?"

"I'm stuck with a bunch of old boring people, but maybe I can fix something."

I reach the third floor. It's blissfully cool. "Thank you for the air-conditioning, by the way."

"They came?"

"Yes, thank God."

"Good. It's on me. Your birthday present."

"Thank you."

"Happy to help."

I go into my room and do a mental inventory of the outfits I brought with me. Nothing appropriate comes to mind, so I go to the closet. It's full of the things I left behind when I moved out at twenty-two. "Maybe there isn't even a seat for me."

"Sorry to say I'm pretty sure there is. Charlotte bought a table weeks ago."

"Sigh." I flip through the dresses, a paved road down memory lane. I stop on one. The dress I wore to my birthday dinner when I turned sixteen. "Fuck it."

"What?"

"Nothing. I'll see you tomorrow."

We say goodbye and hang up. I take the dress and slip the hanger over my head, then stand in front of the full-length mirror. I look a lot more like myself than when I arrived. Color has returned to my cheeks from the daily exercise, and I don't seem so haunted now that I'm eating regular meals and drinking less, despite last night. The dress suits me—it always has—and it feels like a small act of defiance to wear it.

Little victories.

* * *

"And this is my daughter, Olivia," my father says to Fred twenty minutes later. I'm wearing the dress and minimal makeup, just lip gloss and mascara. My hair is loose down my back, and I'm wearing flat sandals so I don't tower over the shorter guests. There are more people here than last week, the effect, I assume, of my father's leave-taking combined with the better cash flow. I make a mental note to ask Tracy when the annuity is going to be purchased. The sooner the better, before he drinks it all away, or his friends do.

"We've met," Fred says.

Lucy has wandered off onto the lawn, so it's just the three of us. Fred's staring at me like I'm a puzzle, like he's seen me before but he's not sure where.

"Ah," my father says vaguely. "In New York, I assume." He's on his third gin and tonic by the sound of his voice. It always gets slurry at that point, like it's been diluted.

"No," Fred says gently. "Here."

"William," I say, touching his elbow. "Come on now—you remember Fred. His aunt and uncle—the Crafts?"

His forehead creases in concentration, then clears. "Oh, Jill's boy."

"Not quite," Fred says. "But close enough."

"How is Jill? I haven't seen her recently."

"She moved to Florida a few years ago. Something about the winters."

"That's where Tracy spends her winters," William says vaguely. He hates the entire idea of Florida, a place where it's impossible to know who's who, according to him.

Lucy walks casually back to our group. "Hi, Olivia."

She looks breathtaking as always, wearing a lime-green wrap dress that hugs her in all the right places, and gold drop earrings that brush her shoulders.

"Hi, Lucy. Thanks for coming."

The other night, at Sophie's, I was sure she and Fred had just met. But seeing them together again, I can see that it's more than that. Maybe it's new between them, but it's not innocent.

"I've always loved this place."

"It's special."

There's an awkward pause as it occurs to all of us that the tables will be turned soon—my father, the guest; Fred, the host. Or maybe it will all be rubble, work crews digging up the lawn the way I've been digging up the past.

"Well, you'll have to keep up the tradition, Fred," William says, rattling the last of his ice in his glass.

Fred frowns. "The tradition?"

"He means the cocktail hour." I turn to my father. "Fred can do whatever he wants to the house, the grounds, all of it."

William grumbles his assent.

"And you shouldn't feel any obligation to do anything to please us," I say to Fred. "But I would suggest we change the topic."

Lucy smiles at me. "I love this dress, Olivia. Where did you get it?"

William rocks back on his heels. "That's my cue to leave. When the women start talking about clothing. Escape, Fred, now if you can."

We all laugh, and then William walks away.

"A nice man," Lucy says, watching him go.

"He is," I agree. "And I found this dress in my closet. I think the last time I wore it was the summer of 2003."

Fred's head snaps up at the date, and I feel a small, petty sense of satisfaction.

"Everything old is new again," Lucy says, oblivious to the tension.

I tear my eyes away from Fred. "Precisely."

"Speaking of . . . if I remember correctly, it's your birthday tomorrow," Lucy says, touching Fred's arm. "Fred, her birthday parties were always so great. These July Fourth parties on the beach. They were wild! This one time, these guys in my class decided to streak, and the Beach Police arrested them."

That was my eighteenth birthday. I hadn't wanted to celebrate, but Ash had insisted. It was the first time I'd been to one of those bashes since the disastrous one with Fred, and part of me kept expecting him to show up, like the lure of my big birthday would be enough to pull him back to the Hamptons. He didn't come, and I ended up making out with some guy whose name I don't remember, then throwing up in the bushes at the exact same spot.

"I remember," Fred says, in a tone of voice I can't decipher.

Lucy's surprised. "You've been to one of Olivia's birthdays?"

"I have."

She looks at me, then at Fred. "You two know each other?"

Fred grimaces. "Why does no one around here know that?"

"Not sure. Anyway, Lucy, it was a long time ago."

"You dated?"

"Briefly," I say firmly, wanting to be the final word on this. "But it was no big deal."

Fred's red in the face now, and I'm not sure if it's embarrassment or anger. Maybe both.

"Right," Lucy says. "So, what's the plan for tomorrow night?"

"I don't really—"

"You should join us." She holds onto Fred's arm, more tightly than earlier. "There's still room at the table, right, Fred?"

"I think my sister has a table."

"That's the same one. She invited us. Ann will be there too. And Sophie and Colin. But they're eight-person tables. Room for you and Wes."

Now it's my turn to blush. "I . . . I thought Sophie would have told you. We've separated."

"I'm sorry to hear that."

"It's fine."

"I hope you'll join us. Truly. You should celebrate your birthday, even if it's a tough time."

"I'll think it over—thanks."

She nods and now we lapse into silence, the sounds of the cocktail party breaking up around us. In a moment, one of us will make an excuse to go, but right now we're bound up together in tensions we don't fully understand.

"What did I miss?" Charlotte says a minute later, coming up next to us with Ann in tow, and all I can do is laugh.

CHAPTER TWENTY

July 2008

After he climbs through my window, Fred and I have a week where I'm so happy, I could burst, but where I'm also nervous that it will go away at any second.

Fred tells me and tells me that things have changed, that we've learned the lessons of the past and we can start planning our future again. But it's hard to hope. I've had other things snatched away from me—my mother, him, tennis—that I didn't see coming, and I prefer to think about what might happen, so I won't be taken entirely by surprise.

So, I'm happy, but it's tinged with something else too. A darkness.

But oh, we have fun. Neither of us has any responsibilities, so we explore together, from one end of Long Island to the other. We take a tiki boat tour in Peconic Bay. We walk around Montauk, our hands glued together. We stand on the point in East Hampton and stare out into the ocean as the wind whips our skin smooth. We go to Shelter Island and ride bikes around it, taking in the wildlife.

At night, Fred climbs up the trellis to my room, and we spend hours exploring each other, finding new ways to please and touch and feel—all the things I'd read about in the romance novels I used to secret away in my room as a teenager. I feel those things, I am those things, a woman, needy, and comfortable enough with Fred to ask for what I want and to give in return.

When I'm not with him, I'm tired and distracted. He has to spend some time with his aunt, which I understand and support. But, but, *but*. It's hard to be alone. Ash has her own boyfriend—she's started dating Dave, the guy who worked with Fred five years ago. I don't see it lasting, but stranger things have happened.

Sophie is away for the summer, working as a counselor at a summer camp with Colin where his sister, Lucy, goes too. Charlotte is interning with a magazine in the city. So, it's just me and William and Aunt Tracy in the house, asking for details of my "summer romance" as she keeps calling it, despite my assuring her that it's something more.

And now it's my birthday. Fred and I were occupied when the clock ticked over, but I wake with the sun and bury my face in his arm, drinking him in.

"Morning, birthday girl." His hair is mussed, and there's a trace of stubble on his chin. I like him like this in the morning. Rumpled, sleepy.

"Morning."

He kisses my arm. "Twenty-one."

"That's right."

"Legal for everything."

I laugh. "I guess."

"What does the birthday girl want for her birthday?"

"Honestly? I'd love a big pancake breakfast."

"That's what you'd love?"

"Hmm." We've started doing this. Tossing the word *love* into conversations about everything but each other. I assume it means we're about to say, "I love you," but I've never said that to a person I'm not related to, so I'm not one hundred percent sure.

"I would."

"You want me to make these pancakes?"

"Aunt Tracy will make them."

"Am I at least invited to this breakfast?"

I kiss him. "Yes."

He smiles against my mouth. "I assume I shouldn't arrive from up here for that?"

"Definitely not."

"All right, then." He starts to sit up, but I pull him back down.

"Breakfast isn't until eight."

"Oh yeah?"

"There's something else I'd love before you go."

"Hmm?"

I run my hand along his stomach. I love its ridges and warmth. I love how it feels against mine, how it fits when we come together. "You know."

"Do I?"

"I hope so."

He presses his mouth to mine, and I want to say it, I want to say that I love this, I love *him*, I want this and him and us forever.

But I don't. Instead, I let our bodies say it for us, and hope we have enough time later for the words.

* * *

After Fred leaves, I take a long shower, then trip down the stairs, feeling light and happy. I kiss Aunt Tracy in the kitchen and put in my order and tell her there will be one more for breakfast.

"This boy who's been sneaking into the house every night?"

"How did you know about that?"

"Please. I'm not your father." Aunt Tracy has a smudge of flour on her cheek, and she's wearing an apron that says "Kiss the Chef."

"Is this a good thing?"

"I think so."

She puts her arms around my shoulders. "I hope so, my child."

"It is. I promise. You'll love him."

"Only you need to love him." She kisses me on the cheek. "Now, go into the dining room—your present is waiting for you."

I kiss her back and follow her directions. The dining room is already set for four—her, William, Fred, and me. I decided long ago to stop wondering how Aunt Tracy always knows what this family wants or needs.

There are fresh-cut flowers at my place, and also a card. I pick it up, imagining something humorous and silly, but it's got my mother's handwriting on it.

The last card I got from her was on my sixteen birthday, the one with the tickets to the US Open. I thought it was the only one I was going to get, because it was a birthday we'd talked about so much. Maybe when I turned eighteen, I had a small expectation, but when nothing turned up, I tucked that away.

But now, here it is. Another message from the grave. Just looking at her handwriting makes me want to cry. There's no way I can read this now, with Fred about to arrive. We haven't even talked about the US Open, how I went with Charlotte and had to listen to her complain about everything from the sun, to the food, to the noise. I tried to cancel her out, but my heart was still raw, and I couldn't enjoy anything, not even Roddick's thrilling ride to the trophy. Afterward, I threw myself back into tennis with a renewed energy and purpose. Watching him win made it feel attainable. I could be a professional; I just had to put in the time. So I worked and worked and tried not to think about Fred. But it hurt, missing that experience—no mom, no him there to share it with.

I tuck the card into my pocket. I'll open it later when I'm alone and can deal with whatever's inside.

The doorbell rings and I go to answer it. Fred's holding a bouquet of wildflowers that he's picked from the garden, and his hair's still wet from the shower. He kisses me on the cheek as he hands me the flowers.

I take them, burying my face in their fresh scent. "Come in, come in."

He walks through the threshold. "It still looks like the lobby of a hotel."

"My ancestors had grand designs."

"On what?"

"The future."

"Olivia!" My father calls from the dining room, tinkling the little bell that sits next to his seat. Sometimes he likes to pretend he's living in a Regency novel, a semi-invalid who needs to be coddled and wrapped in woolly blankets like Mr. Woodhouse.

"Is that your dad?"

I pop the flowers into an empty vase on the entrance table and take his hand in mine. "What's the matter? You've met him before."

"That was five years ago. And I'm pretty sure he hated me."

"He didn't. My dad may growl a little, but he's mostly bark, not much bite."

"Olivia!"

"Coming!"

*   *   *

Breakfast is a success as these things go. My father is surprised to see Fred, despite the extra place setting, but he's mostly polite, especially after he exhausts his questions about Fred's "lineage" and learns (again) that he's related to the Crafts. He then expounds on our own family history for another half an hour, but I mostly ignore him as I make my way through the enormous stack of pancakes, fruit, and syrup Aunt Tracy puts in front of me.

I need to get back on a tennis court soon or I'm going to hear about it from my college coach when I go back in the fall. But for now, I mop up the carbs and sugar with as much satisfaction as I can.

Then we spend a lazy day at the beach with Ash and Dave. Dave seems like less of an asshole than he did in the past, and Ash is happy, so I'm happy for her. It's so much easier to be happy for someone when you're in love.

And I am. I am. Every time I look at Fred, I want to shout it out, but not yet, not yet.

We both know enough to avoid a repeat of the lobster dinner at the club. Instead, Fred and Dave get supplies for a "real" clambake, digging a deep hole in the sand to build the fire in, and then putting a large pot filled with fresh seafood on it as the sun sets down low.

The smells are amazing, and when they pull the pot out of the fire and fill thick paper plates with crabs and lobster tails and corn, I sink into the sand and breathe it in.

Fred sits next to me, his own plate piled high. "You want a bib?"

"Ha ha."

"I'm serious. I have some in my backpack."

144

"I'm good." I kiss him. "Thank you for this."

"My pleasure."

I dig in and it's honestly one of the best things I've ever tasted in my life. The simplicity of it—fresh seawater, the only seasoning—is what I love, I think, but it's also the company, the night, the light from the fire, the darkening sky above.

We eat mostly in silence, all of us greedy with our food. There are other parties down the beach, and maybe when we're done, we'll join one of them and watch the fireworks pierce the sky, but for now I'm content with my small crew, Fred next to me, and Ash across the fire, eating more than usual and sharing small jokes with Dave.

"You all done with that?" Fred asks when my plate is mostly husks of seafood and corn.

"I don't think I could put another thing inside me," I say, and he raises his eyebrow suggestively. "Yikes, that came out wrong."

"Don't worry about it." He takes my plate and puts it in a black garbage bag. He puts his own mess inside too, then rises and passes it to Dave. Then he reaches into the cooler and pulls out a bottle of champagne and four plastic flutes. "Everybody want?"

We all say yes, and he pops the cork and fills the glasses, then passes them out. I take mine and he sits next to me. He holds his glass toward mine. "Happy birthday, Olivia."

"Everything was wonderful." I click my glass to his, but they're plastic, so there's no sound, only a soft thud, and then I take a sip. It's good champagne, not the cheap brand that gets passed around my college dorm sometimes after we win a big match.

Fred sips at his, then makes a face. "Still don't like this stuff."

"Don't drink it then."

He smiles at me, then takes another sip.

"This all must have cost you a fortune," I say. "I want to contribute."

"Don't be silly."

"I'd feel better if I did."

"Ash and Dave split it with me, and that's enough. I want to do this for you."

"Thank you."

"I got you a present too."

"You didn't have to."

"Stop. It's your birthday."

"Okay," I say as I feel the echo of conversations past. I reach for my wrist, to the charm bracelet he gave me five years ago that I put back on after our first night together. I'd almost thrown it out after the breakup, the idea of collecting memories without Fred more than I could take. Instead, I'd tucked it into the back of my jewelry box and tried to forget it was there.

Fred catches my hand and starts to play with the tennis racquet, a mini version of the one I'll need to pick up again soon.

"When I was in the Navy, I went to a lot of places."

"That sounds great."

"It was, mostly. I don't recommend sleeping in a ship's hull with five hundred guys, but when we'd go into port, I always saw everything that I could. When I could, I collected memories, mementos."

I look up at him. "You have a charm bracelet?"

"No, Olivia. For you."

My throat tightens. "You did?"

"I did." He reaches into his pocket and pulls out a small velvet bag. "I never forgot about you, not for a minute. I hoped that someday we'd find our way back to each other." He opens the bag and tips its contents onto my hand. It's a charm of Big Ben, an enamel flag where the clock face should be. "I loved London most of all. I wanted you to be there, to show it to you. So I got you this."

I run my finger over it. "I love it."

"I love you."

I lift my head and stare into his eyes. "I love you too."

"That's lucky."

"It is."

I kiss him and we seal our words, gently, slowly, like we have all the time in the world. "Happy birthday," Fred says when we pull apart.

"Thank you," I say, my hand closing around the charm.

I'm so touched that Fred has done this, but that small dark cloud of doubt is there too.

The bracelet was supposed to represent our future together, not the time we spent apart. When I add this charm to the other, their weight will be equal, a reminder that there was a gap between our time together where there shouldn't have been.

And though we still have most of our life before us, it feels like a bad omen.

Like seeing high, thin clouds in an evening sky, knowing that tomorrow they'll bring rain.

CHAPTER TWENTY-ONE

July 2023

My thirty-sixth birthday morning starts with a call from Wes.

I hold the phone in front of my face, watching his name flash there along with a photo we took years ago, back when we were happy.

I don't answer it, but I don't send it to voicemail either. I don't want Wes to know I've seen his call, and so it rings and rings, then eventually stops. I breathe out a sigh of relief, but then the phone starts ringing again, Wes trying a second time. I ignore this call too, and finally it also stops. A moment later, I'm alerted that I have a voicemail. I'm surprised because Wes never leaves voicemails. I wonder if it's an emergency. But if it were, Wes would text me too, and when he doesn't, I know I can ignore his message.

I'd like to ignore today too, but no one lets you do that when it's your birthday. Between Facebook and calendar reminders, I know I'll be getting a steady stream of alerts and Happy Birthday texts, balloons floating up along the screen when I check them.

I don't want to deal with that, so instead I get up and put on some tennis clothes and head to the club.

"What are you doing here, Birthday Girl?" Matt asks when I walk on court. "I thought I told you to rest today?"

I shrug. "Didn't feel like it."

"How's the rib?"

"It's fine."

He gives me a look like he knows it isn't, and I stare right back. No professional athlete plays pain-free all the time. And though it's been a minute since I could feel every muscle in my body, I prefer this version of myself.

"All right," Matt says. "But take it easy."

I walk onto the court where Cindy's waiting for me. She's happy I'm here, I can see, thinking she's going to beat me today since I defaulted yesterday. And maybe she will. But this old girl still has some tricks up her sleeve, and Cindy shouldn't count her wins just yet.

*   *   *

When I get back to the house, having split sets with Cindy, much to her frustration, I shower and then come down for a late breakfast. Aunt Tracy's set a place for me at the kitchen island, and I can see my favorite pancake mix sitting ready on the counter.

"You didn't have to do this."

"It's your birthday. I always make you pancakes."

I take a seat and look down at my plate. There's an envelope there, and my heart catches in my throat. My name is written on the front, but it's not my mother's handwriting. It's Tracy's. "Thanks for the card."

"Of course."

I open it. It's one of those silly cards, full of puns and jokes about aging. Innocent. I smile and tuck it next to my plate. Aunt Tracy's heating up a pan for the pancakes, and there's a pot of syrup warming on the stove. It smells heavenly.

"I've always meant to ask you," I say, popping a raspberry into my mouth from a large bowl that's full of them. "Those notes that Mom left for me, did you know about those?"

Aunt Tracy turns from the stove. She's wearing a benign smile, part sad, part reminiscing. "She gave them to your father before she died. I think that there were three or four for each of you."

"Three or four? I only got two."

"Perhaps I'm mistaken."

"Or William forgot to give them to me?"

Lauren Bailey

She shakes her head. "I'd always remind him, each year."

I want to cross-examine her. Was it three or four or two? But what's to be gained from that? She didn't hide anything from me. And if my father let a card or two slip through the cracks, it's hard to blame him. My mother died over twenty years ago. That's a long time to keep the faith, especially for a man like him, always thinking of himself first. But it also feels odd knowing that there might be other messages for me somewhere in this house. I still haven't been able to bring myself to go into her private room, the most likely location. I know I can't avoid it forever.

"Where's William?" I ask as Aunt Tracy pours several large rounds into the smoking pan.

"Charlotte took him to check out one of those retirement communities in Quogue."

"I'm shocked."

"At what?"

"Not sure. That Charlotte did it. That he was willing to go."

She flips over the pancakes. "Not much choice for both of them. Time is ticking away."

"I have to find somewhere to live myself."

She bends and pulls a plate from the oven, then stacks the pancakes onto it, adding syrup and then berries. She puts it down in front of me.

I inhale deeply, then pick up my knife and fork. "This smells amazing. Thank you."

"Of course, my dear. It is always my pleasure."

I take a bite and close my eyes at the memories. My birthdays stack on top of one another. "Why didn't you go with them?"

Aunt Tracy puts a pancake on another plate and sits next to me. "I went the other day and picked out the house that I want. Charlotte is showing your father to let him pick it for himself."

I laugh. "You've managed it perfectly. But you don't have to move there if you don't want to."

"He needs me." She cuts into her pancake. "And we're used to each other. I'll keep up the old rhythm, spending the winter down south, coming here for the summer." Tracy sold her apartment in New York ten years ago and bought a condo in a retirement village in Florida.

150

October to April, she flies there with the Canadian snowbirds and nurtures her tan. I'd seen her down there once or twice when I was playing. I'm fairly certain there's a man in her Florida life, but she's never mentioned him.

I put down my utensils and put my arm around her shoulders. "I don't know what we would have done without you. Truly." I kiss her weathered cheek. "I love you. I don't tell you that enough."

She squeezes her body closer, then pulls away. "Enough with that now."

We return to eating, and before long half my stack is gone. I have that uncomfortable feeling in my stomach, like I've eaten too much, but I can't stop myself.

"Where will you live?" Aunt Tracy asks.

"I'm not sure. I thought I was going to have to find a place I could afford on my teacher's salary, but now . . . I guess I have more options."

"You don't have to go back to teaching if you don't want to."

"You're right. I like lots of it. The kids are special, and being a part of their life is mostly great. But there are bad parts, like any job. Too much to do, too few resources . . . But I couldn't do what Charlotte does . . ."

"You mean nothing?"

"It sounds awful to say that."

She puts her hand on mine. "She doesn't think that, though. Charlotte is happy in her life."

I sit back in my chair, this information a surprise. But it shouldn't be. Tracy's right. Charlotte is perfectly content, and I shouldn't judge her. I'm the one who's unhappy. "I'm glad she's happy."

"Me too."

"You think things will work out with Ann long term?"

"I'm not sure . . ." She frowns. "She's an interesting one, that girl."

"Why do you think Charlotte's never come out to us?"

"Does she have to?"

"You're right, she doesn't."

Tracy smiles. "Now, what are you going to do with the rest of your birthday?"

"Clean out another room of the house?"

"I hope you're joking."

I wasn't, but she's right. Today of all days, I shouldn't lock myself in this house. "How about a bike ride and then I'll go to that dinner everyone wants me to attend?"

"That sounds better."

"It's a plan, then."

We touch shoulders again, and then I rest my head on hers. Sometimes I forget, when I'm missing my mother, that I've got one here, next to me, and I've had her all along.

* * *

I show up to dinner at the club nervous and armed with the past. I decided to wear my mother's dress, the one I found when I was cleaning out the clothes in her bedroom. I'm wearing my hair loose again, enjoying the feel of it on my back. After I applied my makeup, I stepped back and appreciated what I saw. A healthier version of me, a younger version, like old paint had been stripped away in a restoration. And I do feel partially restored. I'm happy I came home, despite the minefields. I needed this time to make some decisions about my life that are more than just a flight reflex.

Before I left the house, I went through my jewelry box, looking for something to add. My engagement and wedding ring were there, and also a small bag I don't remember putting inside. When I opened it, I found the tennis bracelet Ash gave me for my sixteenth birthday. The diamonds glowed in the sunlight swimming in through my window, and I put it on my wrist. And then, impulsively, I opened another bag and took out Fred's charm bracelet. It has four charms on it. I questioned myself as I slip it on my other wrist. What am I doing? Last night the dress, today the bracelet?

But *Shh, Olivia,* I told myself. *Two can play at this game.*

I closed the jewelry box and finished getting ready.

The club is lit up and vivid. There's a band playing on a raised dais, and waiters passing champagne and hors d'oeuvres. Matt's here, looking dapper in a summer suit, and I wave to him across the lawn. He gives me a thumb's-up, then makes a complicated hand gesture that indicates that we'll talk later.

We've arrived at the end of the cocktail hour, and it's almost time to take our seats. We find Sophie and Colin in the crowd. Sophie is glowing, pregnant with a secret, while Colin is holding the long neck of a beer, peering out at the dunes and the ocean.

"You look happy," I say to Sophie.

She gives me a spontaneous hug. "Happy birthday."

"Thanks. What's going on?"

"Colin agreed to look for a job elsewhere. He's going to tell his dad tomorrow."

"That's good news."

"Right? I'm so happy. Somewhere else, he can really succeed, you know? Be at the level he's supposed to. And now that we have the money, we don't have to be so beholden to them."

"That's great, Sophie."

"Did you have a good day?"

"Not bad."

"I'm glad you came tonight."

"Me too." So far, anyway. I take a glass off a passing tray. "Can I ask you something?"

"What?"

"Did you get cards from Mom on your birthday? I mean after she died?"

Sophie purses her mouth. "Yes, a few."

"Do you remember how many?"

"Three? Four? I have them somewhere." She takes a sip of her wine. "How many did you get?"

"Two."

"Huh. Maybe I'm remembering wrong."

She's being nice, but I can feel the sadness of the slight creeping up my neck. "Maybe."

"What's this about, Olivia?"

"I don't know . . . being back here, I guess. Going through all of her things." I motion to what I'm wearing. "This is her dress."

"You look like her."

"No, you do."

"Can't we both look like her?"

My throat tightens. "Of course we can."

The lights above us dim, the universal signal to take our seats. Sophie gives me another quick hug, then pulls me to our table, somewhere in the middle of the crowd. Fred and Lucy are already there, their heads tipped toward each other.

I stifle a burst of jealousy and sit down next to Lucy.

"Olivia! You look fabulous."

"Thanks, you too." Her makeup is flawless, and she's wearing a peach-colored chunky necklace around her neck that accentuates her skin tone and pairs perfectly with the sea-green halter dress she's wearing. "The dress was my mother's."

"How perfect. Fred, doesn't Olivia look fantastic?"

He turns his head slowly toward me. "Lovely as always."

Lucy gives him a playful tap on his chest. "Fred! What's wrong with you? She's glowing."

"It's fine, Lucy," I say. "I do look a lot older than the last time Fred saw me."

"What? No. You're one of those ageless beauties."

Fred and I make eye contact. I raise my arm slowly to tuck a lock of hair behind my ear, so that Fred can see what I'm wearing on my wrist. "You're sweet."

Fred's pupils contract, and I know I've wounded him.

"Happy birthday, Olivia," he says, his eyes still on my wrist.

"Yes," Lucy says. "Happy birthday!"

"Thanks."

Lucy grabs a bottle of champagne from the bucket in front of us. "We have to toast to Olivia!"

Charlotte and Ann smile. They're holding hands under the table and giving each other these adorable looks, and I'm both happy for her and sad. The empty seat next to me is like a symbol of my failure. Thirty-six, separated, soon to be divorced.

It sounds like the beginning of a Bob Dylan song.

Lucy pours the champagne and everyone raises a glass. We drink and then the subject turns away from me, and for that I'm grateful. I ask Charlotte about the visit to the retirement community, and she tells me that William says he'll be happy to move there. Though it's farther away from Southampton than he'd like, he thinks it might be best to live somewhere else, likely because he doesn't want all his old friends to see his reduced circumstances.

I can feel Fred listening to our conversation, his head angled toward us, though he's talking to Lucy, and I wonder if he's uncomfortable. But when I sneak a peek, he averts his eyes.

"Any idea where you're going to live, Charlotte?" I ask.

"I've been thinking of Sag Harbor."

"I know some great properties there," Lucy says. "In fact, I have the perfect place for you."

Charlotte leans forward. "Where?"

She mentions an address. "I helped do the interiors a couple of years ago, and I heard they want to sell. It isn't officially on the market yet, but it's near the water and totally your taste."

"Can you get me in before it goes on the market?"

"I think so."

Lucy turns to Fred. "Weren't you saying you wanted to check out a winery in Sag Harbor?"

"Oh, um, yes, my friend James bought it a year ago. I haven't had a chance to go. The Benedict Winery."

"Oh!" Sophie says. "I've heard their wine is wonderful. We should all go." She turns to Colin, who's been uncharacteristically quiet all night. "Shouldn't we, Colin? Doesn't that sound like fun?"

"Yes, it does."

"So, we'll make a day of it? Next week, or the week after? We can check out this house for Charlotte and then go to the winery . . . if you don't mind us tagging along, that is?"

Everyone looks at Fred. "I'll have to check in with James about the date, but yes, I'm sure he'd love to have all of you."

"You'll come too, Olivia?"

"Can I think about it?"

"What's to think about?" Sophie says. "Wine, Sag Harbor. Sounds perfect."

"I agree," a voice says above me as two hands rest heavily on the top of my chair. "Room for one more?"

My heart freezes, and the smiles around the table fall like dominoes as they take in who's standing behind me.

Wes.

CHAPTER TWENTY-TWO

August 2008

The rest of my twenty-first summer passes in a love haze.

I can't tell you what we do every day. The days bleed into one another, one overlapping the next. We explore more—each other and Long Island. My rib repairs itself, and I get back on court, slowly at first, Matt taking it easy on me for the first time ever. Fred and I talk a lot about the future, but not the immediate one—what will happen when Fred and I go back to school in the fall. Instead, we dance around the topic, not quite going back to our old habit of detailed plans, more talking about places we want to go, things we want to see together.

I never end up reading the card my mother gave me for my birthday. Instead, I prop it on my vanity, so her handwriting greets me every morning. I'm not sure why I avoid the inside, only it feels like the last time I'll ever hear from her, and I want to postpone that day as long as I can.

And now it's late August. The days are getting shorter, imperceptibly at first, but our time out by the summer house each night is more in the dark than twilight. It's colder too. We've taken to bringing a blanket and wrapping ourselves in it, our lovemaking creating the heat we need to stay out there as late as we want. We don't talk about what the colder weather means, just push past it, like our breath that appears in a mist as the night encroaches, then disappears in an instant. *Tomorrow*, we're both thinking. *Tomorrow we'll talk about the fall.*

The weekend before Labor Day I interrupt a tense conversation between Aunt Tracy, my father, and Charlotte. Something about the housing market and some bad investments my father made. This isn't the first time we've had issues with money, but it was always shrugged off before. This time, I can tell from Tracy's tone, and even Charlotte's, it's more serious.

"Olivia, can you come in here?" Tracy asks.

I walk into William's study feeling nervous. He hasn't said that much to me about Fred, but I can tell he disapproves. It's nothing he says—more what he doesn't. How he looks at Fred sometimes at the dinner table like he's confused that he's still around.

"What's up?"

"We wanted to talk to you," Tracy says.

"What about?"

"This fall. And whether you can get an additional scholarship for school," Charlotte says, then mouths, "Sorry."

I sit down slowly in one of the chairs in front of William's desk. I'm already on a full sports scholarship, but it doesn't cover a lot of my expenses. Rent, books, food, travel for competitions . . . these are all extras I've paid for in part through work-study but have mostly been covered by William. "There's nothing more I can get. Not now."

William's mouth turns down, and for once he seems focused. "I'm sorry, dear, but there isn't any money for school."

I feel sick and confused. "What do you mean?"

"Surely," Tracy says, "you've been following the news?"

I haven't. Some of the big stories have filtered through: the Beijing Olympics, Obama's run for the White House, but mostly we were in our bubble. Clearly, I should've been paying attention.

"What's going on?"

Charlotte rolls her eyes. "The housing crisis? The markets?"

"Okay."

"The point is, dear," Aunt Tracy says gently, "your father's in a bit of a financial crunch, and we're going to have to retrench."

"Retrench?"

"Like in a war."

"We're at war?"

"It's an expression, Olivia," Charlotte says. "Keep up."

"What am I supposed to do?"

"Can you defer?" Aunt Tracy asks. "For a year while we sort this out?"

"I don't know."

"You should call your school. Your coach. See if there's something . . ."

I bite my lip. I want to cry. All the plans I've been building in my head, the path . . . this isn't how this is supposed to go. "I'll turn pro."

"What?" my father says.

"I'll join the tour . . . I can get paid sponsorships then. Make some money. I won't be a burden."

"Can you do that?" Charlotte says. *Are you good enough?* is what she's asking.

"Yes," I say with confidence because even if I can't, it's what I'm going to do. "I can."

* * *

"So that's the plan," I say to Fred that night. "I spoke to Matt, and he's agreed to come on as my coach. I'll call the school tomorrow."

We're out on the lawn near the summer house. We slipped away from the cocktail party that's going on as if nothing was happening, like one of those doomed parties in *The Great Gatsby*, a book I've always despised.

Fred listened while I spoke, not saying anything, but now, finally, he does. "Can you give me a couple of days?"

"For what?"

"To come up with a better plan."

Our backs are up against the building, our legs splayed out in front of us. Fred's shorts are paint stained. He's been repainting his aunt's porch this last week.

"Plan for what?"

"For you. For us."

I don't say anything because his hurt is evident in his voice. "I have to do it, Fred."

"Let me see, okay? Can you wait a day or two to call the school?"

"Yes, okay."

I want to say more, but I can't get the words out. I don't ask how we're going to stay together with me out on tour. At the ranking I'm going to start at, I'll be leading a wanderer's life, chasing an alchemy of points and prize money and whatever tournament will take me. Fred can't come with me. I won't let him give up his life for mine.

"Thank you." He picks up my hand and kisses it. "I'm sorry about all of this."

"It's not your fault."

"I know, but I can be sorry anyway."

I lean against him. "I thought we'd have more time."

"We will," Fred says with confidence, but his hand in mine is shaking.

*　*　*

"So, here's the plan," Fred says an anxious two nights later, a day that's close enough to September that I can see it on the calendar without having to flip the page. "You'll transfer to my school. I can pay for our housing because I was going to be in an apartment anyway. The team will take you—they'll be more than happy to match your scholarship. Once you graduate next year, you can turn pro, if that's what you want. But this way, you can finish your degree and we can be together. What do you think?" Fred looks at me nervously, but his voice doesn't hold any doubt.

We're in my bedroom. It's late, near midnight. I can hear the crickets outside, grinding their legs in the grass, making that high-pitched whine, and the waves crashing into shore, that metronome beat that never goes away.

"You spoke to your school?"

"Yes, the tennis coach. He knew who you were."

"Okay."

"Are you mad?"

"I don't know, Fred. This is a lot."

"Too much?"

"I wish you'd talked to me before you arranged everything."

He hangs his head. "You didn't talk to me before you decided to go pro."

"You're right." I reach for him. "Come here."

He sits down and wraps his arms around me. I drink him in, his fresh soapy scent, the undertone of sweat because he's nervous. He smells like home to me, and I don't want to lose him. "I love you, Fred. So much."

"I love you too."

"I want to be together. I do."

He smiles against my neck. "I'm so glad."

"Me too. This is good. This is going to be great."

"It is." He sits up. "There's one more thing."

"What?"

"I didn't talk to you about this first either, but . . ." He reaches for my wrist, the one where I wear the charm bracelet. He dips his hand into his pocket and pulls something out. I can't quite see what it is. His eyes are clear and full of certainty. "I love you, Olivia. You're it for me. I want us to be together for always. Will you marry me?" He opens his hand and there's a small engagement ring charm sitting in the palm of it, a perfect little diamond sitting on a silver band.

My heart swells. "Oh my God."

"Is that a yes?"

"Yes, yes, of course I'll marry you." I fling myself into his arms, tears in my eyes, my whole body shaking.

Fred holds me hard against him, then finds my mouth, and we kiss for a minute, both of us emotional. When we break apart, he takes my wrist and attaches the charm. I touch it, marveling at this turn of events.

"Are you happy?" Fred asks.

"So happy. You?"

"Yes. And I'll get you a real ring—"

"No, this is perfect."

We kiss again, then nuzzle into each other.

This is good—this *will be* good. We'll get married and spend the rest of our lives together. I'll move to Boston and play with a new team, and next year I'll turn pro and we'll figure out the times we need to be apart. We'll walk hand in hand together instead of planning for some potential future.

I'm grateful, in a way, that things didn't work out five years ago. If they had, then we probably wouldn't be together now, and this wouldn't be happening.

Married. I'm getting married. To Fred.

It feels like everything I've ever wanted is about to come true.

And that scares the shit out of me.

CHAPTER TWENTY-THREE

July 2023

I sit there, frozen, as Wes slips into the empty seat next to me, like I've been waiting for him to show up all along and he was late, snarled in traffic. He's wearing dark blue chinos, a light gray shirt, and dockers with no socks.

He leans in casually and kisses me on the cheek. "Happy birthday," he whispers in my ear, then squeezes my leg briefly under the table. I jerk it away.

I turn to him with the eyes of the table on us. His sandy hair is longer and curly, due for a haircut. He's been in the sun since we last saw each other, the freckles that come out in summer peppered over his forearms and the back of his hands. I can't help wondering where he's been and with who. "What are you doing here?"

His dark brown eyes are innocent. "Didn't you get my message?"

"No."

Lucy grabs Fred's hand. "Let's go get a drink."

Fred looks grim. "Sure, sure."

They rise and then Ann, Charlotte, Colin, and Sophie do the same. Colin stops and shakes Wes's hand and says it's nice to see him. I can hear Sophie chastising him as they walk away.

All this time I haven't moved. I'm trying to adjust to being near him again. I can smell his cologne and feel his too familiar presence. How can I be so turned off by someone I once clung to?

Wes picks up a fork from his place setting. "Should I not have come?"

"What do you think?"

"I wanted to see you."

"I told you I needed time."

Wes puts the fork down carefully. "But you didn't say anything more than that. Not how much time and if we could talk or if you wanted a divorce. And Olivia"—he reaches for my hand—"I've missed you. I miss you."

It's weird to feel him touching me. Something I used to crave, but now it makes me feel sick. I pull my hand away. "You should've thought of that before."

"This again?"

"Again? Give me a break."

Wes leans forward, his face open and earnest. "I made a mistake. It was a moment of weakness. It meant nothing. And I get that you're mad and disappointed. I wish I could take it back. I never meant for you to know . . . I need you to forgive me."

"*You* need that?"

"Yes. Please, Olivia. Can you forgive me?"

"And then what?" I look away from him, out over the sea of partygoers. Everyone laughing and drinking and swaying to the music, waiting for the moment when the waiters will appear with their trays of lobsters held high over their heads.

"We go back to our life."

"Just like that?"

"No, not just like that. We can go to therapy if you want. We can do whatever you need to change things. Have a baby—whatever."

"A baby, *whatever*?"

"You know I didn't mean it like that."

I turn back to him. I feel weary, that same feeling that weighed me down this last year when Wes was behaving so strangely. How I felt like I was going mad, thinking that things were breaking while he was telling me that everything was fine. But it wasn't fine—I'd been right all along.

"I don't know anything, Wes. Not anymore."

"I'm sorry."

"You said."

"What now?"

"I don't know."

Wes looks down at his hands. He's still wearing his wedding ring, a thick platinum band that he'd picked out himself. *Forever* is engraved inside, and if I'm being honest, even I thought that was a bit over the top when he showed it to me a couple of days before our wedding.

"Is this because of Fred?" he asks.

"What?"

"What's he doing here?"

"That's a good question."

"You didn't come here to be with him?"

"No!" I lower my voice. "I told you William sold the house. He needs help clearing it out. That's why I'm here. I had no idea Fred was around."

"So why is *he* here, then?"

"He bought it."

"What?" Wes sits back. "Wow."

"I wasn't happy about it either."

"Really?"

"Of course not. Come on, Wes."

He crosses his arms, appraising me. "You won't forgive me, but I forgave you."

"What's *that* supposed to mean?"

"You know what it means. Don't make me say it."

"Say what?"

"At least I wasn't in love with someone else during our marriage."

This silences me. It's always surprised me about Wes, how perceptive he is. More than once, he's figured out something fundamental about me without me telling him. I've never had the same insight into him, though.

"That's not true."

"Come on, Olivia—don't do that."

I rub my hands together, feeling the indent in my finger where my ring used to reside. Did I wear it long enough that this is permanent? Like a scar?

"You're saying I should forgive you because you forgave me?"

"Yes."

"I don't know if it's that binary."

"I get that—okay, I do. But I'm not the only guilty party here, is what I'm saying. You and me, we're the same."

I want to snap back at this, to point out the differences. And there are differences. But he's also right. He cheated on us, and I did too. The differences—the how and why and who—don't matter.

"Okay," I say.

"What does that mean?"

"You're right. We both fucked up."

His face clears. "You'll forgive me?"

"I didn't say that. It's hard to trust you right now."

"I understand. But I'm not giving up."

I look away from him, wishing someone would interrupt us. And then, Charlotte and Ann approach the table cautiously, like I'd called them.

"They're about to bring out dinner," Charlotte says.

Our eyes meet. Her face is filled with compassion. "Sit down."

Charlotte waves to the rest of the group, hovering just out of earshot.

"This is Ann," I say to Wes. "She helped broker the deal on the house."

Wes stands and shakes Ann's hand. "Nice to meet you." He lets it go and gives a small bow to Charlotte. "Nice to see you again, Charlotte."

She nods, a chill to her tone. "Wes."

Charlotte has never forgiven us for connecting years after they broke up. It's not rational, but then, unrequited love never is.

Everyone else returns and takes their seats.

"I'm going to go," Wes says.

"You don't have to."

"Are you sure?"

I'm not, but if he leaves, then it feels like I'm telling him that things will never work out, and right now I don't know what I want. We had something good once. Am I ready to throw that all away because of one mistake? I thought I was, but now I'm not so sure.

"Yes. Stay." There's an *ooh* that spreads through the crowd, the lobsters coming out. I reach for my bib and open it up. "For dinner. But not at the house." I say that last part quietly so only he can hear.

"I booked a room here."

Great. Wes and Fred staying in the same place. "Good."

"You can watch Olivia play tennis in the morning," Lucy says. "Fred tells me she's amazing."

Fred's back is to us; he's talking to Colin. But I can see the muscles stiffen in his neck.

"You're playing tennis?"

"In the mornings with Matt. Just to get in shape."

"And Fred is watching?"

"He's staying at the club too. I guess he's seen a few of my matches."

"Ah." Wes picks up his bib and ties it around his neck. He picks up his lobster cracker and breaks into a smile that only I would know is not entirely genuine. "Bring on the lobsters."

*   *   *

After a dinner where the tension ebbed and flowed and settled into unease, the tables are removed, and the band transitions into dance hits for old people. Our group spreads out over the dance floor. Wes drank steadily through dinner, as did Colin, and now they're off in the corner with the bartender, discussing scotch.

I don't mind the drinking. Wes is more gregarious when he has some drinks in him, and I get the need to let loose in the circumstances. I have a few drinks in me too, plus a lot of strawberry short-cake and lobster, and as the evening winds on, the tension starts to seep out of my body. It's my birthday, after all. Shouldn't I be having some fun?

Ash is of the same mind, appearing at my elbow on the dance floor, her thin arms raised above her head, finally free of her "deadly boring table." Her laugh is infectious, and I throw my arms up to meet hers. I shout out the night's events to her over the thumping music, and she gathers me in a hug. "If you want me to punch him, I can."

"That won't be necessary."

She lets me go. "And they're both going to stay here?"

"Apparently."

"Maybe there *will* be some punching."

"Not their style."

She chucks me under the chin. "We'll see."

"Besides, it's not like Fred wants to be with me."

"Sure, right." Ash reaches for the charm bracelet. "And what about you?"

I pull my arm away, embarrassed. "I wanted to get under his skin."

"Mission accomplished, I'd say." She nods to the side of the dance floor where Fred is standing, scowling in our direction.

"I'm sure he's simply reminding himself of his lucky escape."

"Uh-huh."

"He's with Lucy."

"He's not going to marry Lucy."

"Sophie seems to think he might."

Ash puts her arms around my neck like we're slow dancing. "That's wishful thinking on Sophie's part." The song ends and a new beat starts. "OMG," Ash says, "is this what I think it is?"

I listen for a second. "If you think it's 'In Da Club,' then yes."

"Yes! It's perfect! Because it's your birthday!"

"And we're going to a party."

We laugh as the dance floor clears out. But Sophie comes to find us, and we start to do an old routine we used to do as girls, a hip-hop line dance where we thrust our arms out and turn ourselves around while we shimmy. By the time the song's half over, Charlotte, Ann, and Lucy have joined us. I haven't heard this song in years, and yet I still know all the lyrics, as does everyone else. We shout them out, self-censoring the bad parts so we don't offend anyone, and raise our hands to the roof, and by the end, the whole club is watching us as we shout about it being my birthday.

The song ends, and we link hands and take a bow, receiving our applause as is our due.

There's a pause in the music and we disperse. I head toward the bar, thinking I'll find Wes there, but instead it's Fred.

"Can I get a fizzy water?" I say to the bartender. The sound system starts up again, playing "Heat Waves" by Glass Animals. A slow rhythmic beat about late nights and thinking about someone. These lyrics hit a little too close to home. "And a gin and tonic?"

"On my tab," Fred says.

The bartender looks at me for confirmation, and I shrug. "Thanks."

"My pleasure." Fred glances at me. He's holding a glass of red wine. "Having a good birthday?"

"It'll do."

"Some surprises, I guess."

"Yes."

"But you and Wes *are* separated?"

"Yes, we are."

"But working on things?" He lifts his glass to his mouth like his question is casual, but it feels like anything but.

"It's a confusing time." I take my water from the bartender and take a long drink. The glass is sweating in my hand. "How are things with you and Lucy?"

"She's a sweet girl."

"I've always liked her." I put the water down and pick up the gin and tonic. One sip tells me that the bartender made it a double like he knew I needed it, which I do. I take a step away from the bar, wanting to be in a crowd, not alone with Fred.

He follows me as I edge my way to the dance floor.

"Olivia." His tone is intimate, his breath on my neck.

"What?"

"She's not . . ." He stops. "Will you look at me?"

I turn toward him slowly. Someone jostles him from behind, pushing him toward me, and he puts his hands on my shoulders to steady himself. In a second, we could be dancing.

"What is it?"

He touches my bracelet—his bracelet—*our* bracelet. "Why did you wear this?"

"I was feeling nostalgic."

His thumb grazes the tiny engagement ring. The third charm he gave me. "Or to hurt me?"

What's the point of lying? "That too."

"We hurt each other." His fingers touch the skin on my wrist, burning it like his touch always does.

I pull away, but our eyes remain locked. "Yes, we did."

"I'm sorry."

"Me too."

And now I break his gaze and turn back to the dance floor. Ash is there with her husband, Dave, and I want her to glance my way, for *us* to make eye contact so she'll know I need to be rescued. But instead, the music transitions into something slow, and they meld into one with the other couples, and I'm left to save myself.

And oh God. It's the Nora Jones song that was playing when we danced on my sixteenth birthday. When we kissed.

"Olivia," Fred says behind me, so close that I can almost feel his body touching mine. "Olivia."

I close my eyes and breathe him in. I want to lean back, to turn into his arms and spin away with him into the night.

But he doesn't want that.

He doesn't want me.

It's the song and the night, and neither of us are free.

"I've got to go."

"Olivia."

"No . . . I . . . I can't do this . . ."

I start to move away from him, expecting him to reach out, to hold me back, but he doesn't, he doesn't, and that's okay, that's fine, because there's nothing to be gained here, between us.

Only pain and regret.

CHAPTER TWENTY-FOUR

August 2008

"Absolutely not," my father says when I tell him about the engagement with Fred the next day over breakfast.

I'm hurt, but not entirely surprised. "I'm not asking for your permission."

"Olivia, my dear, you are far too young to get married."

"You and Mom got married young."

He glances up at me over the half-moon of his reading glasses. "That was a different time."

"Old people always say that."

"Are you saying that I'm old?" This was the greatest offense to my father, and not the way to convince him to be on my side.

"Older. And about this, maybe yes."

He takes his glasses off and lets them fall to the dining table. He almost never lets anyone see him wearing them, but he can't read his morning paper without them. "This isn't a discussion, Olivia. I've said no. It would be a mistake to get married so young."

I clench my hands "Is this because you don't like Fred?"

"It's entirely about you. I understand that you think you're in love. And perhaps you are. But one summer of flirting isn't enough to build a lifetime on. You will need to trust me on this."

His words descend like a weight on my chest. I hadn't expected him to be overjoyed. I thought I'd get his usual indifference. This was, after all, the man who'd showed zero interest in where I went to college, never asked to see my report cards, and only remembered my birthday because Aunt Tracy reminded him. I thought he might grumble at the expense of a wedding, which Fred and I had already decided we wouldn't put anyone through. I even thought he might be relieved at not having any financial responsibility for me anymore given what was going on.

But an outright refusal? That hadn't occurred to me at all. I was glad I'd told Fred I was going to talk to him on my own.

"You're ruining my life," I say, my lip trembling.

"Be that as it may, this is my final decision."

"And if I do it anyway? If I just run away?"

My father's face registers his exhaustion. "Does my opinion mean so little to you?"

"No, of course not."

"Then why press this?"

"Because we want to be together. We love each other."

"Can you not simply live together like so many of your generation do now?"

I almost laugh. "I'm pretty sure my generation isn't the first to live together before they get married."

"All the more reason to try it out."

He has me here. And if I'm being honest with myself, that's what I thought we'd do. I hadn't understood at first that Fred wanted to get married immediately, in a few weeks. But when I'd suggested to him last night that we live together first after he pulled my calendar off the wall and started talking about dates, he'd looked so hurt that I'd quickly retracted the suggestion.

Fred has insecurities about people leaving, I'm coming to realize, because of his father's death and what happened with that girl Phoebe. He's still mourning his uncle. Whatever it is, he doesn't want to wait—he wants to jump in. Or maybe it's that once you put yourself out there and ask someone to marry you, anything other than an enthusiastic "yes" and an immediate search for a date leaves you feeling vulnerable.

I wouldn't know.

"We want to get married," I say to William. "We don't want to try it out. We want to start our life together now."

"Your Aunt Tracy will feel as I do."

This is a blow, using her against me. "I think she'll be happy for me."

"You talk to her and see."

Tears spring to my eyes. *Now,* I think. *Now is when you decide to suddenly decide to start caring about my life?*

"Mom would be happy for me."

My father stands slowly. His hands are shaking, and I've so rarely seen him in a rage that I don't recognize it at first. "Your mother and I would be of one mind on this issue, of that I'm certain."

I leave the table, running crying to the kitchen to sob out the story on Aunt Tracy's shoulder. She listens to me, and then she surprises me. While she isn't quite as against it as William, she does agree with him.

I wipe my tears away with the back of my hand. "Don't you like Fred?"

"Of course I do," Aunt Tracy says. She's been gardening, and she's gathered an armful of summer roses and was trimming them in the sink, wearing heavy gloves so she doesn't get pricked by the thorns.

"Why shouldn't I marry him, then?"

"You're so young."

"I'm older than Mom was. She was only eighteen."

"Be that as it may, you're very different from her. You have all these plans for your life. What about the tour? How is that going to work?"

"Fred knows I want to do that."

"But does he really understand it?" Tracy starts to arrange her blooms in a vase, a mix of white and pink with a bloodred rose at the center. "You haven't even been training most of this summer. Does Fred have any idea of what your life is like when you're playing tennis?"

"No, but he'll be in class too."

"You barely have time to eat. That's not how to take care of a husband."

"Take care of a husband? It's not 1950."

"Of course not, but relationships need care just the same. You need to spend time together, to build a life. And what you're trying to do is very solitary."

I bite back the angry sentiment that rises in me: to ask her what she knows about marriage because she never made a success of it, the ink on her divorce long dried. But that would be cruel, and I love her so much. Why isn't she on my side?

"We can figure it out."

"Maybe. But what happens next year when you're traveling everywhere?" Tracy says. "And what about the family? I thought you wanted to contribute to your father's finances? To help save this place."

"Is the house in danger?"

"Everything is in danger. Bad things are coming, Olivia. My friends in New York are very worried."

"We should sell it."

"Is that what you want?"

"No, I . . . I just want to live my life."

Tracy pulls her gloves off slowly. "And you shall. But don't rush into this. You haven't even been together for a summer. I don't want you to regret this choice. If you want to change schools and go to Boston, that's fine. But somehow, I don't think you do. You love your team, you're always saying, and your coach."

It's true what she's saying. But. "I also love Fred."

"You can do a year apart. It's not like you'll be in Europe. You can see each other on weekends."

"I play tournaments on weekends."

Tracy nods her head slowly. "Yes."

"Fred can come watch."

"I'm sure he can." *But will he?* she means. "But why Boston? Why are you the one going to him and not the other way around?"

"I . . . " I stutter to a stop. And for the first time, I let myself wonder why the plan involves me uprooting my life to go and be where he is instead of the other way around. If I can switch schools, why can't he?

But no, no. That's not the point. The point is for us to be together. It doesn't matter where. That's a detail we can figure out, like the objections Aunt Tracy and my father are raising. Everyone starts their life together with questions and uncertainties.

"William said that Mom would be against this too."

Tracy's face turns grim. "There's no way of knowing that."

But it turns out she's wrong. Because when I leave the kitchen and go upstairs to my room, to lie on my bed and stare at the ceiling while I play Amy Winehouse's "Back to Black" and try to figure out what the hell I'm going to do, I see my mother's card sitting on my dresser, where I left it six weeks ago. And I'm not sure what drives me to it, but after so many weeks of letting it lie, I pick it up, my heart thrumming. I use my thumb to pry the old glue apart.

My love,

Today you are twenty-one! I'm so happy for you on this milestone. And I'm sad also that I'm not there to share it with you.

But that's selfish. I hope you're living a good life. I hope you're surrounded by love. I hope you and your sisters are a comfort to each other, and your father too.

Are you still playing tennis? I hope that you are. I've never been prouder of you than when I watch you on the court, your concentration, your glee at making a good shot.

Are you in love? I hope that for you too. I hope that you're happy and with a good man. I want to think that we'd have the kind of relationship where you'd tell me all about it. That you'd want my advice on love, like when you used to ask me about the color of the sky and why rainbows exist.

And what advice would I give you? Love wisely, my dear. Be careful who you give your heart to. I got married so, so young, and I would tell you not to follow my example. Don't be in a rush. If the love is real, it will wait until you're ready for it. Marriage is a blessing, but it's also a challenge. You might feel old today, but you're so young and have so much living left to do.

So live, my darling. Live your life to the fullest.

No one else can do it for you.

Love, Mom

* * *

When I meet Fred at the summer house that night, right away he knows something's wrong. It's after the cocktail hour, and I've had a few, sipping gin and tonics on the veranda as the party whirled around me, tasting the bitterness of the tonic as I watch the usual crowd wander around as if there's nothing out of place.

"No one thinks we should get married," I say, trying not to sob.

Fred expels a long breath. "Who's 'no one'?"

"William, Aunt Tracy—even my mom."

"What?"

I gulp back the misery that wants to escape. "It's this card she left me for my twenty-first birthday. It's like she knew. How could she know?"

He takes me by the hand and leads me to one of the moldering benches. The windows are partly fogged, the temperature change from day to night closing us off in this bubble.

"Tell me about it."

I summarize it for him. The conversation with my dad, with Tracy, the card.

"She was just giving you general advice about life. She doesn't know you now, or us . . ."

"No," I say, my voice rising. "She *did* know me. She was my mom."

"I'm sorry." He gathers my hands in his. They're warm and moist. "You're right—I don't know her. And to be honest, my mom isn't thrilled either. But that isn't the point. It's *our* life. It's what we want that matters. They'll get over it."

"But, Fred, I don't want to do this if everyone is against us."

"They won't be, I promise."

"They are." I pause, and then it all comes out in a rush. All the questions and insecurities I'd absorbed that afternoon. "Why do we have to move to Boston? Why can't you come to my school? Did you even consider that?"

Fred lets my hands go and leans away from me. I feel cold, a shiver going through me like when the weather shifts suddenly right before a storm.

"Honestly? I didn't."

"Okay."

"I should have, and I didn't. I'm sorry."

I expel a breath, tasting tonic, my cheeks red with it. "Why are we in such a hurry?"

"Is that what you think?"

"I don't know, Fred. I'm just asking questions."

His eyes darken. "Your own or other people's?"

"That's not fair. I can think of problems all by myself."

Fred laughs, but it's bitter.

"William said we should live together. To make sure."

"You're not sure?"

"I didn't say that."

"You just did."

"No, I—"

"You don't want to get married."

I touch his hand. It's cold. "I only said maybe we should wait. Take some time to figure this out."

His head droops. "So, what, we just call the engagement off?"

"No, I don't want that."

"It sounds like you do."

"Why does it have to be so black and white?"

"Because I asked you to marry me. It was a yes-or-no question, and you said yes."

"I meant it. I do want to marry you. Just not . . ."

"Not now."

"Not like this. Not only because you're scared of losing me."

The words surprise me as I say them, but it's true.

Fred wasn't going to propose until I told him I was leaving on tour. We hadn't even talked about the fall, what it would look like. And we'd both been okay with that.

So what had changed?

"That's not why—"

"Isn't it?" I put my hand on his chin and turn his face toward mine. His eyes are almost black, his face in shadow. The opposite of when he proposed to me. "Fred?"

"I bought that ring weeks ago. I was only waiting for the right time to ask you."

"Oh." I sit back and try to catch my breath.

"Are you going to go on tour?"

"I can't afford school."

"So you'd rather quit than be with me?"

"No, I . . . I have plans, Fred. A path. I need to follow it. I'm twenty-one. My mom is right. I'm at the beginning of my life. And I want to walk through life with you—I do—but I'm too young to get married. You're older than me, you've seen things in the military I can't even imagine, and maybe for you it's the right time, but not for me. But I want to do it with you. I want to figure this out. Can't we?" I slip from the bench and crouch in front of him. "I do want to be with you. I love you. Please believe that."

He shakes his head slowly. "I don't want to do it this way."

"What way?"

"Full of uncertainty." He grips my arms, almost too tight, his eyes wet. "Because I'm certain. I've never been more certain of anything in my life. But you're not, are you?"

Every fiber of my being wants to tell him what he wants to hear, to erase the terrible expression off his face, to make everything back to like it was last night when we were giddy with happiness, and everything seemed perfect. But he's right, I'm not certain, and I can't lie to him even if I wanted to.

"I just want us to take some time to figure this out."

"I can't do that."

I don't have the energy to ask why. I know why in my bones. Because he doesn't want to be with me if I'm not one hundred percent sure that I feel the same way as he does.

Which means that this is the end of us. Again.

"So, we're over?"

"I don't know, Olivia. I'm trying to figure all this out, same as you."

He's saying this to give me hope, but I have none. I've heard this tone before, I've felt this ache in my heart, and I know. Five years later wasn't enough time for us to be the right time.

"You know what you want. You're just afraid to say it."

I rub my hand across his cheek and feel a tear fall against it. My own tears are wet on my face. And my god, *my god*, this hurts. It hurts so fucking much.

I thought things were bad before, the last time, but that was nothing compared to this.

Fred leans down and his lips touch mine, and in an instant, we're wrapped up together.

He pulls me into his lap, and I curl myself around him, hoping that if I get close enough, if there's nothing between us but skin, then maybe all of this will end up differently.

We make love ferociously and more tenderly than ever before. We make love like it's the end of the world, and it is the end—it's the end of us.

Because when we're done, he gathers me close and wraps us in an old musty blanket. I try to keep myself from falling asleep because I'm sure that when I wake, I'll be alone.

But I can't keep my eyes open, I've been through too much today, and sometime in the night, Fred slips away, and when I wake up in the morning he's gone.

CHAPTER TWENTY-FIVE

July 2023

When I get back from tennis the morning after the dinner at the club, Wes is at the house for breakfast.

I couldn't help looking for him this morning out on the court. I thought he might do what Fred has done and watch me, though Fred was absent today as well. When I didn't see Wes on the sidelines, I wondered what part of the club he'd been placed in. Had they put him in a room near Fred, or on the other side of the building?

I both didn't want anyone to know about my personal drama and expected them to rearrange their guests to please me. I was ridiculous.

And then here he is, in the kitchen with Aunt Tracy, teasing her, asking for his special egg-white omelet, which she usually refuses to make, but seems to be fluffing in the pan in front of her. Is this a signal? Does she think I should save my marriage?

"Hi," I say, hanging back in the doorway, unsure if I want to disturb them.

Wes's face breaks into a wide grin. It's one of the things that made me fall in love with him—how his mood is infectious. He's one of those people who walk into a room and change the weather, bringing sun where there's been clouds.

"You look great," he says.

- "I need a shower."

He takes a couple of steps toward me and lowers his voice. "You know I like it when you're messy."

I put a hand up. I might not know what I want from Wes right now, but this intimate tone is not it. "Too soon."

"Sorry."

I step away. "Can I have some of that, Aunt Tracy?"

"You want real eggs, yes?"

"Yes, please."

"Egg whites are better for your heart," Wes says lightly.

Lots of things would've been better for my heart. Him not cheating on me, for one. "I'll take the cholesterol in small doses, thank you."

We take a seat at the island. There's a pitcher of fresh-squeezed orange juice, something I haven't seen since I've been here, and there are newly cut flowers in the vase in the center of the island. Fresh flowers in the entrance way too, come to think of it. We haven't even received the money from the sale yet, and it's already changing things.

"How is the cleanout going?" Wes asks as he pours me a glass of juice.

"Slowly."

"Are you finding anything fun? Like old newspapers or secret letters?"

"Mostly a lot of dust and outdated clothing and furniture."

"Don't forget to check all the hiding places. Didn't you tell me there was some secret cupboard or room in the library, or something?"

"I'd forgotten about that."

"Maybe it's full of buried treasure."

"I highly doubt it."

"What are you going to do with all the furniture?" Wes asks.

"We're going to do an estate sale with Lucy." I explain to him how I'm cataloging everything in the app Lucy sent me. How it's going to take the rest of the summer, probably, to get it done in time for the auction.

"And what's Ann's role in all of this? Where did she come from?"

"Her father is a lawyer in town. She brokered the sale."

He raises an eyebrow. "That all?"

"Pretty sure she and Charlotte are an item."

"Go, Charlotte."

I return his smile. "She seems happy."

"That's great. And Fred is dating Lucy?"

I take a sip of the juice. Bottled sunshine, bright and tart in my mouth. "Apparently."

"How do you feel about that?"

"I like Lucy."

"But all this is weird, you have to admit. Him buying this place . . ."

"Yes."

"He's going to knock it down, I assume? Build something new? Or cut it up for resale?"

Aunt Tracy brings our omelets to us, giving Wes's a distasteful look, even though she made it.

"This smells great, thank you," Wes says. "If you don't want to move on with William, please consider moving in with us."

"Aunt Tracy's going into retirement," I say.

"Of course, well deserved."

Aunt Tracy pauses, like she's considering something. "He's going to move in here."

"Who?" I ask.

"Fred. I heard him on his last walk-through before the sale. He had a woman with him, a designer I think, and he was talking about what he wanted to do with each room. I got the impression he was designing it for someone in particular."

I want to push the omelet away, but I don't. Instead, I force myself to take a large bite. "How come you didn't tell me that before?"

"Didn't I?"

"Don't think so." I take another bite. "Well, it's his house, and he can do whatever he wants with it."

I can feel Wes watching me, but I'm not going to play that game. Besides, what I'm feeling isn't just about Fred. It's about anyone else living here.

"Did he ever say why he bought this house in particular?" Wes asks.

"He did not." I turn to him. "It's not like we've been hanging out. We've barely spoken."

Wes pauses, deciding whether to believe this. "Well, whatever the reason, at least something good has come of it."

"What's that?"

"The money, of course. That's great that William is dividing it between all of you."

I put my fork down slowly. "How do you know about that?"

"Charlotte was telling me last night. I was surprised you hadn't..."

Aunt Tracy drifts away. If this is a fight, she doesn't want to be a part of it.

"I didn't know till I got here."

"Really?"

"Yes, really. You know how Charlotte is with information."

"But it's true? You're all getting a split?"

"Yes. Why?"

He smiles at me again, but this time it doesn't feel warm. "You know why, Olivia. It means we can start over."

"Right."

"And it's great for everyone, isn't it? Sophie said Colin was finally going to leave his job."

"Yes," I say, trying to figure out why my breakfast suddenly tastes bitter.

Money didn't used to be a sore spot with us. Wes had it when we met, and I was comfortable from my years on the tour. Or so I thought; once I retired and sat down with my accountant, I had a lot less money than I expected, and not enough to retire on. I had to do something, and the thought of becoming a tennis coach didn't appeal to me—too many hours, a nomadic life ....

After some deliberation, I decided to dust off my degree and get a job teaching, a move Wes supported because he knew I didn't want to be financially dependent on him. Then, Wes's business failed during the pandemic, and my teacher's salary wasn't going to keep us in Manhattan. Money became a point of contention and conflict.

"Is that what you came here to talk about?"

"No. I wanted to see you."

I push my plate away. I've finished half of it, and that's enough camouflage. "Well, you have."

"Hey, don't be like that."

"Like what?" I stand up. "I need a shower."

"Of course."

"I can't just snap back to the way things were, Wes. Not that they were so great before that either."

He reaches for my hand. "Hey, now, that's not fair. We were having a tough time—everything with my business . . . But we've had a lot of good too, haven't we?"

"There was good."

He smiles encouragingly. "Of course there was. And there will be again. I was thinking, when all this is taken care of, why don't we go somewhere for a long weekend? Before school starts up again. Maybe back to the Bahamas. Didn't we love it there?"

It's where we went on our honeymoon, and we did love it there. We were good there. Happy.

"It's a beautiful place."

"It will be our fresh start. And until then, I'm here for whatever you need. I'm going to stay for the rest of the summer and work from here. I've got a position at that V-Cap I was telling you about. Something more secure. They're okay with me being mostly remote, and I'll go into the city when I need to. So, if you need help in the house, just ask. I know it must be hard for you going through all this stuff. It's getting you down, I'm sure."

"It's a lot."

"Charlotte and Sophie should be helping."

"They should." I sigh. "They are, a bit."

"I can talk to them."

"No, it's fine." I pull away. "I'm going to go take a shower. Aunt Tracy, thank you for breakfast."

She smiles at me. She's stayed silent during out exchange, but I'm sure she has an opinion.

"Will you have dinner with me?" Wes asks.

"Not tonight, okay, Wes? Just give me time."

"When, then?"

I sigh. Taking no for an answer has never been Wes's strong suit. "How about Saturday?"

"Perfect, I'll make a reservation." He kisses me on the cheek, and I let him.

Then he goes to Aunt Tracy and does the same. She shoos him away, but I can tell she likes it despite her protests.

He leaves and I'm still standing there, watching him walk across the lawn, where William is taking his morning walk.

Aunt Tracy puts her arms around me. "He's a smoothie, that one."

"He is."

"You don't have to be with any man, you know."

"I know."

She squeezes, then releases me. I watch Wes talk to William for a minute, wondering what they're discussing, then let it go.

It's not something I do well, but if I want my marriage to have a chance, I'm going to have to get used to the sensation.

* * *

I take my shower and change into an old pair of shorts and a ratty T-shirt. Today is the day I tackle the library with a renewed interest now that Wes has reminded me about the secret compartment behind one of the shelves.

The library itself is large, dark, and daunting, with dark book-shelves up to the ceiling circling the room. There must be thousands of books in here, and I'm not going to be boxing them all up. I'll leave that to Lucy's company. But I do need to go through the shelves and make sure there are no important documents or keepsakes buried within.

I pull open the heavy red velvet drapes, and a cloud of dust flies up. We used to love playing in here as kids, building forts with the furniture and towers of old hardcover books. I run my hand along the spines. All the classics are here: the Brontës, Dickens, Austen.

I pull down the Austen compilation—all six novels in a green hardcover that's almost too big to hold. I remember discovering it when I was thirteen, and sitting in the window reading, reading, reading until I made it to *Persuasion*. I loved all the books, but this one especially. It was my mother's favorite too, and I search the bookshelves for her special copy, the one she'd had since she was a teenager. I don't find it, so I put the large volume aside to keep, and move on down the shelves.

Some of these books are probably valuable, but I'll let Lucy decide that. I text her to ask whether each one of them needs to be cataloged. She answers that no, she'll send her appraiser next week to check if there's anything worth keeping. I sigh with relief and continue browsing.

I pull out the family Bible, with each generation added in a different handwriting on the inside cover. There I am with my sisters, written in by my mother. And beneath Sophie, at some point, my father took the trouble to write in the names of her children, which I find surprising and touching.

I put it in the "keep" pile, then clear off some of the knickknacks into a box—a collection of glass birds, an old vase that isn't worth anything but sentiment, a few drawings Charlotte did that my mother framed.

I'm circling the room, avoiding the place I really want to look. *Await, avoid, attack,* I think, an old admonishment a silly uncle used to give before we went to a banquet in Chinatown when we visited him in the city.

Memory is so funny, what it tosses up, what it discards.

But enough.

I walk to the shelf that hides the secret compartment. It's a large recess behind a block of shelves that was probably meant for a safe. I can't think of the last time I looked in here.

No, no, I can. My mother caught me. I was twelve or thirteen, and she was already sick. I remember because she was in her nightgown, even though it was the middle of the day. I'd slipped away from my piano lesson when my teacher had fallen asleep in her rocking chair, a common occurrence. Charlotte had been keeping something from me—I can't remember what, now—and I was determined to find it. I pulled half the books off the shelves, and then I opened the cabinet.

"What are you doing, darling?" my mom said, moving into the room like a ghost.

"Charlotte hid something from me."

"What, dear?"

"She won't tell me—only I know it's mine."

She walked toward me, her dressing gown billowing around her. Her skin was pale, and the color seemed to have been bleached out of her hair. She wore it long and loose, and it tickled my neck as she gathered me close.

"You shouldn't let Charlotte get to you so much, darling."

"I know."

"Maybe she didn't even hide anything."

I cocked my head to the side. "That sounds like Charlotte."

"Aren't you supposed to be playing piano?"

"Mrs. Carson fell asleep again."

My mom laughed, a melodious tinkle that sound like the piano she loved but didn't play much anymore. She took my hand and led me to the couch. "Sit here and tell me all about it."

I leaned my body against hers. I didn't get to do that very often with her anymore. She was so tired all the time, and sometimes even her skin hurt, she said. "Did you find anything in the secret compartment?"

"No, just some old books."

"That's the past, my love. And sometimes it should be hidden away."

"What do you mean?"

She kissed me. "Nothing. Sometimes I say silly things."

"Sophie is *always* saying silly things."

"She makes me laugh."

"She's such a *baby* still."

"You're all my babies." She kissed me again. "Now, go back to your piano lesson, and be nice when you wake Mrs. Carson. You'll see when you get old, sometimes you get tired in the middle of the day."

"Okay." I got up from the couch, and she rose slowly.

"Go on, now—shoo."

I walked to the threshold, then looked back. She was staring into the secret compartment. Then she took out a book from inside, like it was a treasure, but it didn't look like anything valuable to me.

"Olivia."

"I'm going!"

I press the mechanism to open the compartment. It's at eye level with me now, though the last time I looked inside, I'd had to pull a chair up to get to it. As it was then, it's mostly empty except for a thick leather-bound book that says "Journal" on the outside. I take it out and open it slowly, my mother's handwriting greeting me.

The early entries are sporadic and benign, starting a few years before she got sick. I flip to the end, past several ripped-out pages, the leftover edges ragged. The entry I find was written a few weeks before she died. But how did it get in here? Did she put it here? Why?

The details don't matter, it's the words that will haunt me forever.

It's soon, I can tell. A few days, a few weeks.

I can measure my life in hours now instead of the years I should have.

And it feels like it used to when I couldn't sleep. When I'd watch the clock and with each half hour that passed, I knew it was a deduction. That soon I'd cross the threshold of what was acceptable, that if I didn't fall asleep immediately, the next day would be ruined. Each hour is like that now, only I can barely stay awake. I want to take it all in—I don't want to miss a minute, but I'm missing most of it.

I'm missing my girls. I'm missing my life.

And oh God, I'm afraid.

CHAPTER TWENTY-SIX

June 2013

I did it!

I made it into the qualifying rounds at Wimbledon! A whole year of planning and working on my ranking and eating meals that felt tasteless in their repetitiveness and adding strength workouts and never having anything to drink, and now here it is! The All-England Club in June. Strawberries and cream and people in linen suits and fancy hats. And if I win these next three rounds, then I'm in the main draw.

Matt's traveled with me, and we're staying in a two-bedroom apartment near St Paul's Cathedral. When I'm not practicing or thinking about my next shitty meal, I'm taking in the city. The Thames. The Globe. The river walk. Every corner has a pub on it, and every afternoon as the offices empty out, those pubs turn into a party. It's not a party I can join, but I like listening to it. The barks of laughter, the happy chatter of friends, the cheers, the songs, the flirting.

This city has baby fever. William and Kate are expecting their first child in a month, and the British are betting on everything: date, weight, sex, name. The papers are full of it, like everyone's whole future depends on it, and I guess it does in a way. If the future is the monarchy.

And me? I feel anxious and excited and confident. A lot of the bigger names in the women's draw are out with injuries, and I've been having a great year. Momentum is an important force in tennis, and I have it. I can tell by the way my opponents—women I've known for years—look at me when I walk on court. Like they've never seen me before. Like they're scared of me now.

It's because of the myth—the qualifier one. Every once in a while, someone comes out of obscurity to take it all, winning ten matches instead of seven. It's never happened at Wimbledon in the women's draw. But like an elusive win by one of those famous baseball teams, it's only a matter of time before someone breaks the curse and wins.

I'm determined to be that person.

I'm turning twenty-six this year, and it feels like my last chance to make it. So, I went to Matt in January and asked him what I had to do. Was it possible to turn my career around? He told me that it was, and we made a plan. I've carried it out to a T, practicing smarter, sleeping as much as possible, and praying to the injury gods that I stay healthy.

And then, the night before my first qualifying match against a woman I've beaten several times already this year, I go to a patron's reception and walk right into someone. Hard.

"Ouch," I say, feeling shaken by the impact.

I wasn't looking where I was going, trying to get across the room to where Matt is waving me over, and the person I've run up against is tall, solid.

"It was my fault," he says, and now I'm shaking. Because I know this voice. I know this man.

"Fred?" I say slowly as I look up, praying that he has a voice doppelganger.

But no, it's him. Those deep blue eyes, that dark hair with the slightest curl to it. His face is tanned, like that of someone who spends a lot of time in the sun. His cheekbones are sharp, his features chiseled, and he's wearing an exquisitely tailored blue suit that fits his thin, athletic frame perfectly.

"Olivia," he says, his voice slow and measured, "did I hurt you?"

What a question to ask.

"No, I'm fine."

"I'd feel horrible if I did anything to keep you from winning tomorrow."

He smiles, and his teeth are whiter than I remember. I check his hands—no ring, but the nails are manicured. Fred at twenty-eight has changed in some fundamental way from Fred at twenty-three. I'm not sure how I feel about it.

"What are you doing here?" I ask.

"My company sponsored this event." There's a slight British tinge to his voice now, his Boston accent buried under the Queen's English.

"Your company?"

"The company I work for, rather. I'm the vice president of shipping for de Keurig."

I know the name. It's one of the biggest shipping companies in the world, swallowing up its competitors in splashy deals that are spread out over the business press.

I didn't know Fred worked there when I agreed to attend this event. I've heard only the barest of whispers about him since we broke up five years ago. That's been deliberate. No googling. No checking for his name on Facebook or Twitter. I didn't want to know if he'd found someone to replace me.

"I'm impressed," I say. "Congratulations."

He smiles modestly. "It's not as impressive as what you've done."

My heart picks up. He's been following my career. He must've known I'd be here. He could've avoided me, but he chose to attend.

And then it occurs to me: maybe he's the reason I was invited to this event in the first place.

I shake the thought away. "I haven't done anything yet."

"Of course you have. You're going to do great."

"Thank you. How long have you been in London?"

"Three years. Since I graduated."

"You finished early?"

He picks a glass of champagne off a waiter's tray. "Do you want?"

"Not for me, thanks."

"Of course. You were saying?"

I look past him to Matt, who's watching us. Matt knows something about Fred—he used to come watch me practice when I was

rehabbing after my rib injury five years ago. And he saw me after Fred
and I ended things.

Oh! Matt wasn't waving me over. He was waving me off.

"You finished college early?"

"Yes, in three years rather than four."

"Impressive."

"I had no distractions."

I bring my eyes back to Fred's. They're clear and so blue, like the
summer sky at twilight. But I can't see past that. I used to be able to read
his thoughts like they were written out. Now, it's all an urbane mask, like
this party, which is full of women in pastel dresses and men in linen suits.

"And then three years to VP? They must like you."

"Mr. de Keurig—Tomas—has taken me under his wing."

"That's great, Fred. Congratulations."

"Thank you." He sips at his champagne. "Ready for your match
tomorrow?"

"I hope so. Will you excuse me?"

"Of course."

I walk past him and go straight to Matt. He's in coaching mode,
still wearing the track suit he favors.

"Are you all right?" he asks.

"I'm fine."

"I didn't know he'd be here."

"I wasn't worried you did."

I reach for a cucumber sandwich, then stop myself when I catch a
look from him. "Just one?"

"Go ahead."

I pop it in my mouth and savor it. The cold butter, the crisp
cucumber, the fresh cress. I want to eat a thousand, but just the one
will have to do.

I turn so that Matt and I are watching the room together. Fred is
moving around, glad-handing this powerful man, then that gracious
lady. He's comfortable, secure, at home. The piped-in chamber music
lends a sophisticated air to the event that would otherwise be just some
canapes and drinks in a fancy viewing box.

"Do you think that he arranged for me to be invited to this?" I say
to Matt quietly.

"I've been wondering that."

"Why, though?"

"You'd have to ask him."

"I doubt he'd tell me."

Was it to get in my head? To get revenge for the way things ended? Did he hate me? He didn't seem to, but that morning five years ago, when I woke up cold on the floor of the summer house, that had been the last time I'd heard from him. That had been my choice too. I hadn't reached out because I didn't want to know if he'd answer me. If I kept silent, then I could tell myself it was my decision, not his.

"Don't let it get in your head," Matt says.

It's already in there, buried deep. "Of course." I kiss him briefly on the cheek. "I'm going to go."

"I think that's a good idea."

"I'll see you back at the apartment later?"

"Sure."

I weave my way through the crowd, avoiding Fred on the other side of the room. I leave the reception room and start to walk down the hallway. It feels good to absorb the silence as my feet fall on the thick carpet.

"Olivia!"

I stop, close my eyes, sigh.

Oh, Fred. Why can't you just let me sneak away?

I turn around. Part of me wants to rush into his arms and pick up where we left off. The other half wants to run away in a childish display.

I do neither.

"What, Fred?" I say in a voice that's harsher than I want it to be.

He stops short. "I wanted . . . Good luck tomorrow."

"Thank you."

And then I walk away from him as fast as I can before the past catches up to me.

* * *

The Wimbledon qualifying rounds take place at the Roehampton Sports Center. It's a beautiful stretch of Kelly-green lawn divided into courts separated by low net fencing. There's no proper stands, just corridors where the few people who come to watch the matches roam around. All the players are in white, and I've got a special outfit for the tournament, provided to me by my first top-tier sponsor.

My opponent is a woman named Olga. She's nineteen, tall and stocky, with a serve that sounds like a bullet. But she's a one-trick pony, a fast-serve out wide so she can try to place the return down the line, and I cracked her code the last two matches we played. She doesn't deviate today. The *BOOM* of her serve draws a crowd, but the points play out with a certain sameness. So much so that I'm almost coaching her in my mind, telling her to surprise me by serving down the middle once in a while.

She doesn't, and I break her early in the first set, and the match quickly starts to feel inevitable. She fights harder in the second set, but she doesn't change her strategy, and before long that set is over too, and I've done it.

I'm into the second round of qualifying.

One match down, nine to go, I think as I shake her hand across the net. I go back to my chair and drape a towel over my head. It's midday and hot.

Matt hugs me from behind. "Great match."

"Thank you. The plan worked." I pull the towel off and wipe off my very red face.

"Indeed, it did."

"Tougher match tomorrow."

"Probably," he says. "But you know what to do."

I smile at him, feeling a confidence I haven't felt in a long time.

Matt mentions that there's some media that want to talk to me. I do a few quick interviews, giving the same platitudes that athletes have for time immemorial. When I'm done, I take a cab back to my apartment. The cabbie is chatty, telling me the history of the street we're driving down. I listen politely, struggling with his northern accent.

When I get back to the apartment, I shower, change, stretch. I take out one of the prepared meals and heat it up, then sit down at the kitchen table to eat. It's part of my decompression routine, so I don't focus too much on what's coming up tomorrow. Because right now, all I have to do is wait.

My phone pings on the table in front of me.

It's a text from an old number.

Great match today! Fred writes.

My heart accelerates as I read it. Just above the message are the last texts we exchanged five years ago that I never erased, just let be buried in my phone. *Let's meet at the summer house,* I'd written then. He'd texted back a heart.

Thank you. I pause. *Were you there?*

Yes.

I can't believe it. Fred came to my match, but I didn't see him. Not that I paid much attention to the crowd. It's important to focus on the game—the opponent—in front of me.

Is that okay? Fred writes.

It's a free country.

Olivia.

Fred.

What are you doing right now?

Eating boring food. Working on visualizing for tomorrow.

Do you have time for a walk?

I breathe in and out slowly. I do have time, but I can't do it. Any conversation with Fred is an emotional quagmire. I need to keep things cool, calm, and collected so that I can win my next match. I can't walk into a situation I can't control.

I'm sorry, no.

At some point?

I'll have to think about that.

Fair enough. Good luck tomorrow.

Thank you.

I watch the screen, wondering if he'll text again, but he doesn't.

Eventually I put the phone away, our text thread at the top, something that's been unearthed that should've stayed buried.

CHAPTER TWENTY-SEVEN

July 2023

The weeks roll by slowly, that uncertainty of summer settling in, where you never know what day it is unless you check.

Wes and I have dinner at Bonne Amie. I tell him about Ash's and my discovery about Claude, once again attentive with his "oui, ouis" and zero French behind it. He tries to keep the evening light, but it feels heavy.

Not enough time has passed for me to forget the images I saw on his phone. That perfect breast, cupped in an elegant hand. That metal-clasped belt around her waist, with nothing else adorning her delicate body.

I didn't want to know who it was, and Wes didn't volunteer. I didn't press it. The details weren't going to help me; they'd only make me feel worse.

I haven't forgotten, though. I don't know yet if I can.

So I drink the expensive wine Claude brings us and distract us both by telling Wes about some of the early entries I found in my mother's journal.

I've been reading them at night before I go to sleep, loving falling asleep with her voice in my head. She had a deft hand describing the parties they went to in New York and Southampton, gently poking fun at William and his obsession with beautiful people. It feels like it came from love, and it's a nice window into their life together. I haven't found any other revelations. Not yet.

After dinner, Wes drives me home, and I trip out of the car before he can say whatever it is that's playing across his face.

The next morning, I go to the club, play, have a late breakfast with him, and return to the house to spend the afternoon entering data for the auction, cursing my parents for every knickknack and side table they'd collected.

Another week evaporates, and now it's the third week of July. Wes and I are in stasis, but everyone else's life seems to be moving along smoothly. Ann is a constant presence at the house, and Lucy and Fred make regular appearances at cocktails with Colin and Sophie. Colin's parents are finally in town and are more than happy to babysit. The talk often turns to the trip to Sag Harbor, one I don't want to take and I doubt will happen. But I underestimate both Sophie and Charlotte and their determination, and in the end we all go.

Fred and Lucy, Sophie and Colin, Charlotte and Ann, and Wes and me. A foursome. No, that's a golf term. I don't know what a four-couple date is where more than one couple has history with another person in the party, but that's what I'm on.

Sophie took charge of the details, renting one of those large, black SUVs, with a driver, that seats twelve. But even though there are extra seats, we all sit by couple, Wes and I in the front, Fred and Lucy all the way at the back. The drive is uneventful, and Wes does his ingratiating act, telling stories and getting everyone laughing. Everyone but Fred, who simply frowns at Wes every time he looks at him, then brings his eyes back to the road. But Lucy and Ann, especially, are in his thrall, and I feel a prick of jealousy, like I always used to when Wes plied his charm on someone other than me.

I can't decide if it's a reflex, like how seeing Lucy and Fred makes me feel, or if it's a sign that I want to forgive Wes and try to move on.

I'm not going to solve that today, though, so I laugh with everyone else and watch the scenery unfold and try not to remember that summer Fred and I spent roaming these roads.

Our first stop is a house tour so Charlotte can check out the house Lucy decorated. It's a cute beach cottage twenty minutes outside of town. Two bedrooms, a generous living room and dining room, updated bathrooms, airy and light. I can see Charlotte living here. Lucy was right about it being exactly to her taste, all soft hues of gray and taupe, with linen fabrics and a sea glass color on the walls.

Charlotte lights up when she sees it, touching the back of the couch, running her hand along the quartz countertop. In the backyard, there's a firepit and an outdoor kitchen, and part of me starts to imagine living here too, not with Charlotte, obviously, but in a place like this, smaller, cozy. Our apartment in the city, which was Wes's before we met, is all cold surfaces and hard colors, like a magazine piece of a bachelor pad for a man with taste and sophistication.

"You like it," Wes says, coming up to me in the backyard. I'm standing under a grape arbor, and I can smell the ocean, a few blocks away. Even with all the money we're getting, a place right on the beach would be irresponsible, and I'm glad Charlotte seems to be realistic in what she should buy.

"I do. It's great."

"We could get a place like this."

"Could we?" I turn my eyes to him. His hair is curling in the heat, it's ends blonder than when he arrived. His eyes are so open and guileless, I could believe anything he says when he looks at me like that.

I did.

"If that's what you want."

"We can't afford it."

"But we can. Now, with the money . . . and this new job, it's working out. I'm going to be more cautious in the future. Less . . ."

"Cavalier?"

"Exactly."

"Will you be happy, being safe?"

"I will, Olivia. I will."

I wish what he's saying were true, rather than believing it. Wes is a risk taker, always has been, and thinking of him taking the safe path for the rest of his life doesn't fit.

"We don't have to decide anything now," I say.

"No, you're right. But I want you to know that I'm listening to you. I'm paying attention. You don't like the apartment—I know that. We can get something that's more your taste. We can do whatever you want."

He's so earnest, and I want to tell him that it doesn't have to be all about me. It's supposed to be about *us*. What *we* want. But that's never been the way we worked. Mostly, we did what Wes wanted because I thought I wanted that too. Our relationship never felt like a democracy. But I can't say all that in someone else's back garden on a house tour, so instead I say, "Thank you."

"So," Charlotte says coming up to me and linking her arm through mine, "what do we think?"

"I love it, Charlotte."

"I do too."

"Will you put an offer in?"

At that word, *offer*, Ann and Lucy appear at her side. Charlotte laughs at their eagerness, a loose, happy laugh, and I'm so glad for my sister in that moment, I almost start to cry.

"Yes, I think I will. It's still not on the market, Lucy?"

"Not until Monday. I'll make a call and we can do the paperwork tomorrow." She pulls her phone out and ducks away. Wes and Ann drift away from us, walking further into the garden.

"Where's Sophie and Colin?" I ask.

"Arguing in the living room."

"Ah."

"She wants them to buy a place."

"I know."

Charlotte shakes her head. "They need their own life."

I throw my head back and laugh.

"What?"

"You've been living with William this whole time."

"That's not the same thing at all."

"No?"

"All right, all right. But I'm not moving with him now, am I?"

"You're not. I'm happy for you."

"Ann changed my life."

I wrap my arm around her waist and pull her to me. "I'm so glad for you."

She smiles, then glances toward where Wes and Ann are walking in the garden. "What do you think they're talking about?"

"How fabulous you are."

"Wes didn't think so when we dated."

"You're not still mad about that, are you?"

Charlotte lifts her chin. "No, of course not. But Olivia . . . are you sure you can trust him?"

"No," I say. "I'm not."

And then, like Wes knows we're talking about him, he turns and grins at me in this way he has, like a sunbeam, then puts his hand on his chest, our special way of saying *I love you*, and my heart skips a beat.

I can't trust him, but we don't feel over yet.

* * *

Our next stop is the vineyard, and it's out of this world. Fred's friend, James Benedict, who he met in the Navy, bought the five hundred acres from the previous owner in a fire sale and has spent the last year updating it with all of the latest technology, making the old winery modern.

He takes us on a personal tour, limping along next to me as he supports himself on a beautiful carved cane. A "war injury" he calls it, and Fred lets us know quietly about James's act of bravery when they were both in the Navy, saving someone who'd been swept overboard during a bad storm, and how a rope got caught around his leg like a snake and snapped it in two.

The grape fields, the harvesting tents, the manglers, and vast vats where the wine ages—all of it is fascinating to me. James is a good, gentle explainer, and we get along immediately. We have a certain complicity, he and I, and it's nice to have an uncomplicated conversation with a man.

After the tour, he takes us into the restaurant and tasting room that's finished, but not yet open, and we're treated to an amazing five-course lunch with wine pairings.

We're sitting at two round tables, the group divided in two, with James going back and forth between us. Unlike the bus, where we were divided into couples, I'm sitting with Fred, Sophie, and Ann, Fred to my right and Sophie to my left.

"Wasn't this a good idea?" Sophie says as she unfolds her cloth napkin and takes in the room around us. It's a glass box, with two walls made up of enormous wine storage rooms. In front of us lie the grape fields. Behind us an apple orchard. At capacity, the room could hold a hundred and fifty people, James tells us, and its main use will be for weddings.

"A great idea, Sophie," I say. "Thank you."

A waiter bustles around us, pouring us all a glass of white wine to go with our first appetizer of white fish carpaccio with jalapeño and locally pressed olive oil. "All the ingredients are local," James says. "And seasonal if possible. That fish was caught this morning, as was all of the seafood."

"And the beef was slaughtered yesterday," Fred says, lifting his glass, amused.

James gives a belly laugh, and the two grin at each other.

Fred is happier now, his gloom from the house tour and bus ride lifted. He has an easy way with James, I've noticed, and I wonder if he was the one that James saved out there in the ocean.

"How have you not been here before?" I ask Fred, taking a sip from my glass and sighing in pleasure. The wine is excellent—light, effervescent, refreshing. I could drink a whole bottle, but I remind myself that there are four more glasses coming, which is about three past my normal limit and certainly way past my limit for day drinking.

"I kept meaning to."

"I was about to disown him," James says at his elbow. "Can you blame me, Olivia?"

"Not at all. If it were me, you'd have trouble keeping me away."

"You're welcome any time."

"Thank you."

"And maybe you can convince Fred to make it more than a yearly visit?"

"Oh, I . . ." I feel a blush creeping up my cheek as I take a longer drink from my flute.

"You're bugging the wrong woman," Sophie says, a catch in her voice. "Lucy's the one who has to remind him."

A shadow passes over Fred's face.

"Whoever can persuade Fred is a friend of mine," James says lightly. "Now, taste your food and tell me, is it divine?"

We obey, picking up our forks and trying the delicate fish. It melts in my mouth. "It's fantastic, James. Thank you so much for this."

"It's only the beginning." He flits off to the other table, his cane clacking on the floor.

"He's great," I say to Fred.

"I agree."

"Was it you he saved?"

"It was. A stupid training accident."

"I'm glad."

His features soften, but then Ann says something to him, and he turns away. I eat the rest of my food in silence while Sophie chatters away next to me, intent on keeping me from speaking to Fred. I want to tell her to relax, that he's safe for Lucy, if he's interested, but there's no point when Sophie gets this way. Instead, I guide her gently toward real estate, and over the next course of salad and a delicate sauvignon blanc, she tells me that she and Colin are in a fight over whether to buy something or wait.

"He wants to see if he gets a new job first."

"That seems reasonable. And the money hasn't even been transferred yet." I try the delicate greens and strawberries. I'm not a salad fan, having had to eat too much of it in training, but this one is fantastic. "When is that supposed to happen?"

"End of August, I think, on the same day as the transfer."

So, I'm stuck here until then. Or I could leave and come back. I'm not sure why it's so hard to make the decision, only every time I think about leaving, I feel so incredibly sad. It's going to be harder than I thought, saying goodbye to Taylor House for good.

"Charlotte didn't tell me the date."

"Me neither, but I dragged the information out of Ann."

"What's that?" Ann says, raising her head up from her conversation with Fred.

"We were just talking about the transfer. Has a date been set?" I ask.

"August eighteenth, I believe."

"Can you let me know what you need from me before then?"

"Of course. I'm surprised my assistant hasn't already been in touch. I'll write her right now." She takes out her phone and taps at it quickly while Fred eats his salad between us. I can feel his awkward energy, and I wish I'd waited to bring it up. "And done."

"Thank you."

Lucy puts her phone down. "I wonder what the next course is?"

"Lobster bisque," James says, his ear attuned to every conversation about food. "It's exquisite."

Fred turns in his chair and puts his hand on James's arm. "Thank you for this, old friend."

"It's no trouble at all."

"I know that's not true." He stands. "Now, please take my chair and eat some of this delicious meal. I insist."

He leads James into his chair, almost pressing him down into it. Then he pushes it in like he's a waiter, and walks to another table, picks up a chair, and puts it down next to Lucy.

He doesn't look at me as he does this, but I get the message.

One hour beside me is enough.

Too long in fact.

CHAPTER TWENTY-EIGHT

June 2013

My interactions with Fred in London take on the ping-pong quality of my tennis matches.

I face my opponents, trying not to look for him in the crowd, but I know he's there. Somehow, he stays out of sight. Maybe it's because the crowds are bigger each day than the last, a slow buzz building around me, bringing journalists and fans.

I've never really had fans before, not strangers who follow my stats other than the occasional man—always older, always oddly tanned like he's just come from the beach—who feels like I owe him my time because I'm a woman, and I exist in a world he's interested in.

But I've been pegged by the media as one to watch in this tournament, my half-year record and my jump in the standings marking me for special attention. After I win my second match against the other qualifier who's higher ranked than me, there are journalists to talk to, asking me questions about the potential streak I'm on, where it's going to end. I know better than to give in to that talk, so I spin the platitudes I've heard others share about seeing the ball well, and it not being my opponent's day and that I'm taking each match "one by one."

I try not to look over the journalist's shoulder for Fred, but I can sense him around. Somehow, I know that at some point, once I finish my cooldown and go back to my hotel, I'll receive a message from him.

This time, it comes in the cab.

Great match again. I'm impressed.

Our old texts have been pushed off the screen now. I have to scroll up to see them. I don't.

Thank you.

Everyone is talking about you.

Are they?

As they should be.

Don't you have to work?

When I told Mr. Van Keurig that I knew you, he told me to be the man on the ground.

Ah.

It's really great to watch you play again, Olivia.

Have you never . . . since . . .?

No—well, once in a while. Not in person.

I turn the screen over and rest it on my leg. If he watched any of my matches before now, then it was because he sought them out on ESPN 4 in the middle of the night. It's hard to think about that. The idea that Fred was up, maybe not being able to sleep, and he went in search of me. Was there someone sleeping peacefully in the bed next to him? Did he tell her about me?

"You all right, miss?" my cab driver asks in a thick accent that sounds like a song.

"I'm fine."

"I have tissues."

"Oh." I reach up. I'm crying. Not hard, but a few gentle tears. I wipe them away with the back of my hand. "No, thank you."

He gives me a reassuring smile over his shoulder. "Almost there."

He thinks I lost, my tennis bag and whites giving me away. And that's fine—it's fine. I did lose. I lost the life I thought I'd have to get this one, and it's not that bad. Certainly not worth crying over.

My phone buzzes against my knee.

How about that walk? Fred has written. *It's a lovely day.*

I'm sorry. I'm tired.

Summer After Summer

No worries at all. Best of luck for tomorrow.

Thank you.

I'll be watching.

Okay.

Olivia.

Fred.

We'll take that walk one day, yes?

The tears are about to start again, but I push them back. I'm stronger than this.

I can't make any promises right now.
I have to focus on my matches.
I understand. I'll root for you either way.

Thank you.

And now I power my phone off and bury it in my bag. I don't want to be tempted to write him back, to change my mind, to change the course of my life again.

Instead, when the cab stops in front of my apartment, I tip the driver generously, let myself in, and breathe a sigh of relief that I can be alone for a few hours to take it all in.

*   *   *

I win another match, a hard-fought three-setter against another girl, only eighteen and local, that Britain had pinned its hopes on. The crowd is against me, but I try to ignore them as the push and pull of the match drags on. I win the first set, she wins the second, and then it's the final set, and I can feel that I've tired her out. Her energy is draining, and if I can maintain mine, I'll have done it. I dig deep and serve well, and when I win match point, I throw my arms in the air, releasing my racquet in a twirl, and it's this image—my amazed face, the racquet spinning above me—that's above the fold in the papers the next day and is played over and over on the nightly sports roundups.

I'm in the main draw! Because I beat their girl, the British press is on my side now, the crowd too. By luck, I've ended up on the easier side of the draw, filled with women I've beaten before, sometimes only a few weeks ago. I can see my path to the finals.

Seven matches to go.

Fred writes every day, always with the same offer of a walk, and I always decline. There's more time between my matches, though, now—a day off between each one—so he knows that when I decline to rest it's because I'm not ready to see him. He asks anyway, and each exchange lasts a little longer and reveals a little more of his past, what he's been doing these last five years. He asks me questions too, about my life. My sisters, my father, Ash.

We don't talk about romantic partners, and for me there's nothing to talk about. I've had boyfriends, short-term things with tour players or trainers because that's who you meet when you're on tour eleven months of the year, but nothing serious. I continue to resist googling him. If he's been squiring beautiful British heiresses or models around, I don't want to know.

It's a dance we're doing, a game of musical chairs.

When the music stops, who knows where we'll be sitting.

My first-round match at Wimbledon is against Slavenka, a Russian girl who's been on the circuit as long as me, but with more success. In the early years, we were rivals. But then she surpassed me and moved into the top one hundred while I stayed on the challenger circuit, and it's been years since I've played her. We play on one of the smaller courts, and her game is different from how I remember; she's developed a slice backhand that can go deep or turn into a drop shot without notice, and in the first set I'm running all over the court, getting to balls I wouldn't have even tried for last year.

When I win in two sets, I toss my racquet again, sensing that this is what the crowd wants as they stand and cheer. When it cracks as it lands, I pick it up and hand it to a kid on the sidelines, stopping to sign it first. This draws another cheer, and this time, for the first time, I do find Fred in the crowd. He's standing in a row of seats halfway up the grandstand, center court, dressed in a dapper linen suit, and he's clapping hard. I give a small curtsy—more cheers—do a quick interview, then walk off the court.

Six more to go, Fred writes half an hour later during my press conference.

No amount of media training truly prepares you for what they're like. My name is shouted over and over, and the same questions get asked in English, French, Spanish, and languages I barely recognize.

I give the same answers, but when my phone buzzes, I check it, and the smile on my face says something, because now they want to know who's texting me: Is the message from someone special in my life?

I blush and say no.

Ouch, comes Fred's text a moment later.

I flip my phone over and get back to the task at hand, and it's only later, when I'm slipping into a bath that will be followed by an hour of deep massage and stretching, that I realize he didn't ask me for a walk today.

* * *

My next match is a tough one against an American girl who grew up at one of those tennis academies in Florida that trained the Williams sisters and Capriati. Her name is Jenn—a beautiful blonde with modeling contracts and a grunt on each shot, which is distracting. I lose the first set, and I'm down a break in the second, but then Jenn runs for a ball that's just out of reach and twists her ankle. She's not injured enough to quit, but she's hobbling, not as quick to get to the ball, and I decide that it's now or never.

I up the power on my serves and get more aggressive at the net, and I take the set. On the changeover, the crowd is clapping for me, yelling, "Go, Olivia!," and I tap into their energy and make quick work of her in the third set.

Up goes the racquet again, and this time I really can't believe it.

I'm in the third round! The miracle talk is truly starting now, the way it does in sports, full of stats and probabilities, and how unlikely it will be if I make it. The press conference is full of it, and when it's over, I text Fred this time: *Five to go!* And he writes back a string of exclamation points, and I laugh.

Already, I'll make more money in this tournament than I made all of last year, but it's not about the money: it's about finally feeling like I'm living up to my potential, like the sacrifices I've made—no life, no love, no time off—are worth it.

Matt is fielding calls from sponsors, and I've been invited to three tournaments in the next couple of months that I would've had to qualify for, including the Rogers Cup in Montreal and—oh my God—the US Open.

I'm going to the US Open. Not as a guest, but as a competitor. I sit there shaking in the apartment, happy tears falling, and I almost text Fred again and suggest a walk, but no, I can't do that. I'm on a streak, and when you're on a streak, you have to respect it. I have to follow my exact same trajectory. Same boring meal, same stretching routine, same warmup, same hitting partner on the day off in between matches. I even watch the same movie at night to fall asleep.

It's like a magic spell. Any small deviation can break it.

And that's the last thing I want to do.

* * *

But then, in my next match, something's off. Part of it is the setting. They've put us on center court, and as I stood waiting to go out, I looked up at the extract from Rudyard Kipling's "If," and I felt the edge of panic. It says: *"If you can meet with Triumph and Disaster / And treat those two impostors just the same."* I don't know what it means, but the words *triumph* and *disaster* are not the same to me.

I take that uncertainty onto the court and everything feels off from the warmup. I haven't played this many matches in a row in a long time, and I'm tired. I'm playing against the ranking Canadian player, but she was born in England, and the crowd is more on her side than mine. It's hot out. The kind of sun that feels like it's burning your skin, no matter how much sunscreen you have on. I've never played well in the heat, and today is no exception. I drop the first set and try to fight back in the second. I hold my serve, and she holds hers, both of our grunts getting louder and now it's six–six.

Normally, we'd settle this in a tiebreaker, but not at Wimbledon. We'll keep playing until one of us wins this set. I play a sloppy game, and now she's up seven games to my six, and it's her turn to serve. It hasn't been the strong point of her game, this set, and I'm confident that I can get the break back. But she starts to serve well, and to win the points I thought I would. We're at thirty–thirty, and I nod to let her know I'm ready.

BOOM!

The hardest serve she's hit all day flashes past me. I don't even get my racquet on it. And now it's match point.

I'm going to lose, I think. *Shut up,* I tell myself.

I walk slowly to the other side baseline, trying to get that word, *lose*, out of my head. I turn to face her. She's sweating as much as I am, and she has all the pressure on her now to produce another serve like the last one, to win this match. The crowd is on its feet, and it's so loud in here, the noise is distracting. The chair umpire calls for silence and then up goes the ball and *BOOM!*

Another bomb that almost sails past me, but I get my racquet on it this time. It lands short and I run to cut off her angle as she reaches my drop shot. She hits it right to me, and I volley it back, dropping low, trying to put spin on it. I do, but it spins toward her, and I can see the shot she's going to make before she does—a forehand winner down the line. The ball passes me and there's nothing I can do.

I've lost. She drops to her knees, her hands covering her eyes in joy.

I put a brave face on, receiving a standing ovation from the crowd. I mime throwing my racquet up, and that draws a laugh. Then I sign it and give it to a young girl who looks like me. I collect my things and leave the court.

I step into the tunnel. The two men playing after me are there, waiting to come on court. One pats me on the shoulder and says something nice. I thank him, wish him luck, and he slips his headphones over his ears and goes back into his zone.

I shoulder my tennis bag, adjusting it. When I get past the men, there's another person in the tunnel, and I know, without my eyes adjusting fully to the indoor light, that it's Fred.

He smiles at me, shy, consoling and I finally do what I've been holding back since the cocktail party.

I rush into his waiting arms and let him gather me close, and I cry out my disappointment, but also my relief. That he's here. That it can be our time now.

That it's five years later once again, and somehow we've found each other.

CHAPTER TWENTY-NINE

July 2023

After the lunch in James's restaurant, we're all very full and mostly drunk. I'd be more than happy to go home, but everyone else wants to go to Sag Harbor, and so that's what we do, piling back into the van and then out again when we get to town. We walk without discussion to the beach. It's a beautiful half-moon bay with a flat expanse of sand and the blue ocean curling lazily against it. The wind is down, and there are families paddleboarding and a few small sailboats looking discouraged.

"I've heard a lot about you," James says to me as we walk along the seaside. The rest of the group is up ahead, led by an excited Lucy, who's skipping rocks and turning cartwheels like it was ten years ago. Fred's rolled his pant legs up and opened the collar of his shirt, and he's walking just behind her, laughing at her antics.

"Have you?"

"Men on ships don't have that much to talk about other than the girls they left behind."

I laugh lightly. Wes is also ahead with Sophie, Ann, and Colin. His hands are moving in big sweeping motions, a hallmark of when he's telling one of his grand stories. Wes led a peripatetic life before we got married, never staying in one town long, or with one woman, though we didn't focus on that. He's spent time in every major city: Toronto, Boston, London, Hong Kong. He always said he left right before he got bored, but sometimes I wondered whether he had an instinct for when the bottom was about to fall out.

"Was I the girl Fred left behind?"

"Of course."

I clear my throat. "Ah, well . . . ancient history now."

"Are you sure about that?"

He motions to Fred, who's looking back at us. Our eyes lock for a moment before we both turn away.

"I . . . Yes. It should be, anyway." I kick at a shell in the sand. "What about you? Do you have anyone?"

His face clouds. "I lost her."

"I'm sorry."

"Not the way you think . . . she died. She waited for me, and three months before I was going to be discharged, she was diagnosed with leukemia."

"Oh, James. I'm so sorry."

"It's been hard. When you've met the person you're supposed to spend your life with, and then you can't . . ." He sighs. "Well, you know."

I clear my throat. "I think you have the wrong idea about me and Fred."

"I didn't mean to offend you," James says.

"No, it's fine. It's . . . we have a kind of doomed love. And I don't think that's how it's supposed to be."

"Love isn't always easy."

"I know, but it shouldn't be this hard either."

James smiles. "All poets and novelists would disagree with you."

"Maybe they're just romanticizing heartbreak. Telling us that if there isn't pain, then it isn't a love worth having. But what if *that's* the fiction? What if what we're supposed to be striving for is something that's clear and easy? Look at Colin and Sophie." They're walking arm in arm, Sophie's head resting on Colin' shoulder. "They met as teenagers. And I'm not saying they've never had a fight or growing pains and that they don't drive each other crazy sometimes. But they've had their life together without falling apart. That's a love story to admire. To write about."

"They're lucky."

"They are." I link my arm through his. "But, James, surely there must be someone else for you. I know it must be hard to get over . . ."

"Fanny. Her name was Fanny."

"That's a sweet name."

"She was a sweet girl."

"But you're still here. And I'm sure Fanny would want you to be happy."

"I never got the chance to ask her that," he says.

"Yes, of course—how stupid of me."

"It's all right."

"But poems, literature—they're full of second loves too, aren't they? I'm sure they are."

"I have to meet her, though." He gives me a soft look that implies that maybe I'm that girl, that I could be.

But I'm not. I pat him on the hand. "I'm sure you will. Now that the winery is ready to open to the public, take some time for yourself. Travel a bit. Live."

"You're very good to walk with me."

I point to the group. "I've already heard everything they have to say."

He throws his head back and laughs. "Wes certainly seems to be a good storyteller."

He is, and Ann especially appears enraptured by what he's saying. Even Charlotte, never his biggest fan since their breakup, is smiling at him in the way she used to when she was seventeen. He's a magnetic force that's hard to pull away from.

"He is great at storytelling. It's the rest of life that he has a bit of trouble with."

"Olivia!" Lucy calls to me, running up. Her face is red from the wind, and the salt air is making her hair a little wild. "Run with me."

"What?"

"Remember how we used to do it?" She points up ahead to the breakwater, a huge pile of old rocks and pilings that gentles the sea. A memory pops out of the ether—Sophie, Lucy, Ash, and me running through the sand and then up onto similar rocks nearer to home. We'd leap from them, one by one, with Lucy's nanny yelling after us, terrified that we'd slip and fall.

"Do you remember?"

"I do, but . . . it was dangerous then and still dangerous now."

"Who cares? It'll be freeing. Come on—let's do it."

She tugs on my hand, and I feel the pull of it. Why not run along the sand with her? I haven't done anything fun since I've been home, and I've never felt free.

I kick off my shoes and we trot up to Sophie. "Come with us," I say.

"What? No."

"Come on, Sophie. I'll race you."

Sophie's face changes in an instant. She was always the fastest, and though I doubt she's sprinted in years, she has a deep competitive streak where footraces are concerned.

She hands her bag to Colin and kicks off her sandals. "Where are we going to?"

"The breakwater."

"Do you think that's—" But Fred's objection is buried in Lucy's command.

"Three, two, one—go!"

We take off down the beach, the sand flying up beneath our heels. The shore's a bit rocky, and the spray from the sea is wetting the bottom of my pants, slowing me down. Sophie sprints ahead, but Lucy is on fire today, and she starts to catch up with her, inch by inch. I hear shouts in the wind, trash-talking. The breakwater approaches, thirty seconds away, and I dig in for one last push. These last weeks of tennis have made a difference in my fitness but also worn me down. My lungs are screaming at me to stop, but I'm competitive too.

I pull close to Sophie and Lucy, who are battling to an imaginary finish line. Sophie raises her hands in victory as Lucy sprints past her to the breakwater.

I stop.

"Where's she going?" Sophie pants.

"Not sure."

We watch her, our hands on our knees, breathing in and out. She gets to the first rock and scrambles up, then turns, her hands above her head.

"I feel like I'm having a heart attack," Sophie says.

"Seriously."

"That doesn't look safe."

"Agreed."

Lucy starts to hop from rock to rock, a natural parkour course, which seemed like nothing as a child, but now is terrifying me like when I'm watching someone stand too close to the edge of a cliff.

"She should get down from there," Fred says behind me.

"Not sure we can stop her."

Fred steps ahead of us. "Lucy! Come on down!"

She turns, almost pirouettes, and waves to him. "Come catch me," she yells over the crashing waves.

Fred takes a step toward her, then starts to trot, getting closer and closer till he's waded into the water and is standing below her. He's got his arms up to catch her, but as she bends to take off, she slips the wrong way, her body coming down sideways on the rock. I can hear the sick crunch of her head against it from here as Sophie's scream pierces the day.

I run toward them as Fred scrambles up onto the rock and pulls her up into his lap. Her eyes open slowly, then close again. She's bleeding from a head wound that looks nasty.

"Call 911!"

I reach into my pocket for my phone and pull it out. I don't have a signal. It's been patchy all day. "There's a lifeguard just down the beach—I'll go get him."

Fred nods, his face pale. He's holding her so tenderly it makes me want to weep, but I turn on my heel and sprint as fast as I can past our group, all looking stunned. Past the pain in my legs and lungs and heart, heading for the white structure that houses the lifeguards, hoping that I don't get there too late.

* * *

Hours later, in the hospital, we breathe a sigh of relief when the doctor tells us that Lucy is going to be okay. She has a concussion and will need to take it easy for several weeks, but there shouldn't be any lasting damage except for a small scar near her hairline.

It's just me, Fred, and James at the hospital. Sophie and Colin took the van home because they couldn't leave the kids overnight, and

Charlotte and Ann took the opportunity to escape. At the last minute, Wes decided to go with them. He has some important calls in the morning, and he needs his laptop. He felt bad about leaving, but I dismissed his concern. He barely knows Lucy, and he shouldn't blow an important meeting because of her.

I think he was more worried about leaving me with Fred, but he didn't have to be. Fred was too busy beating himself up over what had happened to Lucy, as if she were his child and it was his fault she'd acted impulsively. I told him to cut it out, and we had a short, bitter argument. Fred stalked off, saying he was going to get some coffee, as I sank back into my chair next to James.

"Things are clearly totally over between you two," James says dryly.

"Oh, hush."

"I've got a car waiting to take us all back to the vineyard."

"That's nice of you."

"Lucy shouldn't drive too long to get to a bed."

"No, you're right."

"It isn't your fault, Olivia."

"I know."

"Why so glum, then? She's going to be okay."

"Just a long day."

I can tell he doesn't believe me. And he's right. I am feeling glum. Down, like a deflated balloon. I'm not sure what it is, exactly. Only the way Fred had looked at Lucy when he had her in his lap earlier on the beach—that wasn't the casual thing I'd assumed it to be between them. There was real pain there, the pain of potential loss, and I didn't like how that felt.

Did that mean I wasn't over Fred, or just that I didn't want him to be with someone else?

Was there a difference?

It didn't matter. What I'd said to James on the beach earlier was true. Fred and I didn't belong together. What more proof do I need than the fact that we couldn't make it despite numerous chances?

Only a hopeless romantic would think that there was still a place for us after everything we'd been through.

And I've never been that.

CHAPTER THIRTY

June 2013

Back at my apartment after I leave the Wimbledon grounds, following my defeat, I prepare carefully for my dinner with Fred.

We'd made plans to meet at six, to give me time to shower and change and stretch and get in the right mind frame for whatever is about to happen.

I can't believe it. It feels like I'm caught in a fairy tale, one where the fairy godmother grants one wish, but a different one comes true. Those ten minutes in the hallway changed everything. Fred holding me, kissing my neck, telling me that this is what he wanted, this is what he planned for. In the moment, it felt wonderful, but now I have some questions.

But first, I reach into my jewelry box and pull out his bracelet. It's the one thing I always travel with, thinking, maybe, that I'll find something to add to it, to make it mine instead of ours. I've never managed to, though, so all I have on it are the charms Fred has given me: the tennis bracelet, the one from London, and our engagement ring. I touch the small stone, then catch myself in the mirror. My heart is skipping around, and I have trouble fastening the clasp. I manage it, then run a brush through my hair.

"You're going out?" Matt says when I leave the bathroom.

"Yes."

"With Fred."

"Yes, Dad."

He frowns. "I thought you weren't talking."

"We weren't."

"And now?"

"I'm going to drown my sorrows in a million drinks and a nice man."

"Not so nice."

"Matt." I put my arms around his neck. "You don't mean that."

"What about your training?"

"I can take one day off. One day to have something for me."

"Yes, all right."

"I wasn't asking." I drop my arms and kiss him on the cheek.

"Just . . . be careful, okay?"

"Are we having the talk? Because that ship sailed long ago."

"That's not what I meant. I just meant . . . be careful of your heart."

"I will be."

But I'm not being careful. And for once that's okay. I've spent too long living inside the lines, on a tennis court, in my life, in my family. I want to have *fun* goddammit. I want to live. And if that means making a mistake again, with Fred, so be it.

The doorbell rings, and I grab a light sweater and trip down the stairs. Fred's standing outside, next to a small town car with a driver. He's wearing a light summer suit with a white linen shirt. And when he smiles, he's so handsome I could cry.

"This is fancy," I say, touching the lapel.

"Only the best for you."

"Ha!"

He kisses me, his lips both new and familiar. He smells great, a light spicy aftershave I don't recognize, and that's okay too. If he smelled exactly like the Fred I remembered, like right after a swim on the beach, it would be too much. This Fred is recognizable enough that I feel comfortable with him and new enough that it feels safe.

"You look great," he says. "I've always liked you in white."

The dress I'm wearing is a variation of twenty dresses I've owned in my lifetime, some of which he's seen me in and some not. This one has a light pink overlay of vines and a scoop neck with a slight flare to the skirt. I feel pretty and feminine, two things I don't always feel in my sporty life. "Thank you."

He opens the door for me, and we slip inside the car. He gives the driver an address and reaches for my hand. He's sitting on my left, and his fingers reach up till they find the bracelet. He leans in closer to me and says, "I'm glad you wore this."

"Don't read too much into it."

"Okay."

I turn to him. His eyes are warm, inviting. "What did you mean earlier when you said you hoped for this?"

"I wondered if you were going to ask me that."

"Well?"

"Don't be mad."

"That's not a great beginning."

"But a happy ending, I promise."

I raise my finger to his lips. "Don't say that. Too risky."

"Right. Okay, well, I read that profile of you in *Tennis Magazine*."

"The one in January?"

"That's right. Where you said this was going to be your year and that your goal was to make it to Wimbledon qualifying and beyond."

"You read that?"

"I read everything about you, Olivia."

I want to melt into my seat. My cheeks are flaming. "I . . . I assumed no one read that."

"Well, I did. And then I did some research and talked to Mr. de Keurig."

"What does that mean?"

"I wanted you to achieve your goals. So, I suggested that the company sponsor the event in Miami. With a sponsorship of that size, we were allowed to suggest a couple of wild cards."

"A couple?"

"One."

"That's how I got invited to Miami?"

"Yes."

I'd wondered about it at the time. I'd applied, but my ranking wasn't quite where it should have been to get in. But then I did, and I did well, and that led to the next tournament and the next and eventually to Wimbledon. "What if I hadn't done well there?"

He clears his throat. "There was going to be a second sponsorship. But you made it to the semis so that wasn't necessary."

"Wow."

"Are you mad?"

"No, I . . . Why do you have so much sway over your boss? That must've been a lot of money he spent."

"The sponsorships made business sense. Miami is a shipping port."

"That can't be it, though. Did you hide a dead body for him or something?"

"No, I . . . his son was under my command. Between us, he was a fuck-up, but he turned his life around for a while when he worked for me. He died a few years ago, and Mr. de Keurig . . . he's kind of adopted me in his place."

"Oh, Fred."

"What?"

"You used up that for me? Why?"

"Come on, Olivia. You know." He reaches for my hand and brings it to his lips. "It's five years later. And I kept waiting for you to come back into my life, for our lives to line up on our own. But they never have. You're traveling all over the world, and even then, I was almost at one of your tournaments more times than I can count, but then something would always interfere. I was tired of leaving it in fate's hands."

"There were still so many things that could've gone wrong. If I didn't win, for one."

"But you did. You're playing great."

"And you got me invited to that event here."

"The party, yes. The qualifier, no. You earned that on your own."

I lean back, processing. Outside, London's old white buildings flash by. We've crossed over to the south bank. "Where are we going?"

"A little place I discovered a few years ago. You'll love it." The car stops. "In fact, we're here."

Fred hops out and comes around to open the door for me. He reaches out his hand, and I take it, though I'm not quite sure how I'm feeling about what he's just said.

He ushers us into the restaurant, and the hostess smiles at him and tells us our table is right this way. He comes here a lot, I can tell, and the hostess obviously likes him.

She leads us through the restaurant—vibrant Portuguese plates on the wall and wonderful smells of saffron in the air—and out to a small courtyard where there's one table with lights strung above it and vines growing all over the walls.

"It's beautiful," I say.

"I think so."

Fred says something to the hostess, and she smiles and leaves us. He holds out my chair for me, and I sit down.

"How did you find this place?"

"I was over here for business one night, and hungry, and I walked around a bit, and then I smelled something wonderful, and I walked in. I've been coming back ever since. Best Portuguese cooking that I've had outside of Portugal. You love paella, yes?"

"You remember that?"

"Of course. The seafood rice here will rival it, I promise." He opens his napkin and puts it on his lap. "I remember the first time I had it in Portugal, wishing you were there to try it."

"I've never been to Portugal."

"We'll have to remedy that."

"Sure," I say, but I'm feeling noncommittal. It feels too dangerous to be otherwise.

A waitress appears with a bottle of champagne and some menus.

"Is this okay?" Fred asks.

"Yes, looks lovely."

The waitress uncorks the bottle and explains the menu. Fred asks if they can bring us a selection of dishes, including the seafood rice. She nods encouragingly, pours us each a glass of wine, and then leaves.

Fred holds up his glass to me.

I raise mine. "What should we toast to?"

"Reunions?"

We clink glasses and I take a long drink. The wine is perfect, the setting too.

So, what's wrong with me?

"What's wrong, Olivia?"

"I was just asking myself that same thing."

"It's too much," Fred says. "I did too much."

"You could've called me."

He sips his wine, then puts the glass down. "Could I, though? I thought about it. A million times. Texting you. All of it. But each time I almost did I thought—what if she doesn't answer? What if she tells me to fuck off? The what-ifs always stopped me."

"I get it."

"Same for you?"

"Yes. I've thought about you often. Not that I wanted to, if I'm being honest. I was a . . . mess the last time. It took me a long time to recover."

"Me too."

Our eyes meet and hold. He has a look in his eyes that I don't recognize until I do. Regret.

"We really screwed that one up," I say.

"It was my fault. Being so stubborn. Giving you this." He reaches for the engagement charm. "I don't know why I was so stuck on being married. Everything was great the way it was. We could've made long distance work."

"We were so young. Maybe we would've held each other back. Not achieved all this."

"I've thought about that. It doesn't make up for being away from you, but I do have a good life."

I look around. "Seems like it."

"These are just things. I threw myself into school and then work. I was in a hurry to get it all finished. To arrive wherever I was going. And I got what I wanted, I thought. But something's always been missing. When I was really honest with myself, I knew what it was. You."

"Why me, though? The girl you haven't been able to make it work with?"

"I've asked myself that."

"And?"

"There's something about you. Us. I don't know how to explain it: I've tried with other people, but nobody fits like we do, you know?"

He says this with hope, wanting me to agree, and I do. I do agree that no one's felt like him and me, so no one's felt like us. That something's been missing from my life. And of course, it was him.

But he scares me too.

"I feel that way also, but Fred . . ."

"Yes?"

"We have to . . . I have to be cautious. I . . . I don't know how this is going to work, if it's going to work. And I need you to be okay with that."

"Take it down a notch, you're saying?"

"Maybe two or three."

"I can do that."

"Can you?"

"Of course. I can even pretend we're strangers on a first date."

"Ha!"

"I can. Watch me." He reaches for his glass. "So, tennis? That something you're serious about?"

My mouth twitches. "Little bit."

"And you live in hotels?"

"I have a small apartment in New York. But yes, mostly."

"Interesting, interesting. And what's that like? Do you like hotels?"

I start to laugh. "You should have a talk show."

"No one's said *that* to me before."

"You'd be very good at it. Like everything."

"I'm not good at *everything*." He's hinting at something, and it's then that I decide.

If we're going to get through this evening, we need to stop going over the past. Fred's joke about us acting like strangers was the right one.

"How about this," I say, raising my glass. "How about we have more of this champagne, and we stop talking in meaningful ways alluding to other things and we just have fun?"

"Fun?"

"Yeah, fun. Ever heard of it?"

"Maybe once or twice."

"So, what do you say?" I tilt my glass toward his. "Deal?"

"Deal."

*   *   *

Our deal works because we get very, very drunk. There's another bottle of champagne and then some Portuguese drink I never catch the name of, and plate after plate of food I shouldn't be eating, but I do not give a fuck.

I'm happy.

Happy without an undertow for once, and all it took was a million drinks and the best meal of my life to get there.

We talk and laugh, and laugh and talk. The restaurant empties out, and now the staff wants to go home, so we need to leave too.

We head out into the night and go for a stroll along the Thames. I'm amazed that I'm still awake, still coherent, enough not to freak out when Fred takes my hand and asks if he should call the car. I say yes, and then the night starts to take on an air of inevitability.

He doesn't let go of my hand in the car, just starts tracing circles on the flesh near my wrist. My whole body responds, a pulse beating between my legs. I turn my head toward him and I don't remember making a conscious decision to kiss him—I just do. He responds, our tongues meeting, his hands in my hair as we arch toward each other, feeling constrained by our clothes and the driver.

In a moment, we're at his apartment, and he leads me in, bashful, past the doorman, so British and polite he acts like we've met before, and then the elevator, where we resume our kiss, not able to keep away from each other, and then in his apartment with large, modern windows overlooking the Thames.

We strip items of clothing off each other, one by one, slowly but deliberately, stopping to taste each other, to enjoy this, not rushing. His thumbs repeat their circles on my breasts, then in between my legs, and then I am up in his arms, my chest to his bare chest and he's carrying me to the bedroom.

Everything is new and old at the same time. Our bodies remembering, but we've both learned a thing or two. I push away what this implies, that we've been with others since the last time this happened, and give into the sensation of us. It's never been like this, not with him, not with anyone, and I come so hard against his hand it almost hurts.

Then he's tasting me, telling me what he wants us to do together, and I nod as he reaches into a drawer and pulls out a condom. And then he's inside me, and I press into him as he slides in and out in a slow rhythm that brings me to the brink again.

Slow, then hard and deep, pulling in and out until we both release together, our cries mingling, our bodies slick with sweat.

He gathers me into his arms, and I feel totally at peace. No regrets, no questions, only the sure and comfortable feeling of being with Fred, the way we were always meant to be.

"I love you," he says into my ear as I start to drift away.

I love you too, I say, but maybe only in my dreams.

CHAPTER THIRTY-ONE

July 2023

By the time Lucy gets released from the hospital, James has everything arranged.

There's a car to take us back to his place, and an overnight nurse. Rooms have been prepared for each of us, and James apologizes when he tells me that I've been put in the honeymoon suite. Finalizing the rooms for guests is the last step to getting the winery ready, but he prioritized this room, and the groom and bride suites, for an event that's taking place in a couple of weeks.

Fred is in the groom's room, and Lucy is in the bride's, and when I take off my clothes and step into the shower to wash off the smell of the hospital, I can't help feeling that that's the way things might turn out. Fred was very gentle with Lucy when she was discharged, and so apologetic too, helping her into the car, into the house, up to her room.

I try not to let it bother me, but I can't lie to myself.

I'm jealous.

When I'm done with the shower, I find a pair of cotton pajamas waiting for me. "Brian & Susan" they say in embroidery across the breast, supplied, I assume, for the upcoming nuptials. They fit, and are soft and comfortable. I pull my hair back with a hair tie I find in my purse, then think about going in search of food. That fabulous lunch a million hours ago has worn off.

But first I send two messages, one to Colin to let him know Lucy is all settled in, and another to Wes, to let him know I'm staying the night. He answers me quickly, asking to go to dinner next week. He's secured a reservation at this Greek place he's been wanting to try all summer. I say yes because it's so much easier than saying no. But he was good today, funny and kind, all the best of him, and I made a promise to him—for better or for worse—that I meant when I made it. It feels old-fashioned to get too specific about it, but I feel like I owe him one more chance. I owe us. And maybe all of this—coming home, packing away the past—that can help us too. Because it lingered between us, whether I wanted to admit it or not.

I'm about to leave my room when I remember one last text—to let Matt know I'm not going to make it tomorrow morning. Cindy will be disappointed maybe, but she'll live. Matt answers me too, despite the hour, saying he hopes Lucy is well.

When I find it, the kitchen is large and set up for catering, with massive built-in fridges and freezers and more counter space than anyone could need. One of the fridge doors is open, Fred half inside it, and then he steps back, his arms full of things, too much for one person to carry.

"Let me help you," I say.

I've startled him, and he almost drops the top container he's holding, but I swoop in and catch it before it falls completely. "Got it."

"Thanks." He smiles at me with tired eyes, then walks the containers to the counter.

"What you got there?"

"I thought I'd make an everything omelet," he says. He's wearing the matching pajamas to mine, the groom's pajamas.

"That sounds great. Lucy okay?"

"She's sleeping. The nurse—and I'm quoting directly here—said that my services were no longer required."

"She needs some sleep."

"She does."

"So stupid." He starts to arrange the containers he's pulled from the fridge in a line. They're chef's prep containers, the leftovers of what was used to make lunch. There are onions and shallots, garlic and peppers, lobster and cheese, and a large package of eggs.

"People make mistakes."

"I meant me. I should've caught her."

"You can make mistakes too. She shouldn't have been jumping from there. It was dangerous."

"Yeah . . . Where do you think the pans might be hiding?"

We open cupboards until I find them. Along the way I find a white wine fridge and glasses too. "Do you think James will mind? I could use a drink."

"I'm sure he won't."

"Where is he?"

"He went to bed. He was tired. It was a lot of activity for him today."

So we're alone. If I weren't starving, I might find an excuse to get out of here, but wasn't I supposed to be honest with myself? It's not only the promise of food keeping me in place.

I open the wine, pour each of us a glass, then sit at one of the counters while Fred starts peeling tops off containers. Then he fiddles with the stove, getting it going after a minute.

"This wine is good," I say.

"This will be good too."

His back is to me, but I can read the expression in his shoulders. He's tired, stressed, annoyed.

"Not how this day was supposed to turn out, huh?"

He chuckles. "No."

"I hope there's no lasting damage."

"Lucy's young—she'll bounce back."

Not so young, I think. She's thirty, and I wasn't referencing Lucy, exactly. But all of our conversations are like this. We never say what we really want to, and that makes me tired.

"Why did you come here, Fred?"

"James invited me."

"You know what I mean."

His shoulders sag as he adds ingredients to the pan. "I'm not sure this is the time to get into all of that."

"What should we talk about, then?"

"I have no idea."

I sigh. "Tell me about James. Tell me about his saving your life."

He picks up a spatula as the pan sizzles, the smell of cooking onions already making me ravenous. "We were in a bad swell, and I was topside when I shouldn't have been. James came looking for me, saw me get swept off. He acted quickly, getting the rescue rope, but then it got tangled in his leg. Each time I was pulling it, it was squeezing him, you see?"

He reaches above him for plates, like he knew they were there all along, and then divides the omelet in two, slipping half onto each plate. He turns around and puts one in front of me. There's a container of cutlery in the middle of the island, and I reach for a fork.

"You didn't know what you were doing."

"I didn't. He pulled me out, but his leg was ruined. They wanted to amputate, but he insisted they keep it. He rehabbed it for years, but it hasn't gotten much better."

I dig into the omelet. It's as good as the lunch. Better. "This is fantastic."

He takes a bite, then another one, two, three. "I needed this."

"I was hungry too."

He takes another bite. "Anyway, then his fiancée got sick while he was in rehab oversees in Germany, and he didn't make it back in time. So, he lost everything there for a while."

"That's a lot."

"It is."

"Did you help him with this place? Give him the money?"

"What makes you think that?"

I look down at my plate as I cut the omelet into smaller pieces, then eat them quickly. "It's something you'd do, I think."

"That might be the nicest thing you've ever said to me."

"Really?"

His tone softens. "Top five for sure."

We stare at each other for a beat too long, and a warning bell goes off in my head. I clear my throat and spear another piece of the omelet. "The investment?"

"I did invest in it, yes. I wanted him to be able to start over. And he was always talking about having a winery when we were serving together. It was their dream. His and Franny's."

"A nice dream."

"It was. It is."

Fred finishes his omelet. "Would you think me a complete pig if I made another one of these?"

"I was just working up the courage to ask you to do it."

"Ha."

I hold out my plate. "Please sir, can I have some more?"

"That's a terrible accent."

"Does that mean I don't get the eggs?"

"It does not."

"Good."

We grin at each other, and it feels weird, but familiar.

Sometimes I forget, because of all our tragedy, how well we got along between our problems. If we could only have a stretch of time between catastrophes, maybe we could've made this work. But we never got that, and sometimes you have to listen to the universe when it's telling you something isn't meant to be, no matter how much it might feel like it is.

"Are you making it or . . ."

"What? Oh yes. Coming right up." He whisks my plate away and takes it back to the stove.

The second omelet is just as good as the first—better even, maybe—and I devour it, along with a second glass of wine.

When we're done, I help Fred wash up and put everything away. And now it's late, almost eleven, but I'm awake. I resign myself to a long wind-down to sleep. But Fred has other ideas.

"I'm not tired," he says. "Though I should be."

"Me neither."

"Why don't we take this to the beach?" he says, holding up the half bottle of wine. "It's a nice night."

"Okay," I say, feeling nervous.

"Don't worry," Fred says.

"About?"

"My intentions are pure."

I laugh because he's read my mind, and though I'm not sure I believe him, I cast my doubts aside. "All right, then. Let's go."

* * *

We find an exit into the backyard, then scramble over the dunes to the beach. I can't imagine what Fred and James must've paid for this property—it's four times the size of my father's place.

"Can I ask you something?" I say.

"Sure."

"How could you afford this? With this and my father's . . ."

Fred swings the wine bottle between his fingers. "Remember the shipping company I was working for? De Keurig?"

"Yes."

"Tomas died and left it to me."

"What? The whole company?"

"He said I was like his son and he had no one else. I told him not to—to leave it to charity—but he insisted."

"What did your mom think about that?"

"She was happy for me. My aunt too. They loved Tomas. We all did. And it's enabled me to help them out. And James too."

"And my house?"

He glances at me. "I thought we weren't going to talk about that tonight?"

I want to bat that suggestion away, but there's something in his tone that tells me not to push. "All right."

He walks on ahead, slipping up over the dunes and then back down again, waiting to help me to the beach. There's a good grassy spot on the edge of it, where we can use the dune for a seat back. Fred plops down, crossing his legs, and I sit next to him. The breeze is high, whipping my ponytail around, racing black clouds against the moon. The air is salty, almost fishy, but it's not unpleasant.

He pours me a glass of wine and hands it to me. "Thank you."

"Welcome."

I lean back and tuck my knees up. The moon's reflecting off the choppy water, but the breeze is warm, and I'm not cold. "It's beautiful here."

"It is."

I pull the loose top of my pajamas over my knees. "Who do you think they are?"

"Who?"

"Brenda and Jack. Or whoever's getting married. The names on our pajamas."

"No idea."

"First wedding, I'd imagine."

Fred puts the empty wine bottle down into the sand. "Why do you say that?"

"No one goes to this much trouble for a second wedding."

"I wouldn't know."

"Never came close?"

"Once or twice."

Something in his tone makes me take a deep drink of my wine. I know about the once. Was there truly a twice?

"What about you?" Fred asks.

"Just the once so far."

"You going to work it out?"

"I don't know." I sigh. "This is a bit weird, talking about this with you."

"I get it."

"Because we're not friends."

"No?"

"I . . . I don't think so."

"That's too bad."

I'm not sure what he's saying, but it is. It is too bad.

"Do you think they're going to make it?"

His eyes are dark. I can't read them. "Who?"

"Branda and Jack. The pajama people."

"Hard to tell. On a scale of one to ten, how pissed do you think she's going to be when she learns that her pajamas have gone missing?"

I laugh. "Maybe he's the one into monogrammed clothes?"

"Maybe."

"You don't think so?"

"I can't see Jack being into that."

"Imaginary Jack, you mean. You don't know real Jack."

"Imaginary Jack," he agrees. "Tall, handsome, he's won the hand of Brenda, also tall, also handsome."

"And rich, very rich."

"Naturally."

"Maybe she's marrying him for his money." I tap him on the shoulder. "You should watch out for that. All these houses you're buying for other people . . . You're going to be prey."

"You think?"

"Definitely."

He holds his wineglass in his hands. "Maybe I should do that."

"What?"

"Let someone marry me for money."

I almost choke on my wine. "Excuse me?"

"It would be easier. Everything would be clear and up front. Like a business transaction."

"You can't be serious."

"Maybe I am."

"What about Lucy?"

He finishes his wine. "I should've brought another bottle."

"You're avoiding."

"Am I?"

"Wow, you must really like her." I say this with a catch in my throat that I hope he doesn't hear.

"She's a great girl."

"Beautiful, impulsive, fun."

"Yes."

"Do I need to keep selling?"

"Are you trying to?" He looks at me now, his face brightened by the moonlight. He's staring at me intensely, half amused, half something else.

"I'm sure Lucy doesn't need any help getting someone to fall in love with her."

"No."

"And you shouldn't marry for money," I say. "You should marry for love."

"That's what I always thought."

"Don't sell yourself short."

"Get the full price?"

"I just meant . . . you shouldn't settle. Wait until you feel . . . wait until it feels like you can't stand your life without that person in it."

Our eyes lock and the world slows down. That's what it felt like between us whenever we could manage to be together.

"I only feel that way in the summer," Fred says.

"Summer after summer . . ."

"What's that?"

"Something Ash said about how we tortured each other summer after summer."

"That's not all we did . . ." He shifts his body weight, and now he's tipping closer to me. "Olivia . . ."

I raise my finger to his lips, surprised somehow at the shock of touching his skin, his mouth, though I shouldn't be. It's always like this between us. The one thing that was never in doubt.

But it reminds me too. Of everything that's broken. How we can't seem to make it work. And I don't want to think about that right now. I just want to enjoy this night and this moon and the gentle rock of the ocean at our feet.

"No bad intentions," I say. "Remember?"

He smiles against my finger, and it's almost like a kiss, then leans away. "I remember."

"We should go back to the house."

"In a minute."

"Okay."

He scoots closer to me so our sides our touching. It feels dangerous, but my eyelids are heavy, the sound of the waves lulling me under.

I let my head fall onto his shoulder, blocking out who I'm leaning on.

"Olivia," he says, but he's far away.

"Shh."

I let my head fall further, and then I feel his arm around me, supporting me, and then I feel nothing at all.

CHAPTER THIRTY-TWO

June 2013

I don't know why I count out my time with Fred in days. Maybe it's because we always end up having so few of them.

I try not to think of that as I wake up hours later, naked in Fred's bed, in his London apartment. I have a moment of disorientation when I can't remember where I am, and then it all comes rushing back. His hands, mine. The way our bodies fit together the way they always have. The way we savored and devoured each other and finally fell asleep.

I feel happy, languid, and terrible, a hangover forming from the too many drinks that led us here.

When I check my phone, there's a message from Matt, asking if I'm okay. I text him back and tell him I'm taking the day off; I'll be in touch later. I don't wait for his reply because I only want this morning to be good, not tainted by anyone's regrets, including my own.

My phone is sitting on top of a folded note. There's a gleaming glass of water next to it and two painkillers in a dish. The note says, *"Stepped out for supplies. Fred."*

I pick up the pills, swallowing them down with the cool water. I feel better already, but unsure of whether I should get up. I look around the room for my clothes, but they're missing. Instead, there's a robe slung over a chenille chair, like Fred's left crumbs for me to follow.

I go to the bathroom and find soap, shampoo, and an enormous shower. I use all of them, luxuriating in the warm water, the first "American" shower I've had since I've been in the UK.

When I'm done, I wrap myself in the robe and use the toothbrush and toothpaste left for me. I try not to think what it means that he has all of this available in his apartment, that this might be a routine and means nothing special. But then the words he said last night come back.

I love you, he said.

And I said it back. At least, I think I did.

I run my fingers through my hair, wiping a streak of steam off the mirror. My face is red from the hot water, from too many matches in the sun, from the blush I have remembering last night.

What am I doing here?

I have no idea, but since it's the first time I have no idea what I'm doing in years, I decide to go with it. What's the worst that could happen? Fred and I don't survive this. I know what that is. I've lived through that more than once. So fine. It's fine. All of this is good and fine.

The smell of freshly roasted coffee hits me, and I follow it to the kitchen. Fred's there, in jeans and an old T-shirt, and here he is, teenage Fred—Fred, the way he looked when we first met ten years ago.

He turns to me and smiles. "Do you like omelets?"

"Depends."

"On what?"

"Who's cooking them."

"You're in luck then."

"Oh?"

"You'll see."

He pats a chair under the counter and pulls it out for me. I take a seat, and he gives me a cup of coffee. It's delicious, a level of bean I don't have access to in my normal life, and that's true of this entire place. It's large, even by American standards. I can't imagine what it costs here in London.

I pour cream into my coffee, that fresh full cream of England, and sip on it slowly, savoring it.

"You're doing well," I say to Fred.

He's at the stove, adding ingredients to a pan, and it's already smelling delicious. "Thank you."

"I mean this place . . . it's amazing."

"Corporate housing."

"You're shitting me."

He turns and grins. "I know, right?"

I watch him cook for a few minutes while he fills me in. How the owner of the company he works for has taken him under his wing, which he told me already. How he has a bunch of real estate and he let Fred have this place for nothing. The plans Mr. de Keurig has for him in the company. And then Fred puts the best-smelling eggs I've ever had in front of me. They're full of vegetables and cheese and smoked salmon, and it's a combination I would've thought was disgusting, but it's delicious.

"Amazing," I say. "This is amazing."

"Thank you." He digs into his eggs. "What do you want to do today?"

"I should hit for a while."

"Or . . ."

"Yes?"

He smiles. "Have you been to Bath?"

"Like the town?"

"Definitely the town."

"No, never."

"Will you go with me?"

I look at my plate. "I'd have to ask Matt."

"Ask Matt?"

"I mean *tell*. I have a big tournament coming up in a couple of weeks."

"I heard. But one day? Will it make a difference?"

"It could. Why Bath?"

"Because I think you'd like it."

I take another few bites, considering. A day. A whole day with nothing but Fred in it. That sounds great. "Didn't Jane Austen hate Bath?"

"Did she?"

"*'All the white glare of Bath'* . . . that's from something."

He points his fork at me. "I'm going to say something crazy, I know, but maybe she was wrong?"

"Maybe. Hmm. I think her mother died while she was in school there? Or wait, no, that's one of the characters in *Persuasion* . . ."

"So, is that a yes on Bath or . . .?"

"Yes."

"Good."

*   *   *

So we go to Bath, and it's not what I'm expecting. For some reason, based on movies and books, I had the impression that Bath was flat. But instead, it's built into a mountain, the golden Bath stone that most of the buildings are made of gleaming against the green hills.

It's not like any place I've been in England, and I find it over-whelming in a good way. We visit the Roman baths and walk along the River Avon and climb the hilly streets, passing names I've only ever read about. I feel like a kid in literary Disneyland, and Fred laughs at me and holds my hand, and we swing our arms between us, feeling young and free.

When we get hungry, we go for tea at the Pump Room—a beautiful neoclassical room with a domed ceiling with its famous spa water fountain. I get the pink champagne tea, and Fred is more reasonable, with a beef sandwich.

"You sure you can eat all of that?" Fred asks, eyeing the three tiers of sandwiches and scones and cream and desserts.

"I haven't been allowed to eat this much in years."

"Allowed?"

"I follow a strict diet. I mean, super strict. These last two days . . . I'm going to pay for it when I come back down to earth tomorrow."

Fred's mouth twists. "Is tomorrow the day you come back down to earth?"

"Probably." I lift a cream-filled cake off the top tier. "But for now, I'm going to enjoy every minute of this." I shove it in my mouth, uncouth and uncaring, and oh my god, it's delicious, so rich and sweet my teeth hurt.

"Aren't you supposed to start with the sandwiches?"

"Who says?" I lift my glass of champagne and chase the dessert down. It's delicious too, and I could live like this forever.

"Who's imposing these terrible diets on you?"

"Matt. Me."

"Is it worth it?"

I take one of the sandwiches off the tier. "Honestly?"

"Of course."

"Before this, I'm not sure I'd say it was. Before this year, I mean."

"And now?"

"I made it into the third round at Wimbledon. I paid for my whole year with those matches."

"That's great."

"I don't know how much longer I can keep it up, though."

Fred fiddles with his teacup. "You'd give it up?"

"I have to at some point."

"Do you still love it?"

"I do. Most days, anyway."

I drink some more champagne and eat the sandwich. It's smoked salmon, and like everything, it's incredible. It's funny, but I don't usually think in superlatives. Not in my ordinary life. But here, with Fred, that's always how things seem to be. Strewn with exclamation marks.

"What about you?" I ask. "Do you love what you're doing?"

"I do, yeah."

"That's good."

"What will you do when you finish tennis?"

"Coach maybe."

"And continue traveling all over the world?"

I shrug. "I haven't given it much thought. It might be nice to put down some roots somewhere."

"Do you like London?"

I reach across the table and put my hand on his. "Why do I feel like I'm in a job interview?"

"I'm sorry."

"It's okay."

He fiddles with his spoon. "It's a bad habit I'm trying to get myself out of."

"What's that?"

"Leaping ahead. Trying to see all the possibilities."

Some of the fizz goes out of me. "Of us?"

"Yes."

"Don't do that," I say as gently as I can.

Fred looks pained. "Why?"

"I feel like . . . can we just take this one day at a time? We haven't had much success, you and I, when we try to plan the future too quickly."

"You're right."

"I'm sorry."

"No, no." He picks up my hand and kisses it. "You are perfectly right. We should be cautious."

"Well, I meant more . . . not cautious exactly, but maybe more carefree?"

"Are we not?"

"We got engaged when I was twenty-one, so . . ."

"Is that not what people do?"

"Are you teasing me?"

"Maybe. Maybe I am."

I grip his hand tightly. "I want this to work, Fred, I do, but let's not put that pressure on us, okay? Not yet. Let's . . . I don't know, let's be different this time."

"I liked the way we were."

"I know—me too. But Fred . . . it's been a day."

He smiles. "You're right. It always feels longer with you, you know?"

My heart swells. "I do. I do know."

"Once I counted."

"What?"

"The days we were together. Because it felt like years, but it wasn't that long."

And now I want to cry because I've done that too. And it wasn't enough. It was far too few. "I don't think it's the number of days that are important."

"No?"

"No. I think—" Fred's phone rings in his pocket. "Do you need to get that?"

"No. You were saying?"

"I was saying that I think it's the weight of the days, not the number. But . . . I do want more days. I want a lot of days."

"Good." Fred's phone stops, then starts again.

"You should get that."

"Yes." He stands as he pulls his phone from his pocket. "Give me a minute."

He walks away, and I can't tell what kind of call he's having. A bit testy, based on his body language, because despite having spent very few days together, I do know that about Fred—what the set of his shoulders mean, the way he runs his hand through his hair when he's frustrated or stalling for time.

He ends the call and comes back to the table.

"Everything okay?"

"Yes."

"Who was it?"

"Oh . . . just someone from work."

"Are you playing hooky?"

"What's that?"

"Forget it."

"No," he puts his phone away. "Sorry, I was distracted for a minute. The answer to your question is yes, I am. Which is very unlike me. But that's good, right? If we're going to be different?"

"It is."

"What do you want to do after tea?"

"Shall we go and find Laura Place?"

"Sounds like a plan." Fred flags down a waiter and asks for a gin and tonic. "If today is our day to go wild, let's do it."

I raise my glass. "To going wild."

* * *

And we do. Not crazy for some people, but crazy for us. We find Laura Place—and I recognize it from the movies, a long line of identical white buildings on a curved street. I snap some pictures on my phone, and then we wander the streets, staring into the windows of tourist shops. We linger at one of them, with a bowed, mullioned window. It has pretty local jewelry made of jet and limestone.

"You should get that," Fred says, pointing to a small charm of the Roman baths.

"It's lovely."

"Should we go in?"

I want to, but . . . "Feels like tempting fate."

"How so?"

"Every time we've added a charm to this bracelet, we break up."

"You're saying it's a curse?"

"It's silly."

"No." He puts his arm around my shoulders and pulls me to him. "I believe in the power of magic. But I also believe in the power of choice."

"What's that?"

"We can choose to give something meaning."

"So if I buy that, it won't be the charm of doom?"

"Not familiar with that particular charm." His mouth twists. "I think you should get it anyway."

"Why?"

"A million reasons, but most of all because this day has been great, and it'll be something to remember it by."

"You're right. Plus, I picked it out."

"Wait, wait, wait. Are you saying you don't like the ones I picked out?"

"Ha!" I kiss him. "Wait here."

I dart into the store and buy the charm, asking the saleswoman to attach it to my bracelet. She admires the other charms on it, and I smile at her and nod when she asks if "my young man" is the handsome man waiting outside for me.

I take my receipt and return to Fred, who's frowning at his phone.

"I thought we were playing hooky."

He puts it into his pocket. "We are. Let me see?"

I hold my wrist up. He touches the charm, then lets it go.

"What?"

"Nothing."

"Fred."

"This bracelet should have so many more charms on it."

"It will."

He smiles. "Good. Shall we find a pub?"

"Excellent idea."

He holds out his hand and I take it, and then we find a cozy place with a snug, and we sit and drink the local beer until the world is fuzzy.

We took the train here, but Fred arranged for his car to pick us up, and so now we're in the backseat, like we were last night, our fingers intertwined. I rest my head against his shoulder as we wend our way through the countryside on our way back to London.

"Good day?" Fred asks.

"The best." He kisses the top of my head and I sink further into him.

"I'm glad you liked it. What do you want to do tomorrow?"

"Shh," I say, turning my face to kiss him. "Don't curse us."

He smiles against my mouth. "No."

His hands come to my face, cradling it. Then he kisses me gently, our eyes closed, mouths soft, taking our time. Because we have all the time in the world. And if we don't, I'll turn this charm over three times and say something magic, and we'll be revived and we'll try again.

When we get back to his apartment, we don't speak. Instead, we continue to explore each other slowly, drinking in our reunion in a way we weren't able to last night.

Every time we come together, I remember how much more everything is with him. How his touch makes me respond in a way no one else's has. I don't know for certain if it's like that for him, but it seems to be.

When we finish, I fall asleep in his arms, and when I wake, he's gone again, but I don't worry this time, even though there's no note. I can picture him in the kitchen, making our breakfast, planning our day. Or maybe he's out getting supplies. Yes, that must be it because the apartment is very quiet, too still if he's here.

I check the time. It's after nine, and I'm late for practice and Matt is going to kill me.

I reach for my phone. I turned it off yesterday after I wrote Matt to say that I was gone for the day. I should let him know that I'll be back on court tomorrow. He'll be apoplectic, but this is doing me more good than a couple of days of hitting.

I turn the phone on, holding it against my chest, waiting for my messages to load. It shudders against me, almost angry at being ignored, and I start to feel concerned. I flip it over. The screen is full of notifications from emails and texts and Twitter.

It takes me a minute to make sense of it, but it's a link from Matt that does it.

A story in the *Daily Mail* about me and Fred. It's got pictures of us together from Bath. Walking down the street, hand in hand. Standing outside the jewelry store, looking like we're picking out an engagement ring.

But the story is not just about me and Fred.

It's about me and Fred and another woman named Catherine— some British socialite that he's been dating that he never told me about.

I feel sick as I flip through the photos of them together. This is what I get for never googling him. He's practically engaged to another woman.

And oh God. The toothbrush, the robe . . . are they hers?

Bile rises in my throat, and I rush to the bathroom and heave up whatever's left from yesterday. When I'm finally done, I sit back against the wall, feeling feverish, and go to Twitter. This girl, Catherine, is apparently quite a big deal here, and my name and hers and Fred's along with #cheater are trending. The vitriol I'm receiving is ridiculous. Why does anyone care about a relationship that they're not in? But they do. The country does. And I don't want to be this person, this villain.

I feel another wave of nausea.

I can't be here anymore. I need to leave. Before Fred comes back.

Whatever he's said to me these last couple of days, it's a lie, and I can't bear to hear any more of it.

I pick up my phone and I call Ash. Because, even though she's a continent away, I know I can count on her to save me.

Two days, I think as I dial her number. Two days to add to our total. Two days thinking we could escape ourselves, but somehow I knew underneath that it wasn't going to happen.

Somehow, I knew that five years apart wasn't enough time to fix us.

Because I forgot that things that are brought back to life aren't real.

They're ghosts.

CHAPTER THIRTY-THREE

July 2023

Fred and I don't speak when we wake with the dawn the next morning on the beach at James's winery. We simply get up, return to the house, and act like nothing happened. Because nothing did. Ditto for the drive back to Southampton in the car that Fred arranges.

Lucy doesn't come with us. She's still woozy, and the doctor told her to take it easy, so James says she can stay with him for a while, until she's ready to go home, and it feels like we all breathe a sigh of relief when this decision is made, but maybe that's wishful thinking.

Fred drops me off at the top of the driveway and leaves without saying anything more than goodbye. It's weird—we felt so connected last night, almost like we *were* friends—and now we're back to being nothing. Maybe less than nothing, because if we were nothing, we could make small talk. But we've never done that. Everything between us has always been outsized. We don't know how to be normal together, so I don't look back when the car drives away, I just go into the house.

After a shower and a change of clothes, I go in search of something, I'm not sure what. While there's still a lot of cataloging to do, the only real clear-out left is of my mother's room. That feels like too much for today, and part of me wants to leave it for the estate sale, and let it be someone else's problem.

But that's what I do. I push problems off until they accumulate. A month from now, I won't have a place to live unless I decide to get back together with Wes. I'll have more money than I've ever had, but less sense of what I want to do. Go back on the tennis circuit? Leave teaching and become a coach? Leave it all behind and move to some warm-weather location where I can read books by a pool and play pickleball in the afternoons?

But no. That's never been me, and the part of me that's been slumbering since I retired five years ago is awake now. I'm not ready to check out of life, I just don't know what life I want to lead.

With these thoughts swirling, I end up in my father's study.

He's sitting behind his desk, reading a book. For all my father's oddness and vanity, he's always been a well-read man. Today's entry is a biography of John Lennon, the Beatles being a band I'm sure my dad ignored when they came out but are now far enough in the past to be intriguing to him.

"Learning anything interesting?"

"What? Oh, Olivia, hello." He puts the book down. John Lennon's small, round spectacles look up at me. "To what do I owe this pleasure?"

"I just felt like . . . we haven't talked since I've been home."

"Haven't we?"

"Not really." I sit in the chair in front of his desk. When I was little, I used to sit here, with my legs swinging, if I was in trouble. My father preferred lectures about comportment over real punishments, so I knew I simply had to listen, and when he was done, I'd be free.

"What would you like to talk about?"

"Are you sure you want to move out of Southampton?"

"Yes, I think so."

"It will be different."

William's hand rests on the book's cover. "I think that might be a good thing."

"Oh?"

"I wouldn't want to be reminded . . . Well, let's just say I have some regrets, my dear. Of a financial nature."

"It's funny to think this whole time we were sitting on this enormous asset."

"I knew that."

"You did?"

"I wanted to preserve it for you. For all of you. And I thought, maybe one day, one of you would live here."

"Charlotte did live here. She does."

"Yes, but to be honest, Olivia, I always thought it would be you. When you finished your world traveling. You always loved the house as much as me." His eyes mist over, and there's a lump in my throat. "But instead, you stayed away."

"I'm sorry."

"Why, though? I know I wasn't always the best father . . ."

"No, it wasn't your fault."

"No?"

"No, I . . . I don't know how to express it . . . I do love it here, but it makes me sad."

"Because of your mother?"

"Yes, that's part of it. I always felt . . . lost here, I guess?"

"I'm sorry."

I smile at him. "There's nothing to apologize for. But things would've been different if Mom hadn't died."

"Yes," he sighs. "The great tragedy of my life."

"Were you never lonely? You didn't want to marry again?"

"No one could live up to her."

"You were happy? She was happy?"

He wipes his thumb underneath his eye. I've never seen my father cry. Not one time after my mother died, at least not in front of us.

"I think so."

"Why did you get married so young?"

"Not so young."

"Mom was only eighteen."

"She was the one who wanted to get married."

"She did?"

He rubs his chin. "Did she ever tell you about her father?"

"Grandpa Simon?"

"Terrible man. She never even told me all the details, but he wasn't a good father. Drove your grandmother into an early grave with his rages. Your mother wanted to escape him. Getting married was a way to do that. But that didn't mean it's not what she wanted. What we both did. Sometimes you can make the right decision, even under duress."

"How come no one ever told me that?"

William laces his fingers together. "Not really the sort of thing you discuss with your children, is it?"

"No, I guess not . . . Only . . ."

"You think your mother regretted it?"

"No, I . . ."

"She was happy, Olivia. Maybe in the end, she wasn't, but she was so sick, sicker than you knew. It took a lot out of her. There's this whole thing now about how one has to be brave when one is dying, as if you've failed yourself if you aren't. But not everyone has it in them to be that when they're dying young. I accepted that. She was scared. She didn't want to leave us. But there wasn't anything she or I, or the doctors, could do about it."

"Thank you for saying that."

"You're welcome."

"I love you . . . Dad."

He smiles. "I love you too."

*   *   *

I spend much of the day wandering around the house, trying to see my past through this new lens. I've been blaming William for the way things are in our family—calling him *William* instead of *Dad*, putting distance between us. But he's been here the whole time. He didn't abandon us to nannies. He didn't bring in a new mother and pretend that our real one never existed.

He did the best he could. He was the one who was brave in the face of the terrible thing that had happened to our family. Not that I blame my mother for being afraid. But maybe that's what it was—the advice she gave me in that twenty-first birthday card. Fear.

Did I screw up my whole life because my mother was afraid of dying? Did she think that if I did what she did, I'd end like she did too?

But if I'm being honest with myself, it wasn't only because of my mother that I'd turned Fred down. William and Aunt Tracy were against me marrying him too. More importantly, *I* was against it. I *was* too young, and everything that's happened between us since is proof of that.

But I also know that the answers to my life right now aren't in this house, hidden in the walls, or in the locked-up memories of old men.

The answer to my future is at the club.

Wes.

A man who wants to be with me. A man who made a mistake, yes, a bad one, but who wasn't trying to hurt me. Who's never looked at me with the cold stare that Fred gave me this morning. And if I've given this many chances to Fred, doesn't Wes deserve another chance too? We've both hurt each other, and I'm not innocent in this.

So I go to the club to find him.

And when I do, he's sitting on the veranda, having a drink with Ann. It's not the combination I expected, but it's innocent despite my hammering heart. They don't jump away from each other or look guilty. There isn't an air of complicity about them. If anything, I'd say they were arguing, but that doesn't make any sense either.

"Olivia," Wes says when he notices me standing there. "Join us."

I walk up to them slowly. "What are you two doing together?"

They exchange a glance. "Well, now the surprise is ruined," Wes says.

"Surprise?"

"We were planning a going-away party."

I frown. "Who's going away?"

"For the family. You know, at the house."

"Oh."

Ann tilts her head to the side. "I thought it would be good for Charlotte. Saying a formal goodbye, having everyone over. Maybe for you and Sophie too."

"Doesn't that sound good?" Wes says.

"It sounds sad."

"We don't have to do it."

"No, no . . . I'm sure everyone will like it, including William." I sit down at the table. "What day were you thinking?"

Wes covers my hand with his. "The day of the transfer. Ann asked Fred, and he doesn't mind, even though the house will be his then, technically."

"Four weeks from now?"

Ann smiles. "The estate sale is that day too, yes?"

"That's right." I fiddle with the spoon in my place setting. "A big day."

"It is. You've got the documents for the sale?"

"I . . . I haven't checked yet."

"Plenty of time." Ann stands. "I'm going to go. I'll be in touch, Olivia. Wes." She nods and leaves.

I watch her walk away, feeling off and jealous. I pull my hand away from Wes.

"What's wrong?" he says.

"Nothing."

"Doesn't feel like nothing."

I turn back to him. "I'm just tired."

He raises an eyebrow. "Bad night's sleep?"

"Yeah, I guess."

"Was the rest of the winery not up to standard?"

"What?"

"The beds not comfortable?"

I fold my hands on the table. "Is there something you want to ask me?"

"Is there something to ask?"

"Nothing happened."

He arches his eyebrow slowly. "No?"

"No," I say firmly, and then sink in my chair as I see Fred coming out of the club. He's wearing shorts and a polo, and when he sees us, I can tell he wants to walk the other way, but politeness drives him toward us.

"Olivia. Wes."

"Hi, Fred," Wes says, standing to shake his hand. "We were just speaking about you."

"That right?"

"Wes, stop it."

"Stop what? I want to know what Fred has to say about what you were doing last night."

"Dinner, I believe," Fred says.

"You had dinner with my wife?"

"Wes!"

"I thought you were taking care of Lucy?"

"We were. But we had to eat. Fred made an omelet when we got home from the hospital. We talked and then we went to bed."

"Separately?"

"Of course separately."

"Listen, mate," Fred says. "I think if you—"

But Wes isn't having it. Instead, he stands, cocks his fist, and says, "I'm not your mate," as it connects with Fred's jaw, knocking him back.

Fred stumbles, then rights himself and projects himself forward, his own fist connecting with Wes's face. Then, Wes is on the ground, Fred on top of him.

"Fred! Wes! Stop it! Both of you."

I grab Fred's arm and pull him back. We're joined by one of the club's security men, and they pull Fred off Wes before another blow lands.

I stay on the ground, next to Wes, as he clutches his face. There's going to be a bad bruise, maybe a black eye.

"Are you okay?" I ask.

"He hit me."

"You did hit him first."

"My prerogative, I think."

I help him sit up. Fred is twenty feet away, a security guard on each arm, but he's not struggling. He's just standing there, watching us.

"Leave, please, Fred."

Our eyes connect and I try to press the message home. That he's not helping, being here, that he needs to go so I can try to fix this.

A look of disgust crosses his face, then he turns and goes.

"You don't want to go with him?" Wes asks.

"No."

"Are you sure?"

"Yes. And despite what you might think, nothing happened between us. Nothing."

"Not *this* time."

I sit back on my heels. "What do you want me to say?"

"I don't know."

"How did this become about me? My past?"

"It's always been about you. About *him*."

"That's not fair."

He rubs his face. "Maybe not, but it's true."

"So, what? We just give up?"

"No, I don't . . . Can't we leave? Go back to New York?"

"I have to finish the house."

"Your sisters can do that."

"They won't, though."

Wes takes my hand. "But you could let them. Let go of all of this. It's just things you were happy not to see for the last twenty years. It can't be more important than us. But if it is, then there's your answer."

"So, what—we leave today? What about the transfer? The party? The estate sale?"

Wes sighs. "That's weeks away. We could come back for it."

"We can't run away from our problems. If we're going to make it, we need to figure out a way to do that where it's hard, not where it's easy."

"So we stay, and then?"

"We go home."

"Together?"

I let out my breath slowly. "Yes."

He breaks into a smile. "Really?"

"I think so . . . I'm willing to try anyway." I stand and reach out my hand. "Do I need to take you to the hospital?"

"No." He takes my hand and I pull him up, then he gathers me close to him. "This will be good. This is going to be good for us."

I let him fold me against him, and it does feel good. Wes and I have always felt good together, regardless of everything that's pushed us apart.

"I love you, Olivia," Wes says.

"I love you too."

CHAPTER THIRTY-FOUR

March 2018

I meet Wes again at a low moment.

It's the end of my tennis career. No one's saying it, but my ranking is speaking for me. I'm down in the dumps, lower even than when I started, and I can't figure out what's wrong. I'm thirty—an age that's unusual in professional women's tennis for a reason. I work just as hard and my body responds almost as well, but there's something holding me back. I'm not a killer on the court anymore. I don't care as much if someone beats me—not like I used to—and it was the fear of losing that kept me in the game. It's a word that hovers around me, *retirement*, and I don't know what to do about it.

How do you give up on the thing you did for years and years to the sacrifice of everything else? How do you take that leap into the unknown?

I haven't figured it out yet, so I stick to my routine. I eat my boring meals and travel to the next tournament and the next. I see my friends once in a while, Ash becoming more of a memory than a real presence in my life, though here I am in New York City in March, going to a charity event that she insisted I go to for moral support.

She's six months pregnant with her first kid, and she's a bit lost, too. She's always been a party girl, and here she is, unable to drink, bigger than she's ever been in her life, about to disappear into motherhood. Or that's what she keeps saying.

"Why are you making me come to this thing?" I ask her in the cab as we weave down Broadway, the cabbie pressing on his brake once a block in a way that makes me feel like we're on a boat, stopping and starting like we're crashing into waves.

"Because you need to find a man."

"What?"

"You do. Enough of this single life."

"I can't believe *you're* saying this to me. Of all people."

She pokes her tongue out at me. Her hair is up in a topknot, and she's wearing thick lashes and a bright red lip. Her fuller face suits her, but I can't tell her that because she keeps referring to herself as "fat."

"I know, I know. Sometimes I look at myself in the mirror and I can't believe it's me."

"But you're happy?"

"I am."

"With Dave."

She swats me. "Stop it. I know, okay? I know."

Their wedding was a lavish affair at the club last summer. I'd worn a pink bridesmaid's dress and endured being asked when it was going to be "my turn" by every single person I talked to. She'd sent the bouquet in my direction, and I'd thought about ducking it, but instead I caught it easily because my reflexes are like that.

"I'm happy for you."

"I want you to be happy."

"I am."

Ash puts her arm around my neck. "Um, no, you are not."

"Who says?"

"I say. Ever since London—"

I hold up a hand. "No. No. We are not talking about that ever, remember?"

She pouts. "You should, you know."

"What?"

"Talk about it."

I can't. I can't talk about it. Not about how the tabloids went into an insane frenzy like I'd killed a child with my car. Or how I was followed around for the next six months and called a whore. I got booed at, at my next tournament, and when I was injured and had to miss the US Open, I was *glad*.

"You still haven't talked to him?"

"No. But it was years ago, Ash. It doesn't matter."

I wasn't sure if that was true, but it didn't matter if it was. Fred had given up calling and texting and apologizing long ago. How was I supposed to forgive him? He'd lured me to London when he was in a relationship with someone else. He'd kept her as a backup plan. Not that he said that, but it's what happened. How was I supposed to get past that?

"Fuck Fred," Ash says.

"Yes."

"I didn't mean that literally."

"I know."

"So, find someone else."

"Maybe."

"No, tonight."

She's so earnest and serious, not like Ash at all. "I'm okay, Ash, I promise."

"Hmm."

"Why doesn't anyone believe me when I say that?"

"Because we see your face."

That stings. Maybe Ash is right. I need to forget the past, who I am, and become someone new. Or be with someone new, anyway. That I do need. Not that I've been celibate. But I haven't connected with anyone, not deeply. *And not like with Fred*, my stupid brain keeps reminding me. And I do miss that. The excitement, the comfort.

The cab pulls up to the Gansevoort, and we get out, taking the elevator to the top floor. It's a bit chilly to be outside, but there are heat lamps and votives on the tables, and half the club is inside anyway. Ash gets me a cocktail—for the thrill of ordering it, she says—and whirls me around the room, introducing me to every single man there. When one too many of them has that look cross their face at my name (the one that says they've heard *something* about me, but they aren't sure what) I excuse myself to go to the bathroom.

I put my drink down on the counter, then raise it quickly and drain it. I examine myself. I don't look so different from how I did as a teenager. But my eyes tell a different story.

"Fuck this," I say to myself. I'm going to leave. Ash will understand. I walk out of the bathroom, determined to do so. There's someone blocking my path.

"Can I get by?"

"Yes, sorry, oh . . . Olivia?"

I focus on the face in front of me. Blond hair, blue eyes, handsome. "Wes?"

He kisses me on the cheek, then backs off, a bit shy. "It's good to see you."

I haven't seen Wes since I was sixteen, when he was hanging around with Charlotte the first summer I was with Fred. He was nice to me, I remember, for the rest of that summer, when I was sulking around the club, trying to heal my wounded heart.

"What are you doing here?"

"Ash invited me."

"She did?"

"We're on a board together."

"She didn't mention."

He laughs. "That's funny. She talks about you all the time."

"Don't be silly . . ." I curse Ash in my head, but maybe she wasn't trying to be this specific with her matchmaking. "What have you been up to?"

"That's a long story . . . Why don't we get a drink?"

"I was just leaving."

"We can go somewhere else? There's a wine bar near here that has a great cheese plate."

"That sounds . . . Yes, let's do that."

"Great." He takes my hand and then looks up at me, surprised at himself. "I don't know why I did that. Is it weird?"

"Well, we are cousins . . ."

"That's all been debunked! The last name is a coincidence."

"And you did date my sister . . ."

"Years and years ago, and it was never serious."

"Does she know that?"

Charlotte's heart was broken, too, when she and Wes split that fall. She's never introduced another love interest to the family, though she's had a few women friends who I thought might be more than that. But Charlotte doesn't confide in me, and the one time I tried to ask, she gave me such an icy stare, I stammered to a stop.

"Do you not want to go?" Wes says, then squeezes my hand.

I can feel its warmth. A spark, something connecting us. He's better looking than I remember, his voice warm and low. "No, I do."

"Good." He flashes his smile again, and it does something to me. A man who doesn't make me want to run away. A man who's looking at me like I'm nothing but a good idea. "Should we go?"

"Yes."

We walk to the elevators, our hands still locked together. As we wait for it to arrive, I catch sight of Ash. She smiles at me, like this has been her plan all along. And maybe it was, but for once, I don't mind. All that matters right now is that Wes's hand feels good in mine and that this night that felt like an obligation now feels like one full of possibilities.

*   *   *

The night turns into a whirlwind.

I'd always heard that term, but it had never applied to me. Maybe it means speed. And Wes and I certainly move with speed. That night at the wine bar ends up back at his place, with me staying over. The sex is good and comfortable, like it isn't our first time. None of the usual awkwardness, and maybe not quite the same passion as I had with Fred, but that's a good thing, I think.

That passion had burned me one too many times. I need something that simmers and never goes out.

The next day we walk to the park after I get back from practice, watching a small sailboat race in a pond, buying pretzels and hotdogs, losing our way because we're engrossed in conversation, and I spend the night at Wes's again.

And the next and the next and a week of nexts.

It's weird, how much we have in common. We just seem to understand each other. It felt like that with Fred at the beginning too, in a way, but this is different.

When I met Fred, I was a kid, and now I'm an adult. I know what I like and what I don't, and Wes seems to want the same things I do. The same food, the same routine, to settle down after so many years of travel. He's also an early riser, going to the gym each morning while I hit. He's fine with the meals I have to eat, the time I have to go to bed. My life slots into his without any friction, though I keep waiting for it. But it never arrives.

After a month, he starts coming with me to tournaments when he can. He watches from the stands and learns how to massage my sore muscles and finds other foods I can eat. He's a strong player himself, and sometimes he hits with me, helping me warm up, getting me mentally ready. I start to play better, a product of happiness, and I marvel how easily he fits into my life.

Other people react to us that way too—when they meet us for the first time they always nod, like Wes's the person they expect me to be with.

"Don't you think it's funny," I say to him one night in bed, "that no one ever asks where you came from?"

"Why would they?"

"I don't know. I was single for so long . . ."

"Oh, you were, were you?" He pulls me to him, rubbing his nose against mine.

"You know what I mean."

He shrugs. "People know something right when they see it."

"Oh yeah?"

"Yeah," he says as he puts his mouth on mine, and then we're lost together for an hour.

When we resurface, I bring it up again. "But where did you come from?"

"The Gansevoort I believe."

"Ha."

"Ashley sent me."

"She swears she didn't." When I told her we were together, Ash swore up and down that she'd never even thought about Wes for me.

She'd invited him because she invited the whole board, wanting to raise as much money as possible.

"Is she trustworthy, though?"

"Who cares?" I snuggle against him. "I'm happy."

"Good." He kisses the top of my head. "Why question it, then?"

"Because if you can just show up, you can disappear too."

"I won't."

"Promise?"

"I do."

I fall asleep with a smile on my face. It's May now, and the mornings are light and airy. And though I'm playing better, I've got some decisions to make about my career that I keep putting off. When I wake up in the morning, there's a stack of mail calling to me from the kitchen table. I've had my mail forwarded to his apartment at his suggestion, so I guess I'm living here now, though we've never discussed it.

Wes's arranged the mail neatly because he's the neat one, not me, and on top is an invitation. It's from Wimbledon. A thick envelope with gold embossing on it. I get one every year. Since I made it into the main draw five years ago, it's automatic. Or it has been. This year, my ranking is so abysmal that I was sure it wasn't going to come.

But here it is.

Wimbledon. One more chance.

The tournament starts in six weeks. If I'm going to play, I need to focus up and drop everything else, including Wes.

"You going to go?" Wes asks, coming into the room behind me, like a cat. He does that, Wes—appears out of nowhere.

"What's that?" I tuck the invitation behind the other mail.

"You don't need to hide it. I'm the one who put it on top."

I kiss him. "Right. Thank you for doing that."

"You should go."

"I should?"

"Olivia, it's Wimbledon."

"I've been before."

"But not since that summer, right? Your storied run?"

At night, after I'm asleep, Wes's been catching up on my career, ever since we started dating. Watching old matches and reading interviews. Researching my opponents and scrutinizing my training routine. Sometimes I think he knows my stats better than Matt does.

"Don't be silly."

"Why is it silly? It was storied."

"I didn't win the championship."

"It was still amazing."

I kiss him again. He tastes like toothpaste. "Thank you."

"Are you going to go?"

"I don't know. Things are good here." I reach out and caress his face. "Maybe I don't want to leave you for that long."

"I could come with you."

"What about the business?" Wes runs his own company, a private venture cap firm that invests in cutting-edge pharmaceuticals.

"Oh right, that."

"Yeah, that. Besides, a tournament like that . . . if I'm going to take it seriously, I need to go over early, to totally shut myself off from everything and everyone."

"I understand."

"You've never really seen me like that."

"Are you worried that I won't love you anymore if you're totally focused on something that isn't me?"

"Oh, you love me, do you?" I say it lightly because we haven't said those words. Not yet.

"You know I do."

"Do I?"

"Olivia, yes." He steps closer to me and takes my face in his hands. "I love you. I do. I thought you knew."

"How am I supposed to know it if you don't say it?"

"You're right. I'm going to say it every day."

I laugh. "You don't have to."

"No, I want to. I love you, Olivia Taylor."

"I love you too, Wes Taylor." I kiss him again, and we bend into each other, wrapping our arms around one another. "Okay, then. I love you every day, it is."

"Sounds good to me." He tousles my hair. "So, you're going?"

"To Wimbledon?"

"Yes?"

"No."

"Why not?"

I drop my arms and step away. Why don't I want to go to Wimbledon? Why have I avoided it all these years despite the urging of my coaches, the press, everyone?

It's obvious but unexplainable.

Fred.

"You do remember what happened the last time I went there, right?"

I'd told him all about it one night. I hadn't meant to, but it had all spilled out in a long stream of words. That Fred was someone from my past, that we'd gotten tangled up in a mess, how the press had had a field day.

Afterward, he'd kissed me and said that I was brave to go through that, and that he'd always found Fred arrogant the few times they'd met over the years through common business contacts. He said he wasn't intimidated by our history; everyone had a past, and if we were meant to be with the person we were with at twenty, then he'd be with Charlotte. We'd laughed at that and moved on to other things, but it was one of the things I loved about him. His confidence in us.

"I remember."

"Well . . ."

"I'm sure the tabloids have moved on."

"They don't do that. If I go there, every story will mention it. The Jezebel returns."

"Who cares what the press says? Show them your tennis. Give them something else to write about."

"Yeah."

Wes taps me on the shoulder. "Or you could bring them a different story."

"What's that?"

"If you were engaged."

"What?"

"Think about it. If you came back to the tournament, newly engaged, rededicated to the game . . . the press will eat it up."

"Newly engaged?"

"Didn't I ask you to marry me?"

"I feel like I would remember that."

"Hmm."

"Wes, be serious."

"I am serious." He drops down to his knee and reaches into his pocket. He pulls out a small black box.

My hand flies up to my face. What is happening?

"Olivia, ever since you came into my life, it's felt complete. Will you marry me?"

I start to shake. I can't believe it.

"Olivia?"

"Yes."

I reach down to him, falling to my knees. He pulls me to him, and when we kiss, I can feel the tears on our faces. He slips the ring onto my finger, and it's perfect, a solitary square diamond on a platinum band.

"I love you, Olivia," Wes says.

"You already said that today."

"Feels like today is a two I-love-you-day."

"At least two." I kiss him, feeling the weight of the ring on my hand. It feels right sitting there, like a promise I made a long time ago. "I love you, Wes."

"Well, that's good. Since we're getting married and all."

"We are. We're getting married."

"I know, right?"

We smile at each other, and then my face falls.

"What is it?"

"Charlotte is going to kill me."

"I doubt it. You father might not be thrilled, though."

"He won't care."

"The same guy who barely let me into the house?"

"He's mellowed."

"Has he?"

I touch his face. "He feels bad . . . for last time . . . He won't put up a fuss."

Wes nods, a moment passing through his face. "I'll be glad about that, then."

"About what?"

"That I wasn't here first."

I take a swat at him. "Wes."

"I'm here last, though."

I lean my forehead against his. "Yes, you are."

CHAPTER THIRTY-FIVE

July 2023

After the fight he had with Wes, weeks go by where I don't see Fred.

He's not at the window when I practice in the morning. He doesn't come to cocktails.

I don't ask, but I know that Wes hasn't seen him either, because I'd be able to tell if he had. Eventually, from a side comment that Charlotte drops, I learn that Fred's left town for the moment, maybe for good.

I don't know how I feel about that, but I try not to let it occupy my thoughts. Instead, I spend time with Wes, tentative time, rebuilding time, and I put the finishing touches on the house for the estate sale.

I read the rest of my mother's diary, and there are no big revelations. I feel like I know her better, but my mother needs to be packed away too, as much as it hurts to do it.

Wes's bruises have faded and my thoughts of Fred fades with them. Wes and I aren't quite what we were—I don't know if we ever can be—but we're better. We don't fight, we remember good times, we plan for more. And this is what I always wanted with him. For him to be present like he was in the beginning, for us to be on the same page. I know that what happened to us happens to a lot of couples when they stop taking time, when they stop paying attention, when they take the other person for granted. So we try not to do that anymore, and the more we do it, the more possible it seems, like a muscle that hurts the first day you flex it, and then never again.

And now it's August, our last week here.

The estate sale is Friday, and afterward we'll sign the transfer papers for the money, and then Wes and I will go back to the city. Everything is cataloged and tucked away. Every room is packed up. There's just my mother's room to clear out, the one thing I could never get to.

But today we're going to, come what may—all three of us together.

Charlotte, Sophie, and I stand in front of the doorway like it's the wardrobe to Narnia.

"What do you think is in there?" Sophie says.

"Charlotte?"

"What? I haven't been inside."

"Not in all the years?"

"I'd tell the cleaners to go in twice a year to keep the dust down—that's it."

"It feels like *she* might be in there," I say.

"Yeah."

"We can't put it off anymore."

"You're right." Charlotte pushes on the door handle. It opens easily, my mother's scent rushing out.

"Oh fuck," Charlotte says, and that sets us laughing.

We step into the room. It's the same as I remember it, and also different. Some things—like the couch she used to lie on to read, to reflect, to snuggle—are smaller than I remember. The windows feel larger, the sunlight brighter. But mostly, it feels like a part of me that I was missing, and I'm not sure why I put it off for so long.

"This is weird," Sophie says.

"So weird."

"I guess we put everything in boxes?"

"That's what I've been doing, yes."

"Okay, okay. No need to be bitchy about it, Saint Olivia."

I ignore the comment and walk to the bookshelves. The library downstairs was full of books, but this is where she kept her favorites.

Her copies of *Anne of Green Gables* and *Ballet Shoes* and *The Secret Garden*. She read them to us when we were children, us curled up around her, as she transported us away to the magical worlds within. Each of us had our favorite. I loved spunky Anne. Sophie loved *The Secret Garden*. Charlotte was drawn to *The Borrowers*, liking the miniature world created therein.

I take the books off the shelf, one by one, and flip through the pages carefully. I can hear my sisters remarking on this find or that, but I mostly tune them out. With each book my heart swells in anticipation, but then it crashes back to earth again. The pages are blank, there's no card to me hidden within. The truth of it sinks in. The card I received from her on my twenty-first birthday is the last.

"I can't believe Lucy chose him over Fred," Sophie says, the first words of theirs that register in an hour.

"What?" I say, turning around. They're huddled by the window, a box at their feet. They've cleared one shelf, while I've done ten.

"Lucy. She's dating that guy, the winery guy."

"James?"

"Right," Charlotte says.

"She is?"

"Yeah, she stayed there for, like, weeks after the accident, and I guess proximity or whatever. She told Colin this morning."

"Lucy and James are together."

Sophie's annoyed. "That's what I said."

"What's it to you?" Charlotte asks. "Good for her."

"I thought she was good with Fred," Sophie says, pouting. "He must be heartbroken."

"Potato, poh-tah-to," Charlotte says. "They're both super-rich."

"Lucy's not like that. That's not what she cares about."

Charlotte shrugs. "Everyone cares about money."

"Okay, that's true, but she's not a gold digger."

"What's Fred saying about this?" I ask, trying to keep my voice casual.

"Who knows? He's probably pissed, though. James is his friend. And he's totally into her."

I think back to that night when we all stayed there after the accident. Was there any hint that James was on the make other than his slight interest in me? My impression was that he was still heartbroken about the loss of his fiancée, but what did I know?

"Fred will get over it," I say.

"How do you know?" Sophie says, her hands on her hips. "Maybe he's devastated."

"Because he's a man."

"That's ridiculous."

"Men always get over heartbreak faster than women."

"Just because Wes—"

I put up a hand. "Okay, forget it. But I know Fred. He'll be fine."

"Don't be so sure," Sophie says. "Now are we finishing this or what?"

* * *

Several hours later, the shelves are almost bare and boxed, and all that's left is the furniture. We log it, and Charlotte and Sophie leave me to finish up.

The estate sale is on Friday morning. Once we know the proceeds, then we'll disburse the money to the charity being set up to honor Mom, and then we can all move on. We decided to make it a music scholarship for young, disadvantaged girls. Hopefully, the sale will raise enough money to make a meaningful impact.

I run my hands along the empty shelves collecting dust. What will happen to our family, without this common ground? I've gotten closer to Sophie and Charlotte this summer. I need to do a better job of keeping in touch. I don't need to hide away from here, or the memories that it holds. I don't need to pretend that I don't love it. The sound of the ocean, the smell of the trees, the endless view. Wes and I should buy a place, I decide. I'll talk to him about it in a couple of weeks, once we're settled back in New York.

I smile to myself, and I'm about to leave the room when I see something poking out from one of the bookshelves. I get closer. There's a book wedged behind it. I pull the shelf out, and free the book. It's my mother's copy of *Persuasion*, old, the pages brittle. I flip the pages slowly so I don't break them. It's full of my mother's annotations and underlining. And then, near the middle of the book, her favorite passage is highlighted in a red box—the one about there *"never being two hearts so open"*—and there are two pieces of paper folded over and wedged in between.

I open them carefully with my hand shaking. The edges are rough—the missing pages from her diary. The date at the top is from a few weeks before she died.

My dearest Olivia,

I've been trying all day to write your eighteenth birthday card and failing. I'm not sure why, only I see so much of myself in you. All your goals and plans—I had those too. But then they flew away like a bird headed south for winter, only they never came back again when the weather turned.

I'm not making sense. My head hurts and I'm tired, and my thoughts are full of him.

Sam.

I've never told you about him, have I? The handsome sailor who came into town on shore leave the summer I was seventeen. Oh, how he looked in his uniform! I'm sorry to say that I always did have a weakness for a good-looking man. And Sam was extraordinary. Tall, dark, striking. Talking to him made me feel so . . . it's hard to describe. Nervous, happy, scared. When I worked up the courage to talk to him, he seemed to be made for me, like something out of a novel, our hearts so open to each other, like no one else had ever felt what we did.

Maybe I was naive, but I believed his promises. He was going to save me from my father, sail me away into the ocean blue. I wanted that so much. I wanted him. I hope you feel that wanting someday, Olivia, though not with the consequences I suffered. I'll never forget his face when I told him I was pregnant, like a rat trapped by a light that turned on suddenly in the night. I knew right then that he wasn't going to save me.

I met your father a few weeks later—do you understand? Another good-looking man, but with a gentle heart. By then, I knew the difference. I could trust his promises. Even when I lost the baby, he didn't break them. We ran away, and for a long time, I was happy. But fleeing from something isn't a foundation to build a life on. I wouldn't trade you or your sisters for anything, but for myself, I wish I'd made a different choice. To live on my own for a while, to chase my ambitions, not to let them drain away in a swirl of parties and surfaces and what was easy.

I've had a good life, Olivia. Better than most.

But oh I want more for you.

CHAPTER THIRTY-SIX

June 2018

I go to Wimbledon.

Before I leave, Wes and I have an engagement party. Charlotte and Sophie, William and Ash, Aunt Tracy and Colin and Lucy all attend. Matt is there too. Everyone I've ever known in the Hamptons it feels like—all the partygoers, the cocktail drinkers. The adults who patted me on the head and sometimes cheered for me from the sidelines at the club.

Charlotte is an ice queen, still pissed that I'm dating Wes, angry that my father is accepting of him when he chased him away when she and he dated. Sophie laughs at her, and Colin teases me about the last name, demanding to see the family tree to make sure we aren't related. Ash is glowing and happy, her first baby delivered, and taking credit for all of it. She still can't drink because she's breastfeeding, but there are drinks in her future, she says, and that's enough. And then she takes a sip from my glass and says, "I'm so bad," and we giggle like schoolgirls.

I feel alive, happy. I'm deep into my training for Wimbledon, but that night I'm free to do what I want, eat what I want, drink what I want. One last hurrah before it all turns serious again. One last night of stored memories to shore up against the press coverage I'm sure is coming, whether I want it or not.

I haven't googled Fred. If he's still in London, I don't want to know, because this isn't about him. It's about me.

We stay late and Wes stays over at Taylor House. I sneak into his guest room because my father still insists on separate rooms, and we make love and fall asleep. My flight is at night, so we have the morning to laze away, the day to finish packing and then drive into the city, to the airport. We do all of this lightly—I'll be gone for a month, but when I get home, we'll get married out on the lawn, with these same people throwing rice and cheering for our future.

Married. It's a big word, one that Ash lectured me about the night before.

"This is serious, Olivia," Ash said after she took a second sip of my drink; then said, "No more," like she was banishing it.

"I know."

"But you're going to London."

"I'm going to Wimbledon. For a tournament. Because it's my job."

"Isn't it dangerous, being there again?"

"I don't even know if he lives there anymore."

"He does."

"How do you know?"

"Because I have a Google Alert set to his name."

"What?"

She lifted her thin shoulders. "I need to keep tabs on him."

"Why?"

"Because he's your asteroid, Olivia, hurtling toward you. Keeping track of it makes sense."

"I prefer to remain in ignorance about the end of the world."

"Yeah, well, he's single."

I wasn't expecting to hear that, and I can't deny it. I feel the impact. "How do you know for sure?"

She lifts her chin. "I'm strong in the ways of Google."

"It doesn't matter."

"You're not going to see him?"

"Of course not."

"Olivia . . ."

"Why does everyone always say my name like that? Like a warning?"

Ash laughed and hugged me. "Because you're a danger to yourself."

"I'm not going to see him."

"Just see to it that you don't."

I kissed her on the cheek and found Wes's arm, and I put that asteroid careening through my life right out of my head.

But I should've known you can't avoid an extinction-level event by pretending it's not happening—that the pull between Fred and me wasn't something that was so easily escaped.

Because I wasn't in England for more than twenty-four hours before our paths crossed.

* * *

It was my fault this time. One day in England was all it took for the walls I'd created across an ocean to come tumbling down. Maybe it was the jet lag. Maybe it was the nerves of the impending tournament, even though I was doing a warmup event first. Or the faster-than-fast engagement to Wes.

Maybe it's because it felt like summer.

It's hard to parse out why we do stupid things.

All I know is that after I sleep off the jet lag and go for my hitting session and stretch and cool down and change into street clothes, I panic. I'm alone in an apartment—not *the* apartment I was in last time, but something similar. I can see the Thames out my window, and I can feel it's breeze against my cheek, the way it felt that night with Fred five years ago when we walked around after our magical dinner, like it was yesterday.

What is this cosmic connection between us? Did we doom ourselves to cross orbits every five years with our stupid teenaged promises?

No.

The only one who's dooming herself is me.

That's why I walk across the bridge and past the Globe and through the winding streets until I get to the Portuguese restaurant. I don't know how I know that he's going to be there; I just do.

And I'm right. I'm *right*.

He's sitting at a table in the corner. He's not alone; he's with another man in a suit, and I breathe out a sigh of relief that it's not a woman. A man I can deal with. A woman—I'd be on my heel turning out of there so fast I'd disappear in a puff of smoke.

I ask the hostess for a table but tell her that I know someone in the restaurant I need to say hi to first, then march right past her to Fred's table. I'm shaking and my heart is thrumming, but I don't stop myself, I just barge on through until I'm next to him.

"Hi."

Fred looks up, not expecting to see me, expecting anyone else, and his face goes through a series of emotions when he realizes who it is. I think the first is happy, but it's quickly replaced by shock. "Olivia! What are you doing here?"

"This is Olivia?" Fred's companion says. "*The* Olivia?"

"The one and only," I say, because the idea that there might be another Olivia is too devastating. "But don't hold that against me."

"Certainly not, dear. I've only heard—"

I raise my hand. "I'll stop you there." I hold my hand out. "I'm Olivia Taylor."

He stands and takes it. Seventy, urbane, gray hair in a short cut, plummy accent, expensive suit.

"I'm Tomas de Keurig. Pleased to meet you." He smiles at me, his teeth large and white. He has nice crinkles around his eyes, and he gives off a vibe like a grandfather.

"What are you doing here?" Fred says, rising to join us.

"I was in the neighborhood. Thought I'd stop in for dinner."

His eyes narrow. He knows I'm lying, but what can he say?

"Would you like to join us?"

"Oh no, that's okay."

"No," Tomas says. "I insist."

He motions to the waiter and gives instructions to move us to a larger table. Through the bustle and fuss, Fred doesn't say anything, just stares at me, then looks away, like he wants to say something but can't bring himself to. I'm feeling shy too, so instead I focus on Tomas, asking about his company and what he thinks of Fred. He's effusive in his praise, says that he thinks of Fred as a son, and tells me in vague terms how Fred tried to save his son so many years ago, and the tragedy that befell them all despite his best efforts.

That's how he talks—*"the tragedy that befell them all"*—like an old man in a novel, formal and stiff. I can tell, though, that it's only bravado. He likes to talk about his son, but it's painful, and he loves Fred—I can feel it so clearly, a feeling I recognize because it's what I feel for Fred too. Fred is uncomfortable being the center of attention, but he's also used to having this story told about him, so he puts up with it, though I know he's dying to ask me something, anything—to understand what's going on.

"And what about you, Olivia?" Tomas asks. "What brings you to London?"

"Tennis."

"You'll be competing at Wimbledon?"

"That's the plan. But I'm doing a challenger tournament first."

"You were the one who made it through the qualifiers a few years back, yes?"

"That's me."

"An impressive run."

"Thank you. And I think I have you to thank for getting me the chance."

"What's that?"

Fred rises himself. "You remember, Tomas. We sponsored some of the surrounding events."

"Oh yes, that's right. Fred here is very passionate about tennis."

"I admire the game. The solitude of it. How you're out there on the court, alone."

"It can be lonely," I say. "Never having teammates. Always in conflict with the people you meet on tour."

Fred's eyes lock onto mine, and a blush creeps up my cheeks.

"I hadn't thought about that."

Tomas checks his watch. "Is that the time? I must be going."

"But you haven't had dinner yet," I say.

"I was only ever meeting Fred for a drink." He stands. "It was lovely to meet you, my dear. And how nice for Fred to have you back in London."

He reaches out his hand again, and I take it. "I feel like you're leaving because of me. But I should be the one to go."

"Nonsense. You and Fred can catch up and I can get home earlier, which I would like to do either way." He gives me a weary smile, and I can see it: the pallor behind his tan, the dark droops under his eyes. This is a man who's exhausted, maybe ill.

"It was so nice to meet you."

"Likewise. Frederick."

They nod at each other, and I stand there. We both do.

"Do you want to sit?" Fred asks. His voice has a bit more British in it than the last time, like it's slowly taking over. Otherwise, he wears the five years that have passed easily, with almost no change in his appearance. A handsome man in full bloom, comfortable in his suit and his surroundings.

My eyes flit to his left hand. It's bare. Mine is too. I left my engagement ring in my jewelry box in the apartment. I take off all my rings when I play tennis, and a locker room is not the right place to secure expensive jewelry.

"Sure." I take a seat, and a waiter comes over with a fresh glass and some white wine. He fills it. I want to drink it all down, but I need my wits about me.

"Hi," Fred says, his features softening.

"Hi."

"I can't believe you're here."

"Me neither."

"When did you get in?"

"Yesterday."

"And you came here on purpose?"

"I did."

"Why?"

I think about telling him the truth, then stop myself. "Like I said, I needed somewhere to eat. And I remember our meal here. It was great."

"You didn't know I'd be here?"

"No, how could I?"

He sits back, his hands in his lap. "How long are you in town for?"

"Depends on what happens on the court."

"And where are you staying?"

I tell him, then I look at the menu, trying to decide what I'm going to eat. There isn't much that fits in with my diet plan, and Matt would be pissed that I've even come here, but I need this. I needed to see him, so I can concentrate on what I'm doing.

"How are you?" I ask.

"I'm good."

"Should I go? Is this too weird?"

"No, we should order."

He flags the waiter, and we both order something. Fish in a simple sauce for me, and a rice dish for Fred—the seafood rice he raved about last time. He orders another bottle of wine too, even though I say I'm not drinking. Fred smiles apologetically and doesn't say what's obvious: *he* needs the drinks to get through this.

The waiter leaves and it's just us again. Not the same table where we were five years ago, but I can see it through the windows, outside in the back, pretty lights strung above it, the vines on the wall creating privacy. Another couple is sitting there, holding hands in the candlelight. I drag my eyes away.

"You never answered me," Fred says. "Not any of the times I called or wrote. You never let me explain."

"What was there to say?"

"I didn't mean—"

I hold up my hand. "Fred, no. You were dating her, right? She was your girlfriend?"

He sighs. "Yes."

"That's all that's important."

"I didn't want . . . I didn't expect things to be so complicated so quickly."

I pick up my knife because I need something concrete to hold onto. "Can I give you another perspective?"

"Okay."

"You lured me to London. You made it so we'd run into each other again, and then you pursued me. And that whole time, you had a girlfriend you never told me about. I think she even called you once when we were together. That day in Bath. You didn't break up with her. You waited to see if things would work out between us, keeping her like a backup plan. Did I miss something?"

He expels a long breath. "You make it sound so calculated."

"Wasn't it?"

"I get why it feels like it was, but that wasn't how it was for me. When I arranged for that sponsorship, I didn't know what would happen. I only wanted to help you make your plan to get to Wimbledon come true. I didn't know how you'd be around me, if you'd even talk to me. Every step I took was tentative. And yes, you're right that I should've broken things off with Catherine. I'd already spoken to her about cooling things down, but I never ended things officially. And that was my mistake. One I'll regret forever."

"It was all over the papers. *I* was."

"I saw. And for that I truly do apologize. I mean, I apologize for all of it. Not my finest hour."

"How did they even find out?"

"Catherine told them."

"What?"

His shoulders rise and fall. "It's how she lives, in the tabloids."

"But she looked bad."

"I looked bad, you looked bad . . . She looked like a victim. Which she likes."

"That's messed up."

"Yes."

"She must've been very angry."

"She was. But I didn't care about her, not enough for the time we spent together. And that was wrong of me. I shouldn't have been with her, knowing that. And when you came to London, I should've been clear with her. But I confess, all I thought about was you."

A lump forms in my throat. I might be angry at Fred—I might be furious—but I'm not a robot. "It's always so complicated between us, isn't it?"

He smiles slowly. "And yet, here we are."

"Yes."

"Five years later."

"Yes. But Fred . . ."

He leans forward. I think for a moment that he's going to hold my hands, and maybe he does too, because he stops himself. "Yes, what is it?"

"Don't you think we make the five years happen?"

"What do you mean?"

"We avoid each other in the in-between times. I could've come back to London anytime since then. I didn't."

"Why didn't you?"

"I wasn't ready to face all of this again. The stories in the tabloids. Your tabloids are terrible. Look at what they're doing to poor Meghan right now."

"It was the same with Kate."

"It's worse, though, isn't it? Because she's Black."

He frowns. "Yes, you're right."

"And her name is Catherine."

"Who?"

"The Duchess. Her name isn't even Kate. It's Catherine, but the whole world calls her Kate because the tabloids decided that's what her name is."

"What does that have to do with us?"

"I don't know . . . just that other people's perceptions can become reality sometimes."

"Only if you listen to them."

"Haven't we been, though? Why do we avoid each other for these long stretches? If we really wanted to be together . . ."

Fred goes still. "Is that what you want? To be together?"

"I don't know."

"That's honest, at least."

I put my hands under the table and run my fingers around my missing engagement ring. "Don't you think it would have happened by now? If it was meant to be?"

"I don't think that life works like that. I think that circumstances and timing and stupid decisions can get in the way of what's meant to be."

"That's us for sure."

"Yes."

I try to read his expression, but I can't. "And you? You want us to be together?"

"I do."

"No hesitation?"

"Of course there is. I'm terrified right now."

"You look completely composed."

"It's an act."

"And the Oscar goes to . . ."

He smiles. "So, what now?"

"I think I need to go."

"Back to the States?"

"No, I'm here for a while, like I said."

"Can I see you?"

I sigh. "I need to concentrate on my tennis."

"I'm glad I'm a distraction at least."

"You are."

Fred runs his hands through his hair. "So where does that leave us?"

"Can I think about it? And maybe in a month . . ."

"You want me to wait a month?"

I laugh. "It's been fifteen years . . . what's one more month?"

"Good point. But it seems risky."

"I don't think so."

"Why?"

I bring my hands up to the table and put them flat on the table-cloth. "Because I know what waiting is like. We both do. It's the together part that scares me."

"Olivia . . ."

"No, I'm going to go." I stand, walk to him, and lean over. I kiss him on the cheek. "Wish me luck?"

"Always."

He reaches for me, but I sidestep him. If we touch for real, then I'm going to crumble, and I need to keep myself together. I need time to examine what the hell I'm doing. To think about Wes and whether I want to throw that all away.

So instead, I say nothing and walk quickly out of the restaurant without looking back.

CHAPTER THIRTY-SEVEN

August 2023

There are more people at the cocktail party tonight, sensing that they're about to be over for good. All the familiar faces and ones I've never taken the time to learn.

It took an effort to be here after reading that letter from my mother. I took the pages back to my room and lined them up against the ones missing from her diary. They matched exactly as I knew they would. So now I know why my mother wanted me to wait to get married. Because she wanted me to choose myself and not be trapped by circumstance. I don't know what to do with this information. Tell my sisters? Bring it up with my father? Or tuck it away like she tucked the pages into her favorite book and left them hidden, maybe forever.

When I come outside, Wes is across the lawn, talking to Charlotte and Ann. Colin and Sophie are making the rounds with Aunt Tracy, like a leave-taking. My father is standing on the veranda, drink in hand, looking out over it all. What must he be thinking? Despite our confab in the library, I don't feel any closer to knowing him or his thoughts. But maybe that's okay. I don't have to access the thoughts of everyone around me all the time to know them.

"What do you think they're talking about?" Fred asks, appearing at my elbow like the ghost that he is.

"When did you get here?"

"Just now." He's dressed more casually than I've seen him in a while, more like the Fred on the beach a couple of weeks ago than the Fred of the club, of finance, of stranger.

"Where were you?"

"I had some business in London."

"Ah."

"So?"

I look back out over the lawn. "So, what?"

"Are they plotting?" He nods toward Charlotte and Wes and Ann.

Charlotte has her back to them, talking to one of the neighbors, and Wes and Ann's heads are tipped together. They do look like they're in a conspiracy, but that's silly.

"What would they have to plot about?"

"I don't know . . . Only, Olivia . . . are you sure you know everything about . . ."

"About what?"

He hesitates. "Ann."

"She makes Charlotte happy, that's all I need to know."

"But have you—"

I cut him off, exasperated. "What are you trying to say, Fred? Are you worried she's some gold-digger after my sister?"

Fred doesn't say anything, just stares back grimly.

"She's a lawyer. Successful by the looks of it."

"Appearances can be deceiving."

"Honestly? Who cares? If Charlotte is happy, what does it matter?"

"I just think you should be careful."

"I'm always careful."

"Not always."

We stare at each other, neither of us saying what we want to. This is what there is between us. Undercurrents, tensions, things that mean one thing and are said as another.

"Just because you're disappointed about your own love life . . ."

Fred arches an eyebrow. "What's that supposed to mean?"

"I heard about Lucy and James."

"I see."

"It doesn't bother you?"

"No."

"Come on, you guys were dating, and your friend swoops in and . . . Plus, I thought James was still mourning Fanny? So much for lifelong devotion . . ."

Fred looks me directly in the eye, stopping my thought in its tracks. "Olivia, I could not care in the least what Lucy and James do. No, that's not right. I'm happy for them. James is important to me, and Lucy is a great girl. I hope they'll be happy together."

His voice is full of emotion, but I can't quite tell what it's directed at. Me, them, himself?

"Who's going to be happy?" Wes says, putting his arm around my shoulders and holding me close to him.

"Lucy and James," I say.

"Ann was telling me about that. How delicious." He laughs, but he's the only one. "What? Not a good story?"

"It was rather sudden," I say. "And she's recovering from a concussion."

"Proximity, illness, James fretting over her. It's like something out of a romance novel, them alone in that massive winery . . . Anything could happen. Right, Fred?"

"Wes . . ."

"What? Fred and I are friends now."

"You are?"

"We fought it out and made up, didn't we?"

Fred nods slowly. "We did."

"And where was I when all this happened? The makeup?"

Wes shrugs. "Not sure. Anyway, are you pining for Lucy, Fred? Going to fisticuffs with James?"

"Are you drunk?" I ask him.

"What? No. Just poking fun. This place needs more fun."

"That it does," Fred says. "I'll see you later, Olivia. Wes."

He touches me briefly on the arm, then walks away.

"What's going on?" I say to Wes.

"What? Nothing."

"You talked to him after the fight?"

Wes catches up my hand. "Briefly. The next morning."

"Why didn't you tell me?"

"I didn't think it was relevant."

"And what were you and Ann talking about?"

"Just gossip. The party. Nothing."

"Which?"

"What?"

"Was it gossip or the party or nothing?"

He lets my hand go. "Why are you cross-examining me?"

"Because you're acting weird."

"Is weird so bad?"

"Depends on what it's about."

"I'm just . . . happy?" His eyes dance as he says this, smiling down at me.

"You are?"

"Yes." He reaches for me again, pulling me to him. "Aren't you? Soon, this will all be done, and we can move on."

I rest my head against his chest. Despite everything, my body still reacts to him in the same way, that mixed feeling of being safe and attracted. I close my eyes and try to block out everything. The sounds of the party, the lingering presence of Fred, all the questions that still swirl in my mind when we're together.

I almost get there. I almost do.

But then, deep in his shirt, I catch the scent of something floral.

Someone else's perfume.

And even though I know it's probably nothing, just someone from the party who put a hand on him, or maybe from the club, whoever is doing his laundry, it makes me pull away.

It makes me remember when all I want to do is forget.

CHAPTER THIRTY-EIGHT

June 2018

Against all odds, I make it to the final of the warmup tournament for Wimbledon.

I don't win. I lose in a tight three-set match against a much younger opponent named Kendall. But as I review the match afterward, I know how to beat her. I know that I *can* beat her if I face her again. There were two crucial games where my focus shifted, where I started looking ahead to the match being over rather than staying in the moment. That's when she broke me in the second set and again in the third. That was the difference. So, even though I lost, I feel good. I've avoided the press about me, stuck to my routine, and stayed away from my phone. The only people I speak to are Wes and Matt.

Wes and I talk about benign things, details for the wedding, nothing serious. I miss him, and that's good, if confusing. With each day that passes, the dinner with Fred starts to fade, like sunlight at the end of the day.

When I check my phone for the first time after the finals, I have a raft of messages—from Ash, my sisters, Aunt Tracy, Matt. And from Fred.

I open his first.

284

Sorry about the loss.

Thank you.

He answers before I have time to read any of the other messages.

When can I see you?

After Wimbledon, I write impulsively.

Are you sure?

Yes, I write with assurance, though I'm anything but certain.

Why do I want to go down this road again?

I ask myself this question, though I know the answer.

Because I love Fred.

I always have. And though I love Wes, I do, it's not the same. What I feel for Fred has always been bigger, faster, stronger. That's why we crash. That's why we fall apart.

But oh, in those moment when we're together . . . Those are the moments that are worth waiting for. Worth seeking out.

I put down my phone and it beeps again. I check it. It's not from Fred, but from Ash.

Have you given in yet?

Fuck off.

That means you have.

I haven't.

But you've seen Fred?

I let that question sit there.

You have, haven't you?

So what if I have?

What about Wes?

I didn't do anything.

Wes is good for you.

I know.

Please promise me you won't do anything stupid.

I promise.

I don't believe you.

I have to go.

Don't do it, Olivia.

Bye!

I put my phone down, then turn it off for good measure.

I don't need Ash, of all people, to tell me how to live my life.

If I want to screw it up again, I should be entitled to.

* * *

I spend the week between the warmup tournament and the start of Wimbledon working on my game. My phone stays off. I tell Wes I need to go dark, that the pressure is getting to me and it's the only way I know how to control it. He says he understands, but I know he's hurt. But I can live with his hurt. It's temporary. If I do the right thing and avoid Fred, despite my texts, it will all be forgotten.

And if I do the wrong thing and see Fred, with all that means, then . . .

I hit what feels like a million balls. I run and I eat, and I sleep. I watch tape of my likely opponents. I come into the first round strong and win my game. A day off and then repeat. That buzz is building around me again—I can feel it. Not because I read the press, but because of the questions that get asked at my press conferences, the number of journalists that show up. The buzz in the crowd as I play. The closer my matches get to center court.

Another win and it doubles. Win, repeat, win, repeat and now I've made it one round further than I did the last time. I'm not the phenom—I didn't come out of qualifiers—but it hardly matters. Everyone remembers that's who I am, and it's like it's happening all over again. I'm floating, seeing the ball well, playing without injury, and it all starts to feel inevitable that I'll make it to the final round and then . . . Fred.

It doesn't work out like that.

Instead, my next opponent is Kendall, the woman who just beat me. Again, I win the first set. Again, she wins the second. Again, it's because my mental focus slips, just for one game, but one game is enough.

And now we're in the third set, and it's neck and neck. I don't flinch and neither does she. I hold serve, she holds serve, the games creep up, the crowd is loud and enthusiastic. They're on both our sides, that center court thrall, and it feels like the game will never end. Kendall is tired. Her arms droop between shots, she's hunched over when she serves, and yet the shots are still precise, the serve still a kicker.

It's the third set and we're six and six. There's still no tiebreaker here, so the points mount and mount and mount, and then I miss. An easy shot at the net where I could've won the point goes into the net instead. I can hear the crowd sigh, like I'm in a large lung. Everyone knows what's going to happen. Neither of us has made a mistake until now, and now she's about to break me.

I shake the mistake off, trotting back to the baseline, trying to read her toss. She goes out wide and returns it, but not as cleanly as I'd like, and she rips a forehand winner past me. And now here we are, match point. Everyone is leaning forward in their seats, and I'm waiting too. Her serve is a bit weak and my return lands on the baseline. She puts one up in the air, and I move around to get the overhead. It comes down hard, but without the angle it needed, and now she pops another one up, a lob that goes over my head and lands in. I run to it, turn, hit it, but I know when it leaves my racquet it isn't going in. It lands two feet outside the sideline, and she screams and falls to her knees.

She won. I lost.

I lost; I can't believe it.

The crowd is on its feet for both of us, cheering, recognizing the amazing performance. I'm fighting back tears. I put my stuff away quickly, wave to the crowd, then I'm in the locker room, alone on a bench, surrounded by players getting ready for their matches. It all overwhelms me. The loss. The loneliness. All the choices I've made in my life that have led me to this moment, with no one here to celebrate with because I wanted to keep my options open.

So, I do two things:

I go into the press conference and announce my retirement.

And then I text Fred and tell him to meet me at the apartment tomorrow night at eight.

For once, I feel in control of my fate.

* * *

The next morning, I'm a bundle of nerves and second thoughts. Matt is furious with me for not consulting with him about retiring. I've got offers pouring in, he tells me. I'm walking away from millions, potentially, the millions I haven't made till now. But I'm sick of tennis. Tired of the sacrifices it requires. I want a life, a family, a home. I want to move my life forward.

I wake at my usual early hour and pace the apartment. I could go out, but it's pouring down rain. All the matches are postponed, not that I'd watch them if they weren't. Instead, I take a long bath and order a massive English breakfast from the pub down the road because I can eat what I want now. The man who delivers it tells me, "Too bad about the game," and I peel off enough cash to make him leave happy.

I bring my breakfast to the kitchen table, and as I'm loading up a scone with a heaping of cream and jam, my phone pings.

It's Fred.

Hi.

    Hello.

What are you doing?

    Eating breakfast. You?

Thinking about you.

    Oh?

Eight is a long time away.

    It is.

What if we didn't wait that long?
I smile.

    What did you have in mind?

Long shot, but . . . Do you have your bracelet here?

    Our bracelet?

Yes.

    Yes.

☺

    Did you just send me an emoji?

It's been known to happen.

    Why did you ask about the bracelet?

Can you put it on?

    Hold please.

I go into my bedroom, and fish around in my jewelry box until I find it. No matter how mad I've been at Fred over the years, I've never been able to let it go. My engagement ring is in this box too, but I avoid it. Ending things with Wes over the phone or by text seems cruel. I'll do it when I get home.

I put it on and snap a picture of the bracelet around my wrist and text it to him.

Perfect, he writes. *So, about tonight . . .*

> Yes?

I could come over now?

My stomach flutters. Is that what I want? Why did I ask him to come at eight anyway? To have a day to back out?

> Okay, yes.

☺

> Ha!

See you soonest!

I smile as a text from Ash comes in.

Sorry, it reads. *I had to.*

> Had to what?

It was for your own good.

> Ash, what did you do?

The doorbell rings. I can't believe Fred is here this quickly. I'm still in my robe, but that doesn't matter. I put my phone down, a touch of annoyance at Ash bristling under my anticipation.

The doorbell rings again.

"Coming!" I yell. I get to the door and open it. "That was—"

"Surprise!" Wes says, his eyes tired but his smile infectious and genuine. "Not what you were expecting?"

I recover as quickly as I can, but my heart is hammering and my throat feels dry. "Oh, I . . . Matt said he was coming over."

"For your lecture?"

"Excuse me?"

"Because you retired?"

"Oh yes. He's pissed."

Wes smiles again. "You going to let me in, or . . .?"

I step back. "Yes, of course. Come in, come in."

He reaches for me. My hands go around his neck reflexively, the bracelet tinkling on my arm. I tuck it nervously down the sleeve of my robe.

"It's so good to see you," he says in my ear, holding me tighter.

"You too."

"I missed you." He pulls me to him even tighter. "Are you okay?"

"I am."

"No, really? Because Ash thought . . ."

I pull back from him gently, trying to be composed, though alarms are ringing in my brain. "Ash?"

He looks guilty. "She told me I should come."

"Why?"

"She thought you could use me here. After the retirement announcement. I know you say you're okay alone, but you're not, Olivia. You need someone. You need me."

"I . . . I don't know what to say."

"Are you happy to see me?"

"I am. Of course. I'm just surprised, and still blown over from yesterday. Can I . . . do you mind if I get dressed? Then we can talk."

"Yes, of course."

"There's coffee in the kitchen. And the rest of my breakfast if you're hungry."

"What I'd really like is a shower."

"Of course. Follow me."

I lead him into the bedroom and through to the bathroom, taking a minute to explain the idiosyncrasies of the shower that took me two days to figure out, while trying to keep my voice as normal as possible.

I can tell that Wes wants me to join him, but my brain feels like it's on fire, so I hand him a big fluffy towel and point to where the second robe is, then shut the door.

I speed to my phone.

I text Ash first. *What the fuck?*

It's still nighttime at home, four in the morning, but Ash is up anyway. It must be the baby.

It's for your own good, I told you.

> *What gives you the right?*

Hate me if you want, but Wes is good for you.
All Fred does is break your heart.
Make a good choice, Olivia.

> *We're done.*

What?

> *Never speak to me again.*

Olivia, please, I'm sorry.

But she isn't. She knew what she was doing, and this isn't the first time she's gone too far in my life. I want to throw my phone across the room, but I can't.

Fred is on his way here. I need to head him off.

I'm sorry but I can't see you right now.

I wait for his reply, but there's nothing. Maybe he's driving or in a dead spot.

I send another text.

Please don't come here, Fred. I'll explain when I can.

I wait again, but there's no answer. Nothing.

I pull clothes from the dresser quickly, hearing Wes in the shower. He's not a shower lingerer, and I don't have much time.

I take off the bracelet and put it in the jewelry box, tucking it away. Then I take out my engagement ring and slip it back on. I throw on a pair of jeans and a shirt, then pick up my phone again. I call Fred this time, but it goes to voicemail.

Goddammit.

"What's that?" Wes says as he comes into the room, a towel around his waist.

"Nothing. I was texting Matt, telling him not to come."

"Save the lecture for later."

"What?"

"Don't quit now . . ."

"Oh right."

The doorbell rings. Fuck, fuck, fuck.

"I'd better get that."

"Tell Matt we'll have dinner with him."

"Yes, okay."

I hurry out of the bedroom to the front door trying too hard to breathe. I open it halfway. It's Fred in a polo shirt and a rain slicker, holding flowers, his face full of promise, his hair wet from the rain.

"You didn't get my text?"

"No. What happened?"

"I can't explain right now, but you have to go."

"At least let the man in," Wes says from across the room. "Poor Matt."

Fred's eyes widen as my face turns crimson.

"It's not Matt," I say loudly. "It's my old friend, Fred. This is very nice of you, Fred."

I step forward and take the flowers, then step back into the apartment and let the door fall open.

Wes appears at my side, still in his towel, shirtless.

"Fred, this is Wes Taylor, my boyfriend."

"Fiancée," Wes says, then extends his hand to Fred, who takes it after the briefest of hesitations and shakes it slowly. "We've met a few times in New York over the years. You're a member of Albright's, right?"

"Yes, that's right. I'm sorry, I don't remember you."

Wes's jaw tightens. "I was a guest of Dell's?"

"Ah, yes . . . Did you say Taylor?"

"That's right."

"Funny about the name."

Wes laughs. "Well, technically, I'm Olivia's third cousin."

"Second cousin once removed," I say automatically, because it's what we tell people to tease them.

"Oh, ah . . ."

"We're joking," Wes says. "It's just a coincidence.

Fred's forehead crinkles, then clears. "You dated Charlotte?"

"That's me. And that was a long time ago. Olivia and I reconnected this spring, and—well, one thing led to another."

"I see." Fred rocks back on his heels. "Well, I wanted to congratulate Olivia on her amazing run in Wimbledon. And on her retirement too, of course."

"In the rain?"

"We don't mind the rain in London," Fred says. "When's the wedding?"

"End of August," Wes says. "In the Hamptons."

"At Taylor House?"

"That's right. You've been there, haven't you, Fred?" Wes says.

He's being a bit cruel, though I'm not sure if it's to me or Fred. I've told him enough about Fred that he knows Fred's been to the house.

"Yes, yes I have."

"Remember, Wes, I told you how Fred and I met," I say, my voice a squeak. "That summer you were dating Charlotte, actually. Fred worked at the beach."

"Ah, that's right. A teen romance."

Fred grimaces. "As you say. Those things never work out."

"Almost never."

"Well, I must be off," Fred says. "It was nice to see you, Olivia. And meet you again, Wes."

"You don't want to stay for coffee?"

"No, no. I've disturbed you too early. I'm an early riser, and I forget sometimes that not everyone has my habits."

"Maybe we can have coffee tomorrow?" I say. "To catch up?"

"I'll have to check my schedule."

"Where can she reach you?" Wes asks.

"Oh, at my office. De Keurig Shipping. Have a nice day. And congratulations again."

"Thanks, mate."

Fred cringes again, and I'm sinking into my heels.

Fred is never going to talk to me again.

This is the last time I'm ever going to see him, and it's awful—I'm awful.

"I do hope we have coffee, Fred," I say, because I have to.

Fred nods almost imperceptibly and starts to walk away.

Wes interjects. "How did you know where Olivia was staying, if you don't mind my asking?"

"Oh, I . . . I still had Matt's number . . . He gave me the address."

"That was nice of him."

"Yes."

"And he didn't tell you, Olivia?"

"No."

"I'll have to have a talk with him. He shouldn't give out your address to just anyone."

"I agree," Fred says, "but he knows me from way back."

"Ah yes, you said. Off you go, then."

Fred gives me a fleeting look, then leaves as Wes closes the door firmly behind him.

He turns to me slowly, and for a moment I'm afraid, though Wes's never been violent or even angry.

"All right now, Olivia. Do you want to explain what the hell is going on?"

CHAPTER THIRTY-NINE

August 2023

Today's is the last day in the house—the auction, the closing, the party. And then back to New York in the morning, back to my life.

The day is gray and cool, and I wake up nervous, like I've forgotten to do something. I push the feeling down as I get ready. It's been a hectic few days, finalizing everything. Lucy has been around to help, but the concussion meant that she couldn't look at screens. So, I became her assistant, making a list of suggested prices, looking up the history of some of the older items.

Things were weird between us. I tried to bring it up a few times, and then finally, yesterday, when we were in the dining room, cataloging the china, Lucy closed her eyes and leaned her head back on a chair that I'd just learned was a Biedermeier.

"Your head okay?" I asked.

She was pale and thinner than earlier in the summer. "Just a dizzy spell. They happen."

"We can stop for the day."

"It's fine. I'll be okay in a minute."

"How long do they say that you'll have symptoms?"

"They're not sure. Maybe as long as six months."

"That long?"

She opened her eyes slowly. "Stupid me. Showing off."

"Fred should've caught you."

"It's not Fred's fault."

"Sorry, is it weird talking about him?"

She smiled. "Not at all. It was never serious between us. Not like with James."

"Serious already?"

"Yes, it is."

I reached out and touched her hand. "I'm happy for you."

"Thank you. James is fond of you."

"I like him too."

"And Fred?"

I looked away. "What about Fred?"

"I know you guys have a history."

"We do. But that's what it is."

"Not for Fred, I don't think."

My heart started to trill. Would I never not respond to the idea that Fred might want me?

"Why do you say that?"

"The way he looked at you. And talked about you."

"That's all in the past."

"You say so."

A lumped formed in my throat, and I coughed it away. "Speaking of Fred . . . shouldn't we get back to this?"

Lucy rubbed her eyes. "He never would tell me why he wanted this house so badly."

"That makes two of us." I held up a chipped coffee cup. "Worth logging? Yes or no?"

She laughed and we spent the next hour finishing the job.

Now, everything in the house has a bar code on it. If it all sells for the prices listed, there will be a tidy sum for the charity.

I look around my bedroom, that feeling of something undone niggling at me again. I'm all packed up, everything personal but the things I need for the night in my car. In the morning, all I'll need to do is clean out one drawer and the vanity where I've shoved my phone and makeup bag. Nothing's out of place.

I'm the one who doesn't belong here anymore.

I go downstairs, where Sophie and Charlotte are waiting. We've somehow all managed to dress in black, like we're attending a funeral for the house.

And maybe we are.

William's gone off to the club for the day, and Aunt Tracy is in the kitchen, hiding, though she says she's baking cookies to encourage people to buy more.

There's a line of people forming outside the front door on the gravel. One of Lucy's assistants opens the door and starts to hand out programs. We stand there at the bottom of the stairs, watching them file in. Neighbors, old friends, strangers. It feels like the whole town is here.

"The house smells amazing, anyway," Sophie says twisting her hands nervously. "I think I gained three pounds just walking in here."

"Oh stop, you look great."

"You do too, Olivia." She hugs me and steps back. "Honestly, when you got here in June you looked like you hadn't seen sunlight in a couple of years."

"I was just tired."

"Well, this place agrees with you."

Tears spring to my eyes. "It does. Why did it take me a lifetime to realize that?"

"Everywhere you run, there you are."

"Yes." I hug her. "Everything okay with you and Colin?"

"Fred gave him a job."

"He did?"

"Fred is everywhere, it seems," Charlotte says, and though the tone is biting, she's smiling. "Even at the auction."

"He's here?"

"Wandering around with his phone, scanning things."

"That's odd," Sophie says. "Why didn't he just bid on the house with the furniture?"

"I've given up trying to figure out what Fred was up to a long time ago," I say. But that's not true. I'm deeply curious about what it is that he's interested in buying, and why. "Has anyone seen Wes?"

"He's here," Ann says, drifting over. She's dressed in a bright green dress with pretty flowers on it, an intricate, metal-clasped belt cinched at the waist. "I was speaking to him a couple of minutes ago."

I feel a prick of jealousy, then quash it. Wes moved into the house for the last week, but he's been staying in a guest room because I'm still not ready to let him back into my bed.

"What about?"

"Nothing much. Charlotte, did you want to bid on anything?"

"Lord, no," Charlotte says, putting her arm around Ann's waist and looping her fingers through the belt. Letting go of all of her possessions is proving good for Charlotte, at least. "Do you mind if I go, Olivia? I'm finding this more emotional than I thought I would."

"Sure, sure."

"The caterers will be here at five to set up for the party. After the signing."

"Is Aunt Tracy supervising that?"

"I think so."

I sigh. Do I have to do everything myself? "I'll go check."

I leave them and go to the kitchen, the back of my neck prickling like it does when I've forgotten something. But what?

Tracy's there, pulling cookies out of the oven, and Fred's standing next to her, his hands in oven mitts, ready to accept the tray.

Did I have some premonition he'd be here? Is that what's bugging me?

"What do we have here?"

Aunt Tracy turns around, her face full of guilt. "Fred came looking for you and offered to help."

I cross my arms over my chest. "I was in the living room."

"It's a bit of a madhouse in there," Fred says, raising his shoulders.

"You ready for this?" Aunt Tracy says, pulling out the first tray.

Fred takes it from her, putting it on the island. They quickly remove three other trays, and then Tracy starts piling the cookies on plates.

"You know the house is already sold, right, Aunt Tracy?"

"What's that, dear?"

"The baking cookies thing. That's for open houses."

"It's an open house of sorts."

Lauren Bailey

"You didn't—"

Tracy picks up a cookie and holds it out to me. "I needed something to do, didn't I? I couldn't just sit here and watch everything get sold."

Guilt flashes over Fred's face, and he busies himself with putting the remaining cookies on a pretty flowered plate.

"I'll just take these out to the buyers," Tracy says.

"I can help."

"No, you stay here. Find out what Fred wants."

She pats me on the arm, then disappears through the swinging door with the plates in hand.

I worry about Tracy. What is she going to do when she won't have us all to fuss over all of the time?

"These are good," Fred says. "Amazing, really."

"She's the best. Why didn't you want to talk to me in the living room?"

"Everyone was around."

"Buying all our stuff so *you* can have an empty house."

He holds his hand up in surrender, a half-eaten cookie in the left. "I offered to take it as is."

"You . . . what?"

"I was happy to take care of all of this. But Ann said the family didn't want that."

"Ann said?"

"She wasn't speaking for you?"

"No. I didn't even know . . . No."

"I should've asked you directly."

"Yes. About a lot of things."

"Olivia . . ."

"No, no, don't use my name like that. Nothing good ever comes of it."

"I'm sorry. I wanted . . . I was going to offer to check the transfer papers and make sure everything's in order."

The transfer papers for the house sale, he means. Ann's assistant had sent them to me weeks ago, and I'd let them sit in my inbox, unread.

"No, thank you. I'm going to go now. Don't follow me, okay?"

"Okay."

I walk out of the kitchen, pushing through the swinging door, that feeling of something out of place dogging me. I stop in the crowd and try to think, but my mind won't go there, like a name I can't quite remember of some celebrity on screen.

I shake the thought away. It will come to me if I don't worry about it too much.

I go to the dining room and then out onto the veranda, where I find Wes talking with Ash.

"Olivia!" Ash says. "We were looking for you."

"Here I am."

"Everything okay?" Wes puts his arm around my waist and kisses me on the cheek.

"Yes, fine I think." I lean into him briefly, then pull away, the feeling I've been pushing down even stronger. "I have a few things I need to do before the signing. Can I meet you there?"

"You don't want me to drive you?"

"No, I'll meet you there, okay?"

"Sure enough."

I squeeze his hand, then let go. "I'll see you later, Ash?"

I walk away without waiting for her answer, but she comes after me.

"Olivia, what is it?"

My eyes search the crowd frantically. *What is it?*

"I can't explain right now."

"Is this about Fred?"

"Not directly."

"You sure you don't want to tell me?"

"I can't right now, okay?"

"Okay." She hugs me tightly. "I love you."

"I know."

I squeeze her tight, then let her go.

I don't why I feel so panicked or what's pushing me away from everyone who wants to help me.

I just know I'm not going to figure it out in this crowd full of strangers pointing their phones at my family's history.

* * *

In a minute, I'm up the stairs, headed toward my bedroom, when something makes me stop on the second floor.

Some instinct draws me to the room Wes's staying in.

I find a couple in there, arguing over the bedframe and whether their daughter will like it.

I shoo them out, and close the door behind them, turning the lock for effect.

There's nothing much personal in here—Wes's suitcase, his laptop on the desk, his toiletries in the bathroom, zipped into a small black bag. It smells like his aftershave, and the bed is made neatly like he always does, but something feels out of place.

I fling open the closet—it's full of empty hangers and some dry cleaning wrapping dumped in the corner.

I close the door, feeling insane.

I go to the bathroom to put some water on my face. I look at myself in the mirror, the years this summer has peeled away. I might not have looked like the girl Fred remembered when I got here, but I am her now.

I need to pull it together and get through today. It's just the auction, I tell myself, all these people, *Fred*.

But the anxiety won't leave. I need something to take the edge off.

Wes usually has some Ativan to help him sleep. Half of one would do.

I unzip the black bag, running my fingers through it, searching for the pill bottle but coming up against something else.

A small velvet box.

I open it, my hands shaking, not sure what to expect. A ring? Some apology gift from Wes that he changed his mind about giving me?

Instead, I find a charm nestled against the satin lining. It's a small plate, painted in vibrant yellows, blues, and reds, like the plate on the wall at the restaurant where I had dinner with Fred in London, the place we ate our last night together. It's beautiful and personal and exactly the sort of thing Fred would remember and memorialize.

But not Wes.

I examine the box and find a folded piece of paper in the lid. I open it, Fred's handwriting staring back at me.

Olivia,

I wanted to give you this in London two years ago, but my pride got in the way. But now that the world is torn apart, when we don't know what will come tomorrow, I regret that I let my hurt feelings rule my actions. Because all my thoughts and plans— they're for you. Tell me I'm not too late. That you still love me like I love you. Give me a sign, and I'll be at your side in an instant, no matter what it takes. But if you want me to stay away, if your feelings aren't what they once were, then say nothing, and I'll suffer in silence forever.

I'm half agony, half hope.

Love, Fred

It's dated March 17, 2020, the day the world shut down. I try to think back to where I was that day, how I missed receiving this.

School was closed—everything was—and Wes and I had an argument about whether to go to the Hamptons or stay in the city. He wanted to go, I wanted to stay, and when our words turned angry, I went for a long walk through my oddly silent city, feeling scared.

When I got back that night, Wes was conciliatory and agreed to stay in town. But he was keeping something from me, this message from Fred, and it all makes sense now. How watchful he became, how irritable. I thought it was just his business failing, our forced confinement, but no. He thought that if I got this note from Fred, I'd leave.

And I can't deny that he might've been right.

Was that why he was with that girl, whoever she is? Because he thought I had one foot out the door? He'd said as much when he came here on my birthday. That I was always in love with someone else.

Can I blame him for thinking that?

Can I blame him for doing what I was about to do with Fred when he interrupted us in London five years ago?

Yes, I can.

I can because I didn't do anything with Fred. He's the one who broke the promises we made, who broke us. And knowing what he's held back from me, this note, this charm, so many things, probably, can I trust anything he told me about his affair? That it was nothing. That it's over?

If I hadn't found those photos, that curved waist, that golden skin, that belt slung low . . .

Oh no, no, no, no—it couldn't be.

I unlock my phone and scroll through my pictures until I find it. I almost drop my phone, but there I have it.

The answer to the questions I never even bothered to ask.

CHAPTER FORTY

August 2023

After two hours on my laptop, back in my own room, I feel ready for the closing.

The house is empty now, the smell of freshly baked cookies barely lingering. There's a certain kind of peace that falls over a house after a large party. Like the memory of the chatter makes the silence sharper.

I check in with Aunt Tracy, who's moved into party prep mode, then drive myself to the lawyer's office.

They're gathered in a large conference room. Ann's father, Barry, is there, as are Ann, William, Charlotte, Sophie, Colin, Lucy, Wes, and Fred.

"Olivia," Charlotte says, "you're late."

"Sorry." I take the only empty seat. It's next to Wes.

"Shall we begin?" Barry says.

"Why doesn't Lucy tell us what the total is first?" I say. "From the auction?"

"Yes, of course."

Lucy takes out her iPad. "If all of the sales close, it's over a million."

A murmur goes around the room.

"So much?"

"All that dining room furniture and the rest of the antique side-boards, tables, etcetera, throughout the house, and some of the rare books account for most of it. A lot of it was Biedermeier and some other pieces that are pretty sought after."

"I think it should all go to the charity. Charlotte and Sophie?"

"Yes, yes, of course," Charlotte says, and Sophie agrees.

"Are you sure, Olivia?" Wes says. "Why not divide it among the four of you?"

"We have enough," I say firmly.

"Yes, of course."

Barry rattles his papers. "If that's all taken care of, we can circulate the paperwork for the transfer?"

"No," I say, "we need to discuss some things in there first."

"Surely you've had enough time to do that already?"

I ignore him. "Did you get the papers, Charlotte?"

"I think so . . ."

"But you didn't read them?"

She checks her manicure. "I glanced at them . . . Everything seemed in order."

"And what about you, Sophie—did you get them?"

Colin leans forward. "What's all this about, Olivia?"

"Will you hand me the papers, Barry?"

He hands a set to me, a worried frown on his face. I flip through them slowly, Wes stiff next to me, the air full of tension. The first thing I'm looking for is on page six. I found it that afternoon when I finally bothered to read it carefully before coming here.

"Did you review this, Fred?"

He looks up. "For my own part, of course. All seemed to be in order."

"And what about this here, on page six?" I point to a clause in the middle of the page. "The finder's fee that goes to Barry and Ann's firm?"

"That's standard in these large types of sales," Barry says, though I was asking Fred.

"Charlotte, didn't you tell me they were being paid a fixed fee?"

Charlotte's mouth turns down at the corners. "Yes, I did say that."

"How much?"

"Two hundred and fifty thousand."

"What?" Sophie splutters. "You agreed to that?"

"It's a tiny fraction of the purchase price. I asked around . . ."

"Who did you ask?" I say.

She raises her chin. "Well, Ann, of course, but I did ask the neighbors who bought down the road a few years ago, and they said the closing costs were outrageous. It wasn't polite to ask them what they meant specifically."

"It's one percent of the sale price, Olivia," Ann says. "And all signed and sealed by your father. It's our standard agreement in sales such as these where we also act essentially as the broker. A true broker's fee would be much higher."

"I thought that too," I say, "but I looked into it today, and usually with high-value homes, the parties don't do a percentage, but a fixed amount."

"I don't get your point."

"It's not the one percent that's the real problem."

"What then?"

"Clause twenty. It's all a bit vague, but as I read it, you've also given yourself a finder's fee of five percent."

"One point two-five million?" Fred says, flipping through his own copy. "That can't be right."

"Am I right? Ann? Barry?"

Barry coughs into his fist. "Well, now . . . I do leave these types of details to Ann, but yes, we do also charge a finder's fee in some high-wealth transactions. I'm sure it's in the agreement your father signed."

"William?"

He's sitting at the other end of the table, with that middle-distance look he always gets with financial matters. "Yes, dear?"

"Did Barry or Ann explain to you that they'd be getting six percent of the proceeds of the sale?"

"I don't recall discussing numbers."

"Did you read the documents before you signed them?"

"No," Charlotte says, "he didn't."

"But we've known Barry for years," William says. "I'm sure everything is aboveboard."

"I'm sure they were counting on that."

"What's that supposed to mean?" Charlotte asks.

"That William was an easy mark. Everyone in the Hamptons knows that." I reach across the table to him. "I'm sorry, Dad."

"It's all right, my dear. It's true that I don't enjoy the details of financial transactions. But there's still enough money for everyone, isn't there?"

"Yes, only . . . Give me a minute." I flip through the document again, past more pages of warranties and representations, and then, on page twenty-six, I get to the nitty-gritty: the division of the remainder, minus fees, and commissions, between William's children. Only, it isn't just to us, not Charlotte and Sophie and me, but to Wes and me. Charlotte and Sophie each get five million, but mine is divided in two.

"Fred, why did you insist on putting together the charity documents yourself instead of letting Ann do it?"

Fred meets my gaze. The document in front of him is open to the same page I'm looking at. "It just seemed like . . . a lot of responsibility was being put into her hands."

"You didn't trust her?" I press. "Why?"

"It wasn't based on anything concrete."

"But?"

Fred clears his throat and doesn't take his eyes off me. "But I heard some things in New York . . . rumors, only. I didn't like how quickly she seemed to have ingratiated herself into the family. When she and Charlotte started dating, she should've handed the file off to someone else. It's a conflict of interest."

"What's that?" William says. "Ann and Charlotte are what?"

"They're dating, Dad," Sophie says. "She's gay. Deal with it."

Charlotte's face is bright red. "Thanks for outing me. And for the record, I'm bi. Honestly, Olivia, first you steal Wes, and now this?"

"I didn't steal Wes, and for the rest of it—"

She lifts her chin. "I can choose who I want to tell about my private life."

"You can." I look at my father. "Do you care, Dad?"

"Of course not. Why does everyone treat me as if I were born in the nineteenth century?"

"Sorry, Father," Charlotte says. "I didn't want to upset you."

"It's perfectly all right, dear. Only I don't understand what this has to do with everything."

"A few more questions for Fred," I say. "Then I'll explain."

"Go ahead."

"How did you learn that the house was for sale, Fred?"

"I was approached."

"By Ann?"

"That's right."

"You didn't think that was weird?"

"I had some trepidations, but she said it was Charlotte's idea, and she knew I had a connection to the house. I'd been looking for a property in the Hamptons for several years; that was well known in certain circles."

"Do you know if anyone else was approached?"

"I do not."

"I guess that doesn't matter. It didn't have to be you. Anyone's money would do." I tilt my head to the side. "Then again, I'm sure it was an extra bit of dessert for Wes that it *was* you."

My use of Wes's name ripples through the room.

He's been remarkably silent next to me. But now, as all eyes are on him, he says, "I'm not sure what you're inferring, Olivia. You know I don't have any fondness for Fred."

"No, but you do for Ann."

The room goes still.

"What?" Charlotte says. "What?"

I wish I didn't have to do this, that I didn't have to expose how badly I've been betrayed, and Charlotte too, in front of everyone, in front of *Fred*, but I don't have a choice.

I shift my gaze to Ann. She's wearing that same dress she was wearing at the auction, the one I thought was so flattering. At her waist is the belt she was wearing the day I met her, an intricate metal design. Unforgettable.

"Why is my share divided between Wes and me? I didn't ask you to do that."

She doesn't look worried in the least. "It's for tax purposes."

"I see. But you haven't divided Sophie's share with Colin."

"Why should Colin get half the money?" Sophie says. "Not that I won't share it with you."

"Of course," Colin says, patting her on the hand. "I wouldn't have it any other way."

"Ann?" I say. "What's the explanation?"

"If you don't want it that way, I'm sure it can be corrected," Charlotte says, her voice faltering. "What's the big deal? And what did you mean before about Wes and Ann?"

Wes's leg is moving under the table now, bouncing up and down in a staccato motion.

"They're a couple," I say as evenly as I can. "Ann's the one Wes cheated on me with."

"No," Charlotte says. "No."

"Yes. I'm sorry . . ."

"I thought you didn't know who it was?" Sophie says.

"I didn't, not until today."

"What made you go looking?"

"It doesn't matter."

Charlotte moves her chair away from Ann. She's white to the hairline. "Please tell me."

"It was the belt."

Ann's hand goes to her waist, realizing her mistake.

"Olivia, if you don't tell me what's going on immediately, I'm going to scream."

I tear my eyes away from Ann and focus on Charlotte. "As far as I can tell, Ann and Wes met last year. They're on a board together, a startup that Wes got involved in after his own business went under during the pandemic."

I'd found it by googling their names, and there it was. Wes had told me about the board, but not about Ann. But if I had to pinpoint the moment when I started questioning our relationship—*him*—it was shortly after he met Ann last fall. Assuming that's when they met.

"Wes and I were . . . having trouble. I thought at first that it had to do with the fact that he couldn't get his new company off the ground. He was withdrawn and secretive for months, ever since last fall. Every time I asked him about it, he claimed he was stressed, that it would pass. But then, right before I came here, I found the text messages." I stop to gulp in some air.

Those horrible, explicit messages had turned my fears into reality in an instant.

"He'd given her a fake name in his contacts—a male name—but it was clearly a woman. There were . . . photographs . . . not her face, but other . . . You can imagine. In one of them, she was wearing a belt. The belt Ann's wearing today."

I steal a glance at her. She's staring at me, with her eyes moving back and forth like she's looking for an exit.

"When I found the messages, I confronted him, and he admitted the affair but said it was a one-time thing. He didn't tell me who it was or how he met her, and I didn't press it because I didn't want the details. I didn't want to know any of it. I just needed to leave."

"You came here," Sophie says.

"Yes. I left him. And that was a problem. It put a wrench in their plan."

"What . . . what plan? What do you mean?"

"To get a large portion of the sale for himself. For them."

"How?"

"He knew Dad was going to have to sell the house, that the bank was forcing the issue. I think that's what gave him the idea."

That and the fact that he was furious at me. That he wanted to punish me. Or maybe he never cared about me at all, and I'd been a mark all along.

"But the money could've gone to Father only," Sophie says. "Wes didn't know he'd agree to give some of it to us."

"He knows Dad is suggestable and that he doesn't care about money. So they worked it out together. Ann would befriend Charlotte and suggest that she and Barry be the lawyers on the deal. And it was Ann who proposed that Aunt Tracy convince William to divide the money. Isn't that right, Charlotte?"

Charlotte speaks quietly. "Yes, that's right. It was Ann's idea."

"Then she found a buyer, someone who'd pay top dollar, and maybe a bit more for the satisfaction of getting the house: Fred."

"Why would Fred care so much about getting the house?" Sophie asks.

"Because he knows I love it," I say, keeping myself from looking at Fred. "And he wanted to hurt me."

"Why?"

"Wes knows why."

Wes had confronted me five years ago in London after Fred left. He knew enough about my past that when Ash told him Fred was in London and that he should come to get me, he assumed the worst.

It all came pouring out of me. How I wanted to make sure Fred and I were truly over if I was going to marry Wes. How close I'd come to leaving him. How I still didn't know what I was going to do when Fred came over, but he should assume the worst.

He was quiet for a long time, and then he told me that didn't want things to end. That he still loved me and that if I wanted to be with him, I could. I could put all of my tortured past with Fred away and start fresh, clean.

And because I'd seen the look on Fred's face in the doorway, because I knew Fred wasn't going to have coffee or tea or anything with me, not after I'd hid Wes from him, I'd agreed.

I wanted a clean future, a fresh start. I was sick of tortured love.

I married Wes in August in the garden, just like we'd planned, and I gave our marriage my best. But then that note had arrived from Fred at the start of the pandemic. The charm, the request to run away together. And all Wes's doubts must've come rushing back.

No, *worse*. He'd thought I'd go to Fred if I got that note, so he hid it from me. But then that filled him with doubt and resentment. And then the way we rubbed at each other in the months that followed, his business failing—all of that built into a big ball of hate. He couldn't trust me to pick him, and so it was like I hadn't. He wanted to hurt me like I'd hurt him.

Worse.

"But why come here after you left him?" Sophie asks. "Why try to reconcile with you?"

I keep waiting for Wes to say something, for him to tell me I've got it wrong, to amend the narrative. But he doesn't say a thing, just works the muscle in his jaw and clenches his hands on the table.

"If I got the money after we separated, he wouldn't be entitled to any of it in the divorce. But if we were together, with Ann's help, he could get his half outright."

"But you would've found out," Charlotte says. "We all would have."

"They didn't care about that. Once the wires went through this afternoon, they'd be gone."

It's that word that breaks me.

Gone.

I'm furious at Wes, I hate him maybe, but part of me still loves him too. And whatever I did, it wasn't so bad as to deserve this.

"Is this all true, Wes? Ann?" Sophie asks, her face white, her hands shaking.

"No," Wes and Ann say together.

Charlotte's hysterical laugh is cut off by a sob. "Oh my God, I fell for you. I fell for all of it."

"We both did," I say.

William stands unsteadily and holds out his arm. He points to Wes. "You leave now. And don't you come back here again."

"She has it wrong."

"What part?" William says as his voice gains confidence. "You didn't cheat on my daughter? You didn't try to defraud all of us?"

"I—"

"No. *No.* I never liked you. When you came around with Charlotte all those years ago, I knew something about you wasn't right. But Olivia, she'd been through so much and she seemed happy . . . I didn't want to refuse her twice."

Wes's eyes narrow. "You stupid old man."

"Enough," Fred says, rising to his feet. "Enough."

Wes and Fred stare at each other, both breathing heavily, spoiling for a fight. Fred looks like he might kill Wes if given half the chance, and that's not what I want.

I push my way between them, holding a hand out to both of them. My right hand touches Fred's chest, but my eyes are on Wes, even as I can feel Fred's heart beating against my palm.

"It's over, Wes. It's all come out now. Just go."

Wes's eyes travel from mine to my hand resting on Fred. "I *knew* you'd choose him."

"You didn't even give me the chance to prove you wrong."

He takes a step toward me, and before he can complete it, Fred is there, holding Wes's arm back behind his back.

"You're not going to be wanting to do that, *mate*," Fred says. "I swear to God. Don't test me in this."

Wes struggles for a moment, then goes limp, like he's giving up.

"Let me go," he says quietly. "I'm going."

Fred releases him, and Wes moves toward the door.

"You too, young lady," William says.

Ann rises. "I can explain."

"Don't bother, Ann," Wes says. "She figured it out. I underestimated you, Olivia."

I meet his eyes, and they're empty. I should leave well enough alone, but I have to know. "Was it *all* a lie? From the very beginning?"

"No," he says. "I'm not . . . This wasn't some grand plan. That's not why I married you."

"How can I believe you?"

"You think I'm capable of that? All these years?"

I shake my head slowly. "I don't know you. That's what it feels like."

"I loved you. I loved you for a long time."

"And then?"

He makes a gesture with his hand. "I think you know what happened." He looks at Fred. "What does it matter? You never loved me. He was always standing between us."

"No, I—"

"Don't, Olivia. What's the point?"

This stops me. Because he's right. We're over. And there isn't any point in arguing about it. Maybe there never was. I return to my chair slowly.

Wes hesitates for a moment, then leaves, his shoulders down, defeated. Ann follows him without saying a word.

The rest of us sit there in silence as Fred settles back into his chair.

"What now?" Sophie says eventually.

"I believe I can be of service," Fred says. He takes the document from me and picks up a pen. He makes short work of it, striking through various clauses, explaining as he goes. "I'll be removing your commission and fee. I assume you agree, sir?"

Barry rouses himself. "I'm terribly sorry about all of this. I had no idea."

"We'll let the licensing board sort that out, shall we?" Fred draws a few other heavy lines, initialing each as he goes. "Now, that's all done. Each of you sign and initial where I've initialed, and this will be the right copy." He speaks to Barry. "The money shall only be wired in accordance with these instructions, you understand?"

"Yes, yes, of course."

Fred passes the paper to me, and I do as he instructed. Then I pass the papers to Charlotte. She's crying, her shoulders slumped. "I can't believe this is happening."

"I'm sorry, Charlotte," I say. "I wish it didn't have to be this way."

Charlotte signs, then pushes the papers to Sophie, who signs them and gives them to Barry.

"Good," Fred says. He turns to Lucy, who has been sitting in stunned silence through all of this. "And that house that Charlotte is buying . . . Do you still want it, Charlotte?"

"Yes, I think so."

"Surely there's another lawyer in town who can take care of that transaction?"

"Absolutely," Lucy says. "And I want to apologize for my part in it."

"Your part?" I ask with a sinking feeling.

"It was Ann's idea that I approach you about the estate sale. I should've said."

"They wanted it all," Sophie says. "As much as they could get."

"I swear to you I had nothing to do with this," Colin says, rousing himself.

"I know, Colin."

"But oh God, I'm embarrassed to say this now . . . I do think he was trying to rope me in."

"How?"

"He offered me a job. At a new company he was going to start once he'd raised the funds. As an equity partner."

"What would the buy-in have been?" I ask.

"A million."

"What?" Sophie says.

"I told him it wasn't my money to decide what to do with. And then Fred offered me a job, much more solid and secure . . ."

"Thank God for Fred," Sophie says, standing, pulling Colin's hand. "Can we go now?"

"Yes."

She looks at me. "I guess we're still having the party?"

"Why not? Dad?"

"What? Oh yes, yes. All my friends are coming."

"We better get back, then." Sophie helps him up. "Come along, now. I'll explain everything in the car."

Charlotte stands and I walk to her and hug her. "I'm so sorry, Charlotte."

"I thought this was it, you know? My chance at happiness."

"I know."

"I should've seen through her."

"We were both taken in. That's a good thing."

"How can it be a good thing?"

"Because I don't want to be the sort of person who'd suspect anyone who's nice to me of being a con artist."

Charlotte laughs through her tears. "All right, good point."

"Besides, this is all Ash's fault."

"What? How?"

I glance at Fred, who's pretending not to listen. "It's complicated, and I'm mostly joking. I'll tell you some other time."

Everyone starts to file out, but I linger behind. Fred is standing over Barry as he works on his laptop, giving the wiring instructions, making sure they're carried out correctly.

"All done," Barry says.

"You'll file the papers now?"

"Yes, I'll do that now and bring the formal set to the party?"

"Why don't you bring them by tomorrow morning?"

"Yes, of course."

"And you'll be cooperating with the police."

"The police!"

"If that's what the family decides."

He's shaken. It's hard to know how much Barry knew about what was going on, but the fees, that for sure he knew about. He busies himself, closing his laptop, taking the papers, and leaves.

And now it's just Fred and me.

"Thank you," I say.

"For what?"

"Taking care of the paperwork. And trying to tip me off in the first place a couple of weeks ago."

"Did I do that?"

"You know you did. I was just too stupid to listen."

"I didn't know anything for certain . . . not all of the financial shenanigans."

I search his face. "But you knew something. Something you didn't tell me."

His mouth turns down. "I saw Ann in the clubhouse early one morning."

"Too early?"

"I knew she must've stayed in someone's room, and I didn't think it was Mr. Pinkman, all eighty-two years of him."

"Why didn't you tell me?"

"It wasn't my place. And I didn't want to be in the middle of you and Wes again."

"That was my fault." I take a step toward him. "I'm sorry."

"For what?"

"For London. I should've come clean to you before . . . well, before anything."

"Yes. Though you did owe me that one."

I almost laugh. "Is that what you thought at the time? That I was getting back at you for Catherine?"

"Weren't you?"

"Not deliberately."

"And if Wes hadn't shown up?"

I hesitate. How many times can I put myself out there for this man? "I would've chosen you."

"But you married Wes."

"You didn't seem like an option. And I did love him. I thought I could . . . start again, have a relationship with less drama."

"Boy, were you wrong."

"Right?" I laugh, then stop. "It's not funny, though."

Fred doesn't take his eyes off me. "I know," he says softly. "I'm sorry."

"No, no, I deserve it. Keep it coming."

"I don't want to do that." His tone is different now. His voice deeper.

"I found something," I say.

"What?"

I reach into my pocket and grasp the charm. I pull it out and open my palm slowly. "I only found this today. And your note. Wes hid them from me."

Fred sucks in his breath. "My God."

"He did it because he knew. He knew what I'd do if I got it."

"Would you have?"

I nod slowly as his eyes search my face. "But Fred, that was three years ago . . . I understand if . . ."

"Hmm." He clears his throat. "You had something wrong today."

"Oh? What?"

"I didn't buy the house to spite you."

"Why then?"

"You must know."

"I don't."

"Olivia . . . I bought it *for* you."

My hands start to tingle. "But why?"

"Because I want you to be happy. And this is where you're happiest. I've always known it."

"You bought it for me. Even though you thought I'd ignored your note?"

He takes a step closer, his hands at his sides.

If I take a step, I'll be in his arms.

"But you didn't."

"But you thought I did."

"I know, but . . . I've never been able to move on. I knew from that first conversation on the beach that we were meant to be. And every time we've been together, summer after summer, has confirmed it. There's never been anyone like you. I've tried. More than once. But it was no use."

"Why can't we make it work then?"

"Timing, I think. When you were ready, I wasn't. And vice versa." He takes the charm from my palm, his fingers grazing my skin. "Fifth time's the charm?"

I half laugh, half cry. "Yes, Fred. Yes."

"Are you sure?"

"I've never been more certain of anything."

He pulls me to him, his mouth on mine in an instant.

Our mouths crash together, our arms lock around each other, and oh, oh, *oh*. This kiss. *This kiss.* My god, how could I live without this for so long?

I want to get lost in it. In him. I want to stay this way forever, but we're in a boardroom in daylight, and that seems like a bad idea.

I pull away. "There's one thing."

"Naturally."

"I'm still married."

"I heard you were separated."

"Oh?"

He pulls me closer. "New York is a gossipy place."

"I've never paid attention."

"It's one of the things I love about you."

I feel weak at the word. "This is nuts, you know, us thinking about this."

"I don't think so. I think it's way past time."

He pulls me in again. His arms wrap around me, and his hands slip under my shirt and up my back, his fingers like fire on my skin.

I don't know how long the kiss lasts—not enough time to make up for the past.

"We're idiots, you and I," I say when we break apart again.

"I agree."

"We should get out of here."

"That sounds like a good idea."

"There's a party at my house."

He leans back. "Am I invited?"

"I think I can swing that. But I'm afraid we have to go somewhere else first."

"Where's that?"

"Your room."

"Won't that make us late?"

"Probably. But I'm willing to risk it if you are."

He rubs his nose against mine. "I don't want your father thinking badly of me."

"Are you kidding, he loves you."

"And you?"

"I love you, Fred."

I kiss him again to prove it, to seal it, and when we break apart, he's never looked so happy, not in all the time I've known him.

"I love *you*, Olivia."

"That's lucky."

He reaches for my wrist and attaches the charm. "It will be."

He kisses it in place, then me again for good measure. When we pull apart, I hold out my hand and he takes it.

"You really bought me my house?"

"I *was* hoping I'd get to live in it with you."

"Really? Even before you saw me?"

"Well . . ."

"You can be honest."

"I didn't know what would happen. I wanted to help you. I knew I still loved you—"

"And you were dating Lucy."

"A few dinners. I like her."

"Hedging your bets?"

He takes my hands and pulls me to him. "No. I think I was protecting myself in case you rejected me. But I was lying to myself. From the minute I saw you again at your sister's house, I knew it was you or no one."

My knees feel weak. "Why didn't you say anything?"

"I tried to, but—"

"I told you to shove it."

"Pretty much."

"We always get in our own way."

"We do. Which is why I think my plan to move in is the right one. If we commit, actually commit, then we'll have to work it out."

"I see."

He looks nervous. "Bad idea?"

I pull his hand to my chest so he can feel my beating heart. "When can you move in?"

EPILOGUE

June 2024

By some miracle, our plan works.

Fred moves in and we make the house ours instead of his or mine or my family's.

I learn what Fred is like in the fall—he looks amazing in sweaters.

I learn what Fred is like in winter—like a kid at Christmas, and on Christmas itself, happy in fleece pajamas unwrapping present after present because we've decided to make up for all the Christmases we missed together.

And I learn what Fred is like in spring—a little melancholy from the lack of sun and spontaneous, whisking us away to a sunny weekend so he can lie on the beach and smile; and then, after we get back, so happy to see the world turning green, the flowers pushing through the ground, that he picks me up and spins me around and around.

I love all of the Freds, but I love my summer Fred most of all.

I offer to let my dad live with us, but he prefers to go to the retirement community. He's made some friends there, and there's maybe even a woman, though he's shy about admitting it. Maybe Aunt Tracy will get it out of him when she comes to visit this summer.

I make the same offer to Charlotte, but she's happy with her cottage, and there's a man in her life too. A friend of James's that she meets at the winery when we all gather there for a Friendsgiving dinner. His name is Ben, and he's a bit quirky, but it seems to suit Charlotte. I would've guessed she'd never introduce another partner to us again after what happened with Ann, but I'm glad to see I'm wrong.

Sophie and Colin are still house hunting, but I think that's on purpose. They enjoy the fights, the battles. It's what keeps it fresh between them. Or so she says, anyway. Who am I to judge? Colin's happily working for Fred, and Sophie's on the board of her kid's school, busy and excited to come out to the house on the weekends and let the boys run around the lawn for hours on end. We've grown closer this year, and I'm happy about that.

In the end, we don't call the police on Ann and Wes. I just file the paperwork to end the marriage I never should have agreed to, and we exchange documents through lawyers. He's never reached out, never tried to give me any other excuses than the ones he's already offered, and I am okay with that. I let him go and didn't look back.

I'm trying to look forward.

I don't go back to teaching. Fred was happy to get a place in New York and live there most of the time if I wanted to, but I found I didn't. I liked the kids most of the time, but I never felt easy in that life. The city was too much of everything and probably part of the reason I felt so far from myself.

But I've been keeping busy.

"You all packed?" Fred asks me. I'm sitting on the floor in the conservatory off the kitchen, surrounded by suitcases and tennis gear. It's sunny out, the first day of summer approaching fast. It's light out now after dinner, and the grass is green and lush.

I glance up at him. He's wearing slacks and a light blue button-down that's my favorite color on him. He just got a haircut too, and he looks delicious. "Yes and no?"

"Which is it?"

I look around at the suitcases and tennis bags and boxes of shoes. "I feel like there's too much stuff and also like I'm missing something."

"You are."

He takes my hand and helps me up. I fall against him in a way that would have been awkward a year ago. Now it's just an opportunity to put my arms around his waist and nuzzle into his neck. I drink him in, that mix of woods and the beach.

"Don't distract me," he says.

"From what?"

"From this."

He takes my hand and holds it in front of him. Then he takes a ring out of his pocket and slips it on my ring finger.

It's a solitaire, tasteful, beautiful, exactly what I would have picked for myself.

Like Fred.

I stare at it, surprised, happy, nervous. "Is this what I think it is?"

"What do *you* think?"

"I think I want you to ask me."

He smiles, then drops to one knee. "Like this?"

I laugh. "Go on."

"Olivia Anne Taylor, I've loved you since I was seventeen. Would you do me the honor of becoming my wife?"

I don't know whether to laugh or cry. Not because I'm sad, but because I'm happy. I've been so happy this last year and I don't want to jinx it. I don't want anything to change.

"It won't jinx it," Fred says.

"What?"

"Us getting married. Me proposing. It's okay this time."

"How did you read my mind?"

"I read your face. And also, I know you."

"Are you sure?"

"I am."

I stare into his eyes. There are no doubts there. There never were. The doubts were always mine.

But I know why, now. I've only loved one person as much as I love Fred, and she left me.

I can face that fear. The past doesn't have to repeat itself. That's something else I've learned—my mom was taking stock of her life and regretting some of her choices as she watched her time wind down. It doesn't mean she wasn't happy. And she'd want me to grab whatever happiness I could, I'm sure of it.

"Olivia? I'm kind of dying here."

"Oh, I'm sorry. Yes, yes, I'll marry you—of course I will."

I fall to my knees and we kiss. It's slow and lingering, and if I didn't have a plane to catch in a couple of hours, I'd pull him to the ground and get lost for the rest of the day.

He holds the sides of my face. "One more thing."

"What's that."

"I'm coming with you to London."

"You sure?"

"I am one hundred percent going to be there for the start of your comeback and as far as it takes you."

"I'll probably lose in the first round."

We stand up together. "I don't think even you believe that."

"Okay, I don't, but I'm old for tennis. Especially as a woman."

"You're in the best shape of your life."

I kiss him. "It takes more than that."

"You're happy, though, about going back on tour? Wimbledon?"

"I chose it, didn't it?"

And I had. It had started as a thought experiment. If I gave myself over to it for a year, what could I achieve? And then I'd played in a tournament for fun and won. And then another. Pretty soon I was collecting ranking points. But most of all I loved playing again. I loved the competition. I loved pushing myself to the limit. How my body felt, even though it was sore.

"You did. And you chose me."

"I *did*."

"Regrets?"

"None."

"I have some."

"Oh?" I say, my heart fluttering.

"Only that we didn't do this sooner."

I laugh. "No, no, this was the perfect time. We weren't ready before."

He leans his forehead against mine. "I think sometimes about the lost time."

"I think about all the time we have left."

"That's wise." He brings my hand to his lips and kisses the diamond. "You said yes."

"You were worried?"

"Well . . ."

I look at it sparkling in the sunlight. "When did you buy this, anyway?"

He mouths turns into a guilty smile. "If I say last summer, would that surprise you?"

"Nope."

"Last summer."

"When last summer?"

"I think I'll plead the fifth on that one."

"Hmm. I'll get it out of you eventually."

"I have no doubt."

My watch buzzes with a reminder. "If you're coming, we should get a move on."

"Yes, ma'am. I'll meet you in the driveway in thirty minutes."

"Sounds like a plan."

We grin at each other and kiss again, and it's lighter now because this is not a goodbye, but another step in our next beginning.

Whatever happens in London will be what it is. There's always the clay court season after that if I feel like it. And beyond that, I know that Fred and I will have summer after summer to build our future.

And all the seasons in between too.

ACKNOWLEDGMENTS

It feels like I've wanted to write this book for a million years, and then I did. And now it's out in the world, in your hands. I hope you enjoyed the ride that Olivia and Fred went on.

I didn't get here alone—I'd especially like to thank my agent, Stephanie Rostan, and my editor, Holly Ingram. And thanks as well to the whole team at Alcove for putting this beautiful book together and getting it out there into the world.

Thank you also to Liz Fenton for reading an early draft and her support in general. Thanks also to Matt Norman, Christy Shillig, and Carol Mason for the same.

If you're a massive fan of Jane Austen (like me), you might have noticed that Olivia's story follows Anne's in *Persuasion*. That is intentional, and I can only hope that this novel lives up to the original.

I am half agony, half hope.